A LITTLE IRISH LOVE STORY

AMY FLEMING

A LITTLE IRISH LOVE STORY

AMY FLEMING

AMBASSADOR INTERNATIONAL
GREENVILLE, SOUTH CAROLINA & BELFAST, NORTHERN IRELAND
www.ambassador-international.com

A Little Irish Love Story

© 2014 by Amy Fleming

Printed in the United States of America

ISBN: 978-1-62020-246-3
eISBN: 978-1-62020-345-3

Cover design and typesetting: David Siglin
E-book conversion: Anna Riebe

AMBASSADOR INTERNATIONAL
Emerald House
427 Wade Hampton Blvd.
Greenville, SC 29609, USA
www.ambassador-international.com

AMBASSADOR BOOKS
The Mount
2 Woodstock Link
Belfast, BT6 8DD, Northern Ireland, UK
www.ambassador-international.com

The colophon is a trademark of Ambassador

*For Sean
and in memory of my
Great Papa,
Aunt Mim,
and my Dad*

ACKNOWLEDGEMENTS

THANK YOU TO MY FRIEND, Audra Brown who did the first round of editing- this book would be literally half what it is without you. To Anna Bowick Johnson for author photograph. To my precious pastor, Father Craig, who fed me spiritually through the writing of this book. To my husband, Sean, whose suggestion of a "friendly barkeeper named Sean" gave me the idea for one of my most loved characters. To my mom without whom this book would not exist- nor would I for that matter. To my bestie, Jessy, whose enthusiasm for this project was contagious. To the chamber of commerce in Adare, Ireland. And to those up in Heaven: My dad who always made me believe I could do anything. My Aunt Mim who was indeed my "Sarah Donnelly". But especially to my Great Papa, my beautiful John Henry Oliver . . . you are my hero both in this book and in my life. Thank you for modeling to me how to love Jesus. Your love story inspired this book. Can't wait to hold your hand again one day.

CHAPTER I

ANNA TREMBLED AS SHE HELD on to her mother-in-law's smooth hands. Every time she held Sarah's hands, she marveled at their softness.

She breathed deeply as the bus clamored on. Sarah's head began to droop onto her shoulder. Anna kissed the top of her curly mane lightly and chuckled.

She thought: *She used the bluing on it again.*

Sarah Maeryn had blue eyes which spoke without her saying a word. At seventy, she was so rich in spirit it seemed her age was nothing to her—her heart was much like a child's. Sarah was always busy with an apron on, cooking something for someone. Yet, with sugar rations at a high during the war, she became frustrated with baking. Therefore, she and Anna worked to find new ways to make old recipes.

Sarah's made many people happy through baking, Anna recalled.

She twisted her long, black hair which draped her shoulder. Anna looked out the window to the bleak, grey scenes of London's dilapidated buildings. The bombs had done their worst on the beloved city; the only thing left standing was the strength of her people.

Once in a while, Anna saw an untouched building, an oasis to the devastation which surrounded it. Then, necks all over the bus craned to marvel at God's provincial hand on the edifice.

After a few hours of the quiet bus ride, mothers began to fiddle in their bags for snacks to feed their fussy children. Three hours later, everyone was out of food, except Sarah and Anna. Anna quietly bent down to rummage through her bag for the little food she and Sarah had time to gather.

Sarah awakened and began to immediately help. Anna reached over and gave a seemingly tired mother a small parcel of nuts and another woman some fruit. Sarah reached in and handed the elderly couple in front of them a sandwich.

After their rations, Sarah and Anna stretched their legs before they boarded a ferry at Pembroke. The ferry was slow to depart, but Anna was in no hurry. She breathed in the sea air as Sarah chatted with a few ladies. Anna kept her one suitcase by her feet and held on to the rusty railing. She was nervous, but knew where they were headed was so much better than from where they had come.

Anna held onto Sarah as she regained her land legs. They stepped onto Irish soil in the town of Rosslare. Sarah smiled up at her daughter-in-law.

"We're in Ireland," she whispered.

Then, she put a handkerchief to her lips.

"Fifty-two years," she said to herself.

"One more bus and we'll be there," Anna said gently.

She took her hand and helped her up the stairs. They sat toward the front. On the second bus, Sarah seemed more alive than ever before. She chatted all around as Anna clung quietly to her window. She watched as the scenery began to suddenly change from black and grey to full color as it had in *The Wizard of Oz*. She hated the movie, but it was a fitting impression.

As the colors changed to beautiful, hilly greens, Anna's spirit began to lift. The hills rolled up and down like her heart felt an urge to do. She saw green.

Life!

Anna and Sarah had spent far too much time in the tunnels when the alarms sounded. She had held her hand then—she was not letting it go now, even if the war was over.

That morning, they only had a half hour to decide whether they were to board the bus to Ireland or not. They heard about it and within minutes, people already clamored for tickets. Anna bought three, but they only used two—they gave one to someone who was one short.

Sarah's other daughter-in-law, Opal, had decided to stay behind in London. She had family to return to, Anna did not.

Anna's brother-in-law and husband had died only a month apart in combat while they served in the European theatre. Anna closed her eyes; it was more than Sarah could bear. She had lost *her* husband, Cornilius, and two boys in a two-year span—her husband to a heart problem, her boys to the war.

Anna had only known *her* husband, Jamie Maeryn, two months before she married him. Sarah was left with two young daughters-in-law, barely out of their teens, who had been strangers to her only months before.

Anna closed her eyes and tried to envision her husband's red, curly hair and contagious smile. She knew when he was called to the front it was only a matter of time before he was killed. He was not the type to be a soldier. He was small and had a soft heart. She could not imagine him shooting a gun at anyone.

He made her laugh like no one else—she loved that about him. Sarah had an incredible sense of humor as well, but so much of it had faded like the color in London.

She stroked Sarah's hand. She had known and loved her mother-in-law longer than she had her husband. Anna moved in with her an hour after Jamie boarded a shaking, army truck filled with other young men destined to die horrible deaths.

It was as if God had her fall in love with Jamie to be Sarah's daughter. They needed each other. Sarah had grown dependent upon Anna's wisdom; Anna was dependent upon Sarah's love. It was something Anna had craved her whole life—the love of family.

Some women were left with babies as token remembrances of their brief marriages. Anna was left with an elderly woman.

The bus stopped many times and people got off until finally it reached the main street of a tiny town. Sarah put her soft hand on Anna's and nodded. Anna awoke from her memories of her past life into her present one. Sarah and Anna quickly gathered all they had and tried to regain their land legs as they scurried down the bus aisle.

Anna handed the driver a handsome tip for going out of his way for them. They stepped into the warm sun of the little Irish village: Adare.

Raised in Adare, Sarah was fortunate to have some distant family in the small village. She was actually Irish; although, her accent had become increasingly muddled as her days in England had spun on.

The two stood and watched people go in and out of stores as they led normal lives in a place untouched by war. It was like the first days after a loved one's death when one is astonished the world is able to continue without him or her.

With thatched roofs and colored doors, each cottage had window boxes filled with flowers. Anna held Sarah's hand and they smiled at each other.

"Home," Sarah mouthed as she held back tears.

Anna nodded.

Sarah had returned to her native land. She hoped someone would help them.

Sarah led her to a pharmacy down the road. The little bell rang as they opened the door. The pharmacist greeted them warmly and inadvertently looked at Anna's beautiful face longer than Sarah's. Another man, the owner of the store, came around the corner of the aisle to greet them. The two gentlemen met them with a warm welcome, but Sarah had to reintroduce herself, as it had been so long.

"Sarah," he whispered. "Milton, you remember Sarah, Cornelius' wife?"

"Of course," Milton's tender voice breathed out.

In awe, they finally embraced Sarah and talked with her softly, hand in hand. Anna no longer heard their conversation. The men and Sarah looked up at her as Sarah wiped a tear away. Sarah motioned for Anna who walked toward them.

"This is my daughter now," she said. "This is Anna. Anna, this is Morty and Milton . . . They were my husband's dear friends. They were children together."

Anna took a deep breath. *No one has ever called me daughter.*

"We need a place to stay and some work," Sarah explained.

"Of course, of course," the store owner agreed. "Actually, funny as it may sound, my tenant upstairs just moved out a month ago. It's still a bit dusty, but there are some furnishings. I think it'll do for the time being."

They led the ladies to a small room above the shop. The two men told them to rest, and then brought them something to eat. Sarah and Anna were half starved, yet Sarah slowly and delicately cut the apples and cheese with a sharp knife after she had prayed.

Then, they took turns bathing. Anna fell asleep twice during her bath; Sarah came in to wake her from her lukewarm slumber.

"I'm so sorry to wake you," Sarah said sweetly.

She took a brush from one of their bags and dragged a chair behind Anna as she rested in the tub. Sarah began to brush Anna's gorgeous, long, black hair. She tried to talk to Anna, but she was incoherent. Anna did not even remember going to bed; she was exhausted.

The next morning, Sunday, muffins were left in a basket at their door. They almost missed church because they were so exhausted, but they dressed in haste and ran down the stairs eating the muffins. Sarah's old church, the St. Augustine Priory, was scheduled to begin its service in less than thirty minutes. The walk there would take every bit of that.

They scrambled through a shortcut Sarah remembered. Anna finally laid eyes on the ancient building, surrounded by dusty sunshine and lush, green grass. Anna brushed crumbs off Sarah's dress before they rushed inside the old Protestant church as the last bell rang. They sat in the back pew.

The bell stopped ringing and the pastor began to pray at the entrance of the church before he entered. Sarah and Anna quickly took off their sweaters and sat merely a second before the congregation was asked to stand for the opening hymn. They stood and sang as they fumbled between the prayer book and hymnal.

The pastor finally went to the front and pushed up the huge sleeves on his robe.

"I've not seen him before. He's new," Sarah commented to Anna.

This means he's only arrived within the past fifty years she's been gone, Anna mused.

His white sideburns almost touched his chin. He adjusted his spectacles and looked out gravely at the faces he knew.

"Ooh, he's handsome," Sarah said and smiled widely at him.

Anna smirked and looked ahead.

After church, they started to walk slowly back to the little apartment loaned to them.

"We must look for work in the morning," Sarah said.

She began to cough so hard they had to stop.

"No, you're in no condition, Mum," Anna said as she held her gently. "I'll find something. I'll go out first thing in the morning. Do you have family here who can help us?"

"I have a distant cousin, but he lives a few miles down," Sarah replied and caught her breath. "I'm all right, dear, just a catch in my throat. I'm very tired."

"Perhaps your cousin can help us."

"It's possible. I haven't seen him since he was a small boy. He wrote me several years ago to tell me his parents, my first cousin and his wife, had passed away. I'll walk up with you tomorrow and we'll call on him."

They slept the rest of the day, into the night, until they finally regained their strength and felt human again. The next morning, Sarah told Anna to wear her best dress and carry her best shoes. So, Anna put on her walking shoes and put her heels in a bag, and then they began to walk the prettiest streets she had ever seen.

The main street bustled with horses and carriages as well as cars. They walked through the park over the little bridge and on to the streets with the thatched roofs. Some cottages had flowers climbing up their walls. Anna smiled, having not seen flowers in a very long time.

The two walked down a tree-lined street until it opened into a huge field. There, like a king seated in the middle of a grand throne room, was the Manor. It was more a castle than anything.

Anna gasped when she saw it. *It's magnificent!*

Sarah smiled at her as she adjusted her bag. She fumbled for her best shoes so they were ready as they approached.

The mansion grew bigger the closer they got. It looked like a medieval lord had lived there. Sarah told Anna it was not old at all—during the potato famine, it had been torn down and rebuilt. Subsequently, work was created which saved the lives of the townspeople.

The grey, stone walls peaked in different places as a red vine crawled its way up its structure like long, red hair on a pretty girl.

Sarah nodded at Anna when they hit the stone drive and quickly slipped on her good heels. She tucked a lock of hair behind Anna's ear and nodded again in approval.

There were beautiful cars parked in the drive. Anna touched a white one with her finger as they walked past. Finally, Sarah knocked on the side door.

A man in a beautiful suit greeted them. Sarah stated who they were. He motioned them into the kitchen and went to find the housekeeper. They sat down on a wooden bench as the cook peeled an apple.

"Yes, of course," the housekeeper said.

She extended her hands to Sarah as she bustled in.

"Welcome home, Mrs. Maeryn. I understand you're seeking work for your daughter-in-law."

"Oh, thank you, Mrs. Fitzpatrick. Yes, I like to say she's my daughter, in fact."

Anna shook her hand and Mrs. Fitzpatrick smiled warmly.

"Thank you, Mrs. Fitzpatrick. I'm willing to satisfy any position you have open."

The housekeeper frowned and said, "I'm sorry to say all I have is a scullery maid position."

"I'd be grateful for it," Anna said without hesitation.

Sarah looked at Anna as if to say she should have thought longer.

"May I start tomorrow?"

"Of course, you may. This is Mary . . . Call her Cook. She'll show you the ropes at seven."

"Thank you so very much," Anna said as she eagerly shook Mrs. Fitzpatrick's hand.

The next morning, the sunlight felt alive as it shone through the narrow manor windows and lit up the air as it twirled and danced. Anna straightened her apron and followed Mrs. Fitzpatrick through one beautiful room after another of the great house. "This is the library," Mrs. Fitzpatrick mused as she pushed open the door for Anna to see inside. "Henry loves the library." Anna looked at her a little confused.

Mrs. Fitzpatrick added, "Henry's the master of the manor. He's a young man. You'll probably see him today some time. He's quite unassuming and humble. We all just call him plain Henry because we've known him since he was born. He inherited the estate a few years back when his parents were killed."

After the tour and a brief history about the place, Mrs. Fitzpatrick almost apologetically handed her a sponge and bucket. She asked Anna to scrub the stone floor of the longest, darkest hallway she ever imagined.

Anna began work at once. As any maid can attest, the worst sound while scrubbing floors is footsteps. They were loud and came closer as she tried to keep her humble gaze on the task.

"Please mind your step," she warned without looking up. The footsteps stopped.

A male voice then said, "Miss?"

She looked up and winced as she tried to look into the stream of light which flooded through a window. It hurt her eyes.

The man looked down at her, and then his face backed away. He adjusted his stance and rested his elbow in his hand. He then changed position again and put his hands behind his back. He seemed nervous and fidgeted as she awaited his command.

"Sir, may I attend to you?" She asked gently.

Anna was not sure if this was Master Henry or not. He did fit the description.

"Yes. No. I'll be on my way. I won't mess your floor by walking through," he said awkwardly.

His nervousness did not match his rugged demeanor. He looked as if he was a force to be reckoned with. Yet, Anna's face immediately humbled him.

"It's your floor, sir. Just watch your step so you don't slip, if you don't mind."

"Slip? I just might. I'm a bit clumsy," he chuckled nervously.

She looked back at the floor. Her knees started to ache from kneeling so long.

"I'm so sorry. Forgive me. Let me introduce myself. My name is Henry Oliver. John Henry Oliver as a matter of fact, but please just call me Henry."

"It's very nice to meet you, sir," she smiled at her employer.

The expression on his face was the kindest she had ever seen. It was unusual for an employer to introduce himself by his first name. However, she had reasoned it was because they were roughly the same age.

"I'm very glad to meet you," Anna said and held out a soapy hand for him to shake.

She immediately realized it and drew her hand back, but he hardily extended his nonetheless. She smiled shyly and wiped her hand against her apron before placing it into his.

"Where are you from?" he asked.

"Wales, originally . . . London, the past few years."

He stood for a minute and stared at her. He excused himself, and then walked away.

Mrs. Fitzpatrick stood at the rounded arc at the end of the great hall. She smiled respectfully as he approached her. Anna stopped scrubbing to better hear their faint conversation.

"What are you paying her?"

"The average for a scullery maid. Has she complained?"

"No," he replied.

Anna strained her ear to hear.

"Whatever it is, double it."

Neither of them must have understood the acoustics of the hallway.

"Sir?" Mrs. Fitzpatrick asked astonished.

However, she should not have been surprised. Henry was the most giving person she had ever known.

"Please just do it. I'd like to help this young lady."

"Yes, sir," Mrs. Fitzpatrick said quietly as she looked at Anna.

Anna hardly believed the good fortune she had encountered, or the kindness. She scrubbed faster and harder as she smiled.

Sarah celebrated with her when Anna told her the news that evening. Mrs. Fitzpatrick paid Anna for her services *that* day, something highly unusual. Later, Sarah's friends brought them a basket of food and they shared tea by the fire as Sarah caught up on everyone she knew.

Anna fell asleep in the soft chair she sat in, and awakened early with a sore neck. She did not pay much attention to it. She almost ran down the road to the Manor, anxious to arrive early.

Anna scrubbed pots for hours in the kitchen, pounded out the dust in the long drapes in the dining room, and weeded the vegetable garden. Mrs. Fitzpatrick dismissed her for lunch and she decided to take her small sack outside to walk and breathe a little.

She found a large tree which overlooked the brook and used the last little bit of energy she had to stride toward it. Her back started to ache, so she sat and leaned against the tree. She took a deep breath and was careful not to close her eyes or drift off. Anna wiped the sweat off her neck with her apron and breathed in the stillness.

As she took a bite of her day-old muffin, she heard soft footsteps in the grass and turned to see her employer gently approach a few feet away with a fishing pole in his hand. She got up quickly and brushed the crumbs from her apron.

"Sir?" Anna muffled through a mouth full of muffin.

Henry smiled and said, "I'm so sorry; I didn't mean to disturb your lunch."

"Oh, no, no . . . I was just about to leave."

"Certainly, not. You've hardly touched your lunch. Please, sit down."

She did and ate more daintily than she had alone as he cast his fishing line. Geese flew overhead and he looked up to watch them; he shielded his eyes with his hand.

What's it like to be rich and have anything you can possibly want without having to work hard for it?

Her back was on fire with the pain. She reached up to smooth down the cowlicks in her wavy hair which was tied back.

"Do you want a muffin, sir?" She asked and offered him some of her humble lunch.

He turned so swiftly, she thought she might have scared away his fish. She noted he looked like he did not know what to say. He looked down at her open sack, and then back at her as she held the last muffin toward him.

Henry then reeled his line and put down his pole. He came over slowly as if she was a small animal he tried not to scare. He sat down near her on the ground.

"Did you make them?" He asked as he leaned toward her.

"No, sir," she said.

He smiled, not certain what to say as if he expected her to say yes.

"Please, go ahead and eat."

"Thank you, sir," she said, slightly relieved because she was incredibly hungry.

He pulled at the weeds around him in the grass and gazed at the water. He seemed to not know what to do. She wanted to alleviate some of his nervousness, but did not know how.

"I'm very grateful for this job. I want to thank you for paying me so well and quickly. I know it was your kindness that caused it."

"Oh, no. Not at all. You're a fine worker."

"Sir, you hardly knew that. I've been here only a day and a half."

He turned, looked at her, and then smiled.

"I find it a little strange you call me sir. Will you call me Henry?"

She paused for a moment and giggled.

"No, sir, I don't think I can."

He laughed with her, looked down, and then said, "I'm twenty-eight. I believe we're about the same age."

"We are."

"I'm very bold to ask such a thing and I know it, but it's rare to have a young person about these grounds. I'd very much like to be . . . To have a friend."

"I'm your employee—"

"Yes, yes, of course. I don't know what I was thinking to ask something such as that of you, but I—"

"If it wouldn't bother you, I'd think I'd like to be."

He looked at Anna with shock and gladness which he tried to hide in vain.

"Well, now, that'd be good."

She smiled with her lips pressed together and asked, "Did you come all this way out here to ask me that?"

"Umm . . . Yes, I believe I did have hopes."

"You're so strange," she said and laughed.

"I believe you should be able to say just about anything to your friend. So, what sort of things should we talk about out here at the tree at . . . oh, say . . . one-thirty every day?"

"I should say all sorts of vile things to you if you'd like."

"I'd, actually, very much like that!" he chuckled.

He leaned back and supported his weight with his arms. He became more familiar and less nervous, although not much; he was still very awkward.

"Well, Mr. Henry," she said.

He turned and nodded as she called him by his name.

"I'll say all kinds of things to shock you on a daily basis if you'd like."

He had not realized before how outgoing and open she was. He did not know quite how to react; she decided to reel in her behavior.

"Or we can talk about the weather."

"Why do people talk about the weather? We know what the weather's doing. Why are we discussing something we know about?"

"You're right," she agreed.

Everything suddenly felt quiet and she began to think he had changed his mind about wanting to be friends with his scullery maid. She licked her lips and looked out to where he gazed at the water.

"I'd very much like to know about your life," she said quietly.

He turned and smiled warmly at her, and then looked back over the lake.

"And I, yours. What brings you to Adare?"

"My mother-in-law wanted to come back after the war. This is her hometown."

"Your mother-in-law?"

"Yes, my husband passed away during the war."

She looked at the grass.

"I'm so sorry," he said sweetly as he looked at the water. "Do you have any other family?"

"She's all I have."

Anna did not want to get emotional when she said it, but she was. The words caught in her throat.

"Why is that?"

"I was raised in an orphanage."

Henry immediately felt ill at ease. *How can I possibly share my childhood, knowing hers?*

He looked away and thought of what to say next.

"I'm very sorry to hear that," he said.

"I was a seamstress before the war," she said.

"A seamstress, do you like to make dresses and all?"

"Yes, I suppose. I love clothes."

"What else do you like to do?"

"I like to paint," she admitted cheerily.

"Well, now, that's something."

"What do you like to do, Henry?"

"Well, in my spare time I read, pay bills, write letters . . . I'm incredibly boring."

"You have a manor to run."

"I do, indeed, but, between you and me, I'm incredibly bored."

"Why don't you travel or something like that?"

"I'd have to find someone to run the Manor."

"Mrs. Fitzpatrick can't do that?"

"I suppose she can if I insisted, but I really don't want anyone to be able to go into my family's bank account, but me."

"I can see that."

"It's a big responsibility."

"Do you have family?"

Immediately, Anna felt bad because she remembered what Mrs. Fitzpatrick had told her about his parents.

"My parents passed away. I have a cousin who's more like a sister to me, but right now she's in the Greek Isles."

"What's she doing there?"

"Probably just spending money."

Anna was taken aback by this, but she never understood wealthy people.

"She's just as bored of a person as I am. I wish she'd come home, though. I miss her. She's a good sort of crazy. There's this terribly ugly, enormous picture of some great uncle we have. You know the kind of painting that just scares everyone because the eyes follow you around. When she's here, she keeps moving it around the house. I opened my washroom and there was Uncle Patrick just staring at me—scared me to death!"

Anna laughed and said, "She sounds wonderful."

"She is."

He looked down at the book beside her and asked, "What are you reading?"

"Oh, it's just this," she said and handed it to him.

"You're reading the Bible?"

"Yes."

"Why?"

"Because it's wonderful."

"All right, I've never heard of anyone taking the Bible out with them to eat lunch before. Doesn't seem like the sort of reading material a girl like you'd be reading."

"Well, you don't know me very well, now, do you?"

"I suppose not. Let me ask you something. How can you believe in all that?"

"My late husband was a very devout Christian and so is my mother-in-law. I've learned a lot from them, but I began to cling to God a few years ago during the war."

"I suppose it was a time when everyone was looking for hope."

"Yes. What do you believe in, Henry?"

"You know, good and evil. If you're good, you'll go to heaven and all. If you're a bad person, you pay your dues."

Anna nodded faintly and asked, "Are you a good person, Henry?"

"I should say not."

"Why do you say that?"

Henry smirked, "I was joking."

"Oh. So, you're a good person?"

"I don't know. Is it all right if we just drop this?"

Henry picked at the grass for a few minutes. She knew he was agitated and he, in fact, did not want to drop it.

"I guess everyone needs something like religion as a crutch."

She was slightly offended and commented, "My faith is not a crutch. I can't even stand with a crutch. No, my faith is in a person who carries me."

"Carries you?"

"Yes, He does," she said with a smile.

She looked hard at him as he stared ahead. His face was so rugged as if he had fought a thousand battles and won them all. He had broad shoulders which made his shirts a little small.

"You know, you're rather handsome."

Henry smiled, looked down, and said, "You're not so bad yourself."

Anna smiled the entire walk home at the end of her shift. She finally had something to think about other than war and survival.

She closed her eyes for a few seconds and trusted her feet and the straight road she was on. The breeze threw her hair in her face, but she did not care. She wrapped her old sweater around her and hugged her arms.

Anna did not want to tell Sarah. She did not want to tell anyone, really, because there was nothing to tell. Yet, there was something to feel.

Sarah buzzed around and asked Anna about her day and served her a soup of mostly broth. Anna was hardly able to wait for Sarah to sit down and pray to eat. She barely heard the prayer and almost inhaled her humble dinner. She put the coins on the table she had earned for the day and smiled at Sarah.

"Did they pay you for the week ahead of time? How did you manage to do that?"

"Mum, it's for the day!"

"All of this!" Sarah exclaimed.

"Maybe tomorrow we can have meat?"

"I should say so!"

Anna smiled and relished the feeling of being full. She had not had the feeling in so long. She finished up the soup which Sarah had intended to stretch for a few days, and then fell asleep immediately when she laid her head down on her pillow beside Sarah.

Sarah tried to talk to her, but Anna was unable to think clearly. She was so tired. The day had been physically strenuous, as all scullery maids' workdays. Sarah moved the strands of hair from Anna's face and looked at her beloved daughter.

"Thank you, God, for my sweet girl," she prayed as tears streamed down her face.

During the middle of the night, Anna awakened and sat up straight. She rubbed her eyes. It was pitch black in the room. Sarah put her hand out to her and touched her back. Anna jumped a little, and then lay back down.

"It's all right now, honey. You're safe. Lie down and get some sleep."

Anna put her face in her hands and started to weep. Sarah sat up and put her arms around her.

"One of those dreams again?" She said softly.

Anna nodded.

"You're here now and all is fine."

Sarah hummed and Anna lay back down. She tried to focus her thoughts back on the joy in Henry's face the day before, *He's so beautiful.*

Mrs. Fitzpatrick had quite a list for Anna to do the next morning; the most daunting of which was cleaning the windows. Adare Manor had more windows than an entire apartment complex back in London. The gravity of the project was dizzying.

She poured a bucket full of water and cleaner, and grabbed a bunch of rags. She worked for hours. Her arms hurt from blood rushing out of them as she reached for all the cobwebs in the corners. Her sleeves were soaked. She looked around, and then rolled them up.

Hours later, she heard a rapping straight in front of her in the window she was cleaning; she jumped. Then, she smiled. Henry was dangling a pocket watch in front of the window with a look of puzzlement on his face. He pointed to the watch, and then shrugged.

She shook her head, not understanding at first. Then, she realized she had heard the one o'clock chime on the clock quite a while ago. *It must've been at least an hour.*

She snickered and pointed to the rag in her hand. Henry motioned for her to come outside. She shook her head again. She did not have much time for lunch. Besides, she did not have anything to eat.

Henry's reminder suddenly made her realize how weak she felt. She had scrounged up the last apple that morning and ate it on her way to work. She knew Sarah was very happy to go to the market sometime that day, so she knew she did not have to save it for her.

Henry left the window and Anna resumed cleaning. She smiled to herself.

"If you refuse to pull yourself away from your work," Henry said from behind her and put his hand in the dirty bucket water and brought out another rag, "then, I'll have to speed things along."

She was taken aback, but she grinned widely.

"How do I do this anyway?" he asked.

"Mr. Henry, you cannot help me wash the windows!"

"Last time I checked they were my windows and I can do what I want with them."

"Sir—"

He stood close beside her and began to wash the same window as she was. She giggled as he attempted to clean and only made more of a mess. She knew it was better if he worked on his own window, but she really did not want him to do that.

Then, she realized her sleeves were rolled up. She quickly stopped and turned away from him to pull them back, wet and all, to button them at the wrist. Henry looked at her from the corner of his eye.

"Well, I think this one looks just fine," he remarked at the smeared window with dripping water.

"Best one yet," she agreed and chuckled.

"Now, off to lunch!"

"Oh, I'm afraid I can't today. I have a long list to do and—"

"Nonsense. I'll go get your lunch. Is it in the kitchen?"

"No, really, it's fine. I'm not hungry."

Henry paused and confessed, "I heard your stomach growl."

"You did not!" She blurted and laughed.

"Yes, I did. Come on, it's good to have a break."

She nodded her head and followed him to the kitchen. She did not know how to tell him she did not have any food.

Cook stood over a roast at the counter. Anna instantly licked her lips when she smelled it. Henry smiled at her.

"I don't know why, but I was hungry for a roast today. Do you want some?"

"You're hungry for a roast every day, Henry," Cook snorted.

"Oh, no, I couldn't. . . ." Anna said, embarrassed.

"I can't eat the whole thing by myself," Henry retorted.

"Oh, yes you could!" Cook said with a chuckle.

"Come on, Miss Anna. Just have some with me. It's got to be better than whatever you brought."

"I dare say it is."

Cook served it up and Anna sat next to Henry at the old kitchen table. She tried to eat slowly, but she was half starved. Henry glanced at her a few times.

"You've worked up quite an appetite," he said.

She was immediately embarrassed, as she realized just how much she had eaten.

"I made a tart for dessert," Cook said and plopped it down in front of Anna.

Anna felt her lower lip turn down and tears started coming uncontrollably. She tried to stop crying, but it was no use. Henry put down his fork and looked at her, and then at Cook who was just as puzzled as he.

Finally, he mustered the courage to put his hand on Anna's back and rub it. She leaned into him and put her head on his shoulder. Henry looked at Cook with wide eyes as he held Anna.

"Are you all right?" he asked.

She nodded and tried to stop crying. She swallowed hard and drank some water. She wiped the tears quickly away with her napkin, and then apologized. She picked up her fork, but Henry took it gently from her hands and put it back down. He opened his arms a little and turned to her. Anna embraced him and cried again.

She finally pulled herself together, only because she was so ashamed. She stole away to the washroom. Henry and Cook stared at each other. Anna stood over the porcelain sink and braced herself with her hands. She looked up into the mirror; her face was puffy and eyes red. Then, she returned to the kitchen.

Henry stood up and asked, "Is everything all right?"

"Yes," she said with a gulp. "I'm just so very grateful."

Anna reached out her hand for Henry's and he held it. He looked at her lovely face. He then realized how very little she had.

He wanted to give her the world in that moment. He wanted to cry with her, as he realized how blessed he was. Yet, at that moment, he was unable to move. She was smiling at him.

Anna finally excused herself, remarked about the time, and went back in the main part of the house. Mrs. Fitzpatrick met her in the library as she finished the windows, and then took her into the servant's quarters. She showed Anna a small room decorated in blue and white with sparse, pretty furnishings.

"This is the scullery maid's quarters," she remarked happily. "Henry's mother decorated all the servant's rooms before she passed. Aren't they pretty? She had my room done in lavender. They all have their own fireplace."

Anna did think it was pretty.

"I don't think I'll need this room, Mrs. Fitzpatrick. I'll be staying with Sarah in town."

"Oh, now dear, I realize that, but sometimes—very rarely actually—there's a late party and you won't want to walk back in the darkness. Or you can just use it to freshen up or take your breaks. There's a small wardrobe to put a few things in just in case."

She was a pleasant woman with pretty features, although she was past middle age. She seemed to love her master and the way she was treated at the Manor. Everyone seemed to feel the same as she. There was not a more pleasant staff in all of Ireland, Anna was sure.

Anna thanked her and they began to walk down the hall toward the library. Henry came out and the two of them curtseyed. Henry almost did as well, forgetting to bow. Anna smiled which he found discomforting and straightened his collar. He finally remembered to say hello to them. The ladies smiled at each other as they walked away and understood how nervous Henry became around women, even those he employed.

"Ah, Anna?" he called.

She turned around.

"Thank you, Mrs. Fitzpatrick," he said to politely excuse her.

She curtseyed. Then, she walked into the library, shut the door, and left Henry and Anna in the hall.

"I was wondering . . . if . . . if you'd like to go with me on a little excursion tomorrow?"

Anna did not answer, stunned at the question.

"You see, I'm in need of some fresh air and I go to the Cliffs of Moher. Do you know it?"

She shook her head.

"Well, you see, I go there every year and usually go with my mates, but they won't be back from the universities until next week. I'm told this is the prime time to go."

She had never heard him talk so much. *He's rambling.*

"The weather is very fine right now and they have all whined we go there every year and how boring it is, you see. I'd really still like to go. It's not far."

She stood and looked at him in the silence he had finally created.

"All right, but I'm to work tomorrow though. Can you talk with Mrs. Fitzpatrick about it?"

"Yes, yes, of course," he said.

He was so delighted he did not know which way to turn.

That night, Anna thought Sarah was going to wet herself from the excitement. Her questions were unending.

"Does he know I'm related to him?" Sarah asked first.

"No, Mum."

"Does he know about you coming from London?"

"Yes, I believe I said something to him like that."

"Does he know what you did during the war?"

"No, Mum, and I don't know if I'll tell him just yet."

"Why ever not?"

"It's not something I like to talk about."

"What are you going to wear?"

"My red dress," she finally answered a question happily.

Henry decided to pick her up in his car outside her little apartment. The entire village was in a stir about it as she hopped in.

"There'll be talk about this," he muttered and smiled.

He opened the top of the convertible and let the warm wind in. It was a rare sunny day in Ireland.

"So, Henry, how do you feel about running off with the scullery maid?"

"Very good . . . Is that what we're doing?" He answered as she snickered.

He's so funny, but not on purpose, of course which makes it so much funnier.

"So, I'd like to know about you, Mister Henry."

"What'd you like to know? And *Henry* is just fine."

"Well, Henry, I'd like to know about your life. What can you tell me?"

"I thought we'd covered this."

"We've scratched the surface."

"Well, honestly, there's not a whole lot else to tell other than what you know. I've led an intrinsically boring life."

"Oh, I don't believe *that* for a second."

"Whether or not you believe it doesn't make it less true. I'd like to know more about your life. What was it like—your childhood— growing up in an orphanage like you did?"

She did not want to talk about it, but she knew she needed to if he wondered.

"We were fortunate enough to have caring nurses," she admitted. "It was just there were so many of us. There was little of everything.

I remember every night going to bed in a crowded, usually cold, room. I imagined what it'd be like to have a family. I can't tell you how rare it'd be for a child—not a baby—to be adopted. If you were, it was usually to work on a farm, as a maid, or caretaker of other children."

"I didn't know—"

"Of course you didn't. I'm so glad you didn't know. Then, there'd be two of us with broken pasts instead of just one."

He smiled apologetically and asked, "What was your husband like?"

"Oh, Jamie was a card. He was always making everyone laugh. He was a red-head . . . skinny . . . loved that man to death. I met him when I worked as a seamstress. I was fortunate to be trained as such in the orphanage so I'd have a skill. He'd deliberately buy trousers too long, so he was able to see me."

"I think most men in their right mind would do something like that after seeing you . . . you know . . . For someone they're attracted to."

"Right, it took him four months and thirteen pairs of pants to ask me out."

Henry grinned.

After a conversation about favorite foods, they pulled up to the Cliffs of Moher. Henry turned to her. Anna surveyed the incredible scenery before her—the land was a beautiful green, and then shot straight down one hundred and twenty meters to an angry ocean. The view went on forever. She walked a ways, and then stopped to breathe it in.

"Beautiful!"

"I'm so glad you think so," Henry said.

"Henry," she said as she turned her gaze into his eyes, "thank you so much for bringing me here."

Henry was dumbfounded and replied nervously as he scratched his head, "Thank you for coming."

They stole a glance at each other in one of the most beautiful places in the world. It was certainly the most beautiful place she had ever been.

"Henry, will you hold my hand?" she asked. "That drop really scares me."

She tried to make her request sound more innocent than it was. He smiled and held out his hand for her to take. His large, rough hands were not the hands of a gentleman. They were similar to the hands of a carpenter.

Life shot up her arms like fireworks in the night and signaled the war was finally over. That was the moment she knew. Anna smiled so hard it hurt.

"Tell me about your life before Adare," Henry said as he held her hand tightly.

"Well, you already know some of it."

"Tell me what it was like during the war in London."

"It was terrible, as you know. Bombs fell daily, even hourly. I was so afraid for Sarah I always looked for a place to hide whether it was when I went to the market for our rations or wherever I was. I wanted to protect her."

"Why do you think such a bond with an in-law?"

"I don't have my own family. She became all I had when my husband was killed. She had no one either. We were meant for each other, I guess," she said as she smiled at him.

"She has taught me so many things and I'm forever grateful."

"What did she teach you?" He asked gently.

"About love and God."

"God, huh?"

"Yes."

"What did she teach you about love?"

"She taught me to see a person for who he or she truly is. Then, love the person anyway."

"So, Anna, you like me anyway, huh?"

"Yes!"

However, she did not simply like Henry; she loved him already. It was so immediate she almost did not believe it in her heart. She wondered if he was feeling half of what she was for him. She looked at Henry. There was much more to him than anyone else she had ever met.

"I have yet to find a flaw in you," he said as he felt increasingly nervous as she stared at him with her beautiful eyes.

"I have a temper," she said with a smirk.

"You do?"

He seemed almost happy to know it.

"Does this excite you?"

"It sort of does; I'm glad to hear you have something you deal with."

"Why'd you like that?"

"Because I have too many to count; it makes you human."

"I am, indeed, that."

"No, I don't think so," he sniffed as he looked at his expensive shoes.

Anna decided to change the subject.

"What's your favorite book, Henry?"

"Frankenstein."

"Frankenstein!" She cried out and laughed.

"Have you ever read it?"

"No."

"Well, Anna, it's one of the best written books of all time."

"Are you joking?"

"No. I promise. I love it. I love how Mary Shelley understands the monster's feelings."

They walked hand in hand.

"So, you're relating to a monster?" she teased.

Henry nudged her with his arm. She felt like she was going to fall from the cliff.

"Don't do that!" She said and laughed nervously. "I'm so scared I'm going over the edge!"

Henry switched places with her so he was the closer one to the drop. Even though it was a relatively warm day, the wind beat against their ears mercilessly. Finally, Anna began to shake from the cold and nervousness. She hated she did that. There was one point in her life when she went months shaking like that, but she did not want to think of that—*No, it's a beautiful moment in every way.*

"You're shaking?"

Henry finally noticed. She buttoned the top of her old sweater. She was wearing her Sunday best, but it was considered rags to a wealthy man like Henry. She was trying not to be ashamed of it. She looked down at her best shoes, covered in mud, and wondered how to get it off before Sunday.

"I'm fine," she said as she shook involuntarily.

"You're not fine," Henry said gently with a smile.

He led her to the car and opened the door for her. He went to the trunk and retrieved a blanket for her. He covered her with it and tucked it around her legs. Then, he got in on the other side.

"Looks like a storm is coming; we best be leaving anyhow."

He started the engine of his gorgeous car after putting up the top.

"Thank you for bringing me here," she said.

She wanted to put her head back and sleep in bliss, but she did not want to miss a moment with him.

"It was truly my pleasure," he said.

She closed her eyes and smiled to savor the moment.

"Anna, may I ask you something?"

"Of course."

"Will you hold my hand again?"

She sat, dumbfounded. She wanted to answer right away, but she was unable to even form the word yes. So, she put her hand in his open one. He threaded his fingers through hers.

"This is terribly inappropriate for an employer," she teased.

"But maybe not inappropriate for a friend?"

"Friends hold hands like this?"

He smiled, turned red, and sheepishly replied, "Yes, I do believe they do."

CHAPTER 2

THE RAIN FELL AS A downpour. It almost frightened Anna how it came so quickly. Henry turned up his wipers and muttered he was glad he had put the top up. Then, the car hiccupped, and then began losing power. Henry pulled off the side of the road, yet kept his headlights on.

"What's happening?"

"The car overheated. It happens sometimes. I have a jug of water in the trunk, but I don't want to go get it in the rain. Do you mind if we sit here for a minute?"

"Of course not," Anna said.

They sat in silence for a while. Anna looked down at their hands, and then back up at Henry who stared out the windshield. She wanted, at that moment, to share everything she was with him. She was unable to explain it. It was as if she was bearing her soul. She took a deep breath and closed her eyes. She began shaking again.

"Are you cold?" Henry asked when he looked at her.

She did not answer, but began to unbutton her sleeve on her left arm. Henry looked down at what she was doing. Her fingers trembled and tears were in her eyes. He did not understand, but he was about to.

As Anna slowly rolled up her sleeve, she turned her arm over. He was puzzled until he made out a small number on the soft skin of

her arm. Then, he saw another number and another. The numbers
went on; six terrible little numbers.

"Anna," he whispered in horror.

She nodded her head.

"How?" he mouthed.

"I was arrested trying to help...."

"Trying to help who, Anna?"

"I hid with Sarah in the tunnels as long as I could, Henry. I
heard reports about the Jewish people. I couldn't just do nothing.
I was worried about Sarah, so I didn't do anything for a long time.
Finally, I couldn't rest until I did. I began smuggling women and
children over the channel."

"They found you?"

"One night, I was helping a woman and her four-year-old little
girl," Anna broke off. "They shot them. Point blank."

She stared off for a few minutes.

"And arrested me."

She swallowed hard.

"We were put into a boxcar for days. Then, we waited in a long
line to be inspected. The strongest and prettiest girls were selected.
We were sent to a brothel for Schutzstaffel (the SS). They ...," she
was hardly to speak, "They made us...."

He lowered his eyes. He had not heard about such atrocities, but
he remembered one reporter stated it taking the next one hundred
years to hear all the stories of horror the Nazis had inflicted.

"Eight of more a night came in ...," she finally said.

Henry sat, with his fingers wrapped around Anna's in stunned
silence. He shook his head quickly and tried to not cry, but tears
began to drip down his face just as hers were.

"Here I am, sitting in my fine mansion, having done nothing
to add to the world, and then I look at you, Anna. You're a hero.

And I think . . . Why don't you have the riches? You certainly deserve them."

"No, Henry, no—I'm not telling you this to make you feel guilty. I just wanted you to know."

"Why . . . Why are you telling me all of this?" He asked gently.

"I don't know," she lied.

I love you. That's why.

"You're my friend, aren't you?"

He wiped some tears from her cheeks. She tried to push down all the memories, but she could not.

Anna thought, *So many concentration camp survivors can tell their stories.*

Yet, she found it difficult to tell hers to just anyone. Henry, however, was very special, this she knew.

The rain pelted the car. She looked at him; her tears still came. Henry nodded.

"Yes, of course, I'm your friend," he whispered.

He was unable to imagine Anna going through what she had.

"After the war, I was returned to Sarah."

"Where were you?" He asked quietly.

"I didn't know where I was at the time, none of us did, but I found out later I was in Mauthausen. I was in an elite area for the SS."

"Anna, I'm so sorry."

"I was one of the lucky ones. I was there for forty-five days before the war ended and we were emancipated. I don't think I could've survived another day."

Henry looked at their intertwined hands and said, "I wish I could take all of that away from you."

She smiled at him and said, "You do. When I'm with you, I don't think about it. I only feel happy."

"I make you happy?"

She nodded.

"Anna, can we do this every day?"

"Sit in a car on the side of the road?" she joked.

"Yes. No. I don't care where I am. I just love being your friend."

"I love being your friend, too."

"How about tomorrow?"

"I have to work, you know that."

"I know the boss, though."

She chuckled and conceded, "Yes, I suppose you might pull a few strings for me."

"Do you want to go into town—Shannon—with me?"

"What will we do there?"

"Do you want to see a movie?"

"That'd be fun."

The rain dissipated and Henry reluctantly cooled down the engine with the jug of water. He started the car and they were back much sooner than Anna had liked. They pulled into the village and Henry parked the car in front of the pharmacy.

"Why don't you come up and meet Sarah?"

"Oh, I'd love to," he said nervously.

She was ashamed of her little apartment, but thought it was a necessary thing. She opened the unlocked door and went in. She called Sarah, Henry sheepishly following behind. In the bedroom, she found Sarah, unresponsive, in bed.

"Mum!"

No response. Sarah burned with fever. Henry gained the courage to peep in.

"Please, go get the doctor!" she yelled.

CHAPTER 3

HENRY FLEW DOWN THE STAIRS of the apartment above to the pharmacy below.

"Call Dr. Lannon!" He yelled at the pharmacist. "It's Sarah!"

The clerk immediately got on the telephone as the pharmacist ran upstairs with Henry. He checked her eyes and felt her pulse. He threw off her blankets—soaked with her sweat—and ordered Anna to change Sarah's clothes and get other blankets.

Henry waited in the living room. Dr. Lannon appeared quickly and went straight into the bedroom. Henry sat and tapped his feet on the floor.

An hour went by. Henry knew because he checked his watch every five minutes. Finally, Anna came out, her hair frazzled and cheeks flushed.

"She's going to be fine," she said. "Dr. Lannon thinks she has pneumonia and he's giving her medicine."

Henry immediately answered, "Don't worry. Whatever she needs I'll take care of. If she needs the hospital, we'll do that as well."

He felt her relax in his arms. She was beautiful in every way. He felt so close to her, so quickly. It astounded him. It was like nothing he had ever experienced. He kissed the top of her head.

"Whatever you need, I'll give you," he said to her. "You don't have to worry about anything."

He wanted to give her everything he had. He closed his eyes and breathed her in.

"Thank you, Henry," she whispered into his chest, her hot breath went through his shirt.

The pharmacist and Dr. Lannon came out and caught them in their embrace. Henry and Anna quickly let go of each other and turned to thank them.

"Bill me," Henry whispered to the two men.

Dr. Lannon said, "I'll check back in an hour. If there's no change by night, she has to go to the hospital."

Anna rushed in to Sarah. Henry sat on the sofa and waited again.

Finally, she re-emerged and said Sarah was awake and asked for the priest to come pray. Henry offered to go get him and left for the priory. He was a little nervous; he never darkened a door to church, except for a funeral or wedding.

He hated religion; it bored him to tears. He never understood people's need for it. It bothered him a little about Anna, but she was so full of love, he accepted the fault in her.

He knocked on the front door of the church, unsure of what else to do. There was no answer. Finally, he opened the door and went into the dimly-lit church. He shuffled on the black and white tiles, and called out Father Donnelley's name. The priest came out of a side door and walked quickly toward Henry with a smile on his face.

"I hate to bother you, but Sarah, the new woman in town—"

"Yes, yes, of course, is anything wrong?" Father Donnelly asked.

He held his hands out to Henry as if he was ready to pray with him. It was a habit for him to do so, as so many who would come to him wanted prayer from him.

"Well, she's very ill with pneumonia and asked for you to come pray."

Henry kept his hands by his side.

"Of course," he said and immediately went with Henry.

Father Donnelly slid into Henry's sports car and commented on its beauty. Henry was proud of it, but he was slightly embarrassed about his wealth.

"Has the doctor seen her?"

"Yes, of course. We called him first."

"Yes, yes," Father Donnelly said.

He secretly thought prayer was needed even before a doctor.

"Henry, are you Sarah's friend?"

"I'm her daughter-in-law's employer."

"Oh, very good."

"Anna and I are friends."

"Well, now," Father Donnelly said with a smirk.

Henry smiled back. He liked the priest immediately.

"She's quite something to behold, isn't she?"

"Father!" Henry uttered and laughed.

"Well, I'm not dead now am I?"

Henry laughed harder, but then stopped as he pulled up to the pharmacy. Father Donnelly thanked him for driving and headed up. Once again, Henry waited in the living room alone.

Finally, Anna came out and took his hands. When she did, he wanted to fly through the roof, but her words kept him grounded.

"Father Donnelly prayed for healing. She's sitting up and asking for soup!"

Henry thought for a moment.

"Oh, that's good," Henry said.

Anna ran down the stairs to order soup from the restaurant across the way. Henry left her a brief note and left.

Dear Anna,

Thank you for today. I had a great time. I need to get back to the house. I guess our movie day is not feasible

tomorrow. Please take the day off and be with Sarah. She
may relapse.

Your friend,

Henry

Henry drove home. His mind was full and heart on fire. He
thought about leaving his car on the side of the road and running home, so much energy burst within him. He finally parked
in his incredibly long driveway and walked the green grass of his
expansive land.

He felt alive when he was with Anna. When she was gone, even if
it was for minutes, he missed her. He walked toward the beautiful tree
where they had their first lunch. It seemed so long ago, but it was not.

He touched the tree and watched the glittering waves in the river.
His thoughts turned dark as he remembered the conversation he
had with her as the rain pelted on his car. She was not only married before, but the horrors she endured at the camp were more
than he could process.

He had absolutely no experience with women, being as shy as
he was. Even the girls in Adare scared him, although he went to
school with them his whole life.

He did not remember ever actually having a conversation with
any of them, let alone have one confide in him. He wondered
what such experiences did to a woman.

"Hello!" A voice called from behind.

Henry looked at his pocket watch. He had stared at the brook
for a half hour as he pondered the eventful day, yet it seemed only
a few moments. Henry turned and saw a man dressed in black,
take off his hat as he approached.

"Father Donnelly, good to see you so soon!" Henry chimed and
shook his hand.

"Thank you, my boy! I thought I'd pay you a visit."

"Well, of course, do you want to come in for some tea?"

"Oh, no, that's fine. Outside will be much more to my suiting. Have you caught any fish of late?"

"No, I'm a terrible fisherman, but I love the peace."

"Yes, as do I. Although, I'm quite good," Father Donnelly boasted and winked.

"Are you now?"

"Yes, I can catch a whale by simply whistling at it," Father Donnelly bragged.

Henry chuckled and asked, "What brings you by?"

"I'd like to thank you for taking care of the widow, Sarah."

"Yes, of course."

"Do you know much about them?"

"A little."

"I know little as well. They're good gals."

"Goodness soul, they sure are!"

"Take good care of 'em," Father Donnelly said.

He put his hat on and turned to leave.

"Father Donnelly, do you want to go fishing with me?"

Father Donnelly's eyes gleamed when he replied, "Would I now?"

CHAPTER 4

SARAH GOT BETTER BY THE hour. Anna thanked God at least a hundred times as she tended to Sarah's every whim. She had read the note Henry left and was a little disappointed. She read it to Sarah, but she was not keen enough yet to sort it out.

Sarah had fallen asleep early so Anna sat in the living room where Henry had sat and stared at the wall as she prayed. She finally decided she needed a walk and headed to the main street of Adare. The children were out in the warmth of the night air. They played in the streets with a few balls and moved out of the way if a car approached once in a long while.

Anna walked the muddy road in her oldest shoes as she trudged to the park. She finally stopped and sat on a bench. She normally hated to stop because when she stopped, she remembered terrible things. Yet, that day, she had wonderful memories to ponder.

It was quite a day. She smiled as she rehashed what had happened. A little boy came by and spun a hoop. She smiled at him. Then, Anna felt someone stand behind her bench.

She turned around and saw Henry as the street lights lit. He stood, hat in hand. She smiled and he sat beside her.

"How is she?" Henry whispered.

"Better. How did you know I was here?"

"I didn't. I actually come here quite often. I had a visit from the rector this afternoon. We fished."

"You fished with Father Donnelley?"

"Yes, he's quite a fisherman. He caught three fish in an hour."

"Is that impressive?"

"To me it is. I don't think I've caught three fish in my life!"

Anna laughed and said, "I have to get back."

"I'll go up with you," he said and put on his hat.

"Why do you suppose he came to see you?" She asked as she stood up.

"I'm not sure. Maybe he wants a rich man to pass the offering plate to," Henry said slyly.

As soon as he did, he regretted it. Father Donnelly was not at all like that, Henry knew it.

"Has he ever done that before?"

"No, but I've had very little interaction with the man. Today was the first day I ever spoke to him."

"I find that strange."

"Why?"

"You've lived here your whole life and have never spoken to the rector?"

"My parents were buried at the Catholic church. My mom was raised Catholic, although she wasn't a believer."

"Still—"

"Although it's a small town, we stay in our own circles."

"May I ask you something?" Anna requested, slightly nervous as they walked back to her apartment.

"Of course, do you need something?"

"No, no, it's just that . . . Well, Sarah opened her big mouth to Father Donnelly and told him I sing and—"

"You sing?"

"Yes, and he's asked me to sing the offertory. I was wondering if you'd like to come to church with us on Sunday."

Henry did not know what an offertory was. The thought of going into a church and not knowing what to do made Henry very nervous.

"Of course, I'll be there. What time?"

"It's at 10:30 a.m."

"Sure. I'll be there. Yes. I'll meet you at the priory."

Anna opened the door behind the pharmacy and started to walk up the stairs. Henry followed and closed the door behind him. He stood at the bottom of the stairs. Anna felt he was not moving and stopped at the fourth step.

"Are you all right?" She asked sweetly.

Henry took off his hat and looked up at her. He did not know what to do with himself. He fiddled with his hat, and then looked back up at her.

"Henry?" She probed as she stepped down to him.

He wanted to kiss her, just like he saw men do in the movies. No man was shy around women in movies. Heroes took what they wanted, but Henry had not felt like a hero a day in his life.

Anna smiled at him. She leaned in to give him a hug and he grazed her cheek with a kiss. He was so clumsy and unromantic, but she beamed at him. Then, she walked up the steps quickly. He stood with his hat in his hand for a long time. Then, he gathered himself and went home to a sleepless night.

Henry dressed a half a dozen times Sunday morning. Once he had to change because he was sweaty. He ended up wearing a navy suit and light blue tie. He shined his shoes, and then brushed his teeth.

He went to the bathroom for the umpteenth time and tried to still the butterflies in his stomach. He breathed deeply, but it did nothing to ease his nerves. Mrs. Fitzpatrick and Cook had the day off, but left him lunch in the icebox and cookies on the table. He dared not put any food on his stomach.

He decided to walk to the church since it was relatively close—the Manor was directly across the way. Besides, he did not want to drive up in a car worth more than any cottage in Adare. So, he took the main roads as much as possible so he did not mess up his shoes.

He arrived quicker than he anticipated—almost a half hour early. He did not know what to do with himself. A few parishioners entered, but it was tough for a visitor to enter so early.

He had almost over-analyzed his early arrival when he saw Sarah and Anna. She wore her favorite red dress. She helped Sarah walk to the church. His heart sank as he realized they had walked. It was at least a mile and a half.

I should've picked them up!

Sarah was certainly in no condition to make the walk. Henry hustled to them as they smiled at him.

"I don't know what I was thinking; I should've picked you up!" Henry said apologetically as he approached them.

He wanted to sit down and cry; he was so upset.

"It's all right, Henry," Anna said sweetly.

Henry offered his arm to Sarah and she took it happily. She guided him to the third pew from the front. He was uneasy about their seating and wanted to sit in the back, but he obeyed. Anna sat on the other side of Sarah. He had hoped she would sit next to him.

"Anna, will you be able to see over there?" he asked.

He was happy someone tall had sat in front of her. She was small and he thought maybe she would move by him.

"I'll be fine. There's nothing much to see," she whispered.

Henry read his bulletin for the tenth time as the organ started. Everyone stood.

Really, this entire service is an exercise in sitting and standing.

The rector spoke, and then the congregation responded.

"God be with you," Father Donnelly said with a smile.

"And also with you," the church responded.

The first time the congregation spoke, Henry jumped. He thumbed through the prayer book and tried to make sense of it. The prayer book seemed like a foreign language—as the scriptures were. He did not really understand much, or why people gave their lives for it.

Finally, Anna got up and stood by Father Donnelly on the platform. Henry's stomach flipped. Instead of the tiny flips his stomach had done numerously all day, his stomach experienced whale flips—he was nervous for her.

Father Donnelly reached his hand out to Anna. Henry noticed she was shaking. Anna looked at him. He smiled and nodded.

"This is Anna." Father Donnelly told his congregation. "I'm told by a certain someone she's quite the soloist."

Anna turned as red as her dress.

"Sarah," he said, "we're all so glad you're feeling better. We've been fervently praying."

The congregation applauded. Henry was baffled. *What a strange thing to applaud.*

"Jesus is our Healer," Father Donnelly said.

An older man nodded and said, "Amen."

Henry was mystified people actively participated. It was not at all like the concerts he had attended where people sat and watched.

Then, Father Donnelly left Anna alone on the platform and everyone watched her. She drew in her breath and started to sing. After the first line of the first verse, Henry melted. Sarah took his hand, always sensitive to other's feelings.

Anna was like a stained glass window. She told a story and illuminated his heart. She sang without accompaniment and never missed a note. Then, she walked off the platform silently.

She sat down next to Henry who was positioned nearest the end of the pew. He smiled and burst with pride as she bit her lip in hope she had done all right. Henry thought, *If there was ever a time to applaud, it's now!*

Yet, no one did. They just leaned forward, one-by-one to catch Anna's eye and smiled at her. Henry had put his hands together, ready to applaud with all his might, but Sarah caught them and held them gently. He looked at Sarah; she smiled and winked at him.

I don't understand church, not even a little.

Father Donnelly walked toward the congregation at the conclusion of the service.

"Thank you, Anna. Wasn't that beautiful?"

The congregation agreed.

"I'd like to invite you all to get your picnic baskets and blankets; we'll fellowship together with a picnic."

Anna turned to Sarah.

"And for those of you who didn't know, like our visitors—I see you Anna, worried you didn't bring a basket!"

The congregation laughed.

"We've planned for you as well. We've all brought enough for our families, and then some. I have some extra picnic blankets, so there's no excuse. You must come!"

Father Donnelly smiled at the three of them.

"Let me pray for you," he said.

Everyone bowed their heads. He put his hands out to them.

"And now, may the peace of God, which surpasses all understanding, guard your hearts and your minds in Christ Jesus."

The congregation agreed and immediately turned to gather their things. People surrounded Anna to tell her how beautiful her solo was and welcome her. Henry had never shown up empty-handed to any gathering in his life. He was taken aback by the feeling of the parishioners who rallied around him and the girls.

Father Donnelly brought over a blanket and sat down with them on the lawn as one happy lady after another offered them countless plates of food. Anna had never seen that much food in her life. Father Donnelly's warm, happy presence cheered them all.

"Sarah, you're looking a little weak," Father Donnelly noted.

"I guess I am," she said with a smile.

"Just wait here a minute," the priest said.

He returned after a few minutes with a heap of pillows which he piled around Sarah until she laughed heartedly at how ridiculous she looked.

"I'm Cleopatra!" She said and laughed harder. "Give me some of those grapes, Anna."

Anna gave her a bunch. Then, Sarah hung them over her head as she ate.

After every person in the parish had spoken to Sarah and Anna, and bowed toward Henry, Sarah and Father Donnelly became engrossed in a private story they giggled relentlessly about. Henry stood and offered his hand to Anna. She took it and they walked together.

He led her by the park they had been in the night before. Anna knew she was going to ruin the only good pair of shoes she owned, but she did not care. Henry walked her through the mud, unknowingly, until her shoes were almost black.

They did not speak to one another; they drank in the unusual warmth of the day. Henry stopped and leaned against a tree. He had not complimented her singing and Anna was nervous about what he thought more than anyone. Yet, Henry was oblivious to his oversight and lost in his feelings for her.

He took her hands and rubbed them with his thumb until they felt raw. Finally, he looked at her and was taken aback by how her eyes were filled with tears and face was filled with joy.

"Henry, how is it possible I've already fallen in love with you?"

Henry's eyes searched hers wildly. He wondered if what she had said was simply a figure of speech. A girl he knew once said she had fallen head over heels in love with a tea pot.

He searched her face. Then, as she waited, her smile faded. He wanted to rescue her heart which he knew had started to break, yet he was speechless. No one had ever said anything remotely like that to him.

"I'm sorry," she said.

Anna looked away. He wanted to hold her, kiss her, yell he felt the same, put her arms around his neck, and spin her around. He, however, stood there like an idiot.

"No," he croaked. "Don't apologize."

She was stunned she had said such a thing to her employer. *Have I temporarily lost my mind?*

He did not know what to do. He cleared his throat three times, looked at their muddy shoes, breathed heavily, and then found she had, indeed, put her arms around his neck. Anna had hugged him. He held her tightly, too tight. He kissed her ear, aimed for her cheek, and then held her again.

She's going to be the death of me, he thought with certainty.

CHAPTER 5

HENRY HARDLY REMEMBERED WALKING ANNA back to her apartment. He did not want to; he wanted to take her home with him and never let her go. She was the most frighteningly wonderful person he had ever met. He decided he might always be scared of her. *That's not a bad thing.*

He wanted to kick himself. *Why didn't I tell her how I felt or kiss her?*

"Stupid, idiot," he mumbled to himself as he foraged through the Manor icebox that night.

He was not hungry, but his nervousness compelled him to eat. He took a huckleberry pie out and dug in without cutting it.

Cook will be mad, but I'll smooth it over with her as always. Ah, Cook—there's someone who doesn't scare me . . . And she's a woman! Why can't I be more open with Anna?

She loved him. He wanted to hear her say it again and again; it would never get old. He stopped eating the pie and stood up.

"I'll go see her," he said. "No, no, you dummy. Give her time."

He continued the conversation with himself the rest of the night.

The next morning, Henry was up before any of the help. He sat at the kitchen table and watched the door for Anna's arrival. Cook found the crumbly remains of her pie and yelled at Henry who was oblivious; he did not try to smooth it over. Cook noticed he was distracted and threw an old muffin at the back of his head. Henry turned around immediately and smiled.

"That's for eating tonight's pie, you hooligan!"

Henry grinned wider. Cook could not help, but smile, too.

She asked, "What's got your panties all in a wad today, Henry?"

Henry loved her expressions and replied, "Nothin'."

She knew he was waiting for Anna. Finally, the door quietly opened and Anna came in, dressed to work. She smiled shyly at Henry and scurried away immediately.

"Well, now," Cook said, knowingly, "you two had quite a weekend."

Henry ignored her and took off after Anna. He stopped her in the hall.

"I need to talk to you," he insisted.

Anna's heart sank and she thought, *Maybe he's going to fire me for what I said yesterday . . . How I threw myself at him yesterday. . . .*

Anna wanted to crawl under a rock somewhere and die.

"I'm not good with all of this—" Henry began clumsily.

"It's all right, Henry. I don't know what I was thinking yesterday. I need to be more respectful. You're my employer and I—"

"Stop, Anna, I'm trying to say something."

"Sorry."

Yet, he still said anything. He just stood there again. He finally mustered up the courage and said, "Lunch?"

She smiled and nodded. Then, she walked away.

Henry tried to psych himself into being manly. He had watched Casablanca in his movie theatre in the basement the night before. He had watched it twice, actually. Still, he was no Bogart. He could not hold Anna in his arms and talk to her so his lips almost touched her nose.

"Bogart's so rough with women," he commented aloud as he watched.

Henry hated he was gentle and thought, *I want to be manlier.*

Henry tried to think of a plan. None came to mind, but he

hoped he had one before lunch. He went to think in his library. The one o'clock chime on his grandfather clock was like a bad omen. He had a plan and met Anna in the kitchen.

Cook served up lunch for the two of them. Anna did not look at him.

"I have an idea for today," Henry announced.

She looked at him with her gorgeous, light eyes. He almost forgot what he was going to say.

"Let's eat in the dining room."

Cook almost dropped her ladle. Henry gathered up his plate and cup. So did Anna. They walked into the huge dining room. Anna marveled at the incredible chandelier which hovered over the thirty-seat table. He picked a seat at the far end and she sat to his right. Then, she ate without a word.

He wanted her to be in awe of the incredible room, but he realized it was just another room to clean to her. He took a deep breath and did not touch his food.

Henry summoned his inner hero and grabbed her face. He planted a kiss on her lips. Unfortunately, her mouth was full of food and she pulled away at once. She put the napkin to her lips and tried to chew as fast as she could.

He looked at her in horror and thought, *I've ruined it. Our first kiss and I've ruined it!*

Then, Anna drank her entire cup of water. He sat on his hands and stared at his food.

"Henry," she began, but then started to laugh

Tears rolled down her cheeks. He laughed with her after a few seconds.

"That was truly terrible," she noted as they laughed harder.

She got up and stood beside him. Then, she put her hand on his rough cheek and kissed him on the lips. She gave him an Eskimo kiss on his nose, and then kissed him again.

"I love you, Henry," she said and laughed once more.

This beautiful creature loves a total mess, he marveled.

The next few weeks, very little work was done by Anna at the Manor. Anna was so happy she almost forgot every terrible episode of her life. Every time Henry smiled at her, another moment spend in the orphanage disappeared. When he kissed her, the memories ceased about hiding in tunnels while bombs fell around her. Even the most terrible, unspeakable of memories were washed away with the water of joy. Heaven was happening in her heart.

Mrs. Fitzpatrick also knew what was happening. She tried to protect their interests by being in their presence as much as possible.

Soon, the spring holiday was upon them. Anna was busy in the kitchen helping the kitchen staff make baked goods for the three other young men who were to befall them from the universities.

Henry was anxious for his three boyhood friends to be with him for an entire week. They had made plans to stay together at the Manor rather than with their families in town. Henry could not wait.

As Anna prepared, though, it became strange to her to work for the man with whom she was in love. She wondered how things would go with his friends about him.

She entered the kitchen early the next morning. There were three young men around the kitchen table where the staff usually ate. They were picking through the baskets of sweets Cook had made the day before. When Anna entered, they quieted, and then started to snicker.

She felt a little uncomfortable and Mrs. Fitzpatrick knew it. So, she scurried her away with a tray of tea for Henry who was in his library, as he usually was. Anna stood with a tray of his mother's china. She put it down, picked up his cup and saucer of tea, and handed it to him black—the way he liked it.

"Thank you," he whispered.

Then, she kissed him on the lips softly.

"Thank you again," he said and smiled.

He quickly looked at the doorway where his three friends stood with mischievous faces. Anna ran out of the library through the side door and closed it. She heard them erupt into laughter when she left, so she stood and listened.

"How come I don't have a scullery maid?" One of them asked.

The rest laughed harder. Henry silently smiled.

"*She* kissed *you*, Henry. I don't care how much of your money she wants, she's worth it!" Sean joked and laughed.

Anna clung to the other side of the door and waited for Henry to defend her, but he said nothing. She ran to the garden by the kitchen.

"Anna?" Cook called out, but she was already gone.

Anna sat and tried not to cry. She hated to cry, but she had so wanted to not be ashamed of who she was in front of Henry's friends. *Why am I still working as a scullery maid for him?*

She sat for a good half hour. Then, Anna felt someone sit next to her in the sunny spot.

"I'm sorry," the tender voice said.

She turned to see a handsome, blonde man with beautiful blue eyes. He was certainly the looker of the group. Henry was handsome in a rugged sort of way, but this one looked like a movie star.

"I'm Tomas," he said as he held out his hand for her to shake.

She did.

"My friends are terrible. I'm sure you heard them."

She did not answer.

"It's just that . . . Anna is it?"

She nodded.

"Anna, we've known Henry since we were toddlers. There aren't many of us the same age in Adare, you know? We know each other very, very well. We're just concerned for our friend. I don't know if you've made this out yet or not, but he's very inexperienced where women are concerned. In fact, we were worried about him for a while because he doesn't even look at women when we're in pubs and all."

Tomas scratched his curly blonde hair and looked at her unchanging expression.

"It's just that . . . A few years ago when his parents died, we—he and I, that is—became even closer. Sean looks like he can be his brother, but they're radically different. Sean's like having a Viking around, ready to pillage your farm, but all in good nature, you know? Then, there's Harry. None of us really like him, we just feel obligated to keep him around."

He chuckled.

"I'm sure you won't like him either. He's analytical and sour. I'm the thinker and Henry, well, he's the quiet one."

He moved his feet on the gravel path and thought about what else to say.

"Henry and I joined the war effort. Harry was in college; I don't think he'll ever not be in college. Sean felt if Ireland stays out of it, he should, too. He's real patriotic. I'm a doctor and I volunteered. They put me in the field. I've seen a lot. . . ."

He squinted in the sun.

"Henry had a very strange job. He was a loader for the planes—he loaded bombs."

Anna looked at Tomas anxiously. He continued, slowly.

"He always believed so many deaths were on him because of that. We tried to reason with him, but he has never gotten over it. He was always this sensitive soul in that massive body. His heart is probably more fragile than yours. We've been worried about him."

"Why?" She choked out.

"I don't know if you noticed his drinking."

She had not. He had not done it in front of her. She wondered if he drank at night.

"So, there it is, Anna."

"Thank you for telling me, Tomas," she said and looked at his beautiful face.

"Just take care of him," he said and got up.

She busied herself with her work the rest of the day as she pondered what Tomas had said. Anna had never seen Henry drink. She was sure he had before, though, because the icebox was packed with Guinness.

That night, Henry and his friends gathered around the fire drinking and playing cards. Mrs. Fitzpatrick commented she had never seen Henry in such high spirits.

"Do you mind terribly staying late?" Mrs. Fitzpatrick asked Anna while she ate a small dinner in the kitchen.

She agreed and told Mrs. Fitzpatrick she would probably take the room for the night after all.

"I'll ring down to your mother-in-law and tell her," she said as she called the store below Sarah's apartment.

Sarah's friend, who owned the pharmacy below, took the call. Mrs. Fitzpatrick told Anna she was certain Sarah would get the message.

"Henry wanted grilled cheese sandwiches and bacon for some reason tonight," Cook said and chuckled.

"Can you take this tray in?"

Anna picked up the heavy tray and took a deep breath. Her stomach made a flip as she entered the library without knocking. It seemed to be their favorite place.

They all cheered at the food as she arrived and put it down to serve each of them. Tomas held out his hand for his plate, winked at her, and thanked her. Henry did not make eye contact. It was as if he was trying not to stir the pot with his friends.

"Uh, Anna," Tomas called out, "we're trying to settle an argument here. Sean—"

Tomas took a sip of beer.

"Shut up!" Sean said and threw a pillow from the couch at him.

Tomas laughed, shielded himself, and then continued, "Sean thinks he's every woman's dream. Do you agree?"

Anna looked at Henry who ate his sandwich.

"Well, I don't know Sean," she said.

"I don't think he's talking about his personality. Stand up, my man, show the woman your assets!" Tomas cried out.

Sean finally found an unordinary amount of courage and stood up. He made muscles and turned so Anna saw his rear end. They all roared with laughter.

"So, what is the verdict?" Tomas asked her.

Tomas got up with his beer in his hand and walked up to her face.

Then, he whispered in her ear, "Do you think he's quite the specimen?"

She looked back at Tomas who looked at her lips. The laughter subsided and everyone stared at her.

"I think you all have a lot to learn about women," she said coolly.

Henry chuckled under his breath. The rest took a moment, and then erupted in laughter.

"They might need some schooling on women, but I think I've had enough experience for us all!" Tomas cried out.

Anna left. *They're ridiculous. Tomas was gentle and sweet out in the garden, but now I see him for what he is when he's with his friends.*

There was nothing which brought back terrible memories more than when a group of men laughed and drank. *Why didn't Henry come to my rescue? He just sat there with his nose red, drinking and eating. Maybe he isn't who I thought he was after all,* she thought.

Anna retreated to the kitchen fired up and yelled, "I don't want to be here!"

She went out into the vegetable garden to regain her cool. After a few angry minutes, she finally went back inside and started to clean frantically. Cook and Mrs. Fitzpatrick just looked at each other.

Anna's apron was soaked with soapy water as she planted herself in the kitchen for the rest of the night, cleaning dishes. Mrs. Fitzpatrick finally sent all the servants to bed and Anna went down the long, dark hallway to the servant's quarters.

Fortunately, that morning she had put a change of clothes and a robe in the wardrobe. She drank some water, washed her face, and tried to calm down. She still heard commotion come from the main areas. She did not bother lighting a fire because it was still warm. She finally began to sink into sleep.

Suddenly, Anna was startled awake. She heard incessant tapping and turned over. She finally realized someone was knocking on her door. At first, she thought it was Henry, but rejected the idea and thought it must be Mrs. Fitzpatrick. She opened the door and shielded herself from the cold with a robe. Tomas stood in front of her.

"What are you doing here?" She asked as terrible memories of men at her door felt heavy in her fearful heart.

"I wanted to apologize, you know, for earlier. We haven't treated you very well and—" he slurred and reeked of alcohol.

"Can this wait until morning?" She asked quickly.

He hesitated for a minute, and then asked, "Can I come in?"

"No."

"Why not?"

He looked at her with a smirk.

"Because it wouldn't look right."

"Oh, so you're one of those—"

He rolled his beautiful blue eyes.

"One of what?"

"Prudes," he whispered with a devastating smile.

"Goodnight, Tomas," she said and started to close the door.

"Anna," he said as he held the door open, "it's about Henry. I have to talk with you alone."

She sighed.

"It can't wait."

"Well, you're going to have to. I need to get dressed and I'll meet you in the library."

"About ten minutes?"

"I don't know," she said annoyed and shut the door.

She put on her clothes from the day before and looked into the mirror quickly to make sure her hair was not sticking straight up. When she went into the library, Tomas stood up with a drink in his hand.

"Will you close the door?" he asked.

"No," she replied curtly.

"All right, I'll just talk softly," he said, visibly drunk. "Listen, I know you and Henry have formed a little bond and all, but I just want to make sure you know what you're getting into."

Anna folded her arms as he took a sip of his brandy.

"This doesn't sound like the sort of thing someone says about a friend."

"No, it's not that; I love him like he's my flesh and blood. It's just that Henry's a much wounded human being."

Tomas took another sip and eyed Anna's every movement.

"I think we've covered all of this," she said and started to walk away.

He grabbed her arm and sneered, "Here's the thing, Anna. I saw how you looked at me today."

"What are you talking about?"

"I can tell you're torn. You see Henry and he's a broken person; you want to help him, that's very sweet. Yet, you have to think of yourself . . . If he's right for you. The answer, Anna, is no."

"Why say such a thing?" She asked with a seed of doubt.

Tomas looked down at his glass, licked his lips, and whispered, "When I talked with you earlier, your shirt sleeve was rolled up."

She froze.

"I saw the numbers, Anna."

She could not speak. Finally, she turned to leave.

"Wait," he said calmly.

He walked over to her, and then began to roll up his sleeve. She gulped, and then drew in her breath slowly. She exhaled with shaking breath as she looked up at him. He nodded with pain in his eyes.

They stood and looked into each other's eyes for a long time. Then, Anna reached out and touched the numbers on Tomas' arm. Slow and gentle hands reached around his shoulders, and he found her clinging to him. He closed his eyes and embraced her. For the first time in a very long time, neither of them felt alone.

He tucked his face into her neck and she felt his warm tears. He sniffed and pulled her back to look at her face. She hung there for a moment, and then sat in Henry's arm chair as Tomas surveyed the room for a place to sit. He finally settled on the couch nearest her and touched the tip of his brandy glass with his ring finger.

"Where?" she asked.

"I was moved around a lot. I was in the field, then at a camp—as you can see—and a couple of hospitals."

"Were you ever at Mauthausen?"

"I don't think so, no."

He stared down at his cup. It was a lie—he had been there for a short time. It was in the beginning of his prison term. Henry had told him earlier she was in the brothels. He had been there and knew all too well what she endured.

Finally, his gaze caught hers again. He handed her what was left of his brandy and she drank it. She followed the curves of the glass with her finger.

"No one ever wants to talk about it," Tomas said with tenderness to his voice.

Anna nodded, and then looked down again. As she put the glass down, she moved and sat next to him on the couch.

"Henry's never going to understand, is he?" she asked.

Tomas put his finger on her hand. The fire was almost dead and the room was cold. Anna pulled in her robe around her chest. A world she suppressed every day and tried to believe was only a dream, was real. The evidence of it sat beside her.

She rubbed her eyes, and then her face; she sighed. They looked at each other again.

"Henry doesn't have any experience with women, Anna. How can he possibly understand?"

"I believe anyone who has a heart can understand."

"Do you really believe that?" He asked, but knew she did not.

"I need to."

"I'm always here to talk."

"Thank you, Tomas. You know I'll listen as well, but I think we know neither of us is going to talk about it."

He nodded and whispered, "Death was better than life there."

"Yes," she replied.

She shivered and he took an afghan behind them to put it around her. He tucked the edges around her shoulders, and then put his forehead to hers. His nose almost touched hers. He leaned toward her, and then he kissed her.

She pulled back almost immediately and searched his face, shocked.

"I'm sorry," he said.

He tried to hold back a smile. His chest still leaned into hers.

"Back away from me," she said as soft as possible, but with force.

His smile faded. He had thought she was simply shy, but it was obvious she was getting angry. She pushed away and stood up. He stood up with her, embarrassed by her rejection.

"You know I'm interested in Henry. He's your friend. How can you do this?"

Tomas's eyes moved back and forth as if he searched his mind for an answer.

"I thought you felt—"

"Felt what . . . Sorry for you? We have this thing which does tie us together in a sick way, but it's something we each want to forget."

"You were in the brothels, weren't you," he blurted.

Anna held in her breath.

"I can tell by how scared you were just then," he answered her silent question. "I know what they did to you girls at Mauthausen."

"*How* do you know?"

He did not answer.

"I asked you something!"

She was infuriated, but he made a slight reach for her hand. He wanted to take her pain away. She looked at his finger stretched toward hers and took a step back.

"You were there!" she hissed.

He nodded. Her mind swam with memories: *Did he see me there? Did he take part in all of that?*

The area she was in was for the SS, but she knew there were other brothels for prisoners. They were used as incentive to the higher class of prisoners such as doctors.

"Did you go . . .?" Anna did not finish her question.

He nodded again. Her wild eyes transformed into a fierce glare.

She did not wait for any explanation, but ran as fast as possible toward Henry's room.

CHAPTER 6

SHE POUNDED FRANTICALLY ON HENRY'S door. He opened it at once. His hair was messed up and he only had his pajama bottoms on. She dissolved into tears and threw herself at him.

"Please, shut the door, shut the door," she cried.

She was scared Tomas was right there.

"Please lock it," she cried.

He did, and then stood dumbfounded with Anna in his arms against his bare chest as she cried.

"What's wrong . . . What happened?" he asked.

Anna was unable to bring herself to answer.

"Shh. It's all right," he said.

After what seemed an eternity, he finally sat on the floor against the closest wall, exhausted. She sat in his lap as he held her and stroked her hair.

"I'm here," he said. "Please tell me what's wrong."

Anna did not tell him—Tomas was his best friend. They finally fell asleep together. They sat up against the wall and held each other tightly.

The morning came within a few hours and she woke before he did. She looked around at his room—the carved mahogany walls and blue curtains. She stood and looked at him. He was beautiful. At that moment, he was even more beautiful to look at than Tomas.

She heard the breakfast cart come up the hall as Cook hummed.

The dishes clanged together as she served the first guest room. Anna heard her knock next door. This was her only opportunity to sneak away before being seen coming out of the master bedroom. She creaked open his door, shut it again, and pitter-patted quickly away.

"Anna? Come and get the trash in this room," Cook called.

She barely caught Anna in her peripheral vision. Harry's head popped around the corner to see her.

Anna began to run. Cook looked after her, bewildered. Mrs. Fitzpatrick caught her in the kitchen.

"What's wrong?" she asked.

"Please, I'm so sorry, I feel so sick. I have to go home," Anna said as a swell of tears tried to escape.

"You're as white as a sheet," she said and surveyed the young woman. "Go ahead. We'll make due here."

She hurried through the property and the miles down to town. She had to get home. As she almost ran through town, she wished she had called the pharmacy to have them get Sarah to escort her back.

"Child!" Sarah uttered as she stormed through the door. "Whatever happened?"

Then, the flood came out. Anna told her the whole, terrible story. Sarah held her on her bed and thought about what to do.

"Did you tell Henry?"

Anna shook her head.

"Why not?"

"It's his best friend, Mum," she cried.

"That doesn't matter. He'll believe you," she said.

Sarah pet Anna's head for a few more moments, and then asked, "Why did you run to him and not Mrs. Fitzpatrick last night?"

Anna lifted her head and thought, *Is she asking why I jeopardized my reputation?*

"I panicked."

"It didn't look good," she muttered.

"No one saw me," Anna said defensively.

"Henry did," Sarah said with a world of innuendo in her voice.

"Mum, I—"

"Anna, I rejoiced with you on your first date with this man, but since I've become more concerned. You have told me he's not a Christian. I believe this relationship is forming too quickly in someone who's not equally yoked with you."

Anna wanted to scream. *This isn't exactly the right moment to give advice!*

"Go take a bath and lay down," Sarah said in a changed tone.

Anna obeyed. She did, in fact, feel sick. She thought of Henry and how he had held her.

When she slipped into her bath, Anna heard a knock at the door and Sarah opening the door in the front room.

"Henry!" Sarah said, astonished.

Anna's heart sank.

Then, Sarah said, "Come in, I want to talk with you. I'm not exactly happy you've been seeing my daughter-in-law without first telling me what your intentions are."

"Forgive me," his wonderful, low voice answered.

Anna sunk deeper into her warm bath. She had not realized how much she loved his voice until then.

"It has all happened so fast. But, I'm here and I want to talk with you as well. Where's Anna?"

"She's resting," Sarah said to spare Henry the imagery of Anna in a bathtub.

"Anna told me she doesn't have parents," he said softly.

Anna stretched her ears to hear.

"I'm it," she commented sadly. "But, I want to talk with you about that. Anna hasn't told you something. You and I are cousins, second cousins. Your father was my cousin. I knew him quite well."

"I had no idea. Why didn't she tell me?"

"At first, I thought you'd recognize our name."

"Mrs. Fitzgerald didn't tell me and I didn't think to ask."

"You didn't think to ask Anna's last name? She probably didn't tell you because she didn't want any special treatment."

Henry was embarrassed. *How don't I know my girlfriend's last name? Everything happened so fast. . . .*

"I'm afraid she's already had special treatment," he said light-heartedly, "but tell me what can I do for you? How can I help you?"

"My husband and my two sons are gone," Sarah said as her voice caught.

"I'm very sorry to hear that," he answered in a raspy voice.

"Are you all right?" she asked.

"I have a headache, but it's nothing. Is Anna all right?"

"No, she's not. If you don't mind, I'd like to give you two pieces of advice, Henry."

"I need all the help I can get."

"The first is to trust that girl, no matter what. One thing I know about Anna is she's blazingly honest. Whatever she does and says, it's true and reflects her heart. Secondly, you don't show up to see her without flowers."

"Flowers, huh?"

"Yes. She's crazy for flowers. I think she's lost her mind sometimes about them. During the war, she'd rescue her little orchid before we went down to the bomb shelters. It didn't make it very long, but she tried."

They chuckled a little.

"Do you want to go with me to buy some so we can talk a little more?" he asked.

"Yes," Sarah said.

Anna wanted to jump out of the bath and stop them.

Heaven knows what Sarah will say to him.

She sloshed out of the warm water and got dressed. She ran downstairs to meet Sarah just as she came back up. She was startled to see Sarah so fast.

"Where's Henry?" she asked.

"He went home," Sarah said suspiciously.

"Why?"

"He needed to tend to something."

"What did you say to him?"

"I told him about his friend. I wasn't going to have you go back in that house with that man there!"

"Mum!" Anna yelled.

"I'm your guardian and I—"

"I'm a grown woman, Mum!"

"You're in my charge and—"

"You had no right to tell him!" she yelled.

She had never yelled at Sarah who was shocked. Anna went upstairs to grab her purse.

"You can't go back, they think you're sick. They'll send you right back home," Sarah reasoned.

Anna sat down on the bed and put her head in her hands. Sarah continued when she realized she had won.

"Henry needs to do this on his own. He needs some time to talk to his friend."

"Talk to his friend! Mum, do you really think Henry's going to *talk* to Tomas?"

"He'll be fine. He'll handle it well."

"There's a limit to everyone's gentleness, Mum!"

"Oh, stop being so dramatic, Anna. You need to rest. Come on, get into bed."

Anna was exhausted. *She's right. I can't go back right away.*

As the early night approached, Anna became more restless. She was obsessed with seeing Henry. She wanted the entire ordeal with Tomas to go away. Once something of that magnitude was released into the world, there was no erasing it.

Anna put on her best dress and walked back to the Manor as the stars started to come out.

"Are you feeling better?" Mrs. Fitzpatrick asked sweetly as Anna entered the kitchen.

"Thank you, I am," Anna said. "Is Mr. Oliver around?"

Anna tried to sound as formal as possible.

"You've missed all the commotion, Miss Anna," Cook said. "He's thrown one of them out . . . can't imagine what they must've done! It takes a lot for Mister to become angry. I've never, not once, seen it in him before and I've known that lad since he barely stood by himself.

"Anna, dear, wait here, I'll try to find him. He was in quite a state. Maybe you can calm him."

Mrs. Fitzgerald went off to find Henry. Anna waited for a half hour in the kitchen, but she did not come back.

"Are you staying here tonight?" Cook finally asked.

"I might have to," Anna said and commented on the time. "I think I'll be fine enough to work in the morning."

"Good. We need you."

Mrs. Fitzpatrick came in. She looked bedraggled.

"Are you all right?" Cook asked.

"I can't find him."

"That's strange. It's past dinner time for him. Have you seen any of the others?" Cook asked as she held a dripping spoon in her hand.

"No."

Anna got up from the kitchen table quickly. She knew something was wrong. Nothing felt right around the house. She went out the kitchen door and began to walk through the grounds. Mrs. Fitzpatrick said she had been through every room of the Manor.

He must be outside, Anna thought.

She ran through the dark fields, scared she might step on a mouse or something worse, but she had to keep going. Anna ran to the tree they had eaten lunch at her first day, but he was not there. She stopped there for a moment to catch her breath and looked around. She had never seen the grounds at night.

She listened to the brook for a minute and asked God what to do. She sat against the tree with her face in her hands and started to pray. She was so exhausted; she was not able to rest that day for fear of what was going on between Henry and Tomas. Anna's head started to bob as she fought sleep.

Sleep, she heard someone gently whisper inside her as if a breeze had passed. *Just sleep.*

A blanket of pure comfort spread over her. It was so peaceful.

Anna's eyes flew open. Her heart started to race.

"No," she said to nothingness.

She got up to avoid sleep, and started to pace. She thought of going back to the Manor where things were more comfortable to wait him, but she felt driven to be outside. She paced faster, prayed harder. An hour went by . . . two hours . . . three. She rubbed her eyes. She heard the crickets louder than her mumbled prayers. Her hair was damp with dew.

Then, as if it was a judgment sent from heaven, she saw smoke invading the moonlit sky!

It's the barn!

Anna started to run. By the time she reached the barn, the entire structure was in flames.

Henry must be inside!

She ran into the barn and the animals were going crazy. She opened a few stalls as the animals ran out. She screamed Henry's name repeatedly.

She set the horses loose. When she turned, she saw Henry collapsed on a bed of hay.

"Henry, get up!" she screamed.

He only moaned. She smelled liquor on him. She turned him over and his face was covered with bruises, his eye was black.

"Henry! Please, wake up!"

He was too heavy for her to drag and Anna began to panic. Finally, he was semi-awake and put his arm around her shoulder. Anna ran with him as quickly as possible and laid him down on the ground outside.

"Henry! Are you all right?"

"The animals," he mumbled.

It was too late. The barn was in flames and it was too dangerous to go back inside. Anna heard the animals call for help—she wept into Henry's chest.

The fire department came with buckets of water, but it was too late. The barn was gone. Fortunately, it had not spread to other areas of the property. The village physician, Dr. Lannon, ran out to the field where Henry lay; he had trouble breathing. He moved Henry back to the Manor and several servants helped him up to his room.

Cook was put in charge of Anna until Sarah came. She gave Anna a damp rag, a glass of water, and then ignored her for the next hour while Henry was examined. There was still no sign of Sarah. The pharmacy had been closed hours before; a servant was sent to get her.

Mrs. Fitzpatrick finally came out and announced Dr. Lannon said Henry had been lucky because he had been so close to the ground where most of the oxygen was.

Sarah finally heard what had happened and flung open the kitchen door to find Anna. She looked at her, covered in ash. Sarah held her girl while she cried.

"He's asking for you," Mrs. Fitzpatrick gently interrupted. She gave Anna a warm towel to clean up with. "You did a very brave thing today, Anna," she said. Mrs. Fitzpatrick walked Anna to Henry's door. Anna closed her eyes and tried to settle down.

Dr. Lannon met Anna at Henry's door. "He's sobered up. Apparently, he and my son had quite a fight. It's not like either of them. Tomas said Henry came after him un-provoked. Sean and Harry somehow got involved in it and ended up beating the snot out of each other. Tomas and the other boys are at my house with stitches. I picked the three of them up about four hours ago.

"They didn't know where Henry had gone. I was coming back as soon as they were stitched up, which took a while let me tell you. Apparently, Henry had gone to the barn, started drinking, and dropped his lantern. What he was doing with a blasted lantern in a barn, I have no idea. . . ."

"Thank you," Anna said and went in.

Henry sat up in bed and was covered in grey soot. He opened his arms to her. She walked into them, and then sat on the bed next to him.

"Thank you," he said. "You saved my life, you know?"

Anna cried on his shoulder. He rubbed her back as he embraced her.

"Look at me," he whispered as he touched her face.

His eyes were wild, but he seemed sober.

"Anna, I need to tell you something. I heard a voice—don't think I'm crazy—, but I heard a voice in the barn."

"What?"

"It said, 'Anna will pray.'"

"What are you talking about?"

"That's what I heard."

"Who was it?"

"It was God."

"God . . . What are you talking about, Henry?"

"Everything feels so clear," he recalled. "I gave Him my life. Not in exchange to live. I gave it to Him, knowing you'd find me, knowing I'd be all right."

Anna looked at Henry, astonished. She hardly believed what she had heard. Tears ran down his cheeks and formed rivers in beds of ash.

"I feel alive," he cried. "When you laid me down on the ground, I looked up at you and your face glowed like an angel's."

Anna cried with him.

"You saved me," he whispered into her ear.

He kissed her face and whispered, "I love you."

CHAPTER 7

Anna's hands gripped Henry's filthy shirt tightly.

"You love me?" she cried.

He nodded.

"That did not take long," she said as she laughed through tears.

He shook his head, and then a well of emotion burst out of him, too.

"And you . . . you—"

"I believe, Anna. I believe."

"Tell me what happened. What went through your mind?" She asked with excitement.

"I had a fight with the guys."

"I know."

"I drank a lot afterwards and went out to the barn. It was getting dark and I was sloppy, so I lit an old lantern—I know it was stupid. I passed out . . . I don't know how the fire started; I mean, I know it was from the lantern, but everything seemed okay at that point. I'd hung it up in the corner of the barn. I don't know if the hook broke or what."

He looked at her beautiful face framed with ash; she had not yet washed it off. He brushed her face with his hand.

He continued slowly, "I had this dream . . . I saw the Crucifixion. Then, as Jesus hung there, I felt my body go into His like I was crucified with Him. There was no pain, Anna. I just felt like

I was getting what I deserved—death. Then, I heard this voice say, 'Anna will pray.' It was as if a multitude was saying it, as if everyone in heaven was saying it in unison. At once, I believed you'd come for me."

He took her hands and kissed them.

"I awakened and the barn was full of flames. I hardly knew if it was real or not. The dream felt more real than anything I'd ever experienced. Then, I saw your face and I felt this surge go through me—pure light. It was as if all the energy of the sun pushed through me. I felt like I was resurrected from the dead."

She bowed her head, hardly able to take in the beauty of his words.

"I believe with all my heart in what you believe in, Anna."

"I knew I had to pray for you," she choked out.

He smiled gently and pulled her to his chest. He kissed the top of her head.

"Thank you so much, Anna."

Anna slept in the chaise lounge beside Henry that night. Mrs. Fitzpatrick left the door open and checked on him often; she and Sarah agreed it was not good for Anna to sleep in Henry's room, but Anna did not care.

Henry woke several times. He had a hard time breathing and Mrs. Fitzpatrick had not yet stirred. Anna gave him breathing treatments and begged him to let her take him to the hospital. He constantly assured her he was all right.

Finally, Mrs. Fitzpatrick came in early in the morning and told Anna to go clean herself up. Mrs. Fitzpatrick helped Henry do the same. Anna went back to her little scullery maid's room, bathed, and changed into clothes Sarah had brought her for which she was thankful. She heard the grandfather clock chime seven o'clock as she scooted through the kitchen, unable to eat anything.

Her shift started at eight o'clock and she needed to collect her thoughts. The wind blew through her hair as she walked toward a field by the Manor. Wildflowers had grown everywhere and she absentmindedly began to pick them randomly until she cradled a huge amount.

Then, she saw a man walk toward her in the meadow in the corner of her eye. She had not noticed him until he was a stone's throw away. She turned—it was Tomas.

He smiled at her. She began to walk away from him.

"I'm here to apologize," he called out.

She stopped, yet did not respond.

"Henry's my best friend. I hate this has come between us," he said.

Anna looked at his face. He had stitches in the corner of his eye. Anna did not move.

"I guess you finally saw the effects of his drinking last night," Tomas said. "I'm glad he's all right."

Anna began to walk away again. He ran to her and stood in front of her.

"They didn't give us a choice. They called it a reward, but it wasn't. Anna, I only went once."

"Please, leave me alone," she muttered as tears dripped down her face.

"I'm so sorry. I'm so very sorry."

"Leave me alone!" she yelled.

He put his hands up and walked away.

She sat in the grass and cried for about an hour. She wanted to get up and run back to the Manor, but did not want to face Henry. It did not matter the beautiful things which had transpired earlier that morning. She thought, *No, he won't ever understand anything I've been through.*

The thought angered her.

Henry shooed Mrs. Fitzpatrick away, determined to care for himself. He put on his slacks slowly—breathing deeply—and then a button down shirt. It was hard to breathe as he tied his black shoes, but he wanted to look presentable.

Shaving was a luxury he could not afford. He sat in the chaise lounge where Anna had slept and caught his breath. He was weak, but he was ready to fly.

He heard a faint knock on the door, and then Anna opened it. She had brought him breakfast. He smiled at her as she laid it on his lap.

"Thank you, my darling."

"Don't call me that ever," she said quietly.

He was taken aback.

"I hate it. I don't want you to call me that."

"All right. I'm sorry."

"I want you to know I'm looking for another job."

Henry looked at her for a long time.

"I suppose it's odd to work for the man who loves you," he said.

He touched her arm, but she walked away.

"Anna!" He called after her, but she shut the door.

She walked into the kitchen and told Mrs. Fitzpatrick she was going to take another job. She was a little stunned, but nodded.

Anna filled up the bucket with hot water and sloshed some rags into it. It was the day to scrub the floors. As she worked, she prayed about where to go and what to do. She heard nothing from the Lord. She did not thank Him for what He had done or ask what He wanted her to do. She simply informed Him she was leaving and asked for another place to work.

She heard Henry's feet clomp into the main lobby as she worked. It was her least favorite room of the Manor with trophies of hunted animals nailed to the walls. She did not like the color dark red, but had no idea why. The carpet was red and hard to take care of as were the furnishings.

His feet stopped at her crouched body as she continued to scrub. She ignored him.

"What's the matter, Anna?" He asked through labored breath.

He crouched down to her level. She continued to ignore him.

"How can I fix it when I don't know what's wrong?" he probed.

"You can't fix it," she scowled.

"Tell me—"

"Why do I still work here?" She asked angrily and splashed her rag into the dirty water.

He was shamed by her question.

"I saw Tomas out in the field," she added.

"How can he have the nerve to show up!" Henry fumed.

"Well, he seemed to know a great deal about me," she said with fierceness in her voice.

Henry was immediately afraid of her. He had an idea where their heated discussion was going.

"You told him, didn't you? You told him what happened to me! Why, Henry? Two people in the entire world knew—you were one of them!"

Henry had not realized so few people knew. His heart sank. *This is how I repay her trust in me?*

"I'm so sorry, Anna," he breathed out.

He searched for what to say next.

"I was trying to help. After the guys poked fun in the library and you stormed out, they remarked how strange you seem. I wanted to have them understand why you reacted the way you did. Tomas mentioned he had seen the numbers on your arm. He asked a few questions—"

"That's the stupidest reason I've ever heard!" She snapped and stood up.

Henry was more afraid than he had been his entire life.

"This is irreparable, Henry," she said with fire in her eyes.

"Don't say that, Anna—"

"You know what? I don't care if I starve, I'm done!"

She threw the rag into the bucket. The dirty water splashed on Henry's shined shoes.

"Anna . . . Please don't—"

"What . . . Quit? You can find yourself a new maid, Henry!"

"No. No. I *want* you to quit. You know what? Give me that thing."

He wrapped his arms around her and untied her apron. It fell to the ground.

"You don't work for me any longer, Anna. I love you."

She wanted to wrap her arms around him, kiss him, tell him everything was okay, and she forgave him. He tried to hold her, but she wiggled free.

"You've hurt me so deeply, Henry. You've made a mess of things."

"I know—"

"I really want to hurt you right now."

"I hate myself right now, Anna. Please forgive me."

She stood and looked at him, tears streamed down his cheeks. She closed her eyes to think.

He continued, "Please, come with me for the day. I'll make it up to you."

"Dr. Lannon said for you to stay put."

"I'm not very good at following doctor's orders."

"Where are we going?"

"Can't a guy have a surprise or two up his sleeve?" He asked and tried to smile.

She was not amused and wanted to know everything that was going to happen. She hated surprises.

He led her gently out the front door. He grabbed his keys and wallet, and then brought her to the cars in the drive. They slid into one and he drove away. Henry thought, *Maybe she hasn't lost all trust me.*

He rode in silence toward Shannon. She looked down at the terrible state of her clothes. The hem had come out; she had not even noticed. She looked at her work boots which were a mess. Sarah had brought them for her a while ago second hand.

She looked at Henry. He seemed to breathe better. His hair was combed perfectly and his clothes looked brand new. She could barely tell he had not shaved that morning.

She brushed the strands of hair out of her face which had come loose from her bun. She saw her reflection in the side mirror. She looked as if she had not slept in days.

He sheepishly reached for her hand. She initially drew it back, but then touched his hand with her pinky. It was all the invitation he needed. He drew a heart on her palm with his finger. He stole a glance at her and hoped not to scare her away.

"Where are we going?" She asked as she cleared her throat.

"Shannon," he replied.

He stopped in front of a clothing store and walked around the car to help her out.

"I thought we'd get some new clothes for you," he said with a smile.

She had never worn a new garment in her life. She nodded and reached for him to help her out. She brushed off her cotton dress and stood in front of the pretty store. The windows were decorated with manikins dressed in beautiful clothes.

"Is this supposed to make everything better, Henry?" She inquired of him in a whisper as she stood in front of the building.

"No, Anna. I wish it was that easy to regain your trust. No, I've wanted to do this for a while. Are you offended?"

She was a little embarrassed, but she shook her head no. He smiled sweetly and held out his arm for her. Anna was greeted by a pretty lady dressed in fine clothes. Anna wanted to hide behind Henry.

"I was wondering if you'd help us with a new wardrobe," Henry requested nervously.

"Of course," the lady replied.

She tried not to look at Anna's tattered rags.

"Come with me," she said kindly.

Henry settled on a couch and grabbed a newspaper. After two hours, Anna was dressed in a pretty blue suit and hat. The lady finalized Anna's purchases at the register.

"Thank you, Henry," Anna said and smiled at him.

"Are you hungry?" He asked and handed the happy lady a thick stack of cash.

Anna nodded as he put the sales receipt into his wallet. He grabbed the bags and headed toward a place to eat.

"Do you want to go to a movie later?" he asked.

"No," she said, even though she did.

She had not seen many movies.

"I need you to know you and I aren't okay."

"I know," he said quietly. "I don't know what to say or do to—"

"You can't help this situation, Henry. You know this is really, really bad."

Once they settled at a restaurant, they ordered their food, and then sat in awkward silence. Henry excused himself for a few minutes—she assumed to the bathroom—and then sat again in silence. They ate without talking, and then slid into the car.

Anna stared out the window. She caught her pretty reflection in the mirror a few times. She played with her long gloves—it had been her idea to get long ones to go way up her arm, so she could wear a few short sleeves without her numbers being seen.

She folded her covered hands in her lap, anxious for Henry not to reach for them. They rode in silence. Henry pulled up to her apartment where she jumped out without his help. She walked away and up the steps to Sarah who had waited for her return.

Sarah was shocked to see Anna dressed as she was. She cried as she told Sarah what had happened. Sarah gave her a handkerchief and cup of tea, and asked where the rest of her clothes were. Anna's stomach sank as she remembered, *Henry still has them.*

Sarah held Anna as she laid her head on her shoulder and advised, "He's a good man, Anna. There are not many of those in the world. Don't let one stupid mistake of his ruin your life."

She knew Sarah was right, but she did not want to forgive him yet. Anna kissed Sarah's soft cheek and went for a walk. She needed to collect her thoughts.

Men tipped their hats to her as she walked the peaceful streets. She had forgotten how dressed up she was. Women simply stared at her.

She walked into the flower store to look around. She hated to go into a store without buying something.

Red-headed twin sisters greeted her from behind the counter. They welcomed her to the neighborhood and handed her a small flower. She thanked them profusely and tucked it in a button on her blouse.

Anna walked a bit with her pretty, new purse dangling from her wrist. She caught the reflection of herself in a store window; she wished Henry was walking with her.

She looked toward the long road to the Manor. It was a long walk, but she needed to see him and tell him she was all right. So, she walked slowly in her new heels, but stopped at her door. She had an idea: *I'll call him from the pharmacy.*

She went inside and the clerk greeted her with a grin. Anna asked to use the telephone. The operator immediately connected her.

"Mrs. Fitzpatrick? It's Anna. Yes, everything is all right. Can you tell Henry I called for him? Mrs. Fitzpatrick, will you tell him I forgive him?"

She hung up the telephone and sat on a stool at the soda counter. She opened her purse and reached in for a coin to pay for a soda. She found a new wallet she did not remember picking out. It matched her purse, but she did not have much need for it, so she had not asked Henry to buy it. *He must've bought it anyway.*

When she opened it, it contained a lot of money. She did not want to take it out to count it. She had never had that much in her life.

She closed her purse and stared ahead. Then, she opened it again. There was a white piece of paper tucked within the bills. She pulled it out.

It read:

I have nothing without you. You're my treasure.

I love you,

Henry

She gulped and tucked Henry's note back inside her purse. She asked for a coke with chocolate ice cream for herself and a root beer float for Sarah. Anna was pensive as she sat and waited. The soda clerk handed her a tall glass for which she paid. Then, he began to make the root beer float for Sarah.

The bell rang on the pharmacy door as a patron entered, but Anna did not turn around.

"Anna!" Henry called from the other side of the door.

He was obviously out of breath as he approached the front cash register. He had a desperate look.

"I got your message!" he blurted.

She whirled around and grinned involuntarily. He ran to Anna and picked her up from the stool upon which she sat and held her close.

"I love you, Anna!" He said loudly and kissed her ear.

Everyone in the pharmacy laughed. Sarah entered the pharmacy for she had sensed there was something going on when she heard laughter. She clapped her hands together, and then embraced Henry when she saw him with Anna.

Henry ushered her to the corner and whispered, "Can I marry her, Sarah?"

Sarah was silent for a moment. She was not shocked by his request, although it was too soon. She put her hands on his handsome face.

"Henry, listen to me," she said, "I'll give my blessing to you in a few months. You're a new Christian and Anna still has a lot to work through."

Henry's heart sank. He had not thought of his new conversion and how it affected his huge decision.

"Draw close to the Lord, Henry. Then, I'll give you my girl."

"Sarah, thank you for your wisdom," he said, humbly.

She kissed his cheek and settled down to enjoy her float. He ordered one, too. He teased Anna about how terrible her float sounded.

Henry reached for Anna's hand and held it. He had never been so happy in his life.

CHAPTER 8

AUTUMN 1946

ANNA LAY IN BED AS the beautiful yellow gold of the room comforted her eyes. She looked out the huge windows from the bed's vantage point. She wanted to see the stars, so she had not drawn the curtains.

She always had trouble sleeping, but never as much as she had during her month of marriage to Henry. She rubbed her tired eyes, but they did not give in. Henry snored beside her, and then jumped in his sleep. She put her hand on his arm and he shot straight up.

In a panic he uttered, "What is it?"

She turned over.

"You were snoring and jumped again," she said quietly.

He stood up and looked around. It was obvious he was still asleep.

"Lay back down, Henry," she said softly.

He did and immediately began to snore again.

I don't know why I bother to wake him.

Anna got up and strolled over to the huge, beautiful windows and stared out at the incredible, but dark landscape. She held her cold arms and looked around for her robe.

The past month had been less interesting than she liked for their first month of marriage. Henry was a busier man than Anna ever thought. They had argued often about it. Apparently, it was not easy to run a mansion. He often worked late into the night.

She dug for a flashlight in her bedside drawer, grabbed her Bible, and snuck out of the room. The dim lights of the hallway gave her the chills, but at least she had convinced Henry to keep them on, despite the cost of electricity.

Anna found a soft chair in the library and settled down. The heaviness of the Bible on her lap was a comfort.

"God, please help my marriage," she prayed.

Then, she closed her eyes, but opened them almost instantly because she heard a door creak. She thought it might be the kitchen door. Anna's heart thumped loudly, and then she heard a chorus of tired, but happy voices and the clanging of dishes in the kitchen.

It sounded as if someone had arrived at the Manor. She adjusted her robe and pushed open the kitchen door. A young woman with wild, red hair spun around.

"Ah!" She cried out in joy.

Anna recognized who it was as the woman engulfed her in a huge hug.

"I hope I didn't wake you!" The woman said as she happily held Anna's hand. "I made Pearce drive through the night because I was so excited to see you!"

"Well, welcome," Anna said to Ashling, Henry's cousin.

Ashling's handsome husband, Pearce, held a large boy in his arms. Pearce kissed Anna on the forehead as he pushed open the kitchen door with his littlest one. He placed his son, Michael, on the floor. Michael was bursting with inhuman energy after being in the automobile so long. Their oldest son, Peter, walked in slowly as he rubbed his eyes.

"Up to bed with you right away, Peter, darling," Ashling said sweetly to her son of seven.

Peter seemed almost relieved. He pulled his hands through his suspenders and nodded. It was the only time he had not argued with his mother about going to bed.

"I'll take Peter if you take the monster," Pearce said

He smiled at his wife and kissed her. Then, he took his firstborn by the hand and led him out of the kitchen.

"What a deal!" Ashling responded after Pearce sarcastically. "Michael!"

She immediately turned and stopped the eighteen-month-old from chewing on the kitchen bench.

"Good heavens, you'll get splinters. That's all I need, Anna. A baby not only teething, but also with a mouth full of splinters. How is it he isn't asleep?"

"Can I get you something?" Anna asked.

"No," the young woman chuckled. "I think I know my way around here."

"Oh, Ashling, I'm so glad you've come," Anna admitted.

"Well, when Henry wrote and said you wanted to see me, I was simply overjoyed."

I don't remember saying that to Henry.

Ashling grabbed a bottle and filled it with milk.

"It's not warm, but I'm too tired to get some boiling water together," she said to Michael who spit the cold milk out.

"Here, let me," Anna said and started the process.

"Come here, you brat," Ashling said playfully as she took the bottle from Michael. "Are you over the shock of being married yet, Anna?"

"No, I can't say I am."

"Well, you'll get used to it. It took me a while. Then, it took me a while to get used to being a mother. Sometimes I still wake up in the middle of the night in a cold sweat."

They both chuckled.

"It's not what I thought it'd be."

"I'm surprised you say that, being married before and all."

"My first marriage was really a month total of being together. He was oversees longer than we were married. My marriage to Henry has already succeeded my first one by a couple of days."

"Have you been missing Jamie?"

It was an intimate question. Yet, Ashling knew no stranger.

"Yes. I have to admit I have, but that's not something I can talk to Henry about."

Ashling came over and put her arms around Anna from behind. "You can tell Henry anything, Anna."

However, Anna was not sure. Michael started to scream. Anna worked faster.

"Oh, good grief, your highness," Ashling said and picked him up.

"Ashling, you must be exhausted. Let me take him."

"Oh, you gorgeous thing . . . Thank you!" she said.

Ashling kissed Anna's cheek and headed out of the kitchen before Anna recanted. Anna finally got the water to a boil as Michael screamed bloody murder with his hand in his mouth. She plopped his bottle into the water and bent down to get him.

"Mama," he whined.

"Oh, I know," Anna soothed. "The bottle will be all ready in a minute, sweetheart."

Tears dripped down his little cheeks as Anna rubbed his back. She prayed the bottle heated up quickly. She hummed with her cheek against his as he finally quieted.

"Hi," Henry whispered from the doorway.

She spun around without stirring Michael. He walked over and kissed her lips, and then Michael's sweaty head.

"He's tired. His eyes are heavy."

"Can you get the bottle?" Anna whispered.

He nodded and got some prongs to lift it out of the pot of water. "Want me to take him?"

She shook her head and explained, "I don't want to stir him."

He handed her the bottle.

"Let's go into the library. We can sit with him while he has his bottle."

The two ventured out into the dark mansion and found the fire faintly burning in the small library, the room where they truly lived. They sat down together on the soft sofa and laid the large baby across their laps. He took the bottle and sucked its nipple twice before he was completely out.

"I think we're stuck," Henry said and chuckled.

Michael put his arms up over his head and stretched out. Anna smiled.

"I take it Ashling is in bed," he whispered.

"Did she wake you?"

"Of course."

They looked at each other and laughed quietly.

Anna noted, "You didn't tell me she was coming."

"I didn't? I thought I told you about it."

"No. That's all right, though. I just don't know her very well."

"Well, all that's about to change . . . Ashling thinks you're sisters now."

Anna put her head on Henry's shoulder. It seemed like it was the first moment of togetherness they had in a long time.

"I met so many people at the wedding. I actually didn't recognize her for a second when she came in," Anna admitted.

"I thought she might have stuck out, especially with her fiery red hair all over the place."

"No, I'm sorry, she did. It's just . . . I was in the library and fell asleep. She woke me up and I was out of sorts."

"Of course, honey," he said and kissed her cheek. "I should've told you."

"Henry, it seems we're never in the same room anymore."

He looked down and said, "I have a lot going on."

"Can't we maybe plan a trip or something?"

"Ashling is here now and—"

"But we can stay for a while with her, and then maybe leave the Manor for her to take care of for a couple of days and—"

"Leave the Manor in Ashling's hands? I don't think so. Though Pearce, maybe."

There was a long pause and Anna began to hope Henry was possibly thinking it over.

"We're going to have a great time together as a family," he said proudly.

Anna knew he had dropped it. He put his head back on the sofa and started to snore again. Anna fumed. She hated how he fell asleep when they talked anything important.

She slipped a pillow under Michael, covered them both up with a soft afghan, and left the two of them in the library. She crept up the stairs, happy to have a quiet night's sleep alone.

Anna woke up as the sun streamed in through the windows. Mrs. Fitzgerald drew a bath for her and she washed her hair.

She had hoped to avoid company as long as possible. She dried her hair and put on a warm, pretty dress. She sighed deeply at the top of the stairs and descended to the fury which awaited her.

The ruckus of the kitchen rang throughout the downstairs floor. Ashling laughed hysterically. Anna opened the kitchen door carefully and hoped not to hit the crawling Michael with it.

"Peter, I told you not to use those cars on the furniture. They'll scratch everything!" Ashling cried out, Anna's quiet entrance unnoticed.

"Anna, my dear," Pearce said and stood up.

Henry played with Michael on the floor. He acted like a dog.

"Good morning," Anna said as happily as possible.

"Anna, grab that thing for me, will you?"

Ashling pointed to a salt and pepper shaker on the kitchen table. Anna slid it toward her.

"Did you sleep?" she asked.

"Yes, thank you."

"She probably slept better last night than she has this past month without me snoring in there," Henry said.

"You're like a bear!" Ashling said. "I'm so sorry, Anna, I should've warned you."

Pearce picked up the newspaper and poured over it.

"What should we do today?" Henry asked Michael.

"I want to go fishing!" the oldest boy chimed.

"Peter, you'll have to catch the worms."

"Worms?" Ashling said.

"For bait," Henry answered.

"Do you tie them onto the hook or something?" Ashling asked, oblivious.

The men laughed heartily. Anna was not sure either.

"You spear them through, Ashling, darling," Pearce said sweetly.

"What?"

Henry nodded.

"Oh, that's not going to happen!" Ashling said.

"Yes, it is!" Peter said loudly.

Obviously, he thought it was all right to yell at his mother if he smiled. She gave him the stink eye and went on.

"Anna, how'd you like to leave these hooligans to their own devices? We'll go find Sarah and go shopping."

Anna smiled and said, "I'd love that. She probably will as well. She's been lonesome lately. We've tried to get her to move here, but she—"

"Michael, get that out of your mouth!"

Ashling ran and yanked a mouse trap from out of Michael's mouth.

"What do we have a mousetrap around here for?" Anna asked. She was embarrassed one laid around with a baby visiting and thought, *If Henry had told me they were coming, I would've baby-proofed everything.*

"For mice, Anna," Henry said and laughed with Pearce again. Anna wanted to hit him.

"When can you be ready to go, Ashling?" Anna said curtly.

"Ooh, I need to change my undergarments," she said with a mockingly low tone. "Can't have red panties on when I'm trying on things! I have to put on my shopping undies—bone-colored so they don't show through anything."

"Ashling!" Henry snapped, embarrassed.

She ran up the stairs and Anna grabbed her purse from the kitchen hook.

"Bye, Henry," she muttered.

"No kiss?"

"Nope," she said and grabbed the keys to the convertible.

Anna slammed the kitchen door shut; Ashling ran behind her seconds later.

"Pearce, do you have any idea what just happened?" Henry asked.

"Not really."

The two men looked around and realized they were left with the two boys by themselves. Anna sped off with Ashling as Henry held Michael in his arms.

"I don't understand her," he said. "I give her everything, but she's been so cold lately. Before we were married, she was so sweet and open. Now, she's like this force to be reckoned with."

"Anna was always a force to be reckoned with, Henry."

"Can't do anything right, Pearce."

"Welcome to being married."

"It shouldn't be like this so early in the game," Henry commented.

"Where did you take her for your honeymoon again?"

"We didn't go anywhere. I didn't want to leave the Manor."

Pearce began to read his newspaper again. Henry continued to look out the window.

"Let's go catch some worms, Peter."

"Yes!"

Peter jumped up.

Anna parked in front of the pharmacy. She had listened to the morning complaints of Ashling about the boys and Pearce on the short ride over. She was already exhausted.

"I'll go get her," Anna said.

She hoped for a moment of solitude, but Ashling jumped out of the car and went up the steep stairs over the pharmacy to get Sarah. Anna knew Sarah was up for anything. She never had to tell her in advance. The two rounded the corner and headed up, just in time to see Father Donnelly emerge from the staircase.

"Beauty of a mornin'," he said.

He tipped his hat to the two young women. Anna just stared at him. Ashling grinned.

They looked at each other, and then bounded up the stairs to Sarah's apartment. They tapped on the door which Sarah immediately answered with a huge smile. She was obviously taken aback not to see Father Donnelly.

"Well, hello," she said, red-faced.

"Hello yourself," Ashling grinned.

She hugged and kissed her.

"Mum, you remember Ashling."

"Of course, she remembers me!" Ashling retorted.

Anna was not quite sure.

"Yes, dear, of course, I do. She's Henry's cousin."

"Yes! I hear you are as well!"

"Other side of the family."

"Still family," Ashling said. "Who are the flowers from?"

She watched Anna eye them on the table.

"Father Donnelly," Sarah answered as she held Ashling's hands.

Ashling squealed.

"Why ever did Father Donnelly bring you flowers? Has something bad happened?" Anna asked.

"Quite the contrary . . . Father Donnelly and I have been courting. He's asked me to marry him!"

"The priest?"

"If he's a protestant, he's fair game!" Ashling chimed.

"I haven't heard you speak of him," Anna said, annoyed.

"Well, I don't tell you everything!" Sarah said.

Her words stung Anna.

"How did he do it? Wait a minute. Did he do it just now?"

"Yes!"

Ashling jumped and insisted, "What happened? Tell us right now!"

Sarah sat and smoothed out her apron. Anna knew she was happier than she had ever been.

"He brought me flowers and stood in the doorway with his hat off. He said, 'Sarah, my dear. This past month with you has been the best in my life. I don't want it to ever end. Please be my wife.'"

"And you said *yes*?" Anna asked.

"Well, of course, I said yes!" Sarah said, slightly offended.

Anna was in a terrible mood. She did not know if she believed in marriage any longer. Marriage seemed to ruin everything.

"Where will you live?" Anna asked.

She knew Father Donnelly lived with his daughter and her family.

"We'll move in with Ingrid for the time being, but we'll be able to keep the apartment if we want to get away."

Ashling giggled with Sarah.

"Are you going to kiss me in congratulations or what?" Sarah asked.

She stood up and held her hands out for Anna. Anna managed a smile and hugged Sarah. She knew this changed everything, yet again. *I'm not even used to being married. How am I going to get used to Mum being married, too?*

"When's the wedding?" Ashling inquired.

"We'll be married next Sunday!"

"Next Sunday!" Anna snapped, astounded.

"Well, you Adarians don't spend too much time engaged now do you?" Ashling jokingly inferred about Anna's quick wedding.

However, Anna had known Henry for a year before getting married. It was quick, for sure, but nothing like this.

"Well, we better go shopping!" Ashling said cheerfully.

She excused herself to the bathroom to give Anna and Sarah a brief moment alone.

"Mum, are you happy?"

"Thrilled."

"Then, I'll pay for anything you want. Name it, it's yours."

Sarah hugged her girl again and kissed her on the cheeks. She knew it had not been an easy time for Anna in her young marriage, but did not know how to make it better.

"Things will get better, darling. Just you wait!"

"I wish you all the happiness—"

"Let's go, girls!" Ashling yelled.

They set off—scarves on their heads, sunglasses on their faces, and happiness for Sarah settled into their hearts.

That night, Henry had ice cream brought into the library, much to the joy of the boys. Michael's face was covered with ice cream and whipped cream.

Henry ate Ashling's cherry off her sundae without asking. It did not seem to bother her. Anna watched the two of them in awe. She wondered why Henry was so attuned to Ashling and not her.

Anna said nothing as she pushed away the chocolate ice cream, which she did not like, to get to the layer of pistachio—her favorite.

"Henry tells me you're quite the artist," Pearce quietly said to her.

"He has offered for me to take classes in Shannon. I might take him up on it."

"Oh, you should. Artists can only get better in the presence of other artists. May I see some of your work, Anna?"

"You're looking at one," Henry said proudly as he motioned to the oil painting over the fireplace.

"You're joking," Pearce said as he stood.

He was truly taken aback by it.

"It's Ruth in the fields," Anna said bashfully.

"It is, indeed. I love the look on her face."

"Just incredible, Anna," Ashling said.

Yet, Ashling hardly looked at it. Pearce stared so hard at the painting it made Anna slightly uncomfortable.

"I love the shadow on her face as she looks back," he said and looked closer with his glasses.

"Thank you, it's to represent the darkness she came from and the light which was in the Boaz fields of wheat."

"Oh, no, I see it for sure," Pearce said.

Anna was not sure if he made a big deal of it to be polite. She was always embarrassed by her work.

"Henry, you can make a mint off your wife's talent."

"Oh, I'd love to if she'd let me," Henry said in a half-lie.

"I don't want to sell my paintings," Anna said.

"Why ever not?" Pearce asked as a true investor. "I know many people who'd pay for this caliber of artistry."

"I'd like to paint for churches . . . maybe scenes from different Bible stories."

"Well, now. That'd be lovely," Pearce said kindly.

"So, Henry, what do you think of Sarah getting married to a priest?"

Ashling wanted to gossip. Henry looked at Anna. She had told him before they sat down for dinner an hour earlier.

"Whatever makes the wonderful woman happy," he said.

He hoped he had not made his wife angry at him again.

"She certainly deserves happiness," Anna agreed in an effort to sound happy for her.

After saying goodnight, Henry took Anna's arm and they walked up the stairs to their huge room.

"How are you really doing with it all?" he asked.

"I'm getting used to the idea of Mum being married. I wish we could help them."

"Father Donnelly is a proud man . . . I doubt he'd take assistance."

"Can you try?"

"Of course, I'll think of a way to make it easier on him. Maybe a money gift will suffice."

Anna felt Henry was taking the easy way out of the situation, although there was no better idea which came to her off hand.

"She wants me to stand up for her," Anna said. "I bought a new dress."

"Good," Henry said, obviously not too concerned.

"I wonder who'll marry them."

"Oh, Father Donnelly has plenty of friends. Maybe even the bishop will come into town to do it."

"Do you want to see my dress?"

"Yes, of course," he said, but Anna knew he had no interest.

"Anna, I know you think you're being ignored lately. I'm trying very hard to make sure you're well-taken care of."

Anna stopped on the stairs and did not answer him for a while. "It's more than a roof over my head I need, Henry. It's you—I need your thoughts, your soul pouring into mine. I need to feel like a team with you."

"Do you want to help me run the Manor?"

"No, not really."

"Then what do you want?"

"I don't know."

"Neither do I."

He began to walk up the stairs again. She stood still and let her husband go on without her. She felt frozen and he did not turn around to see why she was not with him. He just went to bed. *It's so easy for him,* she thought.

Anna sat on the stairs and started to count. She heard him snore in the master bedroom by the time she counted to forty. She put her face in her hands and began to cry. *Where's my Henry, my love? He's a different person than I thought.*

She wished she was able to search for, find, and hold him. He was hidden somewhere deep within himself. She knew she was unable to rescue someone from within.

She pulled her foot out of her slipper and rubbed it. Her feet hurt from all the walking she had done while shopping. She realized her ankle was bleeding a little and turned her bare foot over.

I hate what new shoes do to my sensitive skin.

"What are you doing?" Peter asked.

He smiled at her from the bottom of the stairs, his shirttail half in. The gap between his teeth was visible when he smiled.

"I think I hurt my foot."

He walked up the stairs and picked up her lone slipper.

"Just like in Cinderella. You know the story?"

"I don't think I do."

There were not a lot of stories told to her when she grew up. "She loses her slipper running away at midnight. I have the book in the nursery. Maybe you can read it to me tomorrow?"

He smiled.

"Of course, darling," she said and touched his chin.

"What should I call you?"

"Well, I don't know . . . Whatever you want. You can call me Aunt Anna or just Anna."

"Aunt Anna is hard to say."

She laughed and conceded, "I suppose it is."

"Mama says you were the maid."

Anna frowned. She was starting to like Ashling increasingly less.

"That's true."

"Like Cinderella!"

"Well, I don't know—"

"And now you live in a castle . . . Like Cinderella!"

"Yes, I do," she said.

She smiled at him and stroked his unmanageable hair.

"I want to call you Aunt Cindie, like Cinderella!"

"Okay!" she agreed.

She was not sure she really liked the name, but was overcome with the boy's enthusiasm.

He straightened his glasses.

"Do you like it?"

"Well, I think we need to read the story of Cinderella for me to decide."

"How about now? I'm not tired."

"I think your mum will be mad."

"Not at you," he replied.

"Let's do it tomorrow."

"Okay," he said and hugged her.

She watched as he trudged up the steps and thought, *He drives*

Ashling crazy, but he sure is cute.

Anna's thoughts returned to the strangeness of the day. Her mother-in-law was about to get remarried—something she did not foresee—to their priest. She remained on the steps to ponder the recent turn of events.

I've been married a month. Father Donnelly and Mum must've had a very short courtship. Why didn't she tell me? There's something terrible about deep friendships when one person holds secrets.

She thought about why Father Donnelly had not come to her, *He should've had the honor to at least talk to Mum's only relative.*

The thought made her very angry. She poured her anger into him for this reason. Yet, she knew deep down she was really hurt by Sarah who had not thought enough of her to tell her about their relationship. *This is a deep wound.*

When Anna had asked Sarah at the store why she had not told her, she had responded, "It never occurred to me."

It never occurred to her?

Anna did not even have a comeback for that response. What Anna really heard was *we're not close enough for me to bother to tell you.*

Anna decided to walk to the library. *Maybe there's a book to get my mind off my anger.*

Ashling grabbed her hand. She appeared, it had seemed, from nowhere.

"Sorry, I didn't mean to startle you," Ashling chuckled.

"It's all right. I'm just going to go read," Anna said in an attempt not to sound annoyed.

"No, you're not. I can tell something's wrong."

"Ashling." Anna sighed, agitated.

She wanted to scream, "Leave me alone!" She was angry enough to do it, but she did not. She had learned a long time ago how to calm herself. She acted like she was not angry until she stopped feeling it—her trick served her well.

"Come on up to my room. Pearce is staying in the boy's room tonight; they made a tent in there. We'll talk."

Ashling took Anna's arm and led her up. She handed her one of her nightgowns. Anna reluctantly climbed into bed as Ashling turned on her side to look at her. Anna looked up at the ceiling.

"So, what's wrong?"

"I'm just very taken aback by Sarah getting married," she finally admitted.

She hoped her admission silenced Ashling.

"I sensed it was a shock for you," Ashling said quietly.

"I'm hurt she didn't tell me she was courting our minister."

Ashling was quiet for a while.

"Do you know Father Donnelly well?"

"A little."

"Why don't you go talk to him and vent it out?"

Anna considered her suggestion. The moonlight was incredibly bright. Anna wished Ashling had shut the curtains, but she did not want to get out of bed to do it.

Then, Anna felt Ashling touch her arm. She uttered, "Anna, I didn't know."

Ashling touched the numbers on Anna's arm. Instinctively, Anna jerked her arm away. All her nightgowns were long-sleeved. She had not thought about it when she slipped on Ashling's.

Anna tucked her arm under a blanket. Ashling took Anna's hand in hers, raised it back out, and looked at her with tear-filled eyes.

"Anna, I know you don't like me very much. I've gathered it's Henry who wanted me here and possibly you didn't know anything about it," Ashling continued gracefully without pause, "yet, I came because I want to be your friend . . . Your sister. Anna, I'm not close to my family at all, except Henry. He's my best friend. Anna, he's incredibly boring."

Anna snickered at Ashling's comment, but she was a little hurt when she heard her husband talked about in such as way.

Ashling continued, "I want you to know even though I'm high-spirited—as Mother used to put it—I'm loyal to a fault. You'll see. Once I decide to be someone's friend, I never waver on it. You can tell me anything."

Anna looked at her friend. Ashling's face was serious and determined.

Is she trying to get my secrets so she can tell everyone?

Anna decided to test her. She thought of a small secret no one else knew, *If anyone finds out, I'll know who it came from.*

"I've written letters to all the men who . . . wronged me . . . When I was incarcerated."

Ashling listened.

"I, of course, have no idea who they were or how to get their addresses if they're still alive, but I wrote them."

"Does Henry know?"

"No. No one does."

"What did you do with them?"

"I burned them."

"What kind of things did you write?"

"All the things I remember. I saw their face and what they did to me as I wrote. I wrote each a letter of forgiveness."

"Forgiveness?" Ashling asked, astounded.

"Yes."

"I thought these were angry letters, telling them how you feel and—"

"I feel forgiveness. I get very sad sometimes. Sometimes, I'm angry, but every day I have to choose when I wake up if I'm going to forgive."

"I don't think forgiveness is something you can give to Nazis."

Anna turned on her side and said, "Ashling, I believe with all my heart grace and love are at the center of my faith. If I truly believe that, if I believe God loves all people, then I must forgive."

"How do you do it?"

"I don't. God moves in my heart every morning and does it for me. Forgiveness is free, but it's not cheap. You have to lay down your life to give it."

Ashling reached for her friend's hand. Anna closed her eyes—she felt sleep finally overtake her. She also knew Ashling had soaked in what she had said. So, Anna said a prayer for Ashling and drifted off.

CHAPTER 9

ANNA ATE HER BREAKFAST BEFORE anyone else got up. It was cold that morning, so she decided to put on a coat and take a walk. The sun was coming up. The end of summer still had long days.

She was so tired. She had awakened with her stomach in a knot; it was hard to go back to sleep. Her mind turned terrible memories over and over. She hated to talk about the numbers—it upset her.

She walked through the beautiful grounds of her new home. She still found it unbelievable all she had acquired through marriage. Anna constantly forgot she was no longer poor. So many times, she had awakened in the middle of the night, worried about how to get food the next day.

She mumbled a scripture verse about provision, say a prayer, and then finally realize she no longer had to rely on miraculous provision any longer. She almost missed those days. God had always come through.

She rubbed her burning eyes and walked aimlessly toward the priory. The sun was so warm she took off her coat as she stood in front of her church.

Anna marveled at herself—she had been in the village for over six months, married the richest man, and attended church every Sunday. Yet, she hardly knew anyone, particularly her priest.

Father Donnelly was inside lighting candles for morning prayer for which a few lonely old widows primarily showed up. Anna took a deep breath and checked her dress. She was still in awe of her lovely new clothes.

She opened the door as a tiny, elderly lady came up behind her. She held the door for her, smiled, and went inside to sit at the back. Father Donnelly nodded at her and his faithful group, and then knelt at the altar with his back to them.

Silence.

The five little ladies bowed their heads, scattered around the pews like wildflowers on a meadow. A half hour went by. Anna sat in her seat. She loved to pray, but she felt frozen. She only watched.

One lady wept quietly, another scooted close to her and put her arms around her. Then, a beautiful, wonderful sound—one of them started to sing. Anna recognized she had been a singer in her early years, but her voice had faded and shook.

Anna listened to her wonderful voice as she sang "Be Thou My Vision":

Be Thou my Vision, O Lord of my heart;
Naught be all else to me, save that Thou art
Thou my best Thought, by day or by night,
Waking or sleeping, Thy presence my light.

The words of the song broke the ice in Anna's heart. Tears streamed down her lovely face. Father Donnelly put his arms up in worship.

Anna knew the hymn well. She had sung it so many times in her darkest hours. She remembered how it had pulled her through as she waited each day for the horrors of each night at the camp. She knew every day what was to come as night approached. Finally, she cleared her throat and sang with the beautiful, old voice:

Be Thou my battle Shield, Sword for the fight;
Be Thou my Dignity, Thou my Delight;
Thou my soul's Shelter, Thou my high Tower:
Raise Thou me heavenward, O Power of my power.

As she sang through her sobs, she remembered her faith in His protection. Everyone turned and faced her. They nodded lovingly as tears streamed down. Then, they all sang together with Father Donnelly:

Riches I heed not, nor man's empty praise,
Thou mine Inheritance, now and always:
Thou and Thou only, first in my heart,
High King of Heaven, my Treasure Thou art.
High King of Heaven, my victory won,
May I reach Heaven's joys, O bright Heaven's Sun!
Heart of my own heart, whatever befall,
Still be my Vision, O Ruler of all.[1]

Anna wiped her tears away repeatedly. Jesus *was* heart of her heart, her treasure. Father Donnelly nodded to her as the ladies got up. They gathered around her and placed their wonderful, wrinkled hands on her shoulders.

Then, someone prayed, "Dear God, bless Anna from the souls of her feet to the top of her head."

They all prayed around her with strong, loving, powerful tones. They prayed like Sarah prayed.

Anna barely heard the door to the sanctuary open. Then, she felt a warm, soft hand on the top of her head. She looked up to see Sarah who nodded in serious approval, and then kissed her girl on her forehead.

"Please, God, tell me where I belong," Anna whispered.

She hoped the Holy Spirit magically laid her life's plans before her. He did not. He brought, however, waves of healing.

"Tell them," Sarah whispered and touched her forearm.

Anna felt sick, but she rolled up her sleeve and showed them her secret numbers. They all gasped, began to weep, and held her.

---

1   Words: Forgaill, Dallan, 8th Century. "Be Thou My Vision." Translated by Mary E. Byrne, 1905. "Eriú." *Journal of the School of Irish Learning.* Versed by Eleanor H. Hull, 1912. *hymnlyrics.org.* http://www.hymnlyrics.org/mostpopularhymns/be_thou_my_vision.php (Accessed August 29, 2013)

"She did all of this to save Your people, Lord!" Sarah yelled out. "Heal Anna. Heal her, Lord. Take away the horrible memories of what those men did to her."

The ladies cried openly. Then, as if a blanket covered their camp fire, all was still.

Anna's tears were dried and she looked around at each of their faces. They were radiant. Then, Anna knew Sarah was supposed to be a wife of a pastor.

Each lady kissed Anna and Sarah goodbye. They invited them over for tea, cookies, or whatever they had on hand. Anna accepted every invitation. She felt so much better and so much worse all at the same time. She hated being vulnerable, but this was the place it was safe to be.

Anna told Sarah she needed to meet with Father Donnelly alone. Sarah looked a little shocked, but told Anna she would come by later after she hugged her.

Father Donnelly came over, kissed his fiancé on her cheek, and then sat in the pew in front of Anna. He turned to face her.

"I'm so glad you came, Anna."

"It was a happy accident. I forgot about the prayer meetings in the mornings. I actually came to talk with you."

"Oh?"

"Surely, you can't be surprised."

"I have to say I am."

"You'll soon be my stepfather of sorts."

Father Donnelly had not considered this.

He chuckled and conceded, "I suppose you're right."

Anna looked at him oddly. *Had Sarah not referred to me as her daughter?*

"Father, I'm angry with you," she said without minced words.

Father Donnelly was taken aback.

"Please share with me what I can do to make things right."

"You've been courting my mother for a month, asked her to marry you, and never talked to me."

Father Donnelly thought about this for a while.

"It never occurred to me I needed to."

Anna was infuriated; she sat in simmered silence. Father Donnelly, the good priest he was, immediately knew the depths of Anna's hurt.

"Anna, I'm so sorry I didn't. I can see how wrong that was. Will you forgive me?"

He reached over and touched her shoulder. She nodded her head.

"When I'm with Sarah, I feel like my youth is restored. We were trying to keep our courtship very quiet, for obvious reasons. It gets tricky when you're a rector. I suppose in our quest for secrecy, we did the wrong thing by not bringing you in to our confidence."

She nodded again.

"Anna, may I ask you a question?"

She looked up.

"How are you and Henry doing? Is everything all right?"

He sensed something much deeper was going on.

Anna swallowed hard.

"I didn't think marriage would be like this," she admitted. "I don't know if I even believe in it anymore."

"Why is that?" He asked gently.

She was already thankful he did not scold her. Most pastors would have given her a lecture on God's design for marriage, but not Father Donnelly. He did not lecture; he seemed to really care.

"Before we were married, he paid attention to me. Now, I never see him. He doesn't care. He doesn't talk to me."

Father Donnelly offered his hand. She took it.

"I'll pray, Anna. Marriage is not just a license for intimacy physically. Marriage is a bonding of souls. It doesn't seem like Henry has any earthly idea what he's doing. Do you want me to slap him around a bit?"

Anna laughed.

"No, Father."

Father Donnelly grinned widely.

"He needs more than prayer, though. He needs a spiritual leader in his life to teach him how to be a good husband. I'm guessing he didn't have much of a role model. I knew his father to not only be a distracted man, but then his early death was just awful."

Anna began to understand. *This isn't how marriage is supposed to be.*

"Will you be that for Henry?" Anna asked meekly.

"I'd love to. I'll seek him out on Sunday and we'll do something together. Let's pray he accepts."

"I'll do that."

"Anna. . . ."

"Yes?"

"Again, I'm so sorry."

"It's all right."

"Truly, though, Anna, I was in the wrong. Can we make a pact to be friends?"

"Yes, of course."

Father Donnelly helped her up by the hand and she walked home, the world lifted off her shoulders.

"Where were you this morning?" Henry asked as he cradled Michael to his shirtless chest. He was waiting for the bottle to warm.

"I went to morning prayer."

"Why didn't you tell me?"

She wanted to yell: "Why didn't you tell me your entire family was descending upon us?"

"Why did you go?"

"I just sort of ended up there. It was wonderful, though, Henry—"

"That's good, hon. Can you hand me that?"

He pointed to the towel. Michael had drooled on his bare shoulder. Anna handed it to him, and then started to walk away.

"I would've gone with you," Henry said as she pushed open the swinging kitchen door.

"You would've?"

"Well, sure. I want to be where you are."

His comment surprised Anna. It was as if she had a glimpse of him a month ago. He turned away, his back muscles showed as he held the heavy baby. She smiled.

"I'd love for you to go, Henry. Will you go tomorrow?"

"Of course, it's early enough. I've been doing some Bible study of my own in my office every day."

"I didn't know—"

"I sneak it in when I'm doing paperwork."

"Have you learned a lot?"

"Of course . . . I didn't even really understand the Bible before I became a Christian. Now, I can spend a lifetime on one verse."

"I know . . . It's alive!"

She wanted to dance. He smiled back at her.

"I love you so much, you know that?"

She barely nodded.

"Anna, that nod didn't look confident. You *know* I love you."

She stood still. Michael stirred and put his chubby little arms out for her. She took him and kissed him all over his face. *He's so sweet.*

"Oh, give him to me, you two," Ashling said after she burst into the kitchen.

"I've got his bottle and—"

"Oh, I only use that some times. Give him to me," she said and unbuttoned her shirt.

Anna and Henry looked at each other.

"Well, I've got these for something, don't I?"

Michael nursed happily.

"Ashling, modern doctors have found the bottle is better and—"

"Shut up, Henry. No one's calling you 'mommy.' Then you don't need to make those kinds of decisions."

"You need to follow doctor's orders. They know better. We're not animals, Ashling," Henry said and looked away.

"Well, of course, we are, stupid! Men are so dumb, aren't they, Anna?"

Henry took Anna's hand and went into their library.

"I like how fierce she is," Anna said and smiled.

"Yeah. Until she's mad at you. Then, it gets scary," he replied.

He thought of his crazy times with his cousin.

"Thank you for sitting down and talking to me," Anna said to her husband.

"Of course," he replied.

"I showed some ladies and Father Donnelly my numbers this morning."

He went white and asked, "Why did you decide to do that?"

"It seemed right. They were praying for me and I wanted them to know."

Henry nodded. He did not know what to say.

"Ashling saw them last night as well."

"Why this sudden openness?"

"It just sort of happened."

"I see."

Henry thought about this turn of events, *Other people now know.*

He was scared to ask how much others knew, but said, "I'm glad you can talk about it a little."

He never wanted Anna to talk about it. He did not want it to exist in her mind.

"Sarah was there."

"Oh, how wonderful."

"Yes," she agreed.

Then, there was an awkward silence. Henry thought about the thousand things he had to do that day.

"Did you get some breakfast?"

"No, but I'm not too hungry."

It was a stark contrast to her life of starvation a year before.

"Well," he said and got up, and then tucked in his shirt, "I think I'll see what I can find to eat."

Then, the conversation was over. Anna took a book off the shelf as Henry left.

Well, that was like running into someone I'd been best childhood friends with and now we had nothing to say.

Henry walked through the kitchen hastily without seeing what Cook had made for breakfast and headed out the backdoor. He hopped into one of his cars and sped toward the priory. He had some questions for his rector.

CHAPTER 10

HENRY PUSHED OPEN THE PRIORY door and went in. He wondered if Father Donnelly had gone to breakfast. However, he quickly found him as Father Donnelly knelt at the altar alone.

Henry found a seat in one of the pews and stared at the cross. The cross—Anna had given him a wooden one which he had around his neck at all times. Yet, he hated to look at crosses. All he saw was Jesus hanging on it similar to the way he felt when he looked at Anna's numbers. All he saw was suffering.

Father Donnelly finally got up and walked toward Henry.

"I'm sorry to keep you waiting, my boy," the rector stretched out his hand. "I had a very important meeting just now."

Henry smiled.

"What brings you here?" the priest asked.

He already knew.

"I heard Anna came to prayer today."

"Yes, she blessed us."

"How so?"

"Oh, she sang for us and shared a little about herself."

"Oh."

Father Donnelly sat beside Henry on the front row.

"Why am I getting the feeling this makes you nervous?"

"It's just hard to have others know."

"Why is that? Those numbers are a badge of honor."

Henry had never thought of them like that.

"Those numbers are ruining my life."

Father Donnelly was intrigued.

"I thought I'd be able to handle it. I think I convinced myself I could've handled anything before we married. I'd look at her beautiful face and became a ridiculous buffoon," Henry said with a chuckle.

"Aren't we all around the women we love?"

"By the way, congratulations are in order. Forgive me. Welcome to the family!" Henry said and put his arm around his minister.

Father Donnelly put his hand on Henry's shoulder, squeezed, and chimed, "Thank ye, thank ye. I couldn't be a happier man. But, I'd very much like for us to go back to you being a buffoon."

Henry smiled. *He's so easy to talk to.*

"So, when she told me . . . When she told me they had selected her for the brothels . . . Have you heard about them?"

"I dare say not."

"Well, when the girls were stripped down, before they shaved them, they'd select the prettiest ones. Those went to a different concentration camp. Hitler believed homosexuals were undesirables, so he wanted to make sure his soldiers were not. So, he provided a service for them—these women. . . ."

Henry barely finished what he had said. Father Donnelly pursed his lips and shook his head. He did not want to listen, but had to.

"My Lord and my God," he said.

"She told me she was raped eight or more times a night."

They sat in silence for a long time before Father Donnelly asked, "How long was she there?"

"Forty-five days."

Father Donnelly leaned forward as if in prayer and breathed into his hands.

"I thought I could handle it. I was . . . I'm so in love with her. On our wedding night she just cried in my arms. I just don't want to hurt her, you know?" Henry cried openly. "I've been trying to avoid her the entire month we've been married because when I see her, my heart goes crazy and I just don't want to—"

"You don't want to hurt her. Now, I understand completely."

"I love her so much. She's this gift, you know? She's like this princess, but she has this terrible, horrible thing that happened to her. I know she's trying to talk to me, to pull me in, but I don't want to talk about this with her. So, I've created work for myself so I can be in my own little world and not have to think about it."

Father Donnelly leaned back, squeezed Henry's shoulder again, and advised, "Henry, we must lay down our lives for our wives. You must put aside your heartbreak of what has been done to your wife. You must focus on her. If she cries in your arms, let her. Draw closer to her through it. She needs you."

Henry nodded as his tears flowed and humbly said, "I'll try."

"She's strong. She'll be healed of all of this, I promise you. However, you must be a balm to her soul, Henry. When you turn away from her, you're turning away from the greatest ministry God will ever give you—the ministry to your wife."

The two manly men slapped each other's backs and wiped away their tears with their fists. Afterwards, Henry returned to his house and searched for Anna.

He found her in the library; she was still reading Frankenstein. He closed the book and sat beside her. Then, he took her into his lap and kissed her.

"Let's go on a trip . . . You're right. Pearce can run things for a while. You should've seen how he looked at me when I told him we hadn't gone on a honeymoon."

Anna smiled and whispered, "Where?"

"I don't know. Wherever you want to go."

"Wales."

"All right, I'll book the trip."

CHAPTER II

ANNA AND HENRY SAT IN the drive and he shut the car off. He looked at his wife. It had been a trip beyond what he had ever expected—life-changing. Three weeks of being on a mountain with God and the beautiful creature he called his wife.

"No one's going to understand," Anna said and took his hand.

"I don't expect them to."

"They'll get used to it."

"Yep."

They walked in, hand in hand, as Ashling and Pearce greeted them warmly. Anna grabbed Michael and remarked how fat he had gotten. Peter zoomed in with a toy airplane and bruised Henry's leg with it. Things were a wonderful, friendly flutter.

Ashling excitedly led them into the formal dining room where she had a beautiful meal put together.

"There's a roast, but Henry, I had Cook make a ton of vegetables for you."

"Thank you, Ashling."

"Even though I think you need to get over it and start eating meat again."

"Ashling," Henry moaned. "I've been here five minutes. Your child has beaten me up and now you're giving me advice."

"Sorry. Just think it's time. Poor animals died in the barn fire, I get it ... I get it. It's just not worth torturing yourself the rest of your life."

Anna understood her husband. She smiled at him and held his hand under the gorgeous table.

"So, talk to me! How was it?" Ashling asked happily.

"Well, we will if you give us a chance to talk!" Henry said.

"Go, then, talk!"

"Okay!" Henry said. "We had a wonderful time. We went to the Bible College in Wales."

"On a honeymoon?" Ashling questioned, appalled.

"It's a place I've always wanted to go," Anna tried to explain.

"Why?" Ashling said.

"It's been such a wonderful hub of prayer during the war. There are a lot of leaders who actually believe prayer is what the secret weapon was."

"So, you went to pray?"

Ashling was getting annoyed. She had never met two less romantic people in her life.

"Yes," Henry said.

"And?"

Ashling passed the beans to Henry.

"God talked back," Henry proudly said.

"I'm related to a crazy person," Ashling sighed and rolled her eyes.

"Honey, let the man speak. This is obviously something which means a great deal to Anna and Henry. We need to be supportive," Pearce said gently.

"Ashling, I'm just going to make this quick. Remember when I pulled off the Band-Aid on our leg?"

"Yeah, and all the skin came off with it."

"Well it's sort of like that."

"Okay," Ashling said and took a deep breath, "One, two, three, go!"

"I'm going into the ministry."

Everything stopped.

"I'm going to follow in Father Donnelly's shoes. He has to retire soon; I want to become the rector. We'll be taking a cottage in town to be close to my parishioners. I'll have to take some classes—mostly distance classes through the mail. Father Donnelly has already agreed to it—to train me, that is. I want to give you the Manor, Ashling."

Ashling left the table. Henry looked at Anna.

"Too much skin," Anna whispered. "Let me go talk with her."

Henry winced and nodded. Anna got up and followed Ashling. She was in the library.

"Hi," Anna said to her.

Ashling was seated on the couch and mumbled, "Hey."

Anna went over and sat beside her. Ashling held her hand. Anna kissed her head.

"It's still us. We'll still be around," Anna said.

Initially, Ashling did not respond, but then said, "I don't understand either of you."

"We don't expect you to. We have made a very strange decision."

"Why would Henry give up his inheritance?"

"We'll still have the accounts—well most of them—some he's donating to the work being done right now in Uganda. It's just that he can't be a servant to others if he lives like a king."

"A servant!"

"Yes, that's what a minister is."

"My cousin is going from a prince to a servant!"

"Ashling, the God we serve did something rather similar," Anna replied.

Ashling stood, walked toward the mantle, and commented, "When you were gone, I found this."

She put her hand on the words inscribed on the mantle.

"Yes, Henry did that the day after he became a Christian."

"Do you believe the words he inscribed here?"

"Yes, I do."

"Is he really hearing from God, Anna?"

"Yes."

"How do you know?"

"Because I heard the same thing."

Ashling was taken aback by what she heard. One thing she knew them each to be, though, was honorable. She knew they were not lying. People don't give up their lives for lies.

CHAPTER 12

AUTUMN 1947

TOMAS RODE THROUGH THE VILLAGE one night in his new car. He parked it at his father's cottage, but he did not go in. Sean had written him about the unusual events of the past year in Adare. This was Tomas' first opportunity to come home and see firsthand.

His college years had gone by quicker than most and he had secured a job with one of the top pharmaceutical companies in the world. He had only worked there a few months before he became bored and simply stopped going to work.

He had made enough money in the few months to keep him comfortable for a year. He thought he would easily get another job next year.

Sean's letter intrigued him, as it was about Henry. It was hard for him to imagine what had possessed him to become a priest. He still did not understand why a beautiful girl such as Anna ever wanted to be with someone as awkward as Henry.

Henry had tried to patch things up a few times with Tomas, but he was not going to do it. As far as he was concerned, he had nothing to say to Henry.

Anyone in my position can't judge me.

Tomas shivered at the thought.

When Henry decided to become part of what Tomas had deemed the "lunatic club of Christians" their friendship ended. A scientist like Tomas and his perception of "an ignorant Christian" like Henry was not a good match. The thing which bothered Tomas so much was Henry's intelligence.

Who'd ever possibly buy the ramblings in the Bible? It has no scientific basis. Tomas saw there was no light on in Dr. Lannon's house. He decided he must have been at a patient's house, so he went for a walk. He stretched out of his car and walked through the dark streets of Adare. Then, he stopped.

Anna was in the window of a yellow cottage with green window boxes. She was working in the kitchen. He gulped and watched her. He heard some music being played inside on a record player. *Is it Bach?*

He crept closer into the garden. Then, he realized she was crying. *Why?*

He checked the driveway. There was a car there, but Henry was able to afford two. *Maybe she's alone*, he thought.

He thought about tapping on her door to tell her what had happened in the brothel.

I can't . . . Some things are too difficult to say unless surrounded by the confidant's unconditional love.

A car pulled up on the other side of the house and Tomas quietly stood behind some bushes. It was Henry; he wore a clerical collar. Tomas wanted to laugh out loud. *It looks ridiculous!*

He continued to watch Anna at the window. She dried her tears with her apron and greeted Henry. He sat down, ate, and then retired to another room.

Anna stood in front of the window and cleaned the dishes in the sink. Then, she started to cry again.

He thought about the terrible afternoon Henry had come home. Tomas thought Anna had kept his secret. It was obvious by the horrible look on Henry's face she had not.

Henry had waited for no explanation. He simply came at Tomas and punched him. It began a war never to be quenched.

Yet, there was a secret Henry did not know. Tomas loved Anna. Love was something different to Tomas than Henry, but it was still there like a magnet which pulled him to her.

For Tomas, she was his obsession. He had never found her equal. Still, it was more than that. She was his comfort. He desperately needed her to understand him, to know everything about him . . . To forgive him.

He watched her unbutton the top button of her crisp, white shirt. She stood, supported by her arms as she leaned against the sink. Her head was heavy.

So, is this what their marriage has become . . . Strangers in their house.

Then, as if she was a young fawn who had heard a sound, her eyes shot up. Tomas moved quickly, but she caught his shape. She dried off her hands with a towel and walked out the back door.

"Is someone there?" She called out.

His heart melted. Her voice sounded frightened.

"It's just me, Anna," he said.

Tomas moved into view. *I'd rather feel the pain of her rejection than to have her be scared.*

"Tomas?"

Her skin was pale.

"Yes, I was on a walk. Forgive me. I wanted to see you, and I—"

"You can't be here, Tomas."

"Please, I want to explain."

"There's nothing to explain."

"Henry told me you were in the one for the SS. The one for the prisoners was different. Please let me explain things to you."

She paused and thought about what he said. He was encouraged by her silence, he continued.

"Go on a walk with me?"

"No. If you have something to explain, try to do it now."

Tomas took in a deep breath and stared at her. He did not know where to begin. He wanted to hold her close and tell her everything in her ear while she held him. He had thought about it a lot over the past year and a half. He craved her touch. No one had ever hugged him like she had.

"We were forced to go in."

She waited and asked, "Is that all?"

He nodded, but it was not.

"Good night, Tomas," she said and walked away from him.

He went back to his father's house and grabbed his bags from his trunk. He broke in where he knew there was an open window. His father was the only one to lock his cottage. He had to, since he kept so much medicine.

Tomas stretched out in his old bed face down. The thought of hurting Anna was more than he could handle. *Yet, I have to.*

What he had found in his lab had been a miracle—if he had believed in them. In fact, the drug he discovered was the closest thing he had come to a miracle in his life. Finding it was as if the God he did not believe in had given him permission to use it on the one person who could benefit from it the most. It was a drug which erased one's memory.

He had thought of using it on himself, but, he could not—his research would be gone. He thought of experimenting with some of the patients who came in—so many had mental problems due to war atrocities. He had sneaked the drug into several of the worst cases. The results were incredible.

He gulped. The one person he wanted to use it on more than anyone else was the one person in the world he loved the most: Anna. *My plan is elegant.*

Tomas had driven back and forth to an unknown location a few days that week to prepare things. Dr. Lannon had noticed, but did not think much of it—Tomas had told him he was visiting friends. What he found odd, however, was how close Tomas kept his medical bag with him at all times. *Doctors do it, but Tomas is a chemist. It's highly unusual.*

Dr. Lannon had his son play the violin for him that night after dinner. It was a farewell song, but neither of them knew it. Tomas was not sure when he was leaving, so he kept a forged letter from a university on him at all times which told of an incredibly opportunity.

Tomas took his nightly walk to Anna's house and stood behind the bush in her garden to watch her through the kitchen window. However, something wonderful happened to Tomas that night. Henry did not come home.

He watched from the window and grew aggravated as Anna watched the grandfather clock which they had moved from Adare Manor. It clearly was too big and grand for their humble dwellings.

It was getting very late. Anna then grabbed her car keys. Tomas sprinted for his car to follow her. He did not care where she went, as long as it was far from Henry.

From a safe distance, he followed her for an hour as she headed to Ballybunion Beach. She parked at the end of the street where there was access to the water. He pulled in at a bar next door. Then, he watched her. *She's magnificent.*

Anna looked all around. Not a soul was in sight, so she stripped down to her undergarments and stepped into the frigid water. Tomas was in his glory.

She finally ran and dove in. He did not know how she withstood the water being so cold. He got out of his car and walked over to where she had dropped her clothes.

She giggled and screamed a little in the freezing water, and then turned to swim back to shore. There, she received the shock of her life: Tomas stood over her clothes with a smile.

Her lips quivered and her teeth chattered. She knew she could not stay in the water much longer. So did Tomas.

"What do you want?" Anna yelled and hoped someone heard her. He did not answer. He silently stood over her clothes.

"Can you please go away so I can dress?" she asked.

She hoped he had a little of a gentleman within him, but he did not. He waited. Anna thought about swimming further to get help down the way, but she started to lose feeling in her feet. She had made the swim often to revive herself in the cold water. She knew it was dangerous, but for those few minutes in the water, she did not think. She needed to have those moments.

Then, she realized she had no choice. She had to go toward Tomas to get her clothes and the keys to her car. She embraced herself and walked out of the freezing water; she stumbled a little from the numbness.

"Hello, Anna," he said casually.

She bent down to grab her clothes at his feet, and then got up. At the same time, Tomas grabbed her—he did not want to hurt her, yet did not want to waste the only opportunity he had. He looked into her eyes, she felt a small stab in her thigh, and then everything went black.

CHAPTER 13

THE NOTE FROM ANNA READ: *I went to the beach for a swim.*
Henry crumpled it in his hands. Even the way she wrote was
lovely. He hated, yet loved how unpredictable she was. She had a
wild heart—charitable, loving, but also mischievous and sometimes
even inconsiderate.

He had been at the bedside of his dear friend as he had gone
on to be with the Lord an hour earlier. He wanted her for once
to be a normal wife, to be there with a cup of tea and a caring
hug. Instead, she was angry he was not there again. She always did
something similar when she was upset.

He sighed and looked out the window. Henry realized it was
already dark. He had not noticed it on the way home because
he was so deep in thought about his friend's death. He wiped
the sweat from his neck. *This is the warmest autumn night I've
ever known.*

He sighed and looked at his pocket watch which indicated it
was ten minutes after ten o'clock. *The warmer the weather, the more
unpredictable Anna becomes.*

He closed the watch and looked out the window and decided
what to do. Fortunately, they were one of the few couples in Ireland who had two cars. Anna had taken the nicer of the two the
hour drive down to Ballybunion Beach. Henry was certain, even
though her note did not say.

Anna had one of her never-ending giggles the day before about what she dubbed "Belly Button Beach." She often went there for a polar bear swim as she called it. He shook his head; he had thought her name game was cute the day before. That night, however, he was exhausted and emotionally spent—he was not amused by her.

He decided, though, it was better to pass her on the road and be annoyed with her lateness than to have something bad happen to her. He thought, *Maybe the car broke down.*

He grabbed his keys.

"Silly woman," he said under his breath

It was the one and only time he ever said anything negative about his wife.

The fog rolled in as Henry drove along the bumpy road. It started to sprinkle. His windshield wipers squeaked and he strained to make out each lonely car that passed him. None looked like hers. Halfway there, he became unsettled. *Surely, she wouldn't have stayed out this late.*

He scanned the sides of the road as he went. He hoped to find her with the car hood up, waiting for him to fill her tank with gas or water in her radiator. Still, there was no sight of her.

Henry arrived in Ballybunion and went through the little beach town. He looked for her car to be parked somewhere, anywhere. He went down to the beach and finally saw her white convertible with the hood still down.

He parked beside it and looked in. He had hoped to see her asleep in the seat.

Where is she?

He scrambled for the flashlight she kept in the trunk and banged it until it came on. He turned on each car's headlights which did little good. The beautiful sound of waves breaking and the breeze would have soothed him had it not been for the terror he felt.

He began to call, "Anna . . . Anna!"

Henry began to run along the shore until he saw something he at first thought was seaweed. Then, it hit him, *Her clothes!*

They were strewn on the beach, licked by the incoming tide.

"Anna! Oh, God, please help me . . . Anna!"

He wanted to hear her giggle behind him, come up, and jump on his back to scare him. However, five long minutes went by and he heard only the sound of the waves.

Henry dropped the flashlight and ran aimlessly into the sea. Then, he changed his mind and ran up the street into town. He thought it was faster on foot than in the car. He headed for the only place open, the pub, and yelled for help.

The bartender called the police. Then, Henry begged him to call the only person he knew in Adare who had a home telephone. More panicked than ever, Henry ran back to the ocean.

"Anna!" He called until his voice cracked.

The police showed up first and questioned Henry who had grown desperate. He pleaded with officers to please help him find her, but they had a hard time piecing together his story. Henry was inconsolable. They even contemplated whether or not he was out of his mind. They called the Coast Lifesaving Service, but Henry refused to wait.

A man from a nearby house showed up with a small rowboat—Henry and two other men he did not know rowed out aimlessly. Fog rolled in thicker and more frightening than ever. After an hour, the other men finally agreed they had better go back or else be lost at sea. Henry sobbed and begged them to continue, but everyone else in the boat knew she was lost.

The Coast Lifesaving Service arrived, and then went out in three boats as more of a courtesy than with hopes of finding Anna. No one could survive in the frigid waters that long.

The townspeople straggled back to their homes and left Henry on the dark beach with two cars. He finally sat in the sand, face in his hands, and cried out to God. At the same time, friends from Adare arrived, including Father Donnelly and Sarah. The Coast Lifesaving Service and police stayed to assist. The Adarians went up and down the beach for any of sign of Anna. Their search effort, however, proved to be just as unproductive as the last. The group finally gathered after combing the beach two hours for Anna. They took each other's hands and formed a circle. There, Father Donnelly prayed.

Sarah wept so hard others hardly heard the prayer. Henry sat alone in the sand and stared into the deep ocean. He clutched Anna's pink blouse and her high wasted pants in his tight fists.

Thoughts of his wife's lifeless body eaten by fish in her pretty lace undergarments made him rise to his feet. He waded back into the water and cried out her name. His dearest friends slowly walked up to him and one by one put their hand on his shoulder as he cried into the night air. Then, all of them left, except one.

Father Donnelly had given his car keys to Anna's trusted friends, as well as the care of his wife to Henry's childhood friend, Sean. He initially put up a small fight and told Father Donnelly they needed to keep looking. Father Donnelly had the rare authority to muzzle Sean.

Finally, they all drove quietly away, leaving Father Donnelly and Henry alone on the beach. Only one set of high beams glared toward them.

"She's gone," Father Donnelly whispered.

Henry shook his head violently. He suddenly had an idea and waded out of the water, and then ran up the street again. The morning sun had barely peaked through the dawn.

He burst into the pub once more where a few drunken inhabitants remained and waved around all the money he had in his wallet.

He begged people to come back out to comb the beach farther than they had searched before. A few people staggered out and accepted Henry's proposal.

Then, Henry began to frantically knock on every door in town to beg them to help him. Soon, a scraggly army of ladies in housecoats and curlers, men tying their walking shoes, and little children in their nightclothes congregated in the center of the road and asked what he was doing.

Father Donnelly, who had tried to stop Henry, attempted to explain to the group of townspeople what had happened. A few people returned to their homes, but most accepted the proposition of ten pounds for two hours' worth of search efforts. They used any transportation they had to scour the beach. They even reached as far as the Cliffs of Moher.

Father Donnelly took Henry aside and asked, "Do you have enough money to pay everyone?"

Henry said flatly, "I need a bank."

Father Donnelly went to find a banker to open a bank for him.

Henry handed out money to the search party as promised after a couple of hours. Once again, he begged the townspeople to continue the search—most did not. By mid-morning everyone was gone again. There had not been a trace of Anna found other than her clothes.

Father Donnelly sat beside the exhausted widower and put his arm around his shoulders. They gazed into the sea

"Let's go get something to eat. We'll continue looking as long as you want."

Henry's body shook. Father Donnelly coaxed him up—Henry did not have the strength to argue.

Father Donnelly sat across from Henry in a small diner and held his hand. A coarse middle-aged man sneered at the two of them.

"We don't smile on that kind of affection with two lads," he said as his teeth hung on to an old cigar.

"This man has just lost his wife!" Father Donnelly retorted harshly. Henry's heart sank and he pondered, *Does he really believe she's gone?* He felt betrayed.

The man stood stunned for a moment as Henry pulled away his hand. Then, the man made the sign of the cross.

"Jesus, Mary, and Joseph," he recited solemnly.

"Please step away," Father Donnelly said callously.

His conduct was completely out of character from his usual patient demeanor. The man whispered something to the waitress, and then left as he put his hat on.

Henry did not remember either of them placing an order, but soon tea and porridge were served to them by the waitress. Henry looked at both items and thought about eating.

"She's not gone," he whispered.

He could not bear the thought.

"My son," Father Donnelly said affectionately, "I believe she is."

"There's still hope."

Father Donnelly finally nodded, although all his faith for Anna's return had gone. Yet, Henry's intense love for his wife fueled the engine of his faith.

CHAPTER 14

Winter 1947

ANNA OPENED HER EYES AND peeled them apart like broken cocoons. They were dried with old tears. Pain stung her arms and she pulled them to her chest like precious, old love letters. As she did, she felt herself start to fall. She reached out quickly for something to grasp and thought, *A branch....*

The blur of the moment was transposed into terror when she finally realized where she was. She clung to a small, bare tree in the middle of an endless sea of marshland. She felt dizzy and held the skinny branches of hope with her sweaty, cold hands.

Anna took stock of what she had. She had on a makeshift dress. She was cut up and bled a little. *Can I move? Yes!*

She moved her hands. Yet, she had no feeling below her waist. Her legs were dead weight. She looked around and tried to locate any shred of land. Her eyes blurred the farther they tried to focus. She looked down again. Finally, she saw below her where oysters were perched, ready to devour her like hungry crocodiles.

They'll rip me to shreds; bleed my feet to death before I make it to any shore. If I can see one . . . If I can walk. . . .

She stretched her neck and searched around desperately—confused, horrified. Anna tried to make sense of anything, *Where am I? How did I get here?*

Cold sweat trickled down her neck; her eyesight was almost gone. All she saw were dark blue shadows like a photograph negative.

Her ears rang as the true pain began in the blindness when Anna tried to remember something. Nothing came. *How did I get out in the middle of such a place? Why am I here?*

It was as if the heavens had spit her out and dropped her upon the little tree.

Anna cried out, "Help! Is anyone out there?"

Her throat hurt and she began to choke on her tears. The wind carried her voice to far off places where no one lived. Anna's teeth began to chatter. The sharpness in the air cut through her like the branches.

Hours went by. She stopped shaking. She slept for a minute or two, and then awoke often, startled. She grasped the tree as she felt as if she was about to fall.

The sun was bright, the air was still chilled, and nightfall was coming with no hope in sight. Anna rearranged her body on the tree and tried to find security. Yet, none was to be found.

A few dead branches broke beneath her which made her even more uncomfortable during her quest to hold on. Then, she felt the sensation of a thousand ants crawl on her feet and up her legs. She gasped and tried to brush them away, but there was nothing there. Anna rubbed her legs and the crawling sensation grew worse like little demonic spiders.

She cried in fear and suddenly moved her foot slightly. *I can move a little!*

She concentrated hard, wiggled one of her toes. *Feeling is coming back!*

An hour had passed and more feeling returned until she almost felt able to walk. Anna desperately thought she might step through the oyster beds very slowly and somehow find land. *It's my only hope.*

She crouched down to the cold waters and stuck her foot in. What seemed like a soft, sandy area was actually another oyster, covered in gray mud, waiting for his prey. Streams of blood flowed down the side of her foot. The oyster gaped at her, jaw drawn open in stilled shock.

Saltwater seeped into the deep gash on her foot; she cried in pain. Anna desperately searched, but there was nowhere to even carefully plant a small foot down. It was as if she was surrounded by knives. *It's better to freeze to death.*

She clung to the tree. The soft blue of the sky taunted her. Anna thought, *I wish I could turn my world upside down and nestle in the clouds.*

However, she was trapped, a prisoner of nature. She tried to surmise theories about how she came to be in such a predicament, but there was no memory from which to pull. She desperately searched her mind for anything—any small shred of a passing memory to surmise what had happened—, but nothing came. The nothingness was slowly killing her.

The sunset was pink like the cheeks of a blushing bride, but it was foreboding to her and prophesied her long walk down the aisle of death. She knew she could not survive the night.

Am I to only live for one terrifying day?

"God," she wept instinctively.

She tried to find a memory when she had prayed before, but there was nothing.

"God!" She cried in anger.

She tried to remember a time when she was angry. She shook her head in silence.

Maybe I'm dreaming.

She tried to think of a way to wake up. She shook herself; the branches below her cracked. She reached way down, almost losing her hold, to splash cold water in her face. Then, she screamed out, but her voice was almost entirely gone. She did not wake.

Anna searched her mind for knowledge. She began to count. *I remember how to count!*

She was able to run advanced mathematical problems in her head and solve them. She saw words in her head and was able to read them. She remembered countries and where they were located on the earth. She was sure she was able to remember more of what she had learned.

Why can I remember nothing about my life, yet still retain knowledge?

The marsh began to change—the color of the grass went from green to brown. The water rose from muddy puddles to dark trenches. Then, nightfall came. She waited to die. The water had risen to barely touch her.

Anna wondered, *Is drowning the best way to die? Surely, the water can't be, but a few feet off the oysters. It'd be impossible to swim in.*

The moon rose high, full, and white. It lit up the death bed she clung to and played with the licks of waves which rippled beneath her. She bowed her head in reverence to it.

She felt her body relax and finally accepted what was to come until the faint whisper of water movement perked her head up, curious at the sound. It was rhythmic, but not steady. She looked around and tried to find its source.

Then, she saw a small boat. *My salvation!*

The small boat headed toward her. She smiled slightly and hung her head down, too weak to reach or call out. Then, she felt hands around her as she clung to the man in the dark hood.

Anna thought for a moment, *Maybe it's death coming to take me.*

Her rescuer's voice soothed her when he said, "Shh, I've got you. Hold on. I'm here."

She cried in whimpers as she clung to him. He draped his hooded cloak around her and held her like an infant on his lap.

"It'll be all right now. I'm going to take you home."

He shook in uneasiness almost harder than she did as he wrapped her and tried to rub warmth into her body. The stranger looked at her face in the moonlight. Her eyes were closed in pain. Her skin was pale. He brushed his hand against her cheek and felt how cold she was.

Then, he tried to row home with one hand as he held her with his other—an almost impossible feat. He kept switching hands as he pulled the paddle over her little body on his lap every time he made another stroke. Otherwise, he would have kept going in circles, which is how he felt until that moment—as if his life kept going in circles.

His life had been one of utter loneliness. He had lived for the next challenge to solve, the next scientific riddle to break. He wanted to stop remembering his past life.

As the stranger held Anna, even though he was frightened for her life, he did not recall a more perfect moment. He knew he needed to go home to warm her as quickly as possible, but the feeling of her wrapped around him was so perfect, so wonderful. *I don't want this moment to end.*

He peeked back at her face under the dark cloak. He lost his breath when he saw her face. She was the most perfect human being he had ever beheld.

"It'll be all right," he said to the semi-conscious girl. "I'm here."

Anna turned her head into his chest, anxious to breathe in warm air. He trembled as he cradled her beautiful head in his hand. His heartbeat fell and raced at her touch. He stopped rowing—he closed his eyes, wrapped his arms around her, warmed her for a few moments, and provided her a brief feeling of comfort to continue. Then, he began to row again, anxious to get her inside his warm house to truly help her.

The thud of the boat against the shoreline startled her, she was awakened. He soothed her with his gentle whispers and laid her down on the boat's seat while he waded through the water and pulled the boat to shore. She clung to the cloak the stranger had put around her.

At first, he was unsteady; he hoped to not drop Anna, but he soon managed to carry her out of the boat. He hurried onto dry land, pulled open the door to his little hovel in the ground, and went down the steps into a small, underground room.

He had left a fire going with stew bubbling atop the flames. His mind wandered for a small moment to avoid truly taking in the unfolding events, *I hope I haven't burned dinner.*

He shook off the thought: *She'll die without my help*, as he focused on the more important task at hand.

His bed was carved out of the earth from which he had dug his house. It was a shelf of dirt with layers of old quilts atop. He thought it was not fit for her, but had no other choice than to place her in his bed.

Then, the stranger looked down at her for a few moments; he made the cloak she clung to more snug. He stared at her blue lips, and then rushed over to a small cabinet. He pulled out a change of clothes for himself and put everything else he had on top of Anna to keep her warm.

Then, he stirred his stew briefly. He brought over his small, wooden chair kept by the fire; placed it in front of her; and stared at her beautiful face. She began to shake again, so he put his hand on her arm. *She's ice cold.*

He bit his lower lip and gulped. He needed to warm her with his body heat. Therefore, he carefully and quietly maneuvered because he did not want to awaken her. He finally slipped down behind her and put his arm around her.

Anna immediately calmed down and soon the shaking stopped. He had never felt anything more beautiful—his blood rushed through his body, his heartbeat quickened, and he had to catch his breath.

He propped up his head on his elbow and watched her face from behind. As the night progressed, her lips and cheeks became pink. The stranger started to fall asleep, but realized it would not be good for her to wake up in a strange bed next to him. So, he got up, moved the chair back by the fire, and sat down.

The next morning, Anna woke in a soft bed, cradled in old, white quilts and layers of clothes. She looked around. She was in a small, underground room. *Had I dreamed about the tree?*

She felt the hard, dirt wall, and then turned to survey the rest of the dwelling. She was startled to see a man crouched by a fire; he tended to some food in a pot. She tried to quiet her breathing, yet grew anxious to what this man intended do to or had already done to her.

Anna forced herself to remember the little tree she had clung to, and then the man in the row boat who came to rescue her. It was the only memory she possessed.

The chimney reached out above the small hovel. On the opposite side of the little room, there was a table, two chairs, and a few little pots. She adjusted her dress and twisted her dark, wavy hair back behind her shoulder. He heard her and immediately stood up. He turned and she saw his handsome face for the first time.

He stared at her as if she was a wild animal which had awakened in his little house. She looked him straight into his eyes.

Her eyes are grey.

The stranger swallowed hard. He barely formed his words.

"Are you all right?" He finally asked.

She looked around the room, and then back at him to take a good look. He had short, blonde hair. His eyes were blue—she wanted to sink into them like the sky the day before.

He's young, she thought, *maybe in his early thirties.*

Anna nodded as she finally remembered he had asked her a question.

"Do you want something to eat?" He asked as he turned his eyes back to the fire.

He was afraid to look at her. She rubbed her eyes as she still tried to focus them.

He spooned some soup into a bowl, and then handed it to her. She adjusted the blankets, anxious to be appropriate. She smiled at him, drank the soup, and then looked back at him.

He stared at her. The fire crackled in the fireplace—the only sound in the room.

"I'm so cold," Anna said weakly as he took the bowl from her.

She nestled underneath the blankets. He set the bowl down beside him and quickly helped her to cover up. He pushed the covers around her and sat close to her.

She wanted to ask him so many questions, but was too exhausted to listen to any answers. The sweet rubs of his hands on her arms through the thick blankets lulled her into sleep once more.

He watched Anna sleep the rest of the night and throughout the next day. He forgot to eat or do anything else. Fortunately, he had cut down enough wood for the week the day before.

She did not sleep soundly. She babbled, turned and cried as she slept. Anna dreamed she was lost in a great forest:

She desperately ran to find the way out. She tried to cry out for help, but her voice was gone. She finally stopped, cold and exhausted.

She sat, arms crossed over her chest, close to the base of a tree. She heard a man's voice whisper which did not come from one place, but echoed from every space around her. The trees radiated his voice, the wind rustled with its tone.

"My love," he urged. *"You must find the way out! You must wake up! You must come to me! You're not safe here!"*

"I can't," she uttered. *"I'm trying!"*

"Follow my voice," his voice echoed around her.

The stranger brushed her hair out of her face numerous times. He covered her back up when she threw blankets off in her sleep. He finally found the courage to sit close and take her hand to his lips. She immediately calmed down. He marveled as he turned her elegant fingers in his rough ones, *Even her hands are beautiful.*

He played with her fingers. Finally, her eyes fluttered open and he quickly adjusted his seated-position nervously.

Anna winced at the lightness of the room. She looked at her hands and waved them. Light seemed to follow her hands. She rubbed her eyes and looked over to the stranger. Light propelled out of him. He glowed.

"Where am I?" she asked.

"You're in my home."

"Who are you?"

It was the question he had longed for her to ask. He smiled shyly as he looked down.

"My name is Daire."

"Anna," she heard herself say.

She had remembered her name. She was so confused, yet, somehow she knew it. He looked at her with wide eyes.

"Do you know what happened to me?"

He lowered his gaze. He paused for a great while and stared at the fire.

"I found you last night hanging on a little tree in the middle of the marsh."

"Do you know how I got there?"

"You don't know?" Daire asked.

Anna shook her head.

"I remember nothing."

"Nothing?"

"I don't remember anything at all—not how I got on that tree in the middle of the marsh, not *anything* about my life. . . ."

She looked back down at her hands which still glowed. She waved them again and watched them trail the same streams of light. Daire wanted to put his arms around her, hold her. He knew she must be scared. The few inches from her seemed cavernous. Anna sat up and pulled the blankets close to her chest. She looked down at the piles of clothes on top of her. Then, she looked back at him.

She licked her dry lips. He blinked nervously.

"May I have some water?" Anna croaked.

Her rescuer quickly scurried to retrieve water from a pitcher on the table. When he handed a cup to her, she looked down at the water. It sparkled like diamonds. She drank and handed it back to him. He filled it again, and she drank again.

She sank back under the covers. He grabbed the cup from her hands so she did not spill it.

"Thank you," she mouthed.

Her eyes searched his.

"Do you want me to talk to you a little or just rest?" Daire asked sweetly.

"Talk," she said faintly.

He smiled gently at her.

"Last night was very frightening."

He played nervously with a string attached to his pant leg.

"I go out on my little boat on clear nights."

"Why?" she mouthed.

"Why? I like the stars," he admitted nervously. "I know all the constellations and I try to see the planets."

"Telescope?" Anna whispered.

"No, no. I haven't one of those. I don't know if I really need it for the kind of amateur star gazing I do."

He chuckled lightly and stopped to look at her. He did not truly believe she was really there, talking to him. He took a deep breath.

"Last night, I almost didn't go out because it was so cold, but I had to stretch my legs. Then, when I looked around, the tree in the middle of the marsh looked strange in the darkness. I paddled closer only to find you."

Daire nervously scratched his forehead.

"Do you have any recollection of how you got there, Anna?"

She shook her head. One large tear ran down her face.

"I'm so scared," she whispered, yet felt oddly safe with the stranger.

He hesitated for a long while. He wanted to go to her, put his arms around her, but he was afraid of her. The tears kept flowing down her white cheeks. Her pain made him brave. He finally stood and walked over to her.

She wiped away her tears, and then reached for his hand. Daire almost did not believe the miracle of her reach for him. He was so desperate for her touch his hand believed enough to reach back. He clasped her little hand in his and sat next to her.

"Daire?"

Anna looked at him, eyes heavy with tears as she tried to find comfort in the only person she knew. She finally let go of his hand and in one stunning movement wrapped her arms around his neck. She pulled her body closer to his. He put his arms around her as she clung to him.

"It's all right," he finally managed to say. "We'll find the answers together."

She finally let go. He looked away from her immediately.

"Are you hungry? I have some food here," he offered.

Anna shook her head no. She wanted the stranger to hold her again.

"How do you think I got in the tree?" She asked with a sore throat.

"I don't know. Maybe you were on a boat and fell into the water. Maybe it was high tide and the waves took you to that little tree. Maybe you hit your head on the side of the boat as you fell. Maybe that's how you lost your memory."

She felt the back of her head.

"I don't feel any bumps," she said.

"You just need to rest more and it'll all come back to you."

"Can you get a doctor? Things look funny, too."

"Look funny . . . How?"

"Like light is coming from everything."

Daire pulled his chair close to her and leaned in close to her face. He took a look at her pupils. He tried to concentrate on them. *Her beautiful eyes, her lips are so close . . .*

He finally answered her.

"It sounds like you've had a very hard hit on the head."

"In the tree it was hard to see," Anna said.

He felt her breath on his cheeks. He backed up finally; there was nothing he was too concerned about.

"That often happens when you're in pain or a stressful situation."

"Where are we? Can you get a doctor?"

He smiled at her.

"I'm a doctor."

She smiled back.

"Do you think I'll be all right?"

"Yes, of course," he said after a pause.

"Should I call you Dr. Daire or something like that?"

"No," he chuckled softly, "Daire will be just fine. I'm not very much older than you. It doesn't seem right for you to address me so formely."

"Thank you for helping me," Anna croaked again.

He handed her back the water.

"You're going to need to drink quite a bit. Who knows how long you were in that tree."

"Are there other people around this area?"

"No. Just me."

"Why do you live out here?"

His mouth twitched a little.

"I'm not very good with people."

She sipped her water.

"You're good with me. Why become a doctor if you're not good with people?"

"I'm not that kind of a doctor. I'm a chemist. I make medicine."

"Sounds like very difficult and important work."

It was good for Anna to think and talk about something else for a moment. He simply smiled and looked toward the fire again.

"You're sounding better, Anna, but you must rest your voice. Do you . . . Would you like me to play for you?"

She looked at him quizzically, and then followed his eyes to a violin leaned up against the wall. She nodded and he quickly went to pick it up.

With the care a mother takes to put a newborn's head on her shoulder, Daire lovingly rested the golden body of the instrument beneath his cheek. He played slowly, delicately.

He watched the bow graze over the stings like the fingertips of a lover. He finally closed his eyes and sank into his song as if it was coming from his lips. He finished with the low hush of a single, lonely voice resounding off the walls of the dwelling. The light Anna saw radiating followed his smooth movements as if it was part of the music he played.

When Daire opened his eyes, they immediately focused on Anna's and she drew back from their intense wildness.

"Beautiful," she finally mouthed.

He watched her lips say it to him and was hungry for her to say it again. He was sure he would never grow tired of her praise.

She closed her eyes and drifted off as she nestled her little cup of water in her soft hands. He took it from her gently and covered her up more.

"Rest, Anna. Everything will be all right."

Daire brushed her beautiful, black hair out of her face.

When Anna woke up, she did not know if it was night or day because there were no windows. Daire was gone and the fire was almost dead. Only glimmers lighting the logs with an eerie, orange glow remained.

She put her feet down on the braided rug by the little bed and winced when she caught the cut side of her foot on the edge of the rug. She looked at it and realized he must have cleaned and bandaged it while she slept.

Anna thought for a while about standing and wondered if she would fall back down. Soon, she grew tired of wondering, finally stood quickly, and balanced herself. She walked a few steps as she held out her hands toward the table close by.

She made it to the little wooden table without much ado and emptied the last bit of water in the pitcher into her cup, drank it, and then looked back at the pile of clothes on the bed. She found a pair of Daire's pants and put them on. She still felt weak, so she sat down again on the bed and surveyed the area.

There were stairs behind her which lead to a small door. Anna stood up and the pants fell down. She gasped and quickly put them back on and held them up.

She put her bare feet on the cold, earthen steps and pushed open the door to the forest. She winced at the light as she still saw streams radiating from everywhere. She heard a small thud and looked to her right where she saw the translucent glow of Daire as he walked toward her with a small basket in his hands.

He stopped and smiled widely at her. With one eye closed, Anna shaded her face with her hands. She was barely able to see in the brightness around her.

"Hi," he said, overwhelmed by her beauty. "Are you hungry?"

She nodded.

"How about a potato?" He asked as he held up the huge, ugly vegetable.

She smiled. Then, she looked around in hopes of finding an outhouse.

He knowingly smiled and scratched his forehead. He pointed to a few trees, and then looked down. He shook his head and grinned.

She slowly headed up the rest of the dirt steps to ground level as Daire walked toward the opening of his underground house. When Anna reached the top, he glanced up at her, and then took a hard look. He chuckled at the huge clothes she wore, but as he laughed at how cute she was, she lost her balance and almost fell back. He immediately ran to her side and steadied her in time.

"I'm sorry, Anna, I thought you'd be all right."

"It's okay," she said, embarrassed. "I think I can make it."

She looked at her goal.

"Do I need to . . . ," she bit her lip, ashamed at the question, "dig a hole?"

Daire laughed at her.

"There's an outhouse," he said, reassuringly.

He let go for a second to see if she was able to stand on her own, but quickly changed his mind. He helped Anna to the little shed despite her protest. Daire waited outside, even though she begged him to leave her. She was quick and almost fell out the door when she came out.

"Whoa! Are you all right?"

"I'm fine . . . just so tired. I need to rest for a second or two, and then I can make it."

Daire took a hard look at her, and then scooped her up into his arms without her permission. *I'll never grow tired of this.*

He carried Anna back to his little home. He set her down by the door, opened it for her, and then went back to get his potato.

"Lunch!" Daire proclaimed when he scurried back.

She smiled at him, and then crawled back into the little bed which she had grown tired of being in. He stroked the fire into a blaze in no time, and then roasted the potato closely over it with a long stick.

"Daire?" she asked.

Her voice was like a kiss to his ears.

"Yes?" He answered quickly, anxious for her to talk more.

"What am I going to do? Where should I go? Nothing has come to me at all about my life."

"You're going to stay here, with me. There's no hurry. You'll remember, don't worry."

He got the big pot and held it. He looked at her for a moment.

"Why are you so kind to me?" Anna asked as she choked back tears.

"Anna," he began carefully, "I'm alone . . . Completely. I consider you . . . I consider you one of the best things to ever happened to me."

Anna searched his face and tried to find answers about why he was so alone in this world. She knew he had a handsome face, though she did not remember any others. *He's so kind and good. Why is he alone?*

She reached out her fingers to him. He looked at them, and then slowly took her hand. *Her eyes aren't beautiful just because of their unusual color, but also because there're a thousand kind words in them*, Daire thought.

"Why have you chosen to be alone, Daire?"

Her words stun him. He did not even know where to begin with such a question.

Chosen to be alone? Few would.

"I'm not alone now, am I?"

He tried to be coy to avoid the gruesome answer to her question.

"No," Anna replied.

Her voice wrapped around his heart like no one else's had. He held her hand tighter.

"What if I never remember?"

He put his other hand atop the one he held.

"Then, you never have to leave."

"How can you make a promise like that? You don't even know me. I don't know myself."

"Anna, do you believe in instinct?"

"Yes."

"What do you believe about it?"

She considered the thought for a moment, and then answered.

"Animals have instinct. Birds know how to build nests, fly, and feed their young."

"If a duck can pick out his mate and stay with her for life, is that instinct?"

She drew back her hand and thought, *Is he saying he wants to mate with me? He's lonely because he's crazy.*

"No, no. I'm sorry. I'm giving you the wrong—"

Daire swore underneath his breath.

"I'm not saying I'm mating with you for life, Anna."

He swore again. Anna began to giggle.

"I don't know what I'm saying. I think it's . . . I know you're good. You're a good person. You can know that about a person instinctually."

Anna tried to stop giggling. He soon gave up his pride and laughed with her.

"I think I remember that being called a Freudian slip!"

"So, you remember psychology classes, but not your address!" he joked.

He laughed with her, and then she punched his shoulder in play. Her laughter, however, soon gave way to tears. Daire put his arms around Anna and held her while she cried.

"Will the tears ever stop?"

He breathed in the scent of her shoulder.

"Yes," he said.

"He shall wipe every tear from their eyes," she whispered.

His muscles froze.

"Did you just remember that?"

"Yes."

"Where did you learn that from?"

"I don't know," she said as she focused on being comforted in his arms.

"Anna, who will wipe away the tears . . . Do you remember?"

She kept holding onto him, and then drew up on her knees. She held him closer, chest to chest. She forgot to answer. He kissed her shoulder.

"All I have is you, you know that? I'm so thankful you saved me," Anna said.

Daire gulped and held her tighter still. He looked up and smelled smoke.

"The potatoes are burning," he muttered into her shoulder calmly.

"Oh, no!" Anna uttered and pushed him back.

He got up, chuckled, and turned them over. He waved the smoke away from her and opened the door. He paused. Daire looked at her smile as she waved her hands. He went back to her and extended his hands. She reached around his neck and they held each other again. Braver, he lifted her up and held her even tighter.

"I like burnt potatoes," she lied.

"Me, too," he answered.

Daire was more happy than he ever thought possible. Anna pulled away and saw his soft expression. He smiled at her and hoped she would kiss him, but she did not.

"You said you worked out here in the woods. Where is your work? Do you have test tubes, a lab, and all?"

He had not expected questions so soon.

"I do," he said plainly.

"Can I see it?"

"I'm cooking *your* potato right now," he said playfully.

"Burning," she added.

He sunk his head in protest.

"My lab isn't very interesting, Anna—"

"Where is it?"

"I have a shed."

"Why do you have a shed for that and a hovel in the ground for your home?"

Daire hesitated for a moment. Her word for his home hurt him somehow.

"It's in case there's an explosion. I . . . we'd . . . be safe down here. Also, it's cooler in the summer and warmer in the winter down here."

"How did you dig so far down into the ground without hitting water?"

"We're on a hill."

Suddenly, he sighed in exasperation.

"You made me forget what I was doing. I was going to get you some water for a bath . . . More for the pitcher, too, I take it."

He looked inside the container.

"Gotta' keep you hydrated. I'll be back in a moment."

He held the handle to the pot and marched out.

Anna looked around the little underground dwelling with new eyes. She wondered about so many things in it, but she did not want him to be upset if she poked around in his belongings: a small hutch and the many quilts seemingly made by hand, shelves with cups and dishes, two chairs instead of one. She thought of all the questions she wanted him to answer, and all the ones she wanted to answer herself.

He re-entered the room suddenly and alarmed her.

"Geez!" She exclaimed humorously.

"Sorry," he said sheepishly.

Daire carted in the huge pot with an enormous amount of water. He took the pitcher and laid it inside as he scooped up fresh water. Doing the same with her cup, he handed it to Anna. Then, he put the heavy pot of water on a large hook over the fire with a grunt.

"Can I see your lab?"

He had hoped the question had been buried, but she was insistent. He wanted to tell her no, but was afraid to make her suspicious of him. He wanted her to trust him completely, he needed her trust.

He removed the blackened potato from the fire with a spear and put it on a plate.

After eating, Daire took Anna's hand and they walked into the woods. He steadied her, constantly, until they arrived at a small shed.

"Here it is," he said without fanfare.

She pushed open the door and peered into the dark little building. There was a table with a microscope and test tubes filled with all sorts of minerals and liquids which lined small shelves on the walls. Everything was immaculately kept. She somehow expected to see a dusty lab with cobwebs like Dr. Frankenstein kept.

"What are you working on?" She asked as she tried not to touch anything.

"I'm working on a secret medicine . . . For the military."

She was stunned by his response. She searched his face.

"Is that true?"

He looked back at her seriously and confirmed in his facial expression it was.

"Can you not even tell me what it is? I mean, I'm living here. What if it kills me or something?"

"It can't, Anna. Just promise me you won't touch anything in here."

"I won't," she said with a casual tune in her voice which worried him.

Anna did not like being talked to like she was a child. She turned quickly, her curiosity quenched. She forgot about her weakened state and wobbled for a moment. Daire's gentle hands rested on her waist and steadied her. She held them the rest of the trip back to the hovel.

"Does the military pay you for your work?" she asked.

"Um," he gulped, "they have in the past. I'm working on something new. We'll see."

They each crawled back into the hovel.

"Want to talk about something else?"

"Sure."

"That water on the fire over there is for you to bathe."

Anna looked at Daire playfully.

"I smell pretty bad, huh?"

"No, no, no. I mean . . . Anna—"

She snickered.

"No, go ahead, Daire, tell me I stink. I can take it."

"Anna, I—"

"I'll bathe immediately!" she joked.

"I'll leave after dinner and you'll have some hot water. It's not like having a bath tub, but I'll give you some towels so you can wash off. I have some soap in that hutch. There's a comb and whatever you can find is yours."

"Thank you, Daire," she said sincerely.

He smiled at her.

"Thank you for taking care of me."

His heart wanted to cry, if it was possible. He wanted to wrap her up in his arms and have her absorb him. He wanted to become part of her. However, he simply sat and smiled at her.

After dinner, without a word, Daire left and Anna was left alone in his home once more. She hobbled over to the little hutch and searched its contents with relish. He had just about everything she needed, including a new toothbrush and toothpaste.

She peeled off his shirt and examined herself. She turned her arms over to inspect them—it seemed for the first time. Then, she saw it—a tattoo with numbers which made no sense. She tried to wash it off, but it was permanent.

She washed herself with precision for about an hour, yet remained mindful of how she used the precious hot water. Anna finally decided to wash her hair, although it was difficult. Daire knocked on the door the moment she was finished.

He walked in and saw the beautiful creature with her black hair in wet strings around the soaked shirt which once belonged to him. He almost fell down the stairs as she looked up. He paused for a moment, captivated, and then went to the hutch and brought out a large comb.

He contemplated handing it to her, but wondered about being close to her again.

"Can I comb your hair for you, Anna?" He asked boldly.

She nodded and smiled at him. He sat behind her on the little bed; she turned away from him. He hesitated for a moment, scared to touch her, but then found courage at the thought of how it might feel.

"Daire?"

"Hmm?"

"What's this?"

She showed him her arm with the strange tattoo.

He paused for a moment.

"I have one, too," he said.

He rolled up his sleeve to show her. The numbers were different, but the marking was definitely the same.

"The government often brands people from birth to tell who is who."

"I don't remember that."

"It's true. How about we see what you remember? Can I ask you some questions?" he asked.

Daire tried not to hold his breath while he combed her hair. Anna did not know if she liked the idea of him questioning her, but finally nodded.

"All right, what year is it?"

He hit a snag in her hair and worked on it with his fingers. She thought for a moment, melted at his touch, and then a number popped in her head.

"Uh . . . 1940, am I right?" Anna confidently asked.

She was not. Daire gathered his thoughts again and tried to think of something other than the steady strands of loveliness spread up his arms.

"Well, that's too easy for you. What country are we in?"

She scratched her chin and wiped away a long, wet hair strand.

"Ireland or England? No, we're in Ireland."

"You know more than I thought you did," he conceded.

She smiled proudly.

"Tell me . . . How old are you?"

"You're not supposed to ask a woman that."

"It's for medical purposes, of course," he teased.

She leaned back a little as he gently pulled at her hair and worked out more tangles.

"I'm twenty-eight."

"Do you work?"

Anna looked at her hands. They were not rough, but she had no idea what she did, if she did anything. She shrugged.

She felt his fingers go up and down her back. They combed through her long hair before the actual comb did.

"Um . . . ," Daire hesitantly asked the next question, but winced as he paused. "Are you married?"

He stopped and waited. His fingers were midway down her back; his was breath close to her ear. She laughed suddenly.

"I don't think so!"

He noticed she looked down at her ring finger and rubbed it as she tried to determine if a ring was once there. It was hard for her to tell.

"Maybe," Anna added quietly, "I *am* in my late twenties—"

"Yes," he said softly.

Daire hoped against all hope and continued with the comb.

"Why do you ask?" she teased.

He shrugged shyly.

"If I don't know or remember him—if I'm married, that is—does it even matter? Does it count?"

They were sobered by the thought. He did not answer.

"Ask me more," she said.

"All right . . . Your accent isn't Irish—"

"That's because I'm Welch," Anna said quickly.

She did not know until it came out of her mouth.

"Do you remember anything about Wales?" he asked.

Daire tried to sound less shocked than he actually was.

"No," she said sadly. "I don't remember my parents or family's home. I don't remember how I came to Ireland either. Are you Irish?"

"Can't you tell?"

"Sorry, I wasn't sure. You are. Where did you go to college?"

"I went to Cambridge, so I know a great deal about England. You mentioned England seconds ago. Do you remember anything about it? I studied chemistry there."

"No, I don't. Why did you pick chemistry to study?"

"I didn't."

"What do you mean?"

"My father was a doctor. He insisted I do something very important with my life. He taught me everything he knew by the time I was fifteen. He didn't know what else to do with me. The teachers didn't either."

"What happened?"

"I went to Cambridge."

"When you were fifteen?"

"Stranger things have happened. My father thought chemistry was a good field for me because I loved helping him with the medicine for his patients. I was quite a pharmacist at a young age."

"That's a lot to ask of a young boy. You could've killed people if you gave them the wrong dosage or something, I'm sure."

"Yes."

"Is your father still living? Do you have family?"

"No to both those questions."

He had stopped combing her hair.

"I'm sorry," Anna quietly added.

He rubbed his eyes and sighed.

"I . . . uh . . . I'm not use to having company. I'm sorry."

She turned and touched his arm.

"Don't be sorry."

"Back to you; I was investigating *you* if you recall."

"Yes, you're quite the interrogator," she whispered with a smile.

"Do you want me to stop?"

"No. Go ahead. This is good for me."

"All right then . . . Do you remember having a hobby?"

She pursed her lips and looked around.

"No."

"Do you remember any books you've read?"

He wanted to know the answer if he had been *reading* the conversation, but he was so close to her. All he had to do was come a few inches closer to kiss her.

"I can't think of any right now," she answered.

He was hardly able to think as well.

"Movies you've seen?"

"No."

"Anna, do you remember . . . The war?"

He reached out and bravely touched her cheek. He was anxious for the answer he dreaded the most. He looked at her lips.

"Silly. I'm too young to remember the Great War."

"The Great War, huh?"

Daire was not disappointed she did not remember World War II. Then, he realized his hand still touched her cheek. Anna finally looked down and politely put space between them once more. They looked at anything besides each other for a few seconds.

"Anna, I know you've slept for days, but I'm so tired. I've kept watch over you and—"

"Oh, of course . . . I'm so sorry! Please, have your bed. I'll find something to lie on."

"No, no, no. Go ahead. Take the bed. I just want to lie down here if that's all right."

He took a few quilts off the bed and made up a little cot on the floor directly below her.

"It's all right if I'm this close to you? I'm on the floor and all. I'd make it up somewhere else, but there's nowhere else to stretch out and I—"

"Of course, I don't mind. I'd rather be near you."

He paused and took the quilts to his chest for a moment. He scratched the side of his face.

"I'm glad you don't mind," he said as he tried to hide a smile.

Daire hardly kept his eyes closed as he sensed Anna's stare. Finally, he playfully opened one eye. She quickly reached out her hand to his. He smirked, but it faded as he realized how profound her affection was for him. He reached up for her hand and felt much less tired.

She was so open and trusted of him. She was almost like a little girl—unspoiled, full of affection. *Can it possibly be this finally worked?*

Anna lay on her side and dangled her arm down to him. They played with each other's fingers until Daire finally went to sleep. Then, her dreams took hold of her, as all dreams did when she thought she was still awake:

Two wolves were fighting each other; she did not recognize the shadowy figures. They were staking their territory, her territory. She tried to squirm away, but each time one noticed and put her back on the tree she had held onto days ago. However, she could never tell which was which.

Maybe it was the same one which pulled her back over and over. Maybe the other had tried to set her free. She tried to make out their faces, but it was difficult to open her eyes wide enough to see.

Finally, one killed the other, and then turned violently to her. He flung her back into the tree she had yet again crawled away from; her little body scraped on the branches.

Then, as if the wind had brought it from a far off country, she heard a voice. The voice was not tender or gentle like Daire's. No, it was harsh, unyielding, and full of power.

"You must leave, Anna! You're not safe where you are!"

"How can I leave? The wolf keeps throwing me up in this tree! Help me!"

"There's no one there," the voice said gentler than before.

She looked around and found no one. She was alone like she had been when Daire found her.

"Still, I don't know how to get out of here."

"Follow my voice," the voice said again.

"Anna?"

She heard a new, familiar voice.

"Anna."

She awoke. Daire looked up at her and held her shoulder.

"You were babbling and crying. Are you all right?"

She looked around.

"I had a terrible dream."

"Have you been having those?" He asked as he rubbed his eyes.

"This is the second."

"What are they about?"

"They're about escaping, I think. Maybe I was in trouble or something in my life. Maybe someone wanted to hurt me. There's this person I have to run away from."

"Do you ever see his face?" He asked as his voice broke with exhaustion.

"No. In fact, this time it was two wolves. This voice keeps telling me to run away, but I don't know why or where to go."

"Maybe you should keep track of these dreams. Maybe it'll help you remember."

Anna settled back down in the covers and looked at the ceiling.

"Daire?" She said after a while.

"Hmm?" He grunted groggily.

"Maybe tomorrow we can walk a ways together and see what we can find."

"Do you think you're up for it? I know these woods very well, Anna. It's a very, very far way to anything or anyone."

"How many days walk do you think it'll take?"

"Very many."

"Ireland isn't enormous, Daire."

"I know."

"Then, why would it take more than a day or two?"

"Because, Anna, we're not in Ireland."

CHAPTER 15

SILENCE.

"Where are we then?"

"We're nowhere."

"What do you mean nowhere?"

Daire was too tired to have the conversation. He was afraid he would make a mistake and tell her more than she needed to know. "We're just out in the middle of nowhere."

"But we're in Ireland."

More silence.

"I'll explain it in the morning. I really need to sleep."

"Now, I won't be able to sleep. Won't you just tell me?"

"It's more complicated than you know."

Anna was angry.

"I'm not stupid, you know!" She finally snapped.

He sat up.

"I'm very aware of that, Anna. I'm so sorry. I don't mean to sound like I'm treating you like you are. The fact is I don't know what country we're in."

She seemed somewhat appeased by his answer. He touched some of her locks which hung down off the little bed and put them on her shoulder.

He continued, "I came here by boat to get away from everyone and everything. I was in a storm and I'm not sure what coast we're on."

"How long were you in the boat?"

"A day and a half."

"Then we must be able to find something within a couple of days."

"I just don't think you're up to this yet," Daire said, extremely concerned. "You can hardly go to the bathroom by yourself."

She had forgotten and agreed, "You're right. I need some more time. You can understand, though, Daire, why I want to know."

Anna turned on her side and faced him.

"Of course, but I don't think you've thought of something."

"What's that?"

"Maybe something within you doesn't *want* to remember."

Anna did not answer. She had not thought of that.

"Sweetheart," he said gently, "I have to sleep, I'm so sorry."

He caressed her fingers once more. Before she counted to five, he was asleep. She was soon asleep, too.

Anna awoke, chilled to the bone. She saw her breath in front of her as she looked around. The dwelling was gray and the fire had gone out, no longer giving the flaming orange breath to the room. She carefully stepped over Daire and hobbled over to the low embers; she grabbed the stick to poke and entice the fire.

She breathed on it, put on a few pieces of underbrush, and then coaxed it to become more violent. It finally lit after about a half an hour. She watched the fire blaze as her heart had done for the past few days.

She looked over at Daire. He was a beautiful creature who was certain, as if he had stepped out of a fairy tale. He had rescued and loved her simultaneously. He was all she had in the world. She wanted to crawl next to him, to feel his arms around her. She wanted him to comfort her, to want her.

She thought about her next bold move for a moment as she tugged on the shirt she wore. She tried to cover more of her chilled legs.

Exhaustion soon won out over her desires, however, and she nestled back into her little bed and closed her eyes. Her feet felt like ice; she had not noticed how cold she was until then. She must have been so concentrated on starting the fire she had forgotten her needs. She piled a few more layers onto her feet and tried to stop shaking.

The fire she had worked so hard on went out without warning, as if an unseen person had snuffed it out. Her eyes stared ahead and thought about how long it would take to start it again. She thought of waking Daire to help her. Suddenly, someone was standing in the middle of the room.

He was made of light. He had dark skin and a robe so light, it looked like it was made of gold. His eyes reflected a fire absent from the room. Anna's heart began to race. She opened her mouth to scream for Daire, but her voice was gone. She held her throat in horror, but all she heard was breath coming out of her mouth.

As the great being stared at her intently, she finally gained the courage to reach down and tried to wake Daire. It was of no use. He was like a dead man. Tears ran down her face, until, finally—as if after years of torture—the being spoke.

"You must leave here," his thunderous voice commanded.

I can hardly walk. Why must I leave? Anna thought.

The being seemed to hear her and frowned down at her.

"You must listen to my instructions and do them very carefully. Fast and pray for an entire day. Then, the man will tell you he needs to tend to his work. That's your opportunity. You must paddle north as far as you can."

He disappeared as suddenly as he had appeared. Anna shook from head to toe. She thought she had gone mad and shook violently. Finally, she opened her eyes and realized she was being shaken.

"Anna!" Daire almost yelled.

She sat up straight quickly.

"Anna, are you all right?"

Was it just another disturbing dream?

"Daire," she cried and fell into his arms.

He held her again while she wept.

"Nightmare?"

She nodded as she clung to his shirt. He held her wet face in his hands.

"You were shaking and muttering something I couldn't understand. I was so afraid you were sick," he said softly.

He was happy she was all right. The thought of losing her was more than he could bear.

"Do you want to tell me about it?"

"A man dressed in light told me to run away," she recalled.

Anna tried to breathe through her tears. Daire kissed her shoulder.

"Why do you think it has hit you so hard, Anna? The other dreams sounded worse than this one."

"It was so real." She said as she gripped him tighter.

"Do you think your subconscious is trying to tell you something? Do you think there was a man you were running from?"

She did not answer because she did not know.

"Anna, I think we need to try to hike tomorrow. We'll go slowly. You can see your surroundings and if you need me to I'll carry you home. What do you think?" He asked in a whisper, and then kissed her ear.

Anna nodded, watched the fire blaze, and thought, *Had it never gone out?*

She picked up her head from his shoulder and looked at his face. Daire stared at her lips and held her face in his hands. He waited because he wanted her to be the one who initiated any romance. He said to himself, *She's gorgeous.* He was spellbound as he waited for her to kiss him. Instead, Anna asked him the only question which scared him more than kissing her.

"Do you love me already?"

Already?

He looked down a little, their lips were even closer. He nodded almost ashamed of his answer. In a swooped Anna's lips caught his.

At first, Daire dismissed the thought she meant to do it: *Maybe she accidently touched her lips to mine.*

Then, she drew in closer, hungrier. He was shocked she had kissed him. She wrapped her arms around him and went up on her knees. Then, she stopped.

She casually looked around the room as if nothing had happened, as if the best news of his life had not been announced with a fifty-man orchestra playing in the background. *Had I imagined everything?* He thought.

Anna looked down and tried to gather why she felt such guilt. Her nerves overtook her and she needed things to be normal again. She glanced up briefly at him. His eyes would not let her ever go back to the way things were before she kissed him.

Daire stared—red-faced—at Anna as she refused eye contact. He thought, *Maybe I'm dreaming. Maybe she wasn't even real. How can a face that beautiful be real anyway?*

"I use to have nightmares, too," Daire finally said.

"What kinds of nightmares?"

They looked at each other for a brief moment. He hoped she would kiss him again, but she was so serious.

"I'd dream I was in danger and ran through forests looking for a way out. It'd get to me so much that sometimes, when I'd wake up, I'd do just that."

He shook his head.

"I also had these terrible dreams about a woman trying to find me, Anna." He said as he touched her hand. "I know you're anxious for answers, but you must give yourself time to heal."

"Did you know the person in your dream?"

"Yes, I did. She was my wife."

Daire's admission stuck like a knife.

"Was your wife?"

"Yes."

Anna embraced him immediately. He did not expect it. He rocked her softly.

"I loved her as no one loved," he added in an attempt to sound pitiful.

"Is that why you wanted to get away? Is that why you're so alone?"

"Yes," he pathetically said, almost inaudible.

She held his hands and led him to sit on the chair at the table. She knelt at his feet.

"This is too strange of a coincidence for us to have similar dreams."

"I agree and I think I've an answer for it."

He took a deep breath and brushed a hair out of her face.

"Anna, you're my wife."

Anna drew back.

"Search your heart, Anna."

She looked hard at him.

"Anna, you're my wife."

She abruptly stood, grabbed a blanket to put around her, and then she backed toward the door.

"Just get away from me, Daire," she warned.

He froze and thought the worst: *I've gone too far, too soon.*

Anna reached for the handle on the door and pulled it. When she turned, a wall of ice was in the doorway. *I'm trapped!*

"Are we snowed in?" Daire asked the white-washed woman who clung to the door.

She did not respond.

"Anna? We'll have to keep this fire going at all times," he said as if nothing had transpired between them the last hour.

"Who are you?" She asked gravely.

He did not look up.

"Tell me!" she screamed.

He threw the fire poker into the fire angrily.

"You tell me!" He yelled back.

"You *know* me," she said with a murderous look.

"Yes."

"You've known who I am from the very beginning," she said quieter.

He did not answer this time. She already knew the answer.

"Who am I, Daire?"

"I think you already know the answer to that, Anna."

She screamed profanities at him. He snickered underneath his breath. He had never heard her talk like that.

"You think I'm your wife? You're insane!"

He clenched his jaw. His face was red and he seethed with anger.

"I'm not the one who doesn't remember, Anna."

"Do you think I'd possibly believe this?"

"You'll believe what you want to believe."

She hurled more expletives. He hid a grin behind his fist.

"Why are you laughing?"

"Because I've never heard you so angry in my life," he said and let himself chuckle aloud.

"You don't know me!" she screamed.

He stopped laughing.

"Look, Anna, you have nowhere to go. You can't even get out of this hole. Just try to calm down and let's just talk this out."

"You want me to calm down and you're telling me we're married? Have you totally lost your mind, Daire?"

"Yes, I think I shouldn't have told you this quickly. I should've let you figure it out on your own."

"I wouldn't have because it's ridiculous, Daire!"

"True or not, Anna, you need to calm down. This is not good for you."

She sat down with a thud in the chair. A long silence fell between them. Anna sat furious as she stared at him.

"We don't have a lot of provisions in here," he said, anxious to have a break from the screaming. "I thought I smelled snow earlier. I don't know what I was thinking. I think I have some jars of food around here."

She rolled her eyes as he searched through cupboards and under planks in the floor. Soon, he had gathered enough food for a week if they were careful.

"There, that'll be good. I'll fix us some vegetables for dinner. I don't know how we're going to go to the bathroom. Maybe we can make a hole in the floor or something."

He's prepared this hovel like a squirrel prepares for winter.

She wanted to scream, even physically hurt him. The frustration was almost beyond what was bearable. He made her supper and put it on the table as she stared at him fiercely. He ignored her gaze and asked her to come eat with him.

Anna went over, grabbed her bowl, and then sat down on the bed. She ate quickly. He never looked up and sat calmly.

Daire took out a game of chess and set it up on the table. It looked as if he had made the pieces himself, whittled out of wood.

"Do you want to play?" He asked without looking at her.

"I want some answers."

She swore again under her breath.

"How about this . . . How about if you win this game, I answer a question?"

"How about you answer my questions and I'll tell you where you can stick your game."

At that, Daire turned to Anna, looked at her, and said, "The more questions I answer, the angrier you become."

She thought about what he said for a moment. She was certainly going nowhere with this madman. She had to try a different tactic. *Who knows how long we'll be stuck together.* She needed as much answered as possible before she left when the snow melted.

"How did I get in the tree?" She asked with hatred in her voice.

"I don't know."

"Why didn't you tell me in the first place?"

"Because . . . ," Daire scratched his growing beard, "you were so confused and I didn't want to confuse you even more."

"Why did you ask me all those questions the first time we spoke?"

"I wanted to see what you remembered."

"Why did I hardly have any clothes on when you found me?"

"I don't know."

"Did I used to live here with you?"

"No. I come here for months at a time to get away and work on my projects."

"Why was I in that tree?" Anna suspiciously asked again.

"I don't know."

"Would I have come looking for you and had my boat sink or something?"

"That's the theory I've been working with."

She looked away for a moment.

"Were there things about my life I would've liked to forget?"

"Yes."

"Such as . . . What was going on with me and you?"

Anna played into it for a moment, but Daire was smarter than she ever thought.

"We were getting a divorce."

"A divorce . . . Why?

"We grew apart."

"Did you know it was me in that tree immediately?"

"Yes. As soon as I made out it was a person, my heart leaped. I knew it was you."

"Why?"

"I'd know you anywhere."

"You told me earlier you love me."

"I do," he said and looked her squarely in the eyes.

"But we were getting a divorce, you said."

He paused and contemplated the thought of telling her the truth.

"*You* left *me*."

"Why?"

"Because, Anna, you'd fallen out of love with me."

She grew extremely tired. The shock of it pressed on her back like a heavy load. Her head pulsated with pain. She reached up and rubbed her shoulders.

Daire wanted to walk over and rub her shoulders for her, to touch her again. However, she would not let him, of that he was pretty sure. She looked up at him, obviously in pain. He knew the look. He decided to take a chance.

"Can I rub your shoulders?"

She thought for a moment, but the pain was so intense she finally nodded. He moved beside her in no time.

"I'm so sorry," he whispered and hoped the blow of what he told her had started to ease.

Daire reached up to her shoulders. She pulled her head back as he squeezed her sore shoulder muscles. He leaned in to touch her hair with his lips. He loved her. He loved everything about her.

"Tell me, Anna," he asked as she started to relax, "why did you kiss me? Why do you feel so much for me if we never knew each other?"

She winced as he dug into her shoulder more violently than he intended.

"That hurts."

"I'm sorry."

He let up a little and hoped she was finally calm. She suddenly grew unresponsive.

"Anna?"

She muttered back slightly. He combed through her hair with his fingertips, and then lay her down on the bed as she quickly drifted off. The drug had worked once more.

He sat and watched her for a while. He hated he had told her so quickly. He wanted to take it all back, to remain as they were for as long as possible. He had been in the position to steer her in other directions for months. He rebuked his actions, *Why did I tell her so fast?*

Daire finally had an idea and opened the door. He stood and stared at the wall of snow, and then went to get the large pot he used to warm water. He grabbed a small shovel from the corner of the room, started to scoop snow, and put it into the pot. When it was filled, he boiled it on the fire until it evaporated into steam. He repeated each step three more times until he had made a tunnel. It took him hours.

He was finally able to squeeze his body out of the tunnel. He sloshed down the deep snow to the outhouse. She made him nervous; he hated how powerless she made him feel. Daire's entire life was held squarely in her little hands. Whether she believed him or not was the pinnacle moment to each of their destinies.

He breathed out heavily in the chilled air. He slammed the outhouse door shut, a pile of snow fell all over him—he swore. He was so angry at that moment, more angry than he ever remembered being. Daire was angry with himself.

He finally made his way to the hut where his experiments waited. He searched through his little lab as if he ransacked someone else's. He grabbed his backpack and filled it with more provisions. He paused for a moment to reassure himself about his newly formed plan.

It'll work, he thought. *It has to.*

He scooted back into his home and closed the door. Then, he sat back down on his chair and stared at her with his arm slung over the back of his chair. He watched her chest as she breathed. He had to somehow regain the innocence they had hours before. He wanted her full of life, affection, and love for him. He wanted her to be his. He chewed his fingernails and waited.

"Honey?" she said.

She did not appear to have awakened. She was still, her eyes remained closed. He rushed to her.

"I'm here."

"Get into bed with me," she said and rolled away from him.

Daire gulped. *She's talking in her sleep.*

He knelt beside her and continued to wait. Her words had stirred him with hope once more. He thought about it, but he knew when she truly woke up, she would have the same cruel look in her eyes.

He fell asleep with his head laid beside her, his body knelt. He saw streams of light come out of the cracks in the door.

If I'm going to do this, I have to wake her.

He touched her shoulder. She breathed in quickly, waking almost in terror.

"Shh, it's just me," he said.

Daire hoped she would think last night's conversation was a dream. Anna gathered her shirt at the neck to cover herself. She looked strangely down at him. He knew she remembered his crazy theory.

"Listen, I want you to get up and have some breakfast. I—"

"Just let me sleep," she said and turned from him. "We're snowed in anyway."

"I dug a hole out."

She turned around and looked at him. He nodded.

"Have some breakfast. We'll go for a hike this morning if you're up to it."

Anna sat on the edge of the bed—still not completely awake—and rubbed her eyes. She looked toward the door. Daire opened it and showed her the round tunnel he had made. She looked around for a jacket. He dug something of his up and placed it around her shoulders and took care to touch her as long as she let him.

She wrapped her feet with rags. He tried to help her up.

"I don't need help," she said as she tried to create space between them.

She wanted to go off on alone, to get away from him, but she knew she was not healthy enough. She carefully crawled through the snow hole until she emerged to the sun hitting all around her—her eyes hurt.

Anna went straight to the outhouse and took her time. Then, she crawled back into the hovel. A breakfast of strawberry jam and porridge was more than she had hoped. Daire smiled as she inhaled it.

"You're getting on fine this morning," he said without eye contact.

She did not answer.

"I need some boots," she stated as if she had ordered them from a servant.

"That we may need to improvise; I have an extra pair, but they're far too big for you."

"I'll stuff the toes."

"No doubt you'll have to."

"I'd like to go alone," she stated.

Her words stung him.

"I don't think that's wise, Anna. I'll be following you anyway, so why not just let me walk with you?"

She conceded to what she considered a terrible notion and began to get ready. He had already packed the night before and handed Anna an extra bag to sling over her shoulder. She had nothing of her own, but he suggested some of his provisions for it.

He put his gloves and hat on her as well as his jacket. He made due with rags wrapped around his hands. He layered on almost everything he owned. She gladly accepted all he gave her and laced up his extra set of boots as tightly as possible to set out on their journey.

The walk in the snow was harder on Anna than she had expected. Daire followed two steps behind her. She grew tired very quickly of the walk and was almost immediately lost. After only a half hour, she stopped and tried to catch her breath in the freezing air. She looked around and knew she saw nothing familiar. She rubbed her eyes and thought, *Everything's so blurry.*

"Are you all right, Anna?"

They were the first words he had spoken since they left.

"I don't know where we are," she admitted.

"It's all right. I do."

He reached into his pack and gave her a small snack. She ate it. Then, after only a few minutes, her face went white.

"Daire?" She said as she tried to push back hysteria.

"Yes?"

"My legs are tingling and I can't feel my feet."

"Try wiggling your toes," he said.

Within a second, her legs gave way and she was sprawled on the snow. His heart jumped.

"Anna!"

She was conscious.

"I can't feel my legs!"

"It's all right—"

"Daire! I can't feel my legs!"

"I've got you," he assured Anna as he scooped her out of the snow. He knew it was too far to carry her back, but he had no choice. She clung to his neck.

"Why can't I feel them, Daire?" She panted in a panic.

"Shh, just be calm. We'll get back in no time and figure this out."

"I couldn't feel them when I was in the tree either, Daire. What's happening?"

"You're still very weak and—"

"I can't feel my legs!" she yelled.

He stopped and looked at her squarely in the face.

"The feeling came back last time, remember? Anna, just stay calm, all right. I'll get you home."

He carried her silently through the snow until he thought he was unable to go further.

"Please talk to me, Anna," he said desperately as he tried not to drop to his knees in exhaustion.

She thought for a moment as she started to get a hold of herself.

"Tell me something you remember about me," she said.

She still did not believe him, but tried to get her mind off the terrible situation they faced.

"I remember one evening," he said in between labored breaths, "there was a dance and you were there in a deep purple dress. I saw you looking so beautiful and you gave me an enormous grin,"

Daire smiled to himself.

"It's one thing to have a gorgeous girl give you a shy smile, it's another to get one of those grins of yours, you know?"

Anna involuntarily smiled a little.

"I looked behind me because I was certain . . . I thought maybe it was for someone else . . . which made you laugh. Finally, I realized you were smiling so big at *me*. I kinda went along with the joke and pointed to myself as if to ask, 'Really, you're smilin' at me?'"

Anna found she was slightly lost in his sweet story.

"Then you asked me to dance?"

"No," Daire replied, almost ashamed.

"No?"

"Someone asked you first and I didn't gain the courage the rest of the evening."

"So, how did we get together?"

He paused to take a few heavy breaths as he readjusted her in his arms. Meanwhile, she felt down at her legs, but felt nothing. Yet, she held on to the fact this had happened before—it soothed her.

"Well, it's kinda embarrassing. I was called to your house because you had a wee fever. We were alone in the room with the door shut. You quickly took off your blouse."

"I what?"

"You just took it off and looked at me. You told me later every doctor you'd ever gone to had done so and you thought it was the custom in Ireland. Apparently you hadn't ever seen a physician, except for when you were a child."

Anna felt the blood rush to her face, she was mortified by the story.

"I told you taking off your blouse wasn't necessary. You just shrugged and put it back on."

"I'm surprised you told me that at all."

"I kicked myself for about a week," he said. "You were the wildest person I'd ever met."

She felt a small pin and needle sensation going through the veins in her legs suddenly.

"I think I'm getting better."

He dropped her to her feet, but held her up.

"I'm so sorry. I have to rest," he said.

Daire took out a heavy, wool blanket from his bag and laid it down like a picnic blanket. Then, he set her down on it and almost fell on his face—his head rested on her thigh. This positioning made her feel uncomfortable, but he was too exhausted for her to make a great deal of it. He continued with his lips pressed against her thigh.

"You had this way of walking. I've never seen anyone more confident in my life. You took command of a room when you entered by the way you walked in. Your tight skirts helped you, too. I love to watch you move."

Her legs started to ache as well as bear the terrible sensation of ants crawling over them once again. She reached into the bags and took out a snack. She handed some to him, but he refused.

He finished his story, "You were the most affectionate person in the world. You never stopped hugging and kissing me—I think we made the whole town sick of us."

"How long were we married?"

"Five years."

"When did the problems start?"

"The problems were always there. I was a busy man. You left me around year three and lived alone."

"Seems a silly reason to leave . . . simply because the other person is busy."

"We can't have children either."

"That's also a silly reason."

"What about my childhood? What do you know about it?"

"You had a pretty happy childhood."

"Are your arms numb from carrying me?" she asked.

"I think I should be asking the same question about your legs."

"They tingle."

"That's a good sign."

"You're a doctor. What's happening to me?"

"It's hard to tell without being able to run any tests."

"I've heard of doctor's gut instincts. You must have one."

"Yes."

He did not want to scare her.

"What then?"

"MS."

"What does that mean?"

"It's nothing to really worry about," he lied.

She thought for a moment.

"What does it do to you?"

"You'll just have spasms here and there," he reassured her without looking at her.

Her legs felt terrible. The numbness was almost better than what she was feeling at that point. She rubbed her left leg. Daire noticed and got up after he realized he made her uncomfortable.

"Do you think we can continue soon?" she asked.

Anna tried to stop shaking from the cold, but deep inside— where Daire never saw—she wanted his arms around her again. She shook off her feelings being as strong for him as they were before he had made his crazy declaration. *How can I possibly want someone like him?*

She mulled it over in her mind for a few minutes and decided she felt the way she did because he had saved her. She mused, *Yes, I'm simply grateful.*

He scooted to the side and tugged the blanket out from under her. She held herself up off the snow as long as possible as he quickly put the food away and slung their bags over his arm. Then, he picked her up and immediately she felt warm.

"How much further?" She asked more for his benefit than hers.

"Not long now . . . Maybe twenty minutes or less."

"I'm sorry you have to carry me."

"It's nothing."

However, it was not. Every muscle in his body hurt. His legs and feet were soaked through with chilling cold. He was more worried he might not be able to make it.

"Daire, I can wiggle my toes!"

With that, he put her feet down and steadied her.

"If you help me, I might be able to hobble home, but it'll take more time."

He nodded, relieved, and held her up while she weakly put one foot in front of the other.

"It's hard, but I'm doing it!" she cried out.

Anna was happy for her sake as well as his. They continued at a snail's pace.

"Anna, what do you feel for me?"

She did not want to answer, but she had to be honest. She cried; his mind raced. He was hardly able to stand, much less help her. He plopped down on the snow and she also fell. He covered his face with his hands.

"You can feel it, can't you, Anna," he said, his voice muffled in his hands. "You can feel what I feel, can't you?"

She looked down.

"You know it's true. You know it!"

"No, no, Daire. That's not true. I didn't . . . I don't know."

"You recognize me."

"No, I don't," she said quickly.

"Your mind might not right now, but the rest of you does. Something inside of you knows me, Anna!"

He forcefully kissed her. She tried to get away, but soon gave up.

Something inside of her *did* know him. He breathed out heavily, held the back of her head, and pulled her to him. Then, he took a hard look into her eyes. She reached up around his neck and hugged him. He was shocked.

"I want to go home, Daire," she said through tears.

"It's all right. I'm going to take you there. I know you're tired, sweetheart. I know."

He picked her up and looked into her eyes. She seemed so much lighter. Everything did.

Anna listened to his feet slosh heavily beneath her. She wiggled her toes continually, afraid to lose the feeling. She brushed his jaw bone with her lips. Daire closed his eyes and marveled. *She's finally mine.*

"Is it possible, Daire . . . I left you because of this . . . Because I'm not well?"

He stopped. He held her tightly and whispered into her ear.

"Please don't ever leave me again."

"Maybe I didn't want you to see me like this. Maybe I changed my mind after a few years, came looking for you, and had an accident along the way or something."

"I love you so much," he cried into her neck.

They regained composure and he forged on with her in his arms.

"We're here," he said.

Daire gently put Anna down at the hovel door and crawled through the tunnel first. Then, he held out his arms to her and pulled her inside. He opened the door, carried her to the little bed, and nervously hurried to stoke the fire. He rubbed his hands together, and then took off his boots. He was soaked.

"Daire?"

He turned and saw she was only wore his long sleeved shirt. She sat with her legs hung over the bed.

"I can feel them."

He smiled at her softly. Then, he walked over to her, pulled her knees apart, and kissed her.

"My wife," he whispered.

CHAPTER 16

THE LITTLE VILLAGE OF ADARE had seen its first glimpse of sun in two weeks. It was like a town straight out of a fairy tale with snow-covered roofs. The little window boxes every resident had were frosted over by the winter fairies, as so many of inhabitants believed.

The roads were covered and some residents shoveled their cars out, cursing. All Father Henry saw was beauty around him. He adjusted his spectacles in the harsh brightness of the morning and blinked at the diamond twinkles from the snow on the ground.

Henry was the gentle king of Adare, or so one thought by the way he was treated by citizens. He had a way with people—he communicated beyond the few words he spoke. His sweet, green eyes twinkled when he talked with people. Yet, it was his heart to which people were drawn—never had there been a resident as beloved or a rector as respected.

The last few months had been miserable, but Henry had taught himself long ago not to think on such things. Instead, he smiled the sweetest smile this side of heaven; shut the door to his little, ancient parish; and trudged up the road as he held his collar to his ears and breathed happy breaths.

He went over the bridge to the village and gazed at his dear friends who bustled through the little shops and eateries. His first stop was for tea at his dear cousin's house just over the bridge and past a few houses.

"Fine mornin', isn't it Henry?"

He was greeted with a kiss from Sarah who wore a filthy apron. Henry warmly smiled.

"Goodness soul, Donnelly," Henry said with a smirk. "What have you been into this early?"

She waved her hands in the air as she led him through the kitchen. It looked as if it had been ransacked by a team of wild horses.

"Goodness soul," he whispered.

In the parlor, Father Donnelly smoked a pipe. He smiled when Henry entered and held his dilapidated hat.

"Henry, my son," he greeted him gently.

He was being groomed for Father Donnelly's position from which he was supposed to be retired. However, Father Donnelly had insisted on staying on as Henry's assistant since he was a relatively new Christian and even newer clergy member.

Father Donnelly had become Henry's spiritual father who listened as Henry tried to explain what he had actually heard the voice of God call him to do—give up his life for the ministry. Besides his wife, Father Donnelly had been one of Henry's only links to save him from thinking he had gone crazy.

"My dear wife has been chasing chickens all morning for tomorrow's supper. I'd have run like that, too, if I'd known I'd become another one of her supper experiments," Father Donnelly joked. "I hear you're quite the cook, Henry. Do you think you can help her out? Oh, no, I forgot you don't kill or cook anything that's got a head."

Father Donnelly slapped his thigh and sucked his pipe. Henry chuckled as he sat in the velvet cushioned straight chair in front of him.

"So, what have you heard from the Lord this beautiful mornin'?"

Father Donnelly always asked the same question. Suddenly, Sarah stumbled in and almost thrust his tea at him.

"Oh, I'm so sorry. Those dumb chickens!"

Henry squint his eyes and laughed with her.

"My poor, Sarah," he said sympathetically.

"The chickens would come running if they knew what capable hands they were in, my dear," her husband ironically cooed.

"Oh, hush now!" She said and slapped him with a kitchen towel. Then, she bent down and kissed Henry on the forehead.

"Now, you teach him a thing or two about how to be a good Christian husband, will you?"

Sarah winced almost immediately and bit her bottom lip. She did not mean to hurt him so.

Henry did not flinch his loving gaze.

"You have one of the best men because you're one of the best women," he reassured her.

"Oh, hush now," she teased and wiped away a tear.

She took hold of his hand, and then left the room. She wiped her dirty face with the towel.

"How are you getting along?" Father Donnelly asked.

Henry inhaled, and then let out a slow, deep breath.

"Every evening my heart breaks in a different place, every morning He heals it anew."

"We wait for Him more than watchmen wait for the morning," Father Donnelly nodded with his eyes closed.

"There's not a place inside my heart where Anna had not touched," he said and smiled at Father Donnelly. "It's good the Lord lives in every room she did."

"Not many invite Him to invade like that."

"I have no choice. I can live broken or I can live perfectly broken as an offering to Him."

Henry smiled at his friend.

"You know, Henry, it occurred to me perhaps you should take a little holiday. I believe a change of scenery will do you good."

"I've also thought it might, but when I inquired of the Lord about it, He said I'm needed here."

"Then, it's settled. No holiday for you!" Father Donnelly joked.

Henry grinned from ear-to-ear.

"Have you made plans for Christmas? Will you be going up to the Manor?"

"I don't know."

"Henry, I hope you know you're most welcome here."

"Oh no, no, no. I don't want to impose."

Father Donnelly grinned. It always took a great deal of coaxing to get Henry to feel welcomed.

"Absolutely. You'll come here!"

"I can't ask such a think of you and Sarah. I'll be fine."

"My dear friend, you're like a son to us. We *want* you here."

Henry looked at Father Donnelly, and decided it was polite to cave in.

"Well, all right . . . If it's not too much to ask."

Father Donnelly smiled around his pipe. Over the past year, he had watched Henry grow to become one of the most wonderful human beings he had ever met.

Surely, there's a young woman suitable for him. Henry, of course, would never hear of such a thing. If Anna hadn't been such a divine appointment, if she hadn't practically thrown herself at him, he probably never would've had her.

Father Donnelly chuckled under his breath and thought, *The boy definitely needs encouragement, that's for sure.*

Henry sipped his tea, shook his friend's hand, and then saw himself out. He was more than happy to spend any holiday with Sarah and Father Donnelly. They were as close to him as his parents had been; closer, in fact. They had understood him when no one else could.

His next stop was the flower shop. He practically kept it in business because he was a faithful patron every day of the week, except the Lord's day. The clerk handed him a new bouquet of yellow daffodils fresh from its greenhouses—each day they arranged something special and different for him.

He looked forward to the moment he saw flowers like he used to look forward to seeing his wife's face every morning. He handed the clerk enough money to cover the week's expense. He smelled the yellow beauties and smiled at each florist.

He tipped his hat to every lady he passed as he made his way around the corner to eat breakfast at Mrs. O'Leary's house. She was a frail, middle-aged widow with a voice as weak as her countenance appeared.

"Now, my dear, let me give you a jug to hold those in for Anna while I go get your breakfast."

She was a hearty cook, but she only ate one egg. She served him a heavy plate filled with fried tomatoes, sautéed mushrooms, baked beans, and toast.

"Beautiful," he said to her quietly as she placed a mug of tea down for him.

In the past, Mrs. O'Leary had grown tired of refilling her dainty tea set for him. He drank more tea than anyone she had ever met. So, she went to a pottery class at the parish, which Sarah led, and made the enormous, ugly mug for Henry to drink from every Monday morning.

"This is the most wonderful mug," he said for the thousandth time.

She smiled sweetly at the young man. He took a bite of the smorgasbord of delicacies she had prepared for him.

"Delicious! You've outdone yourself again, Mrs. O'Leary."

"Nothing doing," she said modestly.

She knew very well she was not the best cook in the world. Henry enjoyed every mouthful because it was made with love.

"What's on the docket today?"

"I'm feeling called to do some studying on Zerubabbel today," Henry said.

"What a funny little name. It's a Bible name I'm assuming?"

"Yes. He rebuilt the walls of Jerusalem."

"That seems like a large task for one person."

Henry smiled and tried to hide his mouth full of food.

"My dear Mrs. O'Leary, he had a great deal of help."

"Well, I should hope so. It's not very nice of our Heavenly Father to ask such a monumental task of one person."

"He almost never does."

"When *my* Henry was alive," she began as she always did, "he planted the church garden. My Henry had a way with the plants—sing to them, he did! He sang up a tree in half the time it took to grow."

Henry had guessed long ago it was the reason she took to him so. His dear friend with the same name had passed away the same day Anna had.

He smiled at her while he chewed his breakfast. The conversation went on until Henry had cleaned his plate and helped Mrs. O'Leary wash the dishes with her pump faucet sink.

As he prepared to leave, she adjusted his clerical collar and told him to bring his things by for a good wash and press. He held her bony little hands and kissed her cheeks. Then, she handed him Anna's flowers and he headed straight for his parish.

The Augustinian Priory - Adare was a medieval monastery before it became part of the Church of Ireland. The St. Nicholas School inside educated the majority of Henry's flock's children. Yet, everyone knew his little abbey as The Black Abbey because the monks who once resided there only wore black—a tradition he had tried to keep up.

He wore his black robes, but had often strayed and worn white robes, especially for weddings and Christmas. He wore black pants and shirts almost always because he was in perpetual mourning. He crossed the street from the priory and walked toward the Manor. The tree overlooking the river brought back such fond memories to Henry. There, he had placed a memorial stone for Anna. He faintly heard the children come in for class and knew he needed to be there soon to pray.

He pushed the snow on top of the tombstone away and warmed her name with his hand. He put the flowers down at her stone and kissed the first name of his wife.

"I miss you," he whispered, "but I'm as much in His arms as you are today."

He closed his eyes tight.

"Give me strength, Lord, my Redeemer, to shepherd your flock with the love of the cross."

With that, Henry stood. His long legs and stride took him back to his parish quicker than the children ran. The children loved how tall he was and sometimes joked about how he was a flag pole in a former life.

He listened to the school maid call them to order, and then rounded the corner in a flash to their cheers. The teachers rolled their eyes as he had wound them up, yet again, just as they had calmed them.

"Shh!" he admonished them as he sat down on the window ledge and tried to make himself smaller.

He barely had control of them; the teachers soon regained order. The children sat cross-legged and waited with anticipation for what he had to say.

"Do you ever wonder, children, how God called two animals of every kind to the ark?"

There was no answer.

"Oh, I'm sorry. You don't know the story—"

They cried out they did know the story, and he chuckled as the teachers calmed the enthusiastic children again.

"Well, now that I know you know my friend Noah, I'll continue with the story."

"You're too young to know Noah!" One of them yelled out.

A teacher gave the child a look worthy of melting an iron pot. Henry continued.

"Well, Noah was putting the finishing touches on his boat when all of a sudden—low and behold—two baby elephant ran up to him! Can you imagine? Well, Noah backed up until he almost tripped over these large eggs! And you know what was inside them?"

The children shook their heads in earnest.

"Neither did Noah, but he helped them up—big, little; you name it—and put them on the boat. You see, children, the animals didn't need to come onto the boat full grown, did they? Onto the ark boarded baby kangaroos—"

"What's that?" A little girl yelled.

"Ask your teacher," Henry teased and everyone chuckled. "Let's see, where was I? Oh, yeah, and baby calves, hippos, and . . . Well, baby everything! I believe they all came two-by-two as the Bible says, but they were baby animals! You know why?"

Again, the children shook their heads with excitement.

"Because the stories in the Bible are about *children*, Jesus said, 'Let the little children come unto me; do not hinder them, for to such belongs the kingdom of God.'² Did you know even I, Father Henry, am a child because I'm God's child?"

They stared at Henry with mouths agape—a captive audience.

"Inside, here, where my heart is, that's where I'm a child. That's

2   Mark 10:14 (English Standard Version)

why I'll always stay a child . . . So, will you. Just remember to always come to Him like that, like the animals in the ark."

He looked around the room at the children's faces, and then settled on the teacher's faces which had softened. They were quiet for a moment. He decided to take the opportunity.

"I know this one little girl who heard about Jesus from a young man who was preaching in a tent. Her parents didn't know about him, but the little girl climbed into her parent's car after the tent meeting and thought very hard in the backseat all the way home.

"Finally, she said, 'Mommy, is the stuff that man was preaching about for children, too?' Her mother didn't know for certain, but something inside her made her nod her head and she wisely replied, 'Yes, my love, it's for children, too.'

"Then, the little girl bowed her head and gave her life to Jesus. Never have I met anyone who ever regretted doing so, not once. My sweet children, the gospel is for *you*."

He stood, laid hands on some of the smallest heads, and prayed for everyone's day to be blessed and full of learning. Then, he closed his prayer.

A deep sigh was heard from one of the teachers as she pushed a tear away, anxious for the children to not see her softness. She clapped her hands and startled them to attention.

"All right, children, line up for lessons."

They scurried away with little conversation. Henry had a way of silencing everything, except the still small voice inside everyone.

Henry's legs ached. He had always taken walks during his study time, whenever his weak eyes failed him and needed to rest. However, that day he was done in and hardly kept his mind focused on the passages. It drifted to memories of his wife. He rubbed his eyes and took three very long walks in the crisp air, yet it did not help; he had fallen behind in his study time. *I have all week to finish my sermon*, he reasoned.

Yet, as a minister Henry never knew what the next day might bring. He routinely finished his sermons on Monday so if someone needed him during the rest of the week he had no need to worry. Many times an emergency had happened as a loved one transitioned to be with the Lord or another parishioner needed a healing prayer. So, he asked the Lord for more time to finish and went to bed in his little room behind the sanctuary.

He had given his cottage to Father Donnelly and Sarah after Anna's death. They had been living with Father Donnelly's daughter—a snug situation. The two ladies, Sarah and her daughter-in-law, squabbled in the kitchen. So, Henry gave his cottage to them and moved into a small space in the back of his parish. He thought it right to be near the Lord's house anyway.

He surveyed the less than cozy atmosphere in which he lived. He knew it was fine; its coldness was only apparent in the evening when he was alone. However, more than his surroundings was his acute awareness of the terrible pain of being alone when all was quiet each evening. He rubbed his weary eyes and suddenly sobbed.

Henry's fragile heart was apparent to all. He was embarrassed for anyone to catch him hurting as much as he was. After all, pastors were not allowed to feel as much as he did.

"I need You," he said aloud.

My dear friend, I'm here, a voice inside him confirmed.

He wrestled for a few moments regarding what he had heard. So many times the Lord's voice sounded identical to his; it was very hard to decipher. The way to determine if God had truly spoken—to know it was not a figment of his imagination or what he wished the Lord to say—was to hear the whole thing out.

Henry found it very disturbing because he had twice caught himself talking, not the Lord. The Lord knew his thoughts, however, and waited patiently for Henry to work it out.

I'm here, the Lord whispered from deep within Henry.

What happened next was a rush of love which welled up from deep inside Henry as if a dam had burst. Then, Henry knew it was the Lord's voice for certain and cried all the more.

When Henry was married, his favorite time of day was the evening. Anna either finished a painting or scribbled in her notebook. She hummed and he pretended to read a book, but he actually watched her. His heart fluttered with every sunset because he knew he was about to spend the evening with his beautiful wife. Those moments were more special to him than he had realized.

Toward the end of Anna's life, even though they were still considered newlyweds, they acted far from it. Henry had grown quieter and was more engrossed in his ministry. Anna had tried daily to pull out some sort of affection from him, but he regressed more which she took as a slight and had given up six months into trying. She no longer reached out, neither had he. It was a terrible cycle: acting like two old married people who hardly spoke to one other.

Henry shook his head quickly and tried to shake away his regrets. He had never truly understood darkness until his first night without Anna. It was not simply loneliness, but darkness.

Henry turned on his side and looked at the grey wall. He squeezed his eyes tight with a world of regret in the pit of his stomach.

"I'm so sorry," he said involuntarily.

He felt like such a failure. Henry looked up to his bookshelf where he kept the ancient books of saints. There, perched like a little bird which awaited a meal from his hand was the book he had put off reading: *Dark Night of the Soul*. He knew he needed to read it, but the thought of its message depressed him more than what was bearable. So, it sat as a testimony to all he felt at the moment.

"My Comforter and Friend," Henry prayed as he pictured the Lord in a chair adjacent to himself, "if this is what You feel . . . The longing for Your church . . . What can I do to ease Your burden?"

God paused for a great while, moved by the beautiful, selfless statement Henry lay before Him.

So many of God's faithful often asked why, and even more had felt anger toward Him. Yet, Henry chose to see things through God's eyes. Only God's closest friends truly knew His pain—Henry was one of them.

The people I love don't remember who they are. They're My love, the Lord's voice whispered as Henry took great note of His tone and was deeply grieved.

"I'll help them remember You, for when they know You, they'll know who they are."

My dear friend, My beautiful John Henry, I need you to do just that.

The presence of God fell heavily in Henry's room like a blanket of thick oxygen. Henry laid his head on his pillow and breathed deeply.

CHAPTER 17

ANNA MOVED HER HEAD SOFTLY on the pillow she and Daire shared, and kissed him awake. She still had so many questions, but one had been answered. She believed with all her heart she was, in fact, his wife.

He smiled with his eyes still shut and marveled at the thought she was finally his. He held her close and kissed her neck.

"Daire?"

"Are you all right?" He asked gently.

She quickly turned to him and answered, "Of course."

"Did you remember something?"

"No," she said.

Anna looked at Daire and he smiled. His eyes almost danced with joy when he looked at her. She loved his expression and smiled back at him.

Yes, it's possible we had a past life together. It's obvious there's something very strong between us. A bond we have can't exist without some sort of foundation, realized or not.

Daire stroked Anna's back and was in awe he was not dreaming.

"Daire?"

"Hmm?" He cooed, preoccupied.

"What sorts of things do I enjoy doing?"

"Well, you like a great many things, but I don't know about telling you about them. Maybe you should discover each thing about yourself one at a time."

"No, I want to know."

Daire looked at the hard, dirt ceiling above his head and cradled his head with his arm.

"You loved flowers. You were terrible at growing them, but you loved them. So, I'd go out and garden for you. I'd cut them and fill the house with them inside."

Anna liked the thought of Daire filling her house with flowers. She wished it was not winter so he could do just that.

"Was I educated?"

"Not in an academic school, but you loved to read."

"What did I read?"

He thought for a moment.

"Oh, you know, history, real and imagined. You liked historical fiction, ancient literature."

She did not think it was very interesting, but she searched her mind for information about historical events and found she knew many. As Daire rubbed her back Anna thought back to the Romans, Egyptians, and Greeks. She tried to remember everything possible, but found she became bored with the knowledge she retrieved.

She found it was a remarkable phenomenon: to bore herself about things which once interested her. Yet, it also proved Daire was right.

"I'd like to see where you work again," Anna said.

Daire thought about it for a moment as he calculated the risks. Then, he got up, took her hand, and, in an effort to help her trust him more took Anna into his little shed where he conducted most of his experiments.

She noticed more this time than last. He had notes up all over the wall, but Anna did not understand them. At first, she thought he just had terrible handwriting, but as she looked closer, she realized they were written in another language.

"Oh, yes, I like to keep my hand in," he commented.

Anna looked at him puzzled.

"You know, I like to keep up with my German so I don't lose it. When I work, I write and try to think in German."

"Wherever did you learn German?" Anna asked, surprised.

"I picked it up during the war," he said.

He limited what he said about World War II. She was puzzled again.

"Neither one of us is old enough to remember the Great War."

"There was another war you don't remember."

"There was a war I don't remember?"

Daire was silent for a moment, and then gravely responded, "Yes."

Anna sighed. She was tired of being unable to remember. Daire, however, thought it was better she did not.

"Did you fight in this war?" She asked with obvious annoyance in her voice.

"I didn't fight. I was a doctor. Sometimes I'd treat German prisoners."

Anna stared at him; however, Daire was reluctant to disclose this part of his life. He hated to recall anything to her because it was essential for her to forget.

Then, Anna touched a few glass strips near Daire's microscope. She did not see anything on the slides.

"What exactly are you trying to do, Daire?"

Daire did not look at her as he fumbled through his stack of paperwork. He wondered, *Why did I bring her here? Can't I even be without her for a few minutes while I work?*

"Anna, I'm working on something . . . A medicine . . . For men with war wounds. However, you can't see."

"I don't understand."

"I'm working on something to help soldiers traumatized by what they've been part of during the war."

Anna looked at Daire, her lips twitched slightly. He knew she was thinking and hoped her thoughts did not go too far off the trail he wanted her on.

"What kinds of things did they witness?"

"It's war, Anna. It's hell on earth."

Anna was unable to fathom the atrocities.

"Daire?" Anna asked. "Do you make them . . . Forget?"

It was the question he dreaded. He did not answer.

"Daire?"

"Anna!" He snapped and threw down the papers he was going through. "Why must you know everything? Can't you just accept it's something to help people? It's a drug to help them deal with mental and emotional pain, okay!"

However, it was not okay. Daire and Anna knew it. Shivers went up Anna's spine and she took a step back.

"Anna," Daire said, "I'm sorry . . . I didn't mean to yell. I feel like you're always putting me on the defense."

Anna did not answer. She was deep in thought.

"Can you . . . Go to the hovel and wait for me? I really don't want to tell you more than I have because this is for the government and I . . ."

Anna left.

Anna paced the dirt floor of Daire's little hovel as her mind searched frantically: *what are the odds of me being here with the man who's working on a drug to help people forget and me forgetting who I am?*

It was no coincidence. She knew it. So, Anna formulated a plan to escape, but had to continue with their charade until she found her opportunity.

Anna gasped as she held back tears. She loved Daire and did not want to believe he had tried to harm her. She wondered, *Is he truly giving me a drug . . . Why? Is there something terrible he's trying to help me forget? Had I asked him to do this to me?*

Then, other thoughts came to her: *What if he isn't drugging me? What if he's trying to reverse the effects of my memory loss by studying me?*

Her thoughts went rambled in circles. Yet, one particular thought remained: she loved him. She did not want to leave him.

Daire came in and shook off his boots. He looked at Anna nervously and tried to think of what to say to appease her. He stirred the soup he was making—he always made soup. She had grown tired of the same food over and over, but she did not complain. It was all he ate during the cruel winter.

"Anna, I'm sure you have questions," he whispered.

She thought about what to ask. If he had been drugging her, he was not inclined admit it. She did not want to reveal her cards to him.

"What happened during the war . . . To me?" She asked pointedly.

He was somewhat relieved as he sat beside her and brushed hair out of her face. He was so nervous about reaching to her. She let him, which made him feel more at ease.

"Anna . . . I love you."

His frankness took her breath away.

"I don't want to share this with you, but will because you've asked me."

She nodded.

"You lived in London. You hid in the tunnels a lot from the bombs."

"London was being bombed?"

"Yes."

Anna thought for a moment.

"Daire, why are you being so secretive about the war?"

"Because, my love, there were many things too horrific for you to deal with. My job is to help people who saw too much. I wanted to keep you as innocent as possible."

Anna wanted to ask if it was why he was drugging her, but she did not. The seed had been planted that maybe he was not. There really was no reason if that was all that happened to her during the war. Daire sat next to her and took her hands.

"Anna, I know what you're thinking."

She looked back at him with fear in her eyes.

"I know you think I'm drugging you."

"No," she replied defensively.

"Anna, I know. I want you so desperately to trust me that I've kept all this from you, knowing it's what you'd immediately think. I hope you feel what I feel for you."

He licked his lips and chose his next words carefully. He paused and studied her hand in his briefly as he changed his tactic.

"I know it's very odd that I'd be working on something that affects the brain and you're having problems with your memory. Maybe it's providence. I work with those who have brain injuries or mental instability. I thought about how the brain works and why we forget. When I began to study, I realized it can benefit people who've been traumatized, who can't even function in society, Anna. What happened to them haunts them."

They finally looked each other in the eye.

"Daire, I'm so scared of what I don't remember."

"Nothing can hurt you here," he said and kissed her.

CHAPTER 18

HENRY WOKE IN THE MORNING, splashed water on his face, and scrubbed his tears off. He had fallen asleep as he wept again. He prayed no one ever found out, and then brushed his teeth. The room began to spin as he spit toothpaste out and he caught himself on the porcelain sink. The stress burdened him.

He put on his spectacles and surveyed his room. He made his little bed neatly and swept the floor. Then, he looked out the window. Warm air had come through and the heavy snow had begun to melt.

"Thank you, God, for this day," he prayed.

He got ready for his morning visits: tea with Father Donnelly and Sarah, his appointment with the florist, and breakfast with Mrs. O'Leary.

"Another day closer to seeing your face," he whispered to the Lord.

He thought about the day he would see Anna's face as well. Henry gulped and knelt down to say his morning prayers which were like none others. He whispered them during the day, but three times a day he did something some people may not even consider prayer: he meditated on the resurrection.

Sometimes, Henry spent an hour in thought about it, but always—even if it was just a few minutes—he arose a new person. It was more of a miracle than explainable to his flock of parishioners.

My beautiful, John Henry, the Lord said deep within him.

Henry waited, always dumbfounded when the Lord called him beautiful.

What's been taken from you will be given back tenfold.

"What's been taken from me?" Henry asked, but he knew. "My Lord, I don't want to ever be married again. It was an honor to have Anna, but Lord you know what a miserable husband I was."

Then, without a whisper or a breeze, God's holy presence left his little room.

Henry was quite shaken by the Lord's statement. He immediately went to Father Donnelly's home to discuss the prophetic statement with his friend. Surely, he would have a reasonable explanation for it.

Anna awoke silently. It was hard to tell if it was night or day. All she knew was she was exhausted. She gazed over at the small, green hutch with windowed doors and marveled at all Daire was able to bring with him on his little row boat.

She then saw Daire's reflection in the glass. He was filling bowls with soup. She smiled faintly and watched his beautiful silhouette in the light of the fire. She almost opened her mouth to tell him she was up when he suddenly reached down and pulled up a small floorboard.

He reached and took out a small vile of white powder and put it into one of the bowls. She squinted and thought, *Surely he's not doing what I'm seeing! Maybe it's the reflection.*

Then, he quickly replaced the floorboard, stirred the soup, and started to turn toward her. Anna quickly closed her eyes quickly because she did not want him to know she was awake.

She knew.

"My dear, Henry," Sarah cooed.

As he scurried into her house, he immediately embraced her.

"Are you all right?"

He squeezed her tightly. She pushed him back a little and took his haggard face in her hands.

"My dear boy!" She cried when she realized how much turmoil he was experiencing. "Let me go get the mister—"

Henry shot back, "No!"

She looked at him, startled by his tone. She had never heard anything, but a sweet voice from Henry.

"I'm so sorry," he apologized. "Sarah, it's you I want to see and speak with if you don't mind."

"Of course not," she said.

She took a cloth and cleaned the kitchen table where she had been cutting vegetables from the garden.

"Sit here and I'll get you some tea."

Henry reached up, took her hands, and guided her to sit by him instead. She was always a busy bee and he needed her to truly listen to him.

"I've heard something from the Lord which is most concerning this very morn."

She asked, "What is it, my dear?"

"He's said what was taken from me will be given back to me tenfold."

She did not understand the statement, for most prophets were only understood by themselves. She gazed at his rugged face and large, muscular frame. She did not notice how intimidating he looked because of his soft demeanor. Her husband sometimes described Henry as "strength under control." He had told her what a rare thing it was to be a powerful and gentle man.

"What do you think He means, my dear?" She asked, visibly confused.

"I believe He's referring to our Anna," he said quietly.

She took in a sudden breath and fought back tears at the mention of Anna's name. She realized what Henry was saying. Tears flowed as she wiped them on her apron.

"My sweet girl," she said absentmindedly.

He admitted, "I'm not happy with this."

"My dear, son," she said as she took his hand, "I love you. God loves you. We want the best for you."

Henry welled up, but controlled his emotions in front of the precious woman.

"This may be the first time God and I have words."

"Henry, you mustn't think of it as happening today, but you must prepare yourself in the future. God will give you another wife maybe in a few years. It'll comfort you as it has comforted me to have Thad."

"My dear, Sarah, I've never known a softer soul than yours."

Anna searched her heart about whether or not she was able to leave Daire. She frantically tried to make the decision as she felt him draw closer to her.

"Anna?" He called to awaken her.

She stretched and sat up. She took the bowl from him, and then looked at it. Then, as she stared at it, she remembered a dream she had weeks before. The man had told her not to eat anything before her escape. Then, she looked up at Daire who was already eating quietly. He finally met her gaze.

"What's wrong?"

"I don't feel very well," she said.

He stopped eating and got up.

"Do you think you can eat a little?"

"No," she moaned. "I feel so nauseous. Can you take it away?"

He did, although she noticed the pained expression on his face. He reached up and felt her forehead.

"You're not hot," he stated, concerned. "What's the matter?"

"I told you," she said and turned away. "I'm so nauseous."

"Do you have any other symptoms?"

"No, I don't think so," she said. "I just need to lie down."

"Do you want me to take the soup outside?" he asked.

He hoped her answer was no. The thought of dragging his bowl and the huge pot into the freezing air was not something he relished.

"If you don't mind."

"Of course not," he said and immediately started to gather his food. "I'm just going to put the pot in my shed and eat in there. I'll save it if you want some later."

"Here's my bowl," she said.

"Oh, thank you," he said.

"Don't you want to just put it back in the pot so you don't waste it?" she tested.

He stopped for a moment.

"No, um, you breathed on it and if you have a sickness of some sort, I don't want to catch it as well."

"That seems an unlikely way to catch something."

"Well, it happens. I'll just be a few minutes. Do you think you'll be all right?"

"Yes, I'm just going to go back to sleep."

Daire brought her a bucket and laid it beside the bed. He told her if she needed it, it was there. Then, he left.

Anna was very hungry, but she was determined to obey what the man in her dream had said. Maybe her subconscious had tried to tell her something for a while through dreams. Maybe somehow she knew she was being drugged. She thought about how to escape; she finally settled on an unrefined plan.

Anna's heart sank as she remembered Daire's every touch, everything she had believed for the past weeks with him, everything she felt for him. It was overwhelming, so she decided to only concentrate on her escape plan.

She knew even though she believed he had very serious issues, he was still extremely intelligent. The plan must be simple, but something unexpected to him. She must keep up with the pretense of staying with him. She sat up and brushed her hair which she found comfort doing.

"Hey, how are you?" he asked.

"I still feel pretty poorly, Daire," she said and reached for him.

He came to her immediately and put his arms around her.

"You do feel slightly warm," he said into her neck, and then kissed it. "I'm worried about you."

"I'll be all right. I just need to rest."

He almost kissed her, but then remembered what he had told her about not putting her soup into the pot. He had to make her think he was afraid of her germs. So, he pulled the blanket over her and made his bed on the floor beside her. He did not want her temperature to go up or be tempted to kiss her.

"Just like old times," he joked.

"I'm sorry," she said weakly.

He chuckled and said, "It's fine."

"I hate how short the days are now," she remarked. "The weather has been terrible lately."

"Yes," he agreed. "Don't worry, it'll clear soon. I was looking at the clouds and the sky looked quite blue earlier."

He dozed off quickly and Anna began to think through everything which might go wrong with her plan. As the evening progressed, she realized she was not seeing the halos of light around everything. She began to see things normally again. She was amazed.

She had actually gotten use to the sensation of light permeating out of everything. She rubbed her eyes; they were less blurry.

She had to concentrate. She tried to remember all of her night-mares since she had arrived at Daire's hovel. One nightmare stuck out: the one she thought least like a dream. She tried to remember what was said.

"Fast," he had said.

That, she was doing. She had not eaten or drank anything for over a day. Her lips cracked and bled. All she wanted was a drink, but she dared not.

She searched her memories: *What else did the man say? "Wait for the man to say he is going to work" or something like that. There was something else? That's right! Paddle . . . The boat!*

She began to think clearly for the first time. It was if the fog was lifting off her memory as the minutes passed.

Anna listened patiently to Daire's snores and breathed deeply. Waiting was the hardest part. Her heart pounded until she thought she would fly out of the hovel. She closed her eyes and tried to sleep a little. She needed all of her strength.

Anna must have slept because morning came faster than she liked. Daire was immediately at her side to ask how she was feeling. She lied and told him she was still unwell and could not possibly stomach eating anything. She even conjured up gagging noises while he tried to eat in front of her. He finally kissed her forehead and told her he would be working in his shed all morning.

She wondered if he would become obsessed with the new symptom of the drug he was giving her. She thought maybe he was, so she knew it was her chance.

She counted to fifty before she went to the outhouse. She was testing whether or not he noticed her walking about. She kept her eyes on the shed where Daire did his experiments. There was no stirring. She wondered if he was even in there, it was so quiet. This made her even more nervous as she contemplated, *Is he watching me?*

The sun was hours away from coming up. The days were very short in winter which worked to her advantage. Anna went back into the hovel.

Her heart sank when she realized all of Daire's boots were in his shed. She wrapped up her feet and grabbed everything to help her on her journey: blankets; a small jar for catching water to drink, as she could not risk drinking Daire's water; and a small lantern. Her heart raced and she shook so violently she constantly dropped things. She was hardly able to carry all she needed. She crawled out the hovel and looked around the forest again and toward the shed. It was if the whole world was frozen in fear with her.

Anna scooted out, stood, and stared at Daire's hut for a minute. She had no plan if he saw or caught her. She had no explanation about what she was doing.

She dropped the blankets twice as she shook with fright. She immediately felt she had to go to the outhouse again, but rejected it as just nerves. She gathered up the blankets again, and then started to run.

Snow began to fall slightly. At first, she feared the cold it might bring, but remembered it would cover her tracks. She barely breathed because it was so cold. Her face started to scream with the pain of cold.

She stopped suddenly, turned abruptly, and thought: *are those footsteps?*

She spun around once and looked for him desperately, and then started to run again. She was sure the sound of her footsteps was so loud; they were like demons which pleaded for Daire to find her.

As if an unseen breath blew away the dense fog, she beheld the salvation of the little boat before her. The thought she might have run into the frigid waters unknowingly if the fog had not cleared at that moment sent sheer terror up her spine. She stopped and looked around again.

There was no sound, no birds, no rustling of trees. There was only the faint lap of the water. Anna wondered, *What if he's near waiting by the banks, or hiding in the fog and shadows?*

Anna gulped and walked toward the bank. She was very weak, but did not notice until she tried to uncover the boat. The rough material Daire kept over it was weighed down with layers of snow.

She lost feeling in her hands as she scooped up, brushed away the snow, and threw the canvas off, but she had to keep going. Daire would look for her soon, if he had not already.

She stuck her foot into the water to get a better grasp on the boat. It was somewhat frozen to the bank. She lost feeling almost immediately in her left foot as she tried to launch the boat. She had forgotten she had one of the blankets in her hand and dropped it for a second in the water. She had one less blanket to cover her in the icy cold.

With every ounce of strength Anna had left to launch the boat, she swung her dead foot in and looked at her supplies for a half a second. She did not want to leave any on the bank. She needed everything.

She held the paddle and shook as she tried desperately to feel the wood in her hands. Anna crunched through the icy edges of the tributary and looked toward the tree. It was high tide which could not have been planned more perfectly.

She took a deep breath and paddled with all her might. She was as silent as possible, even the small lapping of the water against the dingy scared her.

She suddenly dropped the paddles because her hands had lost all feeling. Frantically, Anna tried to wrap her hands, but both paddles slid into the water immediately. She put her hands in and anxiously rowed with them to retrieve one paddle. She could not get the other.

She wrapped her wet, cold hands again and began rowing desperately. She watched the bank with wide eyes and waited for Daire to appear. She looked down at the small compass he kept on the seat and hit it with her finger. It did not move.

The fog was thick until Anna felt as if she had rowed into a cloud. She was barely able to make out the tree of her *birth*, the fog was so thick.

Her back ached as she pulled further away and switched sides with her lone paddle to row. She rubbed her eyes—her eyesight still was not what it could have been. Everything was fuzzy, with or without the fog.

She whispered to reassure herself as she shook in cold, "He doesn't have a boat. He can't get you now."

However, Anna's heart did not let her be at ease: *What if I washed back to him? What will he do if he knew I tried to escape? What if I'm just going in circles and row right back to him?*

She covered her hands with the blanket which had unraveled. She removed the wrappings from her feet and warmed them in the same blanket as much as possible.

She did not know which way to row, but she had to keep going. She finally noticed a small glimmer come from what she believed was a bank. She fought off the terrible fear she had simply gone in circles. She rowed closer.

At that point, Anna had stopped shivering and began to feel the sensation of exhaustion sweep over her. All she wanted to do was go to sleep. She was freezing and had to find shelter very quickly.

Finally on the bank, she realized she had seen a small lantern which hung from a porch.

Is that Daire, trying to find me? No, it's a house! A wonderful, old, blue house!

She stuck her numb foot into the water and dragged up the dingy. She fell in the mud, and then picked herself up. Anna hoped the temporary paralysis had not returned.

She was so happy she chuckled. She crawled, and then attempted get up. She tried to run to the haven before her. As she
crawled up on the steps, Anna kicked and pounded on the door.
Then, she lay almost lifeless on the porch.

CHAPTER 19

HENRY PULLED UP TO THE hospital in Sligo Town. Father Donnelly had received a strange call. The Sligo Town hospital was a full three and a half hour ride away from Adare. Henry and he were baffled by the need for their pastoral services.

He thought, *Are there no other priests in Sligo Town?*

It was a pretty town on the water with a much greater population than Adare. The car squeaked to a halt.

"Better check out these breaks when you get back, dear boy," Father Donnelly suggested.

They straightened their clerical collars and looked for the hospital's main entrance. Once inside, a hospital volunteer greeted them, shook their hands, and asked them to wait in the lobby. Finally, a doctor came out and greeted them.

"Thank you for coming," he said and shook their hands solemnly. "I don't suppose you remember me, Father Oliver."

"Henry," Henry corrected, and then added, "You do look familiar. Forgive me if I can't place you."

"I know your family very well. We actually spent a Christmas together when we were young. The name is Dr. Brendan Carey and—"

"Goodness soul! Of course, I remember the Carey family! How are you? I remember that Christmas so well because I had the flu and you were so loud I thought the whole house would fall apart around me!"

Dr. Carey chuckled politely. Then, he tried desperately to get to his point.

"Father Henry," he continued solemnly, "I heard about your wife's passing this summer."

He licked his lips. Henry awaited his condolences, but they did not come.

"I was invited to your wedding, but I'm sure you didn't see me there. It was a large wedding."

He wondered, *Perhaps he doesn't know what to say to me.*

"Yes," Henry said as he shadowed the graveness of Dr. Carey's tone. "I'm so sorry I don't remember you being there."

"No matter," Dr. Carey said quickly.

Henry and Father Donnelly looked at each other, slightly bewildered.

"Your wife was one of the most beautiful women I've ever seen."

"Thank you, sir."

Dr. Carey stared at the floor for a good while.

"Henry," he finally said as he looked squarely into Henry's eyes. "There's a woman here who has a very strange story. There's nothing much wrong with her, except she doesn't really remember anything. The hospital is pressuring me to release her in the morning, but she has nowhere to go."

Henry looked very concerned about this. He could not imagine releasing this woman who had nowhere to go or a memory of who she was.

"The thing is . . . the reason I called you is . . . She looks very much like your wife. I'm so sorry to do this to you, but she doesn't remember who she is and . . . I'd very much like you to just look at her and just make sure—"

"Where is she?" Henry asked frantically as his heart pounded.

As he started to follow Dr. Carey, Father Donnelly caught Henry midstride.

"Henry, my boy, it's not her," he said.

Henry shrugged out of his grasp and was hot on Dr. Carey's heels. Dr. Carey led him up the stairs and onto a floor for patients. He stopped him before he looked in.

"She said her name is Anna."

Henry nodded, anxiously. Then, he turned and went into the room. Henry stared as his wife looked back at him vacantly. Then, he gathered himself and went back into the hall without saying a word. His face was ashen and Father Donnelly believed instantly.

"It can't be!" Father Donnelly blurted.

Henry was unable to speak or hardly stand. Father Donnelly caught hold of him.

"Are you sure?"

Henry did not answer. Father Donnelly looked at Dr. Carey who held on to Henry as Father Donnelly looked around the corner and into the room. Then, Father Donnelly took a step inside.

"Hello," Anna said.

"Hello," Father Donnelly said, wide-eyed.

"The nurses said they thought it'd be good for me to talk to a priest," she said quietly.

She realized her companion was strangely uncomfortable. She checked her gown to make sure she was appropriate.

"Sir, are you all right?" She asked in her usual, tender way.

"Yes, of course," he replied. "If you'll just permit a moment. . . ."

He went back into the hall. Dr. Carey looked at Father Donnelly wildly. His presumption had been correct. He almost had not called, afraid he was wrong. Henry might not have handled it well, but Dr. Carey had taken a chance. Father Donnelly gulped and looked at each of them. Then, he re-entered Anna's room.

"I'm so sorry there isn't a chair, would you like to sit beside me here?" She asked sweetly.

Father Donnelly did, although he normally stood under any other circumstance. He realized he clutched his small, black Bible tightly. He looked down and deliberately removed his thumb and looked at the dent he had created with his intense grasp.

"My dear, what's your name?"

"My name is Anna," she said.

Father Donnelly paused.

"What may I pray with you about?" Father Donnelly asked, unsure about where to put his hands until he finally settled on his knees.

Anna became as uncomfortable as he was, but she decided it was her only chance to talk to someone who would actually listen.

"Would you be offended if I told you I don't know what to pray for?"

"Not at all," Father Donnelly said.

That's truly an Anna kind of response—honest and open.

"What brings you to the hospital, my dear girl?" He asked gently.

"I don't know how to begin this story, but from what I can remember."

"Just go slowly. We can always back up if you need to."

"There's not much, Father. I don't remember anything before three weeks ago."

"Yes," Father Donnelly said as he looked at his hands which were folded.

"A man found me in a tree in the middle of a marsh."

"What man?"

"His name is Daire," she confided for the first time.

The name did not ring a bell to Father Donnelly.

"He was in a boat and took me down out of the tree . . . I remember nothing else before then. He cared for me three weeks, but last night I saw him put a powder in my food and I got scared and stole—"

She looked up at Father Donnelly and searched for forgiveness.

"It's all right, my dear, if you were in peril. Please continue."

"I stole his boat, and then found a cottage. The next thing I recall is being here in the hospital."

There was a lot she had left out; they both knew it. Yet, there was only so much she could tell a man more than twice her age who wore a clerical collar.

"Are you Catholic?" She suddenly asked.

Father Donnelly looked up and quickly replied, "No. Protestant. We are Church of Ireland."

"We?"

"Yes. Another priest came with me."

Father Donnelly turned and looked at the door frame. Henry was glued to the side of it and only showed a small portion of his body. Anna looked at the man, and then back at Father Donnelly.

"Why won't he come in?" she whispered.

"Oh, well, he's very shy," he answered, unable to find a better response.

Anna slightly smiled and said, "I've never heard of a shy priest before."

"Yes, well God calls all kinds, doesn't he?"

She looked at Father Donnelly and laughed.

"I guess!" she agreed.

"If you don't mind I'd like to pray for you," he said.

Anna frowned and explained, "No, I just wanted to talk to someone if you don't mind."

"Well now," Father Donnelly said, befuddled. "If you don't mind, we've had a long drive. Would you mind us getting a bite to eat downstairs, and then coming back up in about an hour?"

"Of course," she said.

She was happy he was going to return.

"Can I get you something?"

220 A Little Irish Love Story

"If there's any tapioca pudding, I'd greatly like some."

"Well, I shall try!" he promised.

It's surreal seeing her smiling face again.

On his way out, Father Donnelly grabbed Henry by the arm and marched him down the long hall as Dr. Carey raced after them.

"Is it her?" Dr. Carey called out.

Father Donnelly stopped, but did not turn around.

"Yes," he answered flatly.

Then, he continued to escort Henry to the cafeteria where they looked at each other and tried to catch their breaths. Henry rubbed his arm where Donnelly had manhandled him.

"I'm sorry," he said. "I just had to get us out of there. I was afraid you'd stand there all day if I didn't grab you."

"I probably would've," Henry's replied in a daze.

He stared off to where the nurses built trays of food for their patients and checked charts for doctor's orders. Father Donnelly swore, and then made the sign of the cross. Henry stood as if the wind had been knocked out of him.

"It's her," Father Donnelly said.

He paced a little and grabbed his hair.

"Father, forgive me. How can this be?"

"It's her?" Henry asked, dumbfounded.

"Of course, you know it is."

Henry shook his head.

"She's dead. I just accepted she's dead. She's not supposed to be here."

Father Donnelly put his hands on Henry's shoulders heavily.

"My son," he said as tears rolled down his face, "she's very much alive."

Henry took off. He ran up the stairs and almost knocked down Dr. Carey and a nurse who quietly whispered about the situation. Then, he stood once more, totally shocked, in Anna's doorway.

"Anna?" He finally squeaked out.

Anna straightened the blanket around her and said, "You're Father Donnelly's friend."

"Yes, Anna. We're here to help you."

She smiled a small smile which made everything inside him light up like a blazing comet. He tried to hide it, but he smiled back. Anna was taken aback. He looked at her, and then turned to a nurse gaped in the doorway.

"Would you mind terribly much if I got a chair?"

"I'll bring you one," the nurse said politely and excused herself.

"My name is Henry," he said as he held his hat and Bible.

"Thank you for coming, Father Henry," she replied.

She had never called him that before. It felt almost as odd as the circumstance he found himself in. He looked at her in awe. Her lips were chapped and face was raw, her hair fell in dirty waves down her shoulders.

The nurse startled him with the chair he had asked for. He sat as uncomfortably as Father Donnelly had by her bedside.

"Forgive me, I heard the story you told Father Donnelly."

"Yes, I saw you in the hallway."

"Yes. Well, do you remember anything about your life before this person found you . . . in a tree you said?"

"Yes, a tree. It was on a small island. No, I don't remember anything before that."

"May I call you Anna?"

"Of course."

"Well, Anna, the doctor says there's nothing much wrong with you so . . . I suppose my only question at this moment is . . . Do you have somewhere to go?"

"No, I don't," she said and looked down.

"Well, we live a few hours away . . . A small village called Adare. Have you heard of it?"

Anna did not answer.

"Well," Henry continued, quite nervous, "we have some ladies you can stay with, or there's even a small apartment. That is, until you get on your feet. I hear the doctor wants to release you as early as tomorrow."

Anna's eyes grew fierce.

"Tomorrow? They haven't even looked at me! They think because I have no physical injuries I'm fine, but I'm not! I've been drugged! I have no memories! Get the doctor in here!" she demanded.

Her reaction scared Henry. He got up and located Dr. Carey. Henry stood to the side of the room when Dr. Carey entered.

"What can I do for you, Anna?" He asked with a fake smile.

"You can start by explaining why you're releasing me in the morning."

Dr. Carey looked at Henry who said and did nothing.

"There's nothing really wrong with you—"

"Nothing's wrong with me! What are your credentials again? Are you out of your mind? I have lost my memory and no place to go. I told you I was drugged. You're releasing me in the morning? I haven't even seen a police officer yet!"

"The nurse in charge called the police when you first arrived to notify them. They came right away, but you weren't conscious to answer questions at that point," Dr. Carey replied sheepishly. "The hospital kept them informed about your memory loss throughout your stay. The police were waiting to see if your memory returned or not before they questioned you. They called again an hour ago and will be here today to take your statement."

Anna looked at him furiously and yelled, "What am I supposed to do!"

She started to cry.

Henry stepped forward.

"We'll be looking after you," he said.

He understood her anger and frustration for it was how he felt as well. One feeling dominated all other emotions he felt: joy. He was taking his wife home.

Anna looked at Henry, and then back at the doctor.

"Why did you call these two poor priests hours away from their home?"

"I knew they'd help you," Dr. Carey replied honestly.

"Would no other men of the cloth help me?" She asked softly yet bitterly.

"This man is a friend of mine. I knew he'd help you," Dr. Carey said and placed his hand on Henry's back.

"We'd like to help you, Anna, if you're willing," Henry said gently. Anna looked at the strange-looking priest. She pictured priests to look more like Father Donnelly than Henry. However, she quickly dismissed his rugged, young looks and asked for some clothes. All she had were Daire's old, big clothes which were ruined during her escape.

"I'll get you some," Henry said and walked up to her bedside.

Dr. Carey retreated and left Henry to fend for himself.

"Thank you, Father Henry," she said.

He began to leave, but turned back and said, "Call me Henry, please."

She nodded; her thoughts elsewhere.

"I'll be back," he smiled.

Henry felt like a clumsy school boy again who tried to talk to the prettiest girl he had ever seen. He walked out of Anna's room and fell back against the hallway wall. He tried to catch his breath, but his heart raced.

"You did fine," Father Donnelly said as he also shook from head to toe. "I'll call Sarah, God help us, and tell her the news. She has to be prepared. We'll take Anna in."

"Thank you," Henry said; he knew it was best.

"There's a dress shop a few doors down," Dr. Carey interjected as he formed a huddle of very confused men.

"I'll go with you," a nurse said to Henry.

He nodded and smiled, thankful. They departed to buy clothes for his beautiful wife. He went to the bank to withdraw no small sum, and then they headed for the dress shop.

The nurse, who had introduced herself as Beth, helped Henry pick out many items. He remembered Anna's sizes after he pondered them for a few minutes. They selected a light blue winter coat; gray hat; scarf; mittens; boots, two dresses—one red, the other blue; pants; three cashmere sweaters; silk nightclothes; and undergarments.

Henry still felt embarrassed to select the latter wear with Beth, so she went on merrily and picked out everything she wanted for herself. She went across the street to the drug store and bought make up and other essentials with Henry's money.

Henry was almost giddy. The happy saleswoman packed up his purchases in pretty bags with paper. Henry put them into his trunk. He wondered how he would give these to her without it seeming strange, so he devised a plan for Sarah to simply tear off the tags and put them in the closet of Anna's room. She could tell Anna someone had given them to her, but they did not fit.

That might work, Henry thought happily.

Father Donnelly met the two of them at the hospital lobby door. Beth excused herself and went back to work. He gave the news to Henry.

"The police were just here. They took Anna's statement. They wouldn't let me in the room, so I don't know what she told them. Henry, they took my statement as well. They want to see you in the morning at the police station."

Father Donnelly paused.

"Henry, I think it best we stay at the inn down the way and rest."

"I don't think it's possible," Henry said with a smirk.

"Well, *I* can and I need to talk with . . . well . . . Quite a few people actually. I've arranged it already; I think it best we say goodnight and get some supper as well."

Henry did not know what he expected to happen when he returned, but Father Donnelly was disappointing him with his lack of mirth. Henry nodded; he knew he needed to follow the level-headed guidance of his friend.

His mind was lost and heart took over the minute he saw Anna's face. It had always been like that with her. Henry walked up the stairs with a grin on his face to say goodnight to Anna: his wife, friend, and love.

This can't be happening. How can it be?

Anna was eating her supper when he walked into her room. He suddenly remembered she needed something to wear home and excused himself to return when she had finished. He ran down to his trunk and picked out the pretty things, but forgot to tear off the tags as he had planned. He tore back up the stairs with his presents in hand for her.

Anna was finishing the last of her juice and wiped her mouth. Henry was suddenly dumbfounded again.

"Father Henry," she chirped, "It's so nice to see you again."

"One of your kind nurses went shopping and picked up some things for you," he said generously and put the bags down.

"Oh, my . . . Thank her for me, please!"

She looked in the bags with wide eyes, obviously pleased.

"We wanted to make sure you had something to wear when you—"

"We?"

"Yes, well, I helped."

"You paid," she stated with a smile and twinkle in her eye.

Henry smiled back. He adjusted his stance as he took a different grip on his hat.

"Thank you very much," she said as she hugged her new coat.

He nodded, walked backwards a few steps, and tripped over the chair.

"Good night, Father Henry," she said.

He turned to leave.

"Father?"

He stopped.

"I don't even know how to begin to thank you and Father Donnelly."

He did not turn around.

"I'm very scared and confused. You two have made me feel better. Thank you. I hope I didn't scare you off the way I lit into that doctor."

"No, no . . . ," he whispered without looking at her.

He found it unbearable to say goodnight. When Henry left—his heart leaped out of his chest.

Anna was not quite so moved as she looked out the window.

"Fog, always fog," she muttered.

She wanted to see something. She was unable to get her bearings about where she was. She finally asked the nurse if she had a map. The nurse returned with a folding map after about an hour.

"I got it out of the doctor's car," Beth said.

"Maybe Dr. Carey's not an idiot after all," Anna said with genuine laughter.

He must be a kind doctor to ask the priests to come help me.

"I hope not, he's my husband!" the nurse said with a laugh.

Anna laughed, too. It felt good.

"I'm sorry, I'm sorry," she said with a hearty laugh.

The nurse easily forgave her.

Henry paced as he listened to Father Donnelly make telephone calls in the lobby of the inn.

"It's true, my love, it's true!" he sobbed as he told Sarah.
Henry stopped and watched. He wished he could see Sarah's face.
Finally, after the police were called, Father Donnelly took out
his embroidered handkerchief and wiped his blue eyes. With tele-
phone calls finished, the two priests embraced each other. They hit
each other hard on the back, and then kissed each other's cheeks.
"My boy!" Father Donnelly sobbed again.
Then, he affectionately slapped Henry's face and shook his hand.
"I'm going to sleep after a lot of liquor tonight. Want to join me?"
"No, Father, you know I don't drink anymore."
"I just thought this was an exception."
"Quite right, but no. I prefer to be totally aware of every mo-
ment tonight."
"Drink it in!"
"I'm drinking it in!" Henry said, laughing.
"But, try to sleep."
"That's not possible."
"I didn't think so, but it's the sort of thing people say. Good-
night, my boy."
"Goodnight, Father," Henry said lovingly.
"You're both my children, natural or not!" He cried out as he
went up the stairs to his room.
Father Donnelly had tried to get Henry to share a room with
him, but Henry was self-indulgent that night and rented his own
room. He wanted to be alone, pray, and thank God all night long.
Henry paced his room, his emotions switched from laughter to
tears in seconds. Then, he thanked God repeatedly, remembering
what God had told him the previous day.
What was taken from me was returned!
He was scarcely able to take it all in. After every emotion
bombarded his being, he turned cold when he thought of all the

questions he had. He paced for a few more minutes, and then went downstairs to call his friend.

"Dr. Carey, please," he said into the receiver and waited.

"Brendan, listen, I'm sorry to call you like this. I called the hospital and they said you were home. I appreciate it . . . thank you. Well, I have a couple of questions. Well, actually, I have a lot of questions. If you can answer even one of them, it will be of help to me.

"Where was she found? I see. Who do you think this man was who she was rescued by? No, I don't have a clue either. She said the last three weeks, where do you think she's been for three months? It's all right. I know you don't have the answers, but I'm trying to get as much information as I can from you. Right. Did she say he harmed her in any way?"

From that point, the conversation went drastically wrong. Anna had told Dr. Carey she and Daire had been living together as husband and wife. Dr. Carey broke the code of medical ethics to tell his friend. Henry hung up without saying goodbye or thank you. He slid down to his knees. The thought hit him extremely hard. He crouched for an hour until his legs ached and head hurt. It was too much. He could not handle one more thing.

His wife did not remember him, she did not love him. She loved someone else; the one who had apparently drugged her. Thoughts raced as shock took over. He wanted Father Donnelly to find him, but at the same time, he did not. Finally, the innkeeper's wife came in and saw Henry crouched in the corner under the telephone.

"Oh, my goodness!" she cried.

She took stock of the sick-looking priest and asked, "Are you with Father . . . Donnelly?"

Henry nodded.

"I'll go get him."

Father Donnelly was downstairs in no time. He picked Henry

up off the floor and guided him to his room with his arm wrapped around his shoulder.

"My boy, what happened?"

Henry could not answer. Father Donnelly had him sit on his bed. Henry slipped off his shoes and fell sideways onto it. He was not going to tell Father Donnelly. He could not stomach saying the words.

"Just rest, Henry, rest. You'll be all right in the morning. The shock is hitting you hard."

Henry closed his eyes slowly as one tear came down. Father Donnelly covered Henry up, and then retired to his room next door. He opened the door between the two rooms so he could hear Henry if he needed him. Then, Father Donnelly finally closed his heavy eyes.

CHAPTER 20

ANNA WAS DRESSED AND READY by nine o'clock the next morning. Dr. Carey was detained by an emergency surgery. So, she sat on her bed, dressed in her beautiful new clothes, hands folded in her pretty grey gloves, and waited.

Father Donnelly knocked at her open door and smiled.

"Well, Anna, you look very pretty."

"Thank you, Father," Anna said dryly.

Henry came in as well, but kept his eyes on the floor, his hat in his hands. That morning, his heart had been freshly wrecked by his visit to the police station. He hated to recall the events of his wife's disappearance. Reliving that terrible night in his statement to the police was more than he could bear. Between the conversation with Dr. Carey the night before and his awful morning, he was not feeling well.

"Good morning, Father Henry," Anna said slightly brighter.

Henry did not answer. He swallowed hard as Father Donnelly looked at him, puzzled.

"I hear Dr. Carey won't be in for some time to check me out. Why don't you go get some breakfast or look around town?"

Father Donnelly was a little unnerved because Dr. Carey had not yet seen her.

"Have you eaten?"

"Yes, yes, you go ahead. I'm going to wait here."

Father Donnelly looked at Henry who had not yet moved. He needed to talk to him. The change in his behavior last night and this morning worried him. He told Anna they would be back to check on her, and then they left.

Father Donnelly and Henry found a small breakfast café. He kept a sharp eye on Henry as he quietly buttered his toast.

"I remember the last time we ate a meal like this, Henry; just the two of us."

Henry remembered as well.

"I sat across from you that terrible morning after Anna . . . Well, after she disappeared."

Henry looked up at his friend. Any other man would have held it against him, but Henry forgave like no one Father Donnelly had ever seen. He had always thought it came easier to Henry than any other creature, but the truth was it did not. Henry did not understand why Father Donnelly had given up so easily that night, why he had chosen acceptance over searching for her.

However, Henry loved his friend more than words could ever say, so he forgave him. There really was not a choice in the matter.

"I'm so sorry, Henry, I gave up that night."

Henry smiled sweetly and said, "You've been a wonderful friend to me; closer than a brother."

Father Donnelly felt an immediate relief and asked, "Why are you so quiet this morning, my boy?"

Henry thought for a moment. He did not want to share with anyone about what he knew.

"I think the impact of her forgetting me finally hit me."

"Indeed. It's a very difficult thing to swallow."

Father Donnelly took a bite of eggs.

"Where do you think she was?"

"I don't know."

"Who do you think this Daire fellow is?"

"I don't know," Henry said.

He tried not to sound exasperated with his friend. Father Donnelly looked up at him when he noticed Henry's tone.

"I'm sorry, forgive me, I'm just very tired."

"Of course," Father Donnelly said lovingly.

Henry paid for their meals, and then went back up to see his wife. A couple of nurses had pulled up chairs and were talking, even laughing with Anna. He watched as she laughed when Beth related how funny he had been during their shopping excursion.

Although he knew Beth truly liked his manners, even related fondly to him, he never realized how silly he was sometimes. He was always shy and awkward around women. He imagined he must have been at his worst in a women's garment store.

Henry knocked and they turned around. When they saw him, they looked a little red in the face, except his wife who always had the air about her of being above everything. Yet, he knew better. For behind the facade of elegance was a little girl who needed her hand held. He loved the different sides of her: the wildness, royal air, and tenderness.

She was a chameleon; she got along well with anyone. She even shadowed the same movements and expressions her companions had. She changed her accent if she wanted, and if that was not enough, she was also incredibly intelligent.

The previous night, Anna was slightly out of sorts and acted a little different than she had before. He imagined she was right—she *was*, in fact, being drugged—because she looked and acted more like herself than she did the night before.

He had been stupefied she had fallen in love with him once. The thought of it happening again was a miracle he hardly hoped for. All he knew was she breathed before him, her eyes danced being around people. She loved people.

Anna had said she had never heard of a shy priest. She was always his voice, the one who paid the social graces with which he had such a hard time. Losing her was like losing his head.

The nurses smiled and quickly excused themselves. Beth whispered, "I'm sorry for the teasing, it's all in fun. I think you're a wonderful man."

Henry smiled at her with eyes which told stories he was not able to say. He shook Beth's hand gently, and then lifted his soft expression to the love of his life.

"For some reason Dr. Carey wants to speak with you before I'm released. I have no idea why," she said coldly.

Henry recognized the tone. She was always angry when she was treated as a lowly woman. She must have taken his request as a slight about her independence. Henry tried to hide his smile as he knew she had probably informed Dr. Carey of the prejudice he was displaying toward her in a very direct manner.

Henry stepped out in the hall where Father Donnelly had already gathered near the doctor.

"I want to thank you, Brendan. I know it was an act of providence for you to be here and be able to call me. It's really miraculous; God breathed this whole situation," Father Donnelly said thankfully.

Dr. Carey was annoyed by people giving thanks to a deity he did not believe in when he was solely to credit.

"Well, I'm just glad I was here. We have to thank our lucky stars, I suppose."

Father Donnelly chuckled, shook the doctor's hand, and said, "I've never seen stars quite this concerned with people before!"

Dr. Carey almost scowled, but he turned to his friend instead.

"May I have a word with you, Henry?"

"Of course," he said.

However, he did not mean it. He could not take any more news from Dr. Carey.

"She says this man who . . . Well, this man, Daire, told her he was her husband. Henry, I wouldn't tell her anything about her past. I'd just let her memory return to her. If you started telling her things, I worry she'll snap. In any case, she seems very unemotional for someone who has gone through so much."

"Thank you very much, my friend, for your concern. I'll certainly take all of this to heart. As far as the lack of emotion is concerned, if she is still the same person I've known, that's just her way of coping. She keeps a stiff upper lip, and then when she feels safe the walls crash down."

"I hope you'll be there when she needs you."

Henry swallowed hard. She had needed him for all these months and he had not been there for her. He looked down at his hat and tried not to cry. The man she had lived with and who had drugged her told her *he* was her husband. Everything in him began to burn with so many emotions—anger, jealousy, and resentment toward that man; and compassion for his wife.

Father Donnelly held Anna's hand as he led her to Henry's car. Everything Father Donnelly seemed to have had once belonged to Henry.

One day, in a moment when Father Donnelly really felt that fact he remarked, "My dear friend, what you've passed down to me is infinitely and eternally more than any car or house could ever be."

Ultimately, Father Donnelly became more at peace with Henry's incredible generosity.

Henry opened the front door of the car for his wife because he knew she got car sick, so he sat in the back as Father Donnelly started the car. The trunk was full of his wife's new things as if they had been on a shopping trip together.

"Well, my dear, you look very sharp, especially next to the likes of us. We had to sleep in our clothes you know," Father Donnelly said. Henry had not really thought about it. Anna smiled with every part of her face—she always did. She turned back around to see the wrinkled shirt Henry wore and gave him a wink and a smile. He thought he might die right then.

Father Donnelly watched his face in the rearview mirror. His friend was extremely quiet, even more than usual.

"Are you two related?" Anna asked as she looked at the two of them more closely.

Father Donnelly was certainly a handsome, older man. His white hair had gold flecks in it, as if a lot of his strawberry blonde had not turned. She knew he was once a very good-looking young man. Henry was much different with his huge shoulders and rugged looks. It took her a while to see it, but he was actually quite good-looking for a priest. She wondered why someone as young as he wanted to be a clergy member.

"No," Father Donnelly gaffed. "Why would you think such a thing?"

"You both have . . . I don't know . . . Similar expressions?"

"Well, we do spend a great deal of time together don't we, Henry?"

Henry smiled into the rearview mirror, and then looked at his wife who had turned around in her seat to see his expression.

"I call Father Donnelly my spiritual father," he said gently.

She smiled sweetly and looked a little longer at him than he could stand right then. Her grey eyes were haunting.

"I'm retired, so they tell me," Father Donnelly continued. "That precious person in the back seat is taking my place."

Anna turned to look at Henry again. He looked back at her with more warmth and kindness than anyone ever had before.

"Why did you decide to go into church work, Father Henry?" she asked.

It took him aback for a moment. She, in fact, was the reason almost entirely.

"My wife—"

"Oh, you're married?" She asked, surprised in many ways.

"His late wife," Father Donnelly added.

Henry glanced at him. Father Donnelly believed in grey areas of the Bible more than anyone he had ever met. Henry was much more black and white. Anna was certainly not his late wife any longer, but Father Donnelly would reason it is better to lie than to hurt someone. So, Henry honored him by not saying anything in front of her.

"She encouraged me to do so," Henry added tenderly. "You see, my wife knew my heart very well. I'd wake her in the middle of the night and tell her I heard God talking to me. She'd never say it was a dream or my imagination. She'd listen."

Henry looked at Anna and lost his train of thought for a moment.

"She'd ask me what He had said and I'd tell her what I *thought* He had said to me. Then, we started journaling it . . . Well, she did. We found God was giving me sermons. We went on a trip to a Christian college in Wales. A man named Reese Howell was there; he really encouraged me. As I prayed more I realized I was called to be a pastor. My wife was a huge part of my ministry. I'm not very outgoing, as you've noticed—she was."

Anna looked at him for a long time and realized he had heard her previous comments about his shyness.

She then said, "I'm sorry for what I said earlier, Henry. There's nothing wrong with being shy."

"I believe hearts, not personalities, are what God calls," Father Donnelly interjected.

Henry became brave as the three-hour car ride continued. Father Donnelly began to fade away and became more of a fixture in the car than a person.

"Anna," Henry began, "I don't want to pry at all, but I want you to have an opportunity while Father Donnelly and I are together to tell us about your time with this Daire fellow. Maybe we can help you if you open up to us."

As Anna stared straight ahead, she told them a little of what had happened to her. She was ashamed of the details, but she shared a small few. Henry balled up his fists and dug his fingernails into his palms until they almost bled as she told one element after another. There was much he preferred not to have heard.

His wife had always been open with him, whether he wanted to hear it or not. He did not imagine, however, her openness with two strangers—of the cloth or not. She seemed to talk to him directly and almost ignored Father Donnelly. She did not even realize she was doing so.

As the car pulled up to the Donnelly's house it was already dark, although it was not quite supper time. Henry remembered the first time he had pulled up to the little cottage. He and Anna had left their stately home and joined the ranks of the wonderful villagers.

"Just let me go talk to my wife, and then I'll come back for you," Father Donnelly said.

He then gave Henry a nod. Sarah waited impatiently on the front stoop. For the entire day, she paid no attention to any work to be done in her little yellow cottage with the window boxes frosted over. She stretched her neck to see her girl—her sweet Anna—alive and well.

She wanted to run to her, to bury Anna in her bosom and cry over her, but she could not. For the first time in her life, Sarah had to gather in her maternal instinct. Henry smiled faintly and realized the torture she endured at that moment.

Finally, Sarah caught sight of Anna and waved fervently. Then, she covered her mouth. Anna waved as a queen might, calm and serene. Father Donnelly took his wife's hands and talked quietly with her.

"My dear, you must not give us away. You must try to be calm," Henry imagined he was saying.

"Father Henry?" Anna said and suddenly broke the silence. He read a slight panic in her voice. He leaned forward.

"I know the Donnellys are the best sort of people . . . I know it. I just can't stay with anyone tonight. I'll be a terrible guest."

"The Donnellys don't stand on formality, Anna."

"It's not that . . . it's just that . . . I've held it together pretty well today—the last couple of hours especially. I didn't want the doctors to think I was mentally incompetent. I have to tell you," she said as she held back tears, "I very much need a place where no one will question why I'm crying. Where I can just—"

Henry put his hand on her shoulder. It was the first time he had touched her since her return.

"I know just the place," he whispered. "Don't worry. I'll take care of it, all right?"

Then, Henry, finally with a sense of knowing what to do for his wife, went and told Father Donnelly and Sarah his plan. Sarah cried a little into her apron as Father Donnelly led her inside before Anna noticed.

Henry climbed in the driver's seat and handed his wife a handkerchief she had embroidered for him last year. She wiped the tears on her face. The stress was finally getting to her.

"We're going to go a stone's throw away, all right? You can have the small apartment that used to be the choir loft in the church."

Anna smiled through her tears. He pulled up to the church minutes later and parked around back where his apartment was located.

"Just give me a minute. I have to get my things," he said.

He left before she told him it was all right and asked him to take her back to the Donnelly's cottage. Henry ran in and looked around his little home. He pulled out his suitcase from underneath the bed and packed the pictures of Anna first. He laid them face down in his case so if she walked in, she would not see them. Then, he ripped off his bed sheets, changed them, put all the clothes he could fit into his suitcase, and looked around again.

"Dear God, please show me anything she might find that won't be good right now," he said aloud.

Then, he remembered the picture of her he kept in his favorite book. He stuffed it in his suitcase as well and shut it. It was just in the nick of time because Anna was already in the doorway.

"I just can't stand the thought of taking your place, Henry!"

"Goodness soul! Of course, you can!" Henry said. "I changed the sheets and there's a bathroom just through there. No one will bother you here."

"Please, I can't let you give up your bed to me," she begged.

Henry walked pass her and said, "I'm getting the better deal. I'm getting what would've been your bed. Sarah is quite the hostess and I'll be a very happy guest."

Anna smiled. He was actually quite funny.

"Well, goodnight," Henry said as he put on his hat.

He hated saying goodnight to her. On their wedding night, he had whispered in her ear, "No more saying goodbye to each other." It had been such a relief to them.

As he closed the door, Anna began to panic. She no longer wanted to cry herself to sleep and let all her emotions go. She did not want to be alone at all and ran to open the door.

"Henry?" she called.

"Yes?" He answered, shocked as he took hold of the car's door handle.

"Where are you going to be again?" She asked unnecessarily.

"At the Donnelly's house," he pointed and knew she did not want him to leave so soon. "Are you hungry?"

"Yes," she said as she realized she had not eaten supper.

"We have a restaurant here," he said proudly. "I'll bring in your things, and then go order something. I'll bring it back to you."

He knew he could not take her anywhere until Father Donnelly had the town meeting the next morning. It was too dangerous. She did not want to go anywhere anyway. The thought of Henry returning, even to simply drop off food, made her feel immediately better.

"That'd be good," she said.

She then realized she had no things to bring in and opened her mouth to tell him so, but he had already hurried to the trunk. Henry tried to see where her packages were in the dark. He finally gathered them in his hands and shuffled around for the little purse Beth had him buy.

He took out his last five pounds and placed them in her purse. Then, he carried in all the packages. Anna stood stunned at her new things which Henry placed before her.

Henry drove off, but forgot to ask Anna what she wanted to eat. He knew her tastes very well, but he did not want her to know. When he arrived at the Blue Door restaurant, the owner came out, greeted him with a kiss to his cheeks, and commented about how long it had been.

Henry blushed and ordered the spinach and ricotta cannelloni. He decided to order lots of sides, a starter, and even dessert. He simply commented about how hungry he was and smiled to himself.

Anna quickly bathed and looked hard at the numbers on her arm. She had not seen them on anyone else, but her and Daire. She wondered, *Did he tattoo me?*

Although the hot water felt wonderful, she dared not take a long bath because Henry would return soon. She went through the bags he had brought in. Beth had thought of everything. She found the most comfortable pants which were slightly too big, the softest sweater, and some socks.

She took the rest of her items out and laid them on the bed. As Anna went through them, it took her mind off all the terrible things she had suffered. She wanted to stay in the very happy moment she was experiencing.

She wanted to look presentable, but she was too exhausted to obsess about how she looked. She decided to try on the rest of the clothes the next day.

She set the little table and wondered where to get another chair. She finally decided to push the table up to the cozy arm chair and give the spot to Henry. He was tall enough to handle it.

In a hurry to get comfortable, Anna occupied her mind. As she sat at the little table, she let her mind wander back to Daire and thought, *What's he thinking?*

He deserved it, of course, after what he had done to her. Still, there was something in her which did not completely believe he had harmed her maliciously. She started a fire in the fireplace and was immediately reminded of the little hovel she had called home. It was even smaller than the old choir room she was in. She thought of the last second before she knew he had medicated her. His face looked so beautiful in the firelight.

The knock at the door startled Anna and her heart fluttered.

"I've brought you spinach cannelloni. I hope you like it. I didn't think to ask before I left and—"

"That'll be fine," Anna said, less enthusiastic than Henry expected.

"Are you all right?" He asked and realized they may not eat together after all.

He had not considered she may want to be alone. His heart began to sink.

"No," she said.

Then, the tears began. Henry stood in the cold since Anna had forgotten to invite him inside. He put the bag of food down, and then offered his hands as he always had to those who wanted prayer. Instead of taking them, Anna embraced him. She thought he had offered to hold her.

What transpired inside Henry was a rush like he had never felt before, not even before she had disappeared. It made him weak and strong at the same time. He held her in his little doorway as the snow whispered in the darkness.

Anna sobbed into his chest. Henry was freezing, but he did not care. Somewhere inside her darkened mind, she knew he was her safe place. Somehow she knew she was loved by him.

"I'm so sorry," she said as she wiped her nose with her sleeve.

"Don't be," Henry barely croaked.

She finally pulled away. Henry almost forgot the food.

"Do you think you can eat?" He asked sheepishly.

"Won't you come in?" she offered.

Never expecting him to say no, Anna's question was casual, but to Henry it was so much more—he had never been alone with a woman his age as a pastor. Henry hesitated for a moment. Then, he smiled and closed the door. He was with his wife, after all.

Anna dished out the food onto plates she had unknowingly received for her wedding. Henry thought about how Sarah had kept most of the set, but insisted Henry take a set for two to eat on.

"These plates are pretty," she commented nonchalantly as she wiped her eyes.

"Here, let me do that," he said tenderly.

He stood and took the dish and spoon from her gently. She gave up the job willingly and sat down in the straight chair. He silently put the food on their plate, and then sat down next to his wife.

He bowed his head. He did not look over to see if she had done the same. He barely choked out a simple prayer.

"Lord, thank you. Amen."

Anna did not notice Henry's slight lack of composure. She was too worried about what he thought of her emotional state.

"It came over me all of a sudden. I'm so sorry," she said, apologetically.

"There's no need to ever apologize to me for showing your feelings," he said.

"I was thinking of Daire and how I can't believe, even after I saw it with my own eyes, he would hurt me intentionally."

"Let me ask you, Anna . . . If you don't believe he was hurting you intentionally, why did you leave? Why didn't you stay and try to find out what he was doing? You said he was a doctor. Could he have been medicating you to help you?"

Henry decided he had lost his mind and thought, *What am I saying?*

In his efforts to get his wife to open up to him, he had created doubt in her mind. She sat silently and pushed around the food on her plate.

"I had these dreams I couldn't shake."

Henry was unprepared for her answer. He stopped his fork midway to his mouth.

"What sort of dreams?" He asked as he tried to hide his surprise by wiping his mouth.

"These wolves were fighting over me and I didn't know which was good or bad. Then, I had these dreams someone was telling me to escape. Do you believe in dreams, Henry?"

"Some," he said modestly.

"What do you think of mine?"

Henry smiled slightly and replied, "I believe God has warned many people in dreams. He warned Joseph, the father of Jesus. That's just one example."

"Do you think it was God warning me?"

"Yes, I do."

Anna breathed deeply and thought it over.

"I don't really know if I believe in God. Am I allowed to say this to a priest?"

Although Henry was shocked by her statement, he answered calmly, "You're allowed to say anything you want to me."

"What's this on my arm? Have you ever seen it before?"

Anna rolled up her sleeve and showed it to him. Henry paused for a longer time than he should have.

"During the war, they often marked people for identification purposes."

"Why don't you have a tattoo?"

"They didn't get to all of us."

"I thought maybe Daire had done it to me."

"No."

Anna gulped. She was tired of talking about herself. She looked at Henry with curiosity.

"Are you from Adare?"

"Yes, my family goes very far back."

Anna wished she knew her family. She wondered if she ever had one.

"Are you close with your family?"

"Not as much as I'd like to be," Henry said.

He smiled sweetly as he tasted his soup. Her grey eyes looked at his until he thought he might bleed pure joy.

"My parents passed away years ago. I have one cousin. We're very close, but she's out of the country right now."

"I'm sorry for that," she said.

"The Donnellys consider me to be an adopted child. Both were married and widowed before; both have lost children. Only Father Donnelly has a daughter left."

"Oh, that's terrible."

"Yes. I've often wrestled with why those kinds of things happen."

Anna wiped an escaped tear from her eye as she recalled her terrible circumstances again. Henry grew extremely brave as he watched her; her pain took hold of him. He reached out and put his hand on hers.

"We'll figure it all out together. You're not alone," he reassured her.

She smiled at him and was thankful. A few more tears streamed down her face.

"Maybe it's because we're the same age or because you're a priest . . . I don't know, but I'm so thankful I have you to talk to right now."

"I'm very glad to be of assistance," Henry said sweetly.

Anna suddenly laughed. There was something about the way he said it which reminded her of a bell boy at a hotel or a gas station attendant.

"You're so funny, Henry," she remarked.

Henry smiled wide. It was not often he was funny, but when he was it was purely accidental.

"Can I tell you something," he asked.

He let his guard down a little. He had fooled himself into thinking he was sharing old times with Anna again.

"Yes," she said through laughter and tears.

"You're the only person who has ever thought I was funny."

She laughed all the more. He wanted to make her laugh, to see the light in her eyes and how happy he made her.

"I love to see you laugh," he said as she winded down. "Maybe I can think of a joke."

Anna laughed again as she tried to imagine Henry telling a terrible joke. Henry was uncertain why, but he laughed, too, and recognized sometimes in times of great stress, little things seem funnier than they truly are. They let go for a moment as they continued to laugh together at the little table.

"Henry," Anna said, "I can't thank you enough."

"No, no, no—" Henry began to retort.

"No, Henry, listen to me. Do you know what the police said? They said I almost died of exposure after I escaped. I had paddled through such cold weather, you know, and found this little house on the water and crawled up to the porch.

"That's all I can remember, but they told me the people didn't come out to help me. They simply called the police. They didn't cover me with a blanket or try to help me in anyway. The people didn't want to get involved. They thought I was a vagrant and didn't want to be endangered."

Henry drew back, quite shocked. He found it hard to imagine not coming to someone's assistance—it was beyond his thought spectrum. He shook his head and fought back tears as he hung his head. He thought of his precious wife not being helped in her greatest hour of need.

"I would've—" he began.

He wanted to rewrite her history for her. He wanted to make her the most loved and cared for human being in the world.

"I know," Anna interrupted. "You're a good man, Henry."

Anna rose and started to clear the dishes, Henry got up to help. Then, she held her head as if she had forgotten something important.

"Henry, I can't believe what all you gave me! Thank you so much. The clothes—everything is beautiful!"

Henry looked her over and marveled at how pretty she looked.

"You look very beautiful," he said.

Anna was surprised. *Henry* was surprised and wanted to kick himself. It was very easy for him to forget he could not say certain things to her.

"I didn't think priests noticed that sort of thing," she said over her shoulder—brazen, yet bashful.

Henry tried to stop his involuntary smile. Anna laughed again. She carried the few dishes to the sink, and then squeezed the leftovers into the tiny ice box. Henry had put in a fresh piece of ice the day before.

She did not want Henry to leave. The Augustinian Priory was away from basically everything. She felt very alone. She was also scared to think and remember.

"Henry, if I need you . . . or Father Donnelly in the night for anything, is there a telephone I can use?"

"No, there isn't. Father Donnelly has a telephone, but the parish does not. Are you afraid to be alone?"

She gulped and nodded. He loved how she was a queen around everyone else and a scared little girl with him. He had an idea.

"I can sleep in the sanctuary. There'd be only the door between us."

"I can't ask you to sleep there."

Henry looked down.

"You kinda are," he said.

Then, he smiled. Anna was mortified at first, but started to laugh again.

"I'm so sorry," she said and reached for his arms, "but will you?"

They laughed longer than necessary, a way to survive the ordeal before them.

"Of course, I will," he finally said.

He did not care if he had to sleep on a bed of nails for Anna. She had asked him to be near her. There was no other place he wanted to be.

"Henry," she said as he opened the door, "what year is it?"

The thought had suddenly occurred to her everything she knew was wrong.

"It's 1947," he replied.

She looked down and pondered, *How old am I?*

Questions started to come at her as fast as darts thrown at a board. Henry decided her silence meant she wanted to be alone. He bid her goodnight once more, and then went into the cool sanctuary. He gathered cushions the ladies had left on the hard pews every Sunday and put them together on the first bench.

He lay down on the make-shift, bumpy bed and stared at the door to Anna's room. He smiled and thought about every word she had said, how she had said them, and her expressions when she spoke. Then, his thoughts took a very dark turn. The thought of another man with his wife haunted him; it fueled his adrenaline so much he was unable to sleep.

Henry fought hard to keep his mind off of it. Instead, he thought about the town meeting the following day. Father Donnelly had not told anyone, but Sarah and the town police about Anna's return. He was nervous and excited about the announcement and wondered, *Will people keep such a secret?*

He thought of the terrible night at Ballybunion Beach where some of them had come to help find Anna. Then, like a gunshot on a still night, a terrible notion went through his mind.

How in the world did Anna end up in Sligo Town?

On the way to Adare, she had told Father Donnelly and Henry she was found on the bank of the lake. He thought, *There's no way she could've floated from Ballybunion to that area. No. She was taken and moved somehow.*

He turned away from the door onto his side and concluded, *Someone must've abducted her. Was it this Daire person? Did he drug her in Ballybunion and put her in that tree?*

A chill ran up his spine. He raced through every possible scenario and tried to think of the least violent way it happened, but no real hypothesis worked.

"God, what happened to my wife?" He asked in frustration as he sat up and rubbed his weary face. "Lord, I need some answers . . . For both of us. Please show me."

Then, Henry remembered driving to Ballybunion to look for her car. He passed about six cars along the way.

Maybe whoever took Anna drove one of them.

He tried to remember what each one looked like, but the night was such a foggy mess. He did not remember details.

In Ireland, it was still dark at eight o'clock the next morning. *Winter is too dark*, Henry thought.

Henry listened at the door to hear his wife stir, but there was heavy silence. He quietly made his way out the door and left a note on the pew where he had slept to tell her he went to shower and change at the Donnelly's cottage.

She needed to sleep as long as possible. He had a terrible headache and wondered if he could even drive the few miles to the house. He rubbed his temples and thanked God he did not have to shovel his car out of the snow.

He turned the heat on full blast and blew into his hands. He looked at the seat she had ridden in the day before and marveled, *She's alive!*

Henry might never totally wrap his mind around this fact. Yet, while her life breathed into his again, there were more questions than answers.

Henry opened the unlocked kitchen door of the Donnelly's cottage and made his way to the guest room with his suitcase in hand. He unpacked, and then ran the shower.

Sarah was silent—much like the morning after she found out her son had died back in London. She did not chase the chickens out of the garden or get angry when her "blasted stove" burned her biscuits yet again. She quietly worked the dough on her wooden counter.

Henry watched Sarah as he ate his oatmeal. He did not feel much like talking either.

"What's with the long faces in here?" Father Donnelly's voice boomed.

His entrance into the kitchen scared them. Neither bid him good morning. It was the first time Henry had been annoyed in a very long time.

Father Donnelly continued merrily, "The town meeting is at ten, my dear, do you think you can occupy Anna?"

"Yes, dear," Sarah said without looking up.

Father Donnelly cleaned his glasses and wondered into the parlor.

She was very happy and excited to see her girl, but the same thoughts Henry had the night before ran through Sarah's mind. She was actually the smartest person Henry had ever met. She tried to hide it as much as possible with her fairy stories and visions of little people.

Sarah enjoyed being Irish so much she believed the stories even more than Henry did. Often, she and Henry talked about the little people who seemed to misplace things. The two of them sometimes got so wrapped up in their musing it drove Father Donnelly crazy.

She also had a way of seeing the beauty in everything. She had turned a small thimble into a beautiful stool for one of the fairy houses in the garden. It was rare she threw anything away, as she always found uses for things.

Sarah washed her hands in the large, white sink after she put the bread in the stove. Henry smelled the fragrant lavender soap as it overtook the aroma of his oatmeal. He loved how everything Sarah did was beautiful, even how she washed her hands. She made anything pretty.

He remembered the day he gave Father Donnelly and Sarah his house after Anna had disappeared. Sarah cried into her apron and commented on its beauty. Anna had done a beautiful job decorating the little cottage, but Sarah somehow made it homier. Henry smiled warmly at her when she turned around.

"I love you," she said more with her eyes than her words. "You're my boy."

Sarah kissed his forehead.

"Are you nervous?" Henry finally asked; his voice raspy and tired.

She poured him a cup of tea and said, "Very."

It was not like her to be at a loss for words.

The town emerged seemingly at once from their cottages and apartments above stores. The word had spread the night before about an unscheduled town meeting and everyone wanted to know what the fuss was about. Henry looked at his watch—it was already a quarter of ten.

He abruptly got up and grabbed his keys. He had to see if Anna was awake for the drive back to the Donnelly's cottage for breakfast with Sarah.

When he arrived at the priory, Henry knocked quietly and the door flung open. He looked at Anna, a vision in the white sweater Beth had picked out. He smiled shyly.

"Are you hungry, Anna?" he asked.

"Starving!" She answered and grabbed her purse.

He opened the car door for her, and then walked around the car to sit next to her. He nervously fumbled with his keys for a few seconds.

"Sarah is anxious to see you. I believe you two will get along quite well."

"Oh, I'm sure we will," she said brightly.

However, inside Anna felt strange like an eerie fog at night. Henry wanted to tell her she did not have to pretend with him, but decided to wait until another time. She looked out her window to see the townspeople walking down the street. They were headed to the Village Hall where a few cars and horse and carriages were parked, and a crowd of people talked outside.

"What's happening?" She asked as she stepped out of the car upon their arrival.

"There's a town meeting this morning," Henry replied as he tried to usher her into the house quickly.

"What's it about?"

"They call one every so often. People have disagreements and things to talk over," Henry said honestly.

Sarah could wait no longer —she had waited long enough. She bounded out of the kitchen door and before Anna knew it, she was caught up in her loving arms.

"It's wonderful to see you!" She said as she held back tears.

Anna was a little shocked by her greeting, but managed to accept her embrace. She looked playfully at Henry who shrugged with a smile.

"I'm so glad you're here because one of those dumb meetings was called and I'll be lonesome."

"You don't go to them?"

"Of course, I don't. I'm no busybody!" Sarah replied.

Henry knew better. She winked at him over her shoulder and he got back into the car.

"Henry, are you going?" Anna asked, surprised.

"Oh, he has to, dear, being the priest and all," Sarah answered for him.

Anna was disappointed not to share another meal with her new friend. Henry would have spread wings and flown if he had known about her disappointment; however, he did not read women well.

The town meeting was full of excited villagers who were confused about the announcement Father Donnelly was to make. It was the only information they had been told and prematurely guessed it something wonderful or something to anger them. Attendees sat down with their preconceived attitudes and waited as Father Donnelly brought the meeting to order. A few folding chairs squealed across the white-tiled floors as people adjusted their seating.

"Let's pray," Father Donnelly said. "Father, grant us the wisdom and solidarity to deal with this incredible miracle you've brought us. Amen."

Everyone looked at each other. Never was there a more brief prayer from their former pastor. Father Henry sat in the front row nervously, and crossed and uncrossed his long legs. He looked over at and nodded to the Catholic priest, Father O'Dell, who had baptized him as a babe. Henry still felt a fondness for the man, although he was stern.

Father Donnelly firmly disagreed with Henry's appraisal of the man. He had been far too open with Father O'Dell about his political views and even almost came to blows with him about ten years ago. Henry chuckled inwardly at the thought of two priests battling it out.

Father Donnelly began, "I'm sure you all are wondering why we're here, gathered on a Thursday at ten o'clock in the morning."

"Of course, we are. Get on with it, will 'ya?" Someone called out.

Everyone laughed. Father Donnelly held his hand up for peace and closed his eyes in disgust.

"Yesterday, Father Henry and I were called to Sligo Town to minister at the hospital there. Henry's childhood friend had become alarmed about a patient he had who had lost her memory."

Father Donnelly stopped so everyone took in what he had just said.

"The friend had thought the patient could possibly be Father Henry's late wife, Anna."

The audience gasped and looked at Henry. He kept his head down and focused on his hands.

Father Donnelly continued, "On close inspection, we immediately knew . . . It's, in fact, Anna."

The townspeople erupted in whispers.

"Please!" Father Donnelly urged quietness to hear him out.

Finally, the crowd calmed down to the point one was able to hear a pin drop.

"She has no recollection of her life here. An unidentified man had found her, according to Anna, three weeks prior and cared for her. She believes he drugged her for whatever reason, we know very little details. She doesn't know about her life before then. The thing is, my friends, she's scared. We have not told her of her past life with us. She doesn't even remember Henry."

Everyone looked in Henry's direction again. Gasps were heard and a few women wiped away tears. They all sat on the edge of their seats.

"What our dear Henry is asking is . . . For us to treat her as a stranger. We need to be friendly and helpful, but please, we beg you not to tell her prematurely anything about who she really is or that any of us know her. The doctor has specifically asked us to do this. He told me he believes her memory will eventually return and that'll be traumatic enough."

Father Donnelly was particularly concerned about a few women who had always wanted to be the one to tell something. It annoyed him when someone did not hold something in confidence.

"Our police here," he started and glanced at the heavy-set police who sat behind Henry.

Everyone grumbled for they despised Officer Hamm for his laziness. His last name was fodder for jokes since his childhood. He was known as a very lazy, portly man. Even Father Donnelly had said Officer Hamm was in "a perpetual state of hibernation."

"Our officer has agreed to arrest anyone who tells Anna anything prematurely without Henry's sole permission!"

Father Donnelly looked down and smiled at Officer Hamm who was startled. He was not sure if Father Donnelly was joking or not until he heard Henry chuckle underneath his breath.

Some townspeople laughed a little as well while others finally realized Father Donnelly had tried to create a moment of levity in their very serious situation. Father Donnelly grinned to himself, and then continued.

He said somberly, "She does know her name, so you may call her Anna. Just please don't tell her anything more. Remember, your compliance with this request is very important to me, especially to Henry."

Father Donnelly adjusted his stance and tone.

"There isn't anyone who has not been touched by Henry's and Anna's story. There isn't one of us who has not felt their generosity or love. I beg you, please do this for them. I'll be here to answer any questions I can after we convene, but Henry . . . Henry's leaving to take his wife out."

Henry was flabbergasted by his friend's remark. Henry looked up at his friend.

"I'll be taking over as rector for a little while as Henry takes care of Anna."

They had not discussed any of what Father Donnelly had just said. Henry disliked when Father Donnelly took charge, but inside he knew it was best and decided to let it go. He rose quickly and exited the hall before anyone caught up to him.

How can I concentrate on anything, but Anna?

Sarah sat in the parlor with her tea cup in her hand and the saucer in her lap. Anna mimicked her motions. They sat quietly and listened to the tick of the clock Anna had always hated. For once, Sarah had absolutely no idea what to say. They had run out of niceties before Anna had finished her apple turnover.

Anna looked up at the exquisite painting above the fireplace, and then Sarah met her gaze. It was an oil painting of a woman who gathered wheat in her apron. The woman walked away from the painter, but looked back.

Sarah smiled and asked, "Do you like it?"

"Very much," Anna said, pleased to have something to talk about. "I feel like the lady in the painting. I'm trying to find small strands of clues about my life and gathering them one-by-one. Her fist is tightly holding her apron. It's as if what she holds is life and death to her."

"Yes, I believe it is. The woman in the painting is Ruth," she began.

However, they heard someone enter through the kitchen door and slosh through the house with snowy boots. Sarah lost her cool for a moment.

"Thad Donnelly! Don't come in this house with those wet boots!" she yelled.

Henry peaked around the door frame and apologized, "I'm sorry."

He had forgotten, probably for the first time, to be respectful of Sarah's floor.

"Oh, my dear, I'm sorry I yelled."

"I deserved it," he said as he smiled and kissed her cheek.

"Do you want me to clean it?" he asked.

"Clean it? Of course, I don't, you scoundrel. See to Anna. Thad tells me you're taking her away from town for the day," she whispered. "I think it's best until everyone starts getting used to things."

Sarah left the room and Henry took in the scent of apples and cinnamon in the air. Anna smiled when she saw him. He stood with his hat in his hands and his boots melting puddles onto Sarah's clean floor.

"I was wondering if you'd like to go out for the day," he began, more nervous than the first time he had ever seen her.

"Yes," she said plainly.

He lit up. He was not the most romantic of fellows, but, at least, it was a plan.

"There's a really good library in Shannon. Are you at all curious about some things?"

Henry fiddled with his hat.

"Oh, yes, I am . . . Thank you!"

"Maybe we can have some lunch and if you need anything there, we can get it."

"Henry, you've already been so generous."

"Let him buy you things, girl! He has more money than you think!" Sarah called from the kitchen.

Anna blushed. Henry might have killed Sarah if he was not so happy. Anna gathered her coat and walked through the kitchen with Henry.

"It never hurts to tell the girl your assets," Sarah whispered.

She gave Henry a light swat on his backside.

He thought, *She's back to her old self again.*

Anna giggled as she slid into Henry's car. Sarah loved to embarrass him, especially in front of Anna. She loved how he turned ten shades of red when she said anything off color. Henry was always so appropriate and serious. It was "good for him to get messed up," as Sarah often said. Henry sighed and shook his head.

"It'll take about a half hour," Henry said when he changed gears.

"How did the meeting go?"

"I believe well. I left early."

"Were there a lot of problems to be solved?"

"No," he said, and then turned to smile at her.

"Mrs. Donnelly seems to be a very quiet person," Anna remarked.

Henry chuckled.

"What?"

"She's actually quite the opposite."

"Why are you taking me to the library? Are there things you'd like for me to see?"

"I got concerned last night when you asked me what year it was. What did you think the year was?"

"I'm not sure."

"Do you remember anything at all?"

"I remember so much from my school lessons, but I don't know who taught me or where or really anything beyond that. Can you explain that?"

"I can't explain any of this," Henry said solemnly. "Anna . . . I'd have asked immediately, but I didn't want to be out of place on this. We have a wonderful doctor in our little town: Dr. Lannon. He has lived in Adare his whole life, but he studied in America. If you want, I can get him to come see you to assess the situation."

Anna thought for a moment. She doubted a doctor in a small town was much good to her, but she finally thanked Henry for the thought and agreed to it. Henry knew if he had arranged a visit without asking her, she might have been furious. He loved the way his wife was so fiery, but he was scared of her at the same time.

Henry stopped the car in front of a drugstore and told her they needed sunglasses. Henry had noticed Anna constantly shading her eyes from the sun as it bounced off the white snow. He had remembered her complaint about her eyes in the hospital and was concerned.

She picked out a fashionable pair of white ones and Henry picked up the first aviator shades he found.

"Is there anything else you need?" he asked.

Anna shook her head, too embarrassed to tell him about the other items. Before they left, she had opened her purse and expected it to be empty. However, she found he had put five pounds in it. She wanted to buy anything else she needed in town herself.

The library was not as busy as Henry had thought it would be, so he left Anna to look around while he took out an old theology book and sat down at an empty table. He watched her closely as she went through the newspaper racks. She pulled out a few, and then sat at a table alone not too far from him.

Anna was lost in thought, so he did not hold it against her when she had not sat beside him. He tried to concentrate on his book about St. Augustine, or Auggie, as he was affectionately called. Henry loved Augustine's testimony—he was rough and honest.

However, nothing really peaked his interest quite like watching his wife's long black tendril escape and fall into her face while she poured over the newspapers. She brushed it out of the way, blew it out of the way, tried to pin it out of the way, but all attempts were useless. He found the entire scene mesmerizing.

A small group of young men whispered near Anna. Finally, one was nudged out and went to Anna in a stealth-like manner. It was as if he was afraid he might scare her off.

"Hi, there," the young man whispered.

He was tall and gangly. Henry watched him, unblinking. Anna looked up.

"I'm Tim and those are my mates over there. We were wondering if you know where the nearest pub is."

"No, I'm sorry, I don't. I'm new to the area as well."

"Oh, well, actually, that was a line . . . It desperately didn't work," he admitted.

Anna giggled.

"I don't suppose you'd be interested in trying to find a pub together, would you?"

"Thank you very much, but I have a lot of reading to do."

"Oh, okay," Tim said.

He went back to his friends who snickered and punched him playfully on the arms. Henry was relieved. He was not use to witnessing such things, although Anna had often told him about instances when she was by herself and it had happened. He guessed his large shoulders and intimidating glances had kept a lot of men at bay as he walked with her.

She had often commented his collar scared most of them more than his physical attributes—to which he smiled. She always knew how to joke with him. Men often showed affection by making fun of each other—so did she.

Anna got up, locked eyes with Henry, and walked toward him. She never had any idea what her gaze did to him.

"Are you ready to go?" she asked.

He closed his book and followed her out of the library as he thought, *Something's wrong. Something's very wrong.*

Anna got into the car and held her purse in her lap. She looked more put together than ever. When she was unhappy, she often worked on her appearance longer than when she was happy—she was overcompensating.

"I'm not in the paper," she said frankly.

Henry frowned and tried to make sense of what she meant.

"You'd think someone found without memory would be mentioned in the paper."

"It may have been in the Sligo Town paper," Henry said.

"I looked there."

Henry did not know what she meant.

"It's as if someone decided no one needed to know about me."

"Maybe there were other things which outweighed—"

"There's an article about a chicken farmer on the first page," she said.

Henry smiled.

"Do you think this is funny?"

"I have no idea what's wrong."

"Henry, let me ask you something. Do you think I'm stupid?"

"Of course not," Henry said nervously.

"Did you have them keep it out of the papers?"

"No, but Dr. Carey might have."

"Why?"

"Because," he shifted in his seat, keys still in hand, "Anna, we don't know who this person was who had you for three weeks. He could be looking for you. Dr. Carey was worried about your safety, I'm sure."

Henry made an assumption.

"Henry, why isn't anyone looking for me?"

The question stabbed him deeply.

"Why aren't there posters everywhere with my face on them or ads in the paper? Why aren't there pictures of me in the police station as a missing person?" Anna asked in frustration and sobbed.

"We'll figure this out together," Henry said and tried to comfort her.

"Was the town meeting about me today?" she asked.

Henry thought for a moment and admitted, "Yes."

She looked at him surprised.

"This is a very small town, Anna. We wanted everyone to treat you very kindly."

"Then why wasn't I introduced?" She asked vehemently.

"We will. We just wanted everyone to be aware you'd be with us for a while."

Henry was almost breathless. He had forgotten how she noticed everything. He hated to keep things from her, especially things this important, but he had agreed with the doctor. It was too much of a shock and there was hope her memory might soon return.

Anna reached for Henry's hand. Tears streamed down her face. They looked down at their intertwined hands.

"I'm sorry," she said. "I'm very frustrated."

"I know."

Henry found a small café with white linen on the tables. There was a glass refrigerator filled with a hundred different pastries.

"I'd like very much to skip lunch and go straight for dessert," Anna kidded.

"Then, that's what we'll do," Henry agreed and handed the menu back to the waiter who approached them when they were seated.

Anna gasped in pretentious disbelief, and then teased, "Well, rector, that's a bold move."

"Oh, you have no idea," he said as he awkwardly flirted with his wife.

"We have a sample plate of the pastries," the waiter said.

Anna nodded her head and Henry agreed.

"Then, I'll bring you two teas to start."

"Henry, can I ask you something?"

"Anything."

She grew a little serious and asked, "Are you trying to court me?"

He sat back in his chair. He gathered his courage as much as possible and asked, "What if I am?"

"I wish you wouldn't," she said very forthcoming.

"All right," Henry said and wished she had not been so frank. *It'll be a long lunch and ride home.*

"It's not that. Henry, don't . . . Don't take it like that. It's just that I'm in desperate need of a friend right now. Do you understand?"

"I'll always be your friend."

They looked at each other for a long time.

Anna added, "I want to be your friend. I just don't want you to read into it."

"No, no, goodness soul. I won't do that," Henry lied for the first time in years.

"I'm so scared, Henry. Will you hold my hand through all of this?"

Henry thought about all the moments he had held his wife's hand. He smiled inwardly.

"Do you want to know the truth?" she asked.

He wanted to scream, *No, no! I don't want to know the awful truth! I want to stay in my world where you're my angel and you've never sinned!*

"I told you to tell me anything."

"I don't deserve a man like you."

"You don't know me."

"Yes, Henry, I think I do."

"You've known me for what two, three days—," Henry started.

He tried not to cry in front of her. He hated his emotions, so he gulped them down and looked around at the restaurant in an effort to seem casual.

"You're not hard to figure out, Henry," she said.

He was insulted. He wanted to be wild, strong, and brave with her. He wanted to be her fighter, lover, and best friend. He wanted to be unpredictable and romantic. Yet, he was only one thing to Anna: a very faithful, new friend. He had to accept this terrible fact.

"There's a lot you don't know about me," he argued.

"Oh, I know!" she said. "I just mean—"

"It's all right. I know what you meant."

Their pastries came and the waiter picked up on the change in atmosphere.

"Do you want to see a menu after all?" He asked when they frowned as the delectable plate was put before them to share.

"This'll be fine, thank you," Anna said sadly.

Henry unwrapped a small slice of chocolate cheesecake and looked at Anna. He knew it was her favorite.

"That looks good," she said as she eyed the cake.

"It does, doesn't it?" Henry agreed.

He looked at her again as she perused the plate of goodies.

"I know you want this, Anna."

"No, I don't," she retorted.

"I'll make a deal with you. I'll give you this cheesecake if you promise me you'll go back to being light-hearted."

Anna smirked and said, "I don't think that's possible. You've forever ruined me and now I'll go lock myself in a dungeon and waste away."

"Well now, that's too bad."

He took a small bite of the cheesecake. Anna's eyes grew big.

"Mm. Change your mind?"

She smiled.

"I thought you'd come to your senses," he said and put the slice on her plate.

She looked at him and he winked at her.

"I think we need a rule."

"I hate rules," she said.

"Well, this one is a good one. We aren't allowed to talk of anything icky today."

"Did you just say *icky?*" She asked and laughed. "I've never heard a grown man say icky."

"Well, get used to it. It made you laugh, so it's now my favorite word."

Henry knew how to draw Anna out of a funk.

After eating, Henry started the car, and then put his hand on the seat. He cleared his throat and waited. They had spent the last bit of the lunch laughing until they were almost sick. Anna realized he waited for something.

"What?" She finally asked.

"I was informed not too long ago you'd like to hold my hand. If I can't court you, as you say, at least hold up the bargain we've struck."

Anna laughed hard and held her forehead. She slid her hand into his. Henry smiled and drove home.

"Okay, but not in front of anyone, all right?" She said about their hand holding.

"Then, every time there's no one watching, your hand has to be in mine."

"It's settled."

"I have a few demands myself."

"Go on."

"You're not allowed to ogle me the way you do in public," Henry teased.

Anna laughed again and promised, "I'll try very hard not to."

It had been a good idea for Henry to take Anna out when he had because a mob had descended upon Father Donnelly to ask a multitude of questions he was not prepare to answer. He was exhausted by noon as he slowly made his way back home. He finally returned to the shelter of his cottage where he spent the remainder of the day.

Henry held the kitchen door open for Anna when they returned to the Donnelly's house unannounced. Sarah heard them and quickly went to lock the guest room where Henry had haphazardly taken out all of his wife's pictures. Father Donnelly napped in his chair.

"Did you have a good time, dears?" Sarah asked.

"Yes," Anna replied pleasantly.

"If I'm lucky, Anna might let me actually sleep in a bed tonight," he said without thinking.

Anna turned bright red. Sarah smiled.

"I mean, I slept on the pew . . . Oh, never mind."

"I think I'll be fine, *Father* Henry," Anna replied and tried to signal he needed to be more formal around other people.

"You want to stay in my apartment again?" He asked hesitantly.

"If you don't mind," she said.

Sarah left the couple to see what her husband was up to.

"I'll sleep anywhere you want me to," he whispered into her ear.

She looked at him wide-eyed and he asserted, "Oh, you know what I mean! I don't mind being on the pew, I was just teasing."

"I know," she whispered.

"You're coming back for supper?" Sarah asked them as she returned to the kitchen.

"Actually, I thought we'd eat in again," he said.

Sarah looked up at him startled. It was unlike Henry to refuse an invitation.

"Oh, so my food isn't good enough?" She asked, slightly offended because she wanted to spend time with Anna as well.

"It's not that," Henry replied.

"Well, what is it, then?" She asked, unrelenting.

"Mrs. Donnelly," Anna began, "I don't think you've noticed, but Henry's desperately in-love with me and constantly wants to be alone with me. I really think Father Donnelly needs a private word with him. After all, is it really kosher for a priest to be alone in the bed chambers of a young woman such as I being so confused and upset?"

Henry's mouth dropped open. Anna winked.

"Henry!" Sarah slapped him with her dish towel.

Then, he began to snicker.

"You see, Mrs. Donnelly, he portrays this unassuming character who's shy and sweet. But, he's really quite dangerous to be around. I've feared for my innocence twice today alone."

Sarah laughed as well. It was ridiculous.

"Hey, now, I can be foreboding!" Henry finally said in his defense.

"Yeah, sure," Sarah said.

Henry drove Anna to his apartment. He ensured she took his hand before he pulled away.

"I'll see you tonight," he said and he left.

Anna chuckled to herself as she freshened up and began perusing Henry's extensive library which covered an entire wall. The books were mostly about theology or archeology. There were some pretty thick books which read: Old Testament Survey on the cover. She marveled at the amount of study which it took to be a preacher.

A knock on the door startled her. She felt like she had been snooping and was found out. She went to the door, expecting Henry, but instead there was a small, older man who carried a black case. She was drawn to the door.

"Hello," said the man, "I'm Dr. Lannon. Father Henry told me you'd like to me to talk with you."

"That was fast. I just told him it was all right this afternoon."

"Well, I believe he's quite worried."

"Come in," she said warmly.

"Let's sit and chat for a moment, all right?" He suggested so Anna was less nervous.

He pulled up his pants legs and sat in the cushioned chair.

"Tell me, is there anything at all you remember save the last three weeks? Any memory, as faded as it may be?"

"No."

"All right, can you answer a few physical questions for me?"

Anna answered Dr. Lannon's questions. He was not too alarmed by her responses. She seemed in good health. Everything she told him might have been caused by her stressful situation.

"I want you to be comfortable to tell me about anything that arises. I'm going to write, with your permission, a few associates who've dealt with this sort of condition."

"That'd be fine," she agreed.

"I'd like to ask you something for my benefit, Anna. This man you lived with, is he someone the authorities should search for? Is he someone who has harmed you or you believe can harm you?"

Anna did not want to tell Dr. Lannon too much, but he needed to know.

"He drugged me."

"Yes, I've heard Henry say as much," he admitted.

Anna grew hot with anger and thought, *Henry had no right.*

"Please, I can see you're getting upset. Henry didn't want to divulge anything, but I insisted he tell me everything he knew before I agreed to take you on as a patient. I was apprehensive about it because I'm not a neurologist, you see."

"I don't know if the drug he gave me caused my—"

"Amnesia."

"Yes."

"Well, it's possible, although not likely. If it was drug-induced, it'd be out of your system or, at least, less effective on your system by now. You don't seem to have any recollection as of yet."

"So, that's bad news?"

"Yes. It's not good news."

"What do you think caused it then?"

"Well, the hospital said there was no trauma to your head, which would've been my first guess. It's possible trauma can cause amnesia—you went through quite an ordeal."

When he thought further about what could have caused Anna's amnesia, his blood ran cold.

"You think someone hurt me?"

"Yes."

"Is this something I'd want to forget?"

"Yes, if it was bad enough. The human brain shuts down so we can cope. It's a little like when you're upset, laugh, or smile. It's a mechanism you have to deal with things . . . So they don't overwhelm you."

"That makes a lot of sense, but it also makes me feel very nervous about what it could be."

"The fellow you stayed with . . . Do you believe he'd harm you?"

Anna thought hard and sighed, "I don't know."

"Well, what we'll do together is research all we can. We'll do it together, all right? Meanwhile, if anything at all changes or comes back to you, I'd like to know."

Anna thanked Dr. Lannon for his visit and he left. She lay down on the bed and decided not to be angry with Henry. She needed to not skip through her emotions like they were rocks on a river. She had to gather herself to be more like he was.

"Hi," Henry said when he returned to his apartment with a bag of food that evening.

"Hi," Anna replied.

As they worked together to set the plates, they brushed against each other. Then, they sat and looked one another. Henry grinned, Anna looked at him in awe. He was not the same man she had met days ago. He was bold and full of life.

"It didn't take very long for you to open up," she remarked.

"Well, I guess you have a way of bringing out the worst in me," he joked.

He set out the homemade tomato pie Sarah had made. Anna went to find something to scoop it out with. It was still warm and had not solidified.

"I haven't yet seen you eat meat. How does a guy with your stature live without it?"

"One day at a time," he kidded.

"Seriously, Henry."

"I gave it up to the Lord. I fast it."

"Whatever for?"

"Well. There's a story."

"I'm listening."

"I don't want to speak about it."

Anna sighed, exasperated. Henry looked up at her with a playful smirk. Yet, it was the truth. He did not want to tell her.

"Henry, I've been thinking. Maybe I'd like a job."

"You're still recovering. You've only been here for a few days, Anna, I don't know how wise that is."

"Thank you for the pounds you put inside my purse and all you've given me. Henry, I don't want to rely on you."

Henry thought about what she said. He wanted her to take and continue to take from his hand—he had enough money. She was his wife and Henry wanted Anna to totally depend upon him.

"What would you like to do?" he asked.

"I don't know. You know this town. Maybe someone needs help?"

Henry thought. He was not aware of anyone who did.

"I'll see what I can do," he said as he racked his brain.

Then, Anna served the tomato pie in heaps with a giggle. She dropped half of Henry's slice on the table and laughed harder.

"It tastes better than it looks," he said.

Anna poured water from a pitcher and commented, "I haven't seen you drink alcohol either. Is that another story you don't want to share?"

Henry nodded. There was so much he did want to say, but he could not.

"Okay, Henry, this is one question you have to answer. I was joking at the Donnelly's, but it's a little weird. How is it a member of the clergy can eat dinner alone with a young woman?"

Henry almost choked on his water and answered, "The fortunate thing about this particular parish is it's out of everyone's eyesight. Besides, I think this is a very different case."

She did not answer and waited for more.

"Do you want me to stop?"

"No, it's not that. I know pastors are usually very careful to keep up appearances."

"And how do you know that?"

She could not answer.

"Jesus was friends with women."

"Does the Bible say he ate dinner alone with them?" Anna inquired as she cut a tomato with her knife.

"It's possible."

Anna made a dubious face. Henry reached out his hand.

Anna asked, "Do you expect me to hold your hand and eat at the same time?"

"No, I want to pray with you for our dinner."

Anna looked at his untouched plate.

"Oh," she chuckled.

"God," Henry prayed, "bless us as you have every moment we've been together. Thank you for the food. Bless it to us. Amen"

After his prayer, Henry did not let go of Anna's hand and she snickered as he made a mischievous face. They ate quickly; they were hungrier than they had thought. Their lunch in Shannon had not been enough for either of them.

Once they had finished their dinner, Anna cleaned up and commented about the leftovers from the night before when she crouched down to make room in the icebox. He smiled and remembered Anna organizing their refrigerator many times.

Shortly thereafter, Henry put on his coat; he did not want to overstay his welcome. Anna did not share her visit from Dr.

Lannon with him which was a disappointment, but he had no right to pry.

"Are you leaving?" she asked.

"I simply want to keep up appearances. I can't stay alone in this little apartment with a young woman such as you."

"Such as me, huh?" She said, a little hurt.

"No, no, I just meant . . . Anna, you're the most beautiful."

Henry cleared his throat and began to button his coat. He did not believe what he had said.

She smirked and repeated, "The most beautiful what?"

"Just that . . . The most beautiful."

He lowered his head as he finished buttoning his coat. He went back into his shell. He had to break back out if he wanted to win her heart. He knew the next day she would be debuted to the whole village. He worried some of the men might not respect his prior claim to her.

Uncomfortable, she started to stop him, "Henry—"

"Anna, we're friends."

"Of course, we are."

"Well, it's just . . . How will I know if you ever want more than that? I'm not very good at reading people."

Again, he did not believe what he had said. He was going too fast.

"Henry, I . . . I have had a lot to take in. Please don't push me."

His heart broke.

"I'm so sorry. I don't know what I was thinking when I said that," he apologized, more angry with himself than he ever thought possible.

Henry opened the door and walked out. Anna felt a quickening in her heart and called after him. He turned around, four feet into the darkness. The snow fell fast and his breath formed a cloud around his red face.

She called out, "I'll kiss you."

What does she mean? Does she want me to kiss her now?

Anna clarified, "When I want more, I'll kiss you."

Henry smiled faintly, but found it hard to believe her. He took a step toward her.

"Let me clarify here," he began.

She laughed as she held onto the door.

"*You'll* kiss *me?*" he confirmed, "So, it won't be your face is close and you have that look in your eye kind of thing for *me* to kiss *you?* I'm no good at figuring out that sort of thing either."

"Nope!"

"*You'll* kiss *me?* How about that," he said to himself and put on his hat.

He turned toward his car, but then turned to watch as she closed the door and heard her lock it. He turned back to his car, but then decided to walk—rather run—because he suddenly had so much energy.

Henry tried to wipe the smile off his face with his hand, but he could not. Anna was falling for him—he knew she was. Within days of knowing him, it was happening all over again.

He was so lost in his thoughts, he ran pass their house a few blocks.

"What on earth?" Sarah said with a start as Henry opened the kitchen door abruptly.

Snow and darkness framed his silhouette as he held up his hands like a champion. She stopped kneading dough and watched him, awestruck.

"She's falling for me," he announced without holding anything back.

"It's been three days, Henry," she said "The girl is scared to death and only trusts you."

"Exactly," Henry said

He took off his coat and plopped on a stool. Sarah rolled her eyes and thought, *He isn't listening. It's not like Henry.*

"Now, you listen to me," she said as she shook her rolling pin at him. "You need to back off!"

"She's my wife!"

"No, she's not. She doesn't know you from Adam. You need to give that girl some breathing room."

"Some breathing room?" Henry said in disbelief. "This is the first real bit of happiness I've known in a very long time."

"My dear, please," Father Donnelly said as he entered the room. "We already discussed this."

"Well, I don't think it's right . . . The way he's going after her."

"I'm not—" Henry protested like a teenager to his parents.

Father Donnelly put his hands on Henry's shoulders and stood behind Henry. He watched his jealous wife aggressively roll her dough.

"Henry, keep making yourself available to Anna. Go on a walk with her every day or something, but you have to back off the dinners alone."

Henry knew he was right. Anna was already suspicious. It did not mean he liked it, though. Henry was obsessed with being near Anna; he wanted to kiss her and never stop. That was what he wanted, but he knew his heart was not exactly practical.

Father Donnelly retreated into the parlor and Henry followed. He lit his pipe, and then looked at Henry.

"My boy, we have to be moderate. We must give her space."

Henry imagined some of the backlash from Sarah was his refusal of her dinner invitation. He was being selfish. Sarah needed time with Anna as well. They were as close as two people ever were and had a history beyond Henry.

"Forgive me," he finally said as his thoughts and passion settled.

"There's absolutely nothing to forgive," Father Donnelly insisted.

Henry smiled at how Father Donnelly had said it—forceful and sure of himself.

"Now, my wonderful boy, let's set up a plan for you, shall we? I think we need to get our heads in gear. You turned your brain off the moment you saw her."

Henry knew that was not true. He had thought and meditated on so much since he first saw Anna three days ago. One thought plagued him: *who was the man she was with?*

He thought of a stranger touching his wife, holding her, kissing her. It was more than he could deal with, so he pushed the thought away repeatedly. However, it came back and ate at his happiness like locust.

CHAPTER 21

HENRY WALKED TO HIS APARTMENT in the morning. He
was not quite as full of energy as he had been when he had left
her the night before. Father Donnelly had calmed him.

Henry had already accomplished so much that morning, although it was early. He knocked on the door and Anna greeted him
with a smile. His heart soared again with one look into her eyes.

"Have mercy," he whispered into the air as she walked away to
get her coat and purse.

He closed his eyes to still his feelings and thought, *Is it me or is
she even more beautiful?*

She was supposed to eat breakfast with the Donnellys. Sarah had
insisted. Anna got inside the cold car and wondered why it was
not warmer. She did not realize Henry had run to the Donnelly
home the previous night.

He started the car and thanked God he did not have to dig
it out of the snow. He did not say anything or offer his hand to
Anna as they rode in silence. Anna knew something was up and
grabbed his hand on the steering wheel. He did not have the heart
to pull it back.

"Are you all right?"

"Yes, yes, of course," he reassured her as he tried to slow his heart
rate. "I actually have good news for you. I talked with the florists
in town and they're going to let you work there."

"Oh, Henry, that's wonderful! I love flowers!"

"Well, I thought you might like the company as well. It's owned by twin sisters with red hair. They're about your age and very sweet girls."

"This is great news. When do I start?"

Henry had not thought of that small detail.

He had gone over to the florist shop and rang their upstairs bell since they were not yet open for business. He did not know whether Clara or Cara had greeted him. He could never tell them apart.

They had solemnly told him they were unable to hire anyone. Although they swore never to admit it, they were actually quite concerned they had lost him as their best customer. He had kept them in business with his extraordinary floral purchases. Even before Anna had seemingly died, he filled her house with flowers daily.

His offer, though, to pay Anna's salary was more than generous. He also added he wanted her to take a bouquet home daily.

"Just tell her it's part of the pay for the job," he suggested.

Clara, and Cara,—who had joined the conversation as soon as she heard Father Henry's voice—were thrilled. The twins were romantics who were in a vast company of women who secretly wanted to be loved the way Father Henry loved his wife. He gave them a month's salary and separate payment for his daily purchase of flowers. They hugged each other when he left.

Henry also hoped the opportunity presented Anna with some friends. Even though she was known and loved by all when they were married, she had few close friends.

"On Monday," Henry blurted.

Anna clapped her gloved hands and squealed.

"But, Anna, your needs are already taken care of. What'll you spend the money on?"

"Do you expect me to live in your apartment and eat Mrs. Donnelly's food the rest of my life?"

He laughed and thought of the terrible meal they had shared. "I should say not."

"Then stuff it, Henry," she said jokingly.

Anna took off her coat inside and Sarah kissed the "poor dear who had to freeze in this terrible cold." Sarah kissed Henry's face, too. He excused himself immediately to give the ladies time together and headed for the shed.

"I made your favorite!" Sarah said with cheer.

"My favorite?" Anna asked.

Did I let the cat out of the bag already?

"Oh, I was speaking to Thad. Is he not here?"

Anna seemed to buy her explanation.

"I haven't seen him," she answered.

Sarah was thankful to think on her feet so quickly. She pulled popovers out of the oven and put the strawberry butter in a pretty dish. Then, she poured Anna some tea and sat beside her at the dining room table. Sarah folded and played with her napkin nervously.

"Have you lived here your whole life?" Anna asked.

"No, I'm sure you can tell by my accent I haven't. I was born here, but I went to London with my husband right after we were married. I came back here after the war. Henry's a distant cousin of mine; I knew he'd help me when my home was lost."

"Oh, that's terrible! How did it happen?"

"Bomb."

"A bomb?"

Anna found it hard to believe. Sarah did not want to continue the conversation.

"My dear, how do you like the popover?"

"It's delicious," Anna chimed.

Sarah smiled at the memory of Anna teaching her how to make them years before. She took a deep breath with a feeling of completeness as she sat that morning beside her girl again.

"Thad's driving me crazy," Sarah commented absentmindedly.

Anna gulped to avoid spitting out her tea.

"The man is tired, I know. I'm no spring chicken either, but it'd be nice if he helped out here a little more than he does . . . And his incessant whistling."

Anna helped clear the dainty dishes, and then looked out the window as she scrubbed the muffin tin.

Henry shoveled the Donnelly's drive.

"Oh, sweet boy!" Sarah commented as she dried the dishes.

Anna handed Sarah the last dish, dried her hands, and put on her boots, gloves, hat, and coat.

"What on earth are you doing?" She asked, but Anna was already outside.

She went into the shed and got another snow shovel. Henry turned when he saw a scoop of snow fly. He smiled at her as they shoveled snow together. Sarah watched from the kitchen window and realized how wrong she had been the night before.

Henry and Anna shoveled together in silence. Henry thanked her and told her to go get warm as he went to Mrs. O'Leary's home. Instead, Anna followed him and before either of them froze over, they had cleared several drives and walkways in the Donnelly's neighborhood.

The villagers watched from their windows as the couple worked together, once more. Unbeknownst to either of them, they soon had a small, captive audience at every window in the area. Observers were moved to tears at the incredible miracle they witnessed.

Anna was out of breath. Henry stopped and put his shovel down. He watched as she warmed her hands.

"I can't feel my hands," she said and snickered.

He knew the tone which meant she was struggling. He walked slowly to her and paused. He should have listened to Father Donnelly, but he could not. His wife was standing before him, tired from helping him. Moved, he took her little gloved hands into his, and then blew warm air into them. She sighed and so did the other women gathered around their kitchen windows.

Henry decided it was time to stop. He could have shoveled every drive in Adare, but he knew his wife could not. He walked her back to the Donnelly's house and opened the kitchen door dramatically.

"Tea!" He demanded jokingly.

Sarah obeyed at once and put a pot on. Henry helped Anna out of her coat, and then sat beside her. He was giddier than a love-struck school boy. She had helped him. He saw inklings of his Anna return to him.

"I'm sorry," Sarah whispered into Henry's ear as she gave him a mug.

He winked at her. He knew there was a lot of truth to what she had said the night before and made sure he kept it close to his heart.

"Your face is chilled," Sarah said as she hovered around Anna like a mother hen.

She warmed a washcloth and handed it to her. Anna smiled, and then used it. She was terribly tired and sore, but in her heart, Anna was happy to be of use, especially to Henry.

Anna dropped her tea, still unable to feel her fingers. She was mortified, but Sarah's only concern was for her and why Henry had kept her out in the freezing weather so long. The spilled tea was cleaned up before Anna had stopped washing her hands in the warm tap water.

"Hello, sticky fingers," Henry teased when she sat back down.

Anna punched him in the shoulder.

"Get him again!" Sarah cheered as Henry laughed.
Father Donnelly emerged from his "quiet time with the Lord" and entered the kitchen cleaning his glasses. Henry had taken his glasses off that day because they kept fogging up. Father Donnelly stopped and witnessed the gaiety of the moment; it had been a long time since he had seen his friend have a genuine laugh.

"Well, now," he said and kissed Sarah on the cheek.

"Henry has done your work for you, sir—clearing the drive ... And this pretty girl helped him! You should be ashamed, Thad," she quipped.

Father Donnelly was unmoved. He continued cleaning his glasses.

"I hope you got the back path as well, Oliver," he said.

Anna and Henry smiled.

"For shame, Father Donnelly, for shame," his wife scolded.

He stood beside her and pinched her bottom.

"Thad!" She yelped, thoroughly mortified.

"She can dish it out, but she can't take it," he commented.

Father Donnelly gloated over the sight before him: Henry and Anna seated next to each other, laughing over coffee; and Sarah buzzing around doing far less than nothing in all of her hurrying and fussing. At once, he truly felt at home in the environment and was, for a few seconds, convinced the last horrible months were simply a terrible nightmare.

"Henry got me a job!" Anna announced.

Everyone stopped.

"At the florist," Anna added and noticed everyone's shock. "I start on Monday!"

Father Donnelly and Sarah looked at Henry; they instantly knew what he had done to get the job for her. Father Donnelly contemplated whether or not it was ethical for Henry to pay his wife, but managed to come to the conclusion it was fine.

She needed to feel useful, which had become apparent after she shoveled snow that morning.

"Well, that's wonderful, dear," Sarah said, her feminism showed.

Father Donnelly knew better than to share his old fashioned thoughts about women with his present company, particularly his wife's. He left the room without saying a word.

"Maybe we can go dress shopping today?" Sarah asked Henry more than Anna.

Sarah had given all of Anna's beautiful clothes to the widow society in Shannon less than a month before. Henry had cried when she did, for many of the clothes not only held memories, but also the scent of his beloved. They hung in their old bedroom and took up precious room.

Not as sentimental as Henry, she did not understand why it had hurt him so. Henry had a hard time being in the same room as Sarah for two weeks after she had done it, but soon forgave her completely, although it still bothered him at times.

Anna thought for a moment. The idea sounded wonderful, except she had no money. Henry thought about the fact he had just bought Anna quite a bit of new things, but knew it was only enough for a few days. Henry smiled; he knew his wife's thoughts. She loved clothes.

"You know," he remarked, "I think it's a wonderful idea. In fact, I almost forgot. The florist shop is very particular about their employees looking quite stylish. They handed me a stipend to give you for some professional-looking clothes."

Henry reached into his pocket and gave Anna all he had. He had gone to the bank the day before to take out money for the week. Anna looked at it and back at Henry.

"You're a terrible liar," she said with tears in her eyes.

"I have no idea what you're talking about," he said as he blew on his tea.

There was nothing he would not give her.

"Henry, put your money away . . . I'm no pauper, if you recall. I can afford taking this sweet girl shopping."

Henry knew she wanted to repay the damage she had done a month ago. He walked up to her and hugged her.

"It's all right," he whispered and kissed her cheek.

Anna did not know whether or not to refuse the money. Henry understood.

He said, "I want you to depend upon me for something, Anna. Please take the money."

She looked at him with tears in her eyes and shook her head no. She held it back out to him. Sarah left the room and found something to dust in the parlor.

"This isn't right, me taking from you all the time."

Henry sat by her on the stool again.

"Anna, I have no other expenses than what I give to others. My apartment is free, every woman in this village has signed up to feed me every meal for the next ten years or so, and the parish pays me to do what I love. What joy do I have than to give to others? Let me bless you."

Anna sat motionless. Henry got up, grabbed her purse, stuffed the money inside, and simply said, "There."

"Thank you," Anna said and embraced him.

Henry stood still for a moment, shocked once again by his wife's affectionate soul. He would have given her a million dollars if it had been acceptable to her. He would have given everything he had to her, but it was too soon to do such a thing. He only gave her what she was forced to accept.

"I'm ready to go," Sarah said as she re-entered the room unannounced.

Henry and Anna let go of each other. Sarah stood as she buttoned her pretty gloves. Sarah kissed Henry's cheek and Anna smiled at him without saying goodbye.

The two ladies helped each other put on their coats, and then went out the door. Anna climbed into the passenger's side of the car. Sarah rolled over the flower bed at the end of the driveway. Anna did not seem to notice, as she was still buttoning her gloves in the car.

"These blasted things," Sarah muttered as she tore through her frozen lily bulbs.

"It's probably best she not spend a lot of time in Adare right now," Father Donnelly said behind Henry who watched out the window as they drove off. "I just hope they remember the way. If you recall, neither of them is very good with directions, Henry."

Henry wanted to run after them, but Father Donnelly knew they would be fine. Sarah always carried a coin in her purse for a pay telephone.

"You'd think they'd use a map once in a while," Henry said.

"I give it an hour before they ring us."

However, they did not call. Sarah chatted about gardening and cooking until Anna thought she would lose it on the way. Her quick, rhythmic speaking was enough for Anna to interject an occasional "uh-huh" to be polite. Anna was able to let her thoughts go wherever she wanted as they drove through Shannon and looked for stores.

Henry sat restlessly in a big arm chair while Father Donnelly smoked his pipe.

"How do you feel about me preaching for a while?" He asked nonchalantly.

"Fine, fine," Henry replied, although he was not completely.

"I'd love to sing some of the old songs you've forsaken," Father Donnelly said with slight condescension.

"That'll be fine," Henry said as he recoiled.

He wanted Anna to call, to say she was lost, so he had to go get her. Instead, he listened to Father Donnelly drone on about Bach and the old chanter style of hymns. Henry allowed the former rector to take over, however temporary, which Father Donnelly secretly relished. Henry knew he needed to really usurp his leadership later, but for now, it was necessary.

"Seems Anna's always shopping for clothes," Father Donnelly commented.

Henry kept looking out the window. He knew why his wife found so much comfort in clothing. She had told him far too much about her time in the concentration camp brothels. He knew she needed to feel safe by being covered. It hurt his heart to think of her suffering. He would have clothed her with a thousand garments it made her feel better.

Henry finally buried his head in a book. Four hours went by, still no girls. Father Donnelly had spent the early morning preparing his sermon and selecting hymns, so he quietly settled into his chair and started to snore.

Henry, however, was worried. His thoughts raced back to the day she had gone to the beach. He had lost her because he was not with her. To say Sarah was without street smarts was an understatement. *Why did I let them go?*

At the pinnacle of worrisome pain, the door flew open and ladies chattering and fluttering with bags of purchases invaded the cottage. Henry's heart relaxed.

"Show him what you got!" Sarah exclaimed with a new stole wrapped around her shoulders.

"You look quite lovely," he commented to Sarah who blushed as she modeled her blue, velvet stole.

Anna excitedly showed him everything she had purchased, and then handed him back change which he unwittingly put back into his pocket, just as he would have a year ago. He could not picture any of it on her body, but was kind enough to remark on each piece and what a wonderful job they had done together.

Anna looked as if she had been crowned princess and handed the world. Sarah looked more content than she had in years. They had fun which was what Henry wanted.

"Are you tired?" Henry asked Anna.

"I'm utterly exhausted," Sarah answered.

Anna snickered as Henry turned back to her.

"I'm fine," Anna said as Sarah removed her hat and left the room.

"Did you have a good time?" Henry asked.

"I ate a steak and had a beer."

"So, you did have a good time!"

"Aren't you going to try to convict me?"

"Goodness, no."

"Why not?"

"You probably needed it. Want to go for a walk?"

It was cold outside and the snow was very thick, but Anna said yes anyway. Henry offered her his arm.

"We don't have much daylight left and I want to show you around."

Large ladders were in the main strip of town as men in overalls and thick coats shouted to each other as they hung Christmas lights over the street. Henry smiled as he walked with his beautiful wife on his arm. He had not too long ago thought it was going to be a very lonely Christmas.

Everyone was so used to seeing Henry and Anna walk the same way just months ago. Quite often, despite their lack of closeness behind closed doors, the couple had walked together for their weekly errands in town.

"Henry!" A tough-looking woman appeared seemingly out of thin air before them.

"Miss Gertie!" Henry said apprehensively. "This is Anna."

Gertie's eyes bulged as if she had to see the phenomenon to truly believe. She paused, and then shook Anna's hand vigorously. A group of young ladies stopped and one put her hand to her mouth.

"Henry! Get that blasted cord, will 'ya?" One of Henry's buddies called from atop a huge ladder.

Henry ran to help and left Anna standing alone for a moment. His friend had not registered the miracle. It took Henry's friend, Sean, significantly more time to realize the walking dead stood before him.

Sean swore as a spark rose from the connecting cords. He sucked his burned finger, and then he saw Anna. He swore louder, but this time in amazement.

Henry chuckled underneath his breath as he looked up at his friend. Sean always hung the lights for the town. His pub was not very busy in the afternoon, so he had the time. He thought he had the skill.

Anna noticed Sean and Henry were built almost exactly alike. The truth was they were very different. Sean was extremely outgoing and good with women. Sean had wondered—everyone had wondered—what Henry's problem was with women until Anna had come along.

"You watch," Sean had said in his teens, "Henry will meet the one and that'll be the end of him. The rest of us will still be off gallivanting, but Henry will settle down."

Sean was right. He often was, but there were times when he was very wrong. He had not agreed with Henry's choice of occupation and his views as far as alcohol was concerned. The lack of Guinness in Henry's life was as if he slighted one of Sean's dearest friends.

However, Sean had been one of Henry's champions when it came down to Henry's choice of girl. Henry grinned up at Sean who was one of the few in Adare who knew Henry from childhood. The rest of his friends had moved on from the quiet little town.

Sean barely made it down the ladder and actually missed a step right before he reached the ground. Henry steadied him and Sean swore again.

"She's prettier than I remember," he whispered.

Sean had been the only one who had hoped, even believed, Anna had been washed ashore somewhere, alive. Even Henry had gotten angry with him about it at one point. Yet, Sean had instincts Henry did not; he was a smarter man than he was electrician.

"If there was ever a time to have a drink . . . ." he said as he stared at Anna.

Henry agreed and stared, too, as men tipped their hats at the resurrected daughter of Adare. He shook Sean's hand and told him he would stop by, not for a drink, but for his company over the weekend. He wanted someone besides the Donnellys to talk with about everything. There were some thoughts he only shared with Sean.

"Man, she's gorgeous!" Sean said as he gaped.

Henry ran back to Anna and had her take his arm again. She had not moved from the spot where he had left her.

"Everything all right?" The two asked each other in unison.

They smiled and strolled on to the florist shop so Anna could meet her new employers. They immediately embraced her. Anna felt at ease right away as Clara and Cara talked quickly and finished each other's thoughts and sentences.

They were delighted to have Anna join them and showed her around a little. Henry snooped around for what they had new from their lush greenhouse. He was sure there were no better cultivators in all of Ireland.

Henry selected a long, yellow flower. He took out a stem and put some coins on the counter for them. As Anna came back in from the greenhouse tour, Henry handed it to her.

Clara and Cara wanted to faint if Henry had let them right then and there. They looked at each other wide-eyed as if to say, *He's so romantic!*

Anna quietly ripped off the stem and put it in his lapel. He smirked and remembered how she hated he wore black almost always. He actually did not even know he had a button hole in his coat collar until she threaded the delicate flower through it.

"Are you trying to get me beat up?" He whispered to her.

"That's a secret hope I have," she whispered.

He waved goodbye to the florists as Anna stated she would see them soon. Anna looked toward the pharmacy. For some reason, even though they had been in one the day before in Shannon, Anna's thoughts returned to Daire and his experiments with medicine. She froze.

"Are you all right?" Henry asked.

It seemed he was always asking that question. He looked up at the sign and decided to stand perfectly still.

Is she remembering something?

"I'm sorry," she said, just as his hopes were up. "I was thinking."

"It's all right. What were you thinking about?"

She did not want to tell him, but she felt obligated to somehow.

"I was thinking of Daire."

The answer hurt his heart.

Daire? How can she be thinking of him while surrounded by the Eden they strolled through?

"What about him?" he asked.

He tried to form the connection to the pharmacy's sign and Daire.

"He said he was trying to invent a new medicine."

"Did he *make* the drug he gave you?"

Somewhere Henry had lost that very important detail.

"Yes, he had a shed he worked in."

"Do you remember the sort of things he had in the shed?"

"There were things in vials."

"Do you remember what any of them were called?"

"I only remember a few herbs like you'd find in a garden. The rest I didn't know. They looked like chemicals of some kind."

"Huh," Henry said as he contemplated what Anna had said.

If only she remembered. It's unusual for her not to notice everything, but if she'd been drugged, it explains how she'd been so easily manipulated.

"Would you like to go in?"

"No, thank you," she said.

A few more people came up and cheerily greeted Henry and Anna as if they saw a movie star. Anna, however, was lost in thought. The sun was starting to go down even though it was not quite dinner time.

"I think I just want to be alone tonight," Anna said after she realized how exhausted she felt.

She wanted to be alone with her thoughts. She felt as if she had lived in another time and space the past week as she made her new friend, Henry. She wanted to remain faithful, somehow, to Daire and concentrate on all that had happened. She had reacted over something explainable if she had given him the chance.

In the car, Anna was quiet and she did not hold Henry's hand as she looked out the window. She thanked him, got out of the car, and carried her bags of clothes up the couple of stairs without his help. As she waved goodbye, he knew where her thoughts were: not with him.

Henry returned to the Donnelly's cottage after he left Anna in his apartment. Father Donnelly and Sarah saw the change in Henry's demeanor. He hardly said a word during dinner, although he was usually quiet, save the last few days with Anna.

They looked at each other when he retired to his room at eight o'clock that evening. Any excuse to be alone did not come quick enough for Henry. Like Anna, he needed to think, but his thoughts focused completely on Anna.

CHAPTER 22

SATURDAY MORNING WAS A LAZY time for the Donnelly household. Sarah politely told everyone to make their breakfast. Henry sat down to work on a puzzle which remained perpetually out because Anna had asked him to come for her later than usual—she wanted to sleep in.

He realized all the changes must have been exhausting, but he was still concerned about where she was in her head. Father Donnelly took the opportunity to talk with Henry about it.

"Henry, my boy, I want to form a plan with you about Anna."

"With all due respect, it seems you're forming your plans without me quite fine," Henry said as he studied the puzzle.

Father Donnelly was taken aback. It was not like Henry to speak to him in such a way. However, Henry was in a worse mood than he had been his whole life—he was aggravated, torn, and tired.

How can she not remember me at all?

He knew it was only days, but it was not. He had been suffering for months since her disappearance. Father Donnelly held a funeral and Henry had grieved and reasoned he would always grieve. If the truth be told, he had lost Anna the year before. Henry had given his life to his occupation and left Anna—and her independent ways—in the dust. They were strangers living together in the same house.

She was definitely his right hand in all matters of social content. She handled the church suppers, events, and all ladies' outings. They looked like partners in every way, but they were not because their marriage was far from perfect.

Anna was finally his again. Then, seemingly out of nowhere last night, he felt he had lost her again. It was almost unbearable.

"Well, now," Father Donnelly said calmly, yet hurt by Henry's words.

If it had been anyone else he would not have felt the sting, but somehow words coming from such a gentle person let Father Donnelly know he had crossed the line.

"I'd very much like your input."

Henry snapped, "That's a change."

Father Donnelly almost rose out of his seat. He considered confronting Henry about his lack of respect, but realized it was he who needed a lesson in respect. Henry studied the table full of puzzle pieces of Versailles.

He reached for Henry's hand. Henry did not look up.

"I'm sorry, my boy."

Father Donnelly's eyes filled with tears. In that instance, Henry broke and began to cry as his head dropped.

"Come here," Father Donnelly said as he grabbed Henry to cry with him. The table lifted as they stood up. Father Donnelly tossed it aside and embraced Henry. The puzzle pieces scattered on the floor.

Father Donnelly talked into Henry's big shoulders, "I feel the Holy Spirit wants to lift you in His loving arms, cover you with His feathers, and tell you it'll be all right. As for me, Henry, I want you to know how proud I am of you, my dearest son."

Henry cried into his friend's shoulders. Sarah walked in, saw the mess and their embrace, and then quietly left. They finally settled into two massive chairs by the fireplace and stared into it.

"What if she doesn't want me?" Henry asked.

Father Donnelly reached over and put his hand on Henry's knee. He, too, worried about the same thing.

"How can she even think of this Daire?" Henry said angrily. "He drugged her!"

"I know, my boy, I know"

"What's she thinking?"

"It'll be all right, Henry. Calm yourself. Since Anna's death, you've had quite a bout."

Henry looked hard at his friend and thought, *Her death?*

Father Donnelly had not realized what he had said as he looked down at the rose-embroidered rug. He did not want to look at Henry who he had never seen cry like he had before. He did not realize how painful his comment was to him.

Henry was embroiled in anger. He rose immediately and headed straight to Father Donnelly's shed. When he left, Father Donnelly got up and walked over to where Sarah watched Henry from the kitchen window. Henry emerged with a spike driver he had bought long ago from a man who worked on the railroad.

Father Donnelly went out to speak with him.

"Leave me alone!" Henry snapped as he hoofed up the road afoot. "I'm going to do something I should've done a long time ago!"

Henry trudged quickly down the road and Father Donnelly knew how hard it was to keep up. So, he climbed inside his car and drove alongside Henry at a slow pace.

"What are you going to do?" He called out the window of his creeping vehicle.

Henry did not respond. He was a massive man, with a railroad spike. There was only so much anyone was able to say to him.

A few people talked and stared as they watched the two priests make a spectacle of themselves. Henry finally turned at the drive to the Manor. He took a shortcut and walked through the grass in an area where Father Donnelly could not drive. Then, he went another half a mile to the tree by the stream. It was his and Anna's special place where her memorial tombstone was located.

Father Donnelly had parked his car and half-ran to Henry to catch up with him. Henry started to swing the spike driver against the tombstone. When Father Donnelly finally caught up to him, he tried to catch his breath.

"She's not dead!" Henry yelled as he broke the tombstone apart. Then, he threw down the massive tool and looked at Father Donnelly.

"She's not dead!" He said emphatically.

Father Donnelly knew Henry was angered by him giving up the search. He had convinced Henry to stop looking for Anna. Henry locked eyes with him, and then trudged away. He walked to the parish where Anna was just getting out of bed.

Father Donnelly drove back home, his heart was heavy. He had thought with the lightness of the past few days, the storm had passed and a new chapter had begun in their lives. He thought Anna's memory would return and things would be back to normal. He had not expected Henry to lose his composure and sense of reason, he never expected it.

Henry knocked on Anna's door and held his arms for warmth as he stood shivering. In his anger, he had forgotten his coat. Anna answered as she brushed her hair. She stopped and looked at the man before her who dripped in cold sweat.

"What happened? Come in!"

Henry warmed his bare hands against the warmth of the fire-place. She rushed to grab him a blanket. Henry felt peace stream through him as she wrapped it around his shoulders. Then, Anna sat down and waited for him to speak.

"Is it okay if we went away for the day?" He asked as he sniffed.

"Are you well, Henry?"

"No," he said harsher than he liked. "I need to get out of here."

"All right," she agreed.

She looked out the window and asked, "Do you have the car?"

"I walked."

"I'll go get it. Just stay here, Henry, all right? I'll be right back."

Anna layered her warmest outerwear and left Henry by the fire. She was alarmed and needed to talk to the Donnellys. She hurried as she sloshed through the snow and wondered, *What happened?*

The Donnellys were not home, but their house was open. Anna gathered Henry's keys and coat, and then hurried back to him with the car. She re-entered the little apartment and Henry immediately met her with an embrace. She held onto him tightly.

"I'm so worried about you, Henry. Are you all right?" She asked again.

"Father Donnelly and I . . . We have a lot we're working through right now. I'm so stupid to make you go out in that weather to get the car and I—"

"It's fine," she said and rubbed his back quickly.

"No, it's not. You don't even have a license anymore."

"Are you warm?"

He embraced her again. Just knowing she was there comforted him whether she loved him not.

"I got your coat," she said and held it out to Henry.

He put it on and thanked Anna. His eyes were red and puffy.

"Where do you want to go?" she asked.

"I just want to drive . . . Anywhere."

"Okay. Let's go then, all right?"

They got in the car together. Anna looked at him and thought, *He's not himself.*

She reached for his hand and he surrendered it quickly. He held her hand so tightly it hurt. She thought about her night spent thinking of Daire. She loved Daire's passion; however, she never saw any in Henry. Yet, in that moment she realized he was.

She wondered why Henry had come to her and not gone to another friend. She did not have to wonder long when he kissed her hand as he drove.

"I'm sorry," he said finally.

"Better?" She asked, reluctant to pry.

"Better," he said.

Henry had wanted so many times to be comforted by her as he grieved. The reason he could not accept her death was because he was alone without her to get through it. It was a vicious cycle.

"Where are we going?" she asked.

He realized he was on the same road he had taken the night she went missing. He decided to detour from it and go to the cliffs. He needed open space and a place to walk while holding her hand.

"The Cliffs of Moher," he said as he pulled up.

"Sounds foreboding," she said.

"It's actually quite beautiful."

"Scary can be beautiful."

"It certainly can be," he agreed.

He laughed a little and they finally came to a stop. It was incredibly windy and he worried about the weather conditions.

"Just tell me when you get too cold, all right?" he said.

She opened the door and commented she was already cold, but he made her get out to at least see the sights. It was breathtaking with an immediate drop down into the ocean. She held onto Henry's arm, scared she might fall, even though she was a safe distance from the edge.

Henry put his arm around her and remembered the first time they had come to the location together. He smiled. He wanted Anna to kiss him, but she did not. She shivered in his huge arms.

"Thank you for coming out here with me," he said loud enough so she heard him over the wind. "Do you want to get back in the car?"

She nodded. They walked back to his parked car. When the doors of the car shut, it silenced the outside. They warmed their hands when Henry turned on the heater.

"This is beautiful, but why did we come *here*?"

"Oh, it has sentimental value to me. It comforts me to be here."

"Why?"

Henry thought for a moment, and then answered, "This is where my wife and I had our first date."

"What was she like?" Anna asked with compassion.

"Well, she was really beautiful."

"She was?"

"Yes, she was. She also sang and painted. She had a lot of wonderful talents, unlike me. Anna, I know I've been quite charming and handsome," Henry kidded, "so it may've covered the fact I have absolutely no talents."

"What? Come on!"

"No, I don't. I'm a rarity. Few people are born with absolutely nothing at all to give as far as talent goes. My parents tried everything to find my gift to the world. They were very frustrated after spending lots of money on all kinds of lessons.

"My wife, however, was given much more than her share of talents. It was as if God had split our souls like we were a piece of cake and gave her all the icing."

Anna laughed.

"I'm an icing-free cake," he said humbly with a smile.

"You're so quiet with everyone else, but me. It's like I have a secret to your true identity or something."

"Well, I turn into a different person in the pulpit as well."

"Is that right?"

"Yep."

"I'd like to hear you preach."

"Well, it won't be for a while. Father Donnelly is taking over for a few weeks to give me a break."

"So, that's what the fuss was about this morning."

"Somewhat," he admitted honestly.

"How much of a sabbatical is he having you take?"

"Two weeks or so."

"Why?"

"He thinks I'm distracted by you."

"Is he right?"

"Yes," Henry answered.

Anna was flattered. She tried to hide her smile. She turned to him as she held onto the white, leather seats.

"How about you prove him right? How about you let me distract you for a while?"

Henry smiled and said, "I'm listening."

"I'm hungry."

In a small pub a few minutes away, they agreed on potato soup. Anna sipped a beer while Henry blew on his soup. They were tired.

"Tell me more . . . About your wife."

"Why do you want to know about her?"

"I like what your face does when you talk about her."

Henry smiled as he looked down at his soup. He was afraid to talk about her because Anna might figure things out. In fact, he was not sure of her suspicions already. He knew it was best to let her remember on her own since Daire had told her he was her husband. Henry was fearful Anna might put him in the same category as her captor.

"Well," Anna finally said after an awkward silence, "if you don't want to talk about her, how about you tell me more about you."

"What do you want to know?"

"Do you have family besides your cousin, Ashling . . . Anyone else in the area besides Sarah?"

"My parents passed away about ten years ago."

"I'm so sorry. I remember you saying that. Can I ask how it happened?"

"Car accident," he said as he sipped his hot soup.

"What was your childhood like?"

"My parents were distant, but good. They weren't very affectionate, but I always had everything I needed. I had a good education."

"Any siblings?"

"No."

"I had a group of close friends and Ashling came every summer and holidays."

"And you grew up in Adare?"

"Yes, I did."

"What was that like?"

"It was quiet for the most part."

"Did you have girls after you?" Anna asked more seriously.

Henry laughed and admitted, "Um, no."

"How did you meet your wife?"

"She was my best friend."

"Yes, but how did you meet her?"

"She worked for me, actually."

Anna thought about what Henry said. She actually felt a little jealous of the woman who seemed like a goddess in Henry's eyes. Anna did not think she stood a chance competing with such a thing. It made her a little upset. She wondered if she actually felt something for Henry. Yet, every time she let her mind search her heart, she thought of Daire's passion and the rush she felt when he held her.

He sighed involuntarily.

"Are you tired?" Anna asked.

"Yes, I kinda am."

"Do you want to go home?"

He nodded and put some money down for the waitress.

The desolate road back to Adare was straight and narrow.

Anna stole glances at the vulnerable priest next to her. Henry was an odd sort with the body of a lion and heart of a lamb. It was an anomaly. The fact he was shy around everyone else made him more of a mystery. She did not understand why he had opened up to her so quickly, so easily.

He pulled up to the Donnelly's cottage.

Do you want to go in or do you want to go—?"

"I'll go in," he said.

He paused with his hand on the door handle and said, "Time to face the music; I can't stay mad at him, you know."

Anna smiled faintly.

"Do you want to come in? Do you want me to drive you home? I'm sorry. I'm not being very polite am I?"

"You're half asleep. I think I'll walk home. I need the exercise."

"Do you want me to walk you? It's getting late."

She did. She really did.

"I'll be fine."

Henry studied her as she fidgeted with her purse and buttoned her grey gloves. He knew she did not want to walk home alone. He was so tired and out of sorts, he almost leaned over and kissed her, but caught himself.

"Hey," he said and took her hand. "I want to walk you, if you don't mind."

She finally nodded. His eyes were tired, but he thought a walk might do him good. Besides, it afforded him more time with her. Henry and Anna began their walk up the snow-covered road as Anna clutched her purse. She was delicate and looked pretty with her long, black hair and light eyes. She looked over at him. He looked like a mountain man. Sometimes, he almost crouched down to make himself less gorilla-like.

"You're cute," she said.

"I'm cute?" He asked with a smile. "That hurts you know. Tell a guy who's as big as an ox he's cute and it's like a dagger to the heart, Anna."

She laughed and kidded, "Oh, yes, I'm sure."

"You're kinda okay yourself."

"Why thank you."

"I mean, you're tolerable to look at, I guess," he joked.

She hit him and warned, "Watch it, you!"

"*Somebody* wants you, I'm sure," he continued.

"Will I sit by you in church tomorrow?" she asked.

"I'll be up front. Sarah will be in the congregation, though."

He thought for a moment and asked, "You'd want to sit by me?"

"No. Of course, not. I was hoping to avoid you at all costs to-morrow."

"A wise course of action."

"Henry, why are you so outgoing with me and nobody else?"

"Well, that's not true. I have a couple of friends I'm pretty open with."

"You're not like this with the Donnellys."

"No, I'm not. They tend to overshadow me."

"So, who?"

"Well, I was like this with my wife."

"I figured as much."

"And I'm like this with a couple of my friends I've known since I was a lad."

Henry thought of his three friends. His heart hurt when he thought about Tomas and how badly things had gone between them.

"Are you like this with your family?"

"Sure. Ashling and her family are privileged to know me as you do."

"So, why me?"

"Would it upset you if I admitted you remind me of my wife?"

"How so?"

"In a lot of ways; she was fiery like you."

"I hate that about myself."

"I loved it. That is, unless she was mad at me, of course. Then, she scared me to death."

"How did she die?" Anna asked quietly.

Henry looked at her and smiled fondly.

How do I answer this question?

"We're here," he said as he motioned to the church.

"You don't want to talk about it."

"Nope."

She turned to him on the stoop and said, "Henry, thank you for being my friend. Thank you for everything."

She thought for a split second about kissing him, but knew there was no turning back afterwards.

He's still grieving his wife and transferring all his feelings onto me.

Then, she thought about kissing Daire and instantly beat the thought down. Henry was so good and Daire was such a grey figure in her life.

Was he good or bad?

She did not know, nor did she have any hope of seeing him again. *Can I start over with this clergyman?*

Henry nodded, moved she had thanked him for his friendship. Then, he began to walk away.

"Henry?" She called out.

He turned around with his hands in his coat pockets. She wanted to ease his pain, to be close to her friend. She did not know if she was ready for anything more.

"What do you want for Christmas?"

It was a stupid thing to ask, but she could not think of anything else to say.

He wanted to shout, *You!* but he did not. He wanted to tell her he wanted her to kiss him, for Pete's sake, but he did not. He simply shrugged.

"What do *you* want?" He choked out into the cold, night air.

"My memories," she said.

"You'll have them by then," he promised.

Right then, he made a deal with himself. If she had not remembered by Christmas, he would tell her. She might be furious, but he had to set a time limit on the relationship they had formed.

"You're going to put in a good word for me with the guy upstairs, huh?"

"Always."

She stepped in the snow, walked over to Henry, and hugged him.

CHAPTER 23

SARAH DONNELLY SANG THE OLD hymns in a low, almost baritone voice. Anna tried not to stare at her as she tried to read the music in an old, dilapidated book. She could not follow the old chanter. Father Donnelly was dressed in his robes and sang away with the quiet congregation. It seemed no one liked the old songs.

Anna looked over at Henry who rocked slightly on his dress shoes and tried to sing as best as he could. He wore his black robe which she thought made him look like the Ghost of Christmas yet to Come from the neck down.

Henry tried to ignore Anna's beautiful eyes for he knew the entire congregation stared at the back of her head. He did not want anyone to have any further reason to stare. He allowed himself to glance at her once, but he completely lost his place in his prayer book. He was sure everyone noticed.

Father Donnelly's sermon was boring, even Sarah snoozed a little. Anna nudged her a few times and hoped no one heard the faint snore. Father Donnelly droned on about forming close relationships with one's children and parents. Anna, however, kept her eyes on Henry. It was interesting to see him in that light.

The church was packed that Sunday—it was standing room only. She hoped Henry was a better preacher than Father Donnelly, but she doubted it. Anna thought his prayers were short and unpoetic.

She reasoned if Henry's shy demeanor in public was an indicator of what kind of speaker he was, it would be painful.

Henry sat with his thoughts elsewhere as Father Donnelly preached.

On Sunday afternoons Anna and he used to cook a few soups to keep in the ice box for the coming week. She usually made a colossal mess when she cooked.

Henry smirked involuntarily at the memory. He loved the bits of imperfection in her. She seemed more real with her little quirks.

He wondered if Anna wanted to be near him. The past three months, he spent his Sunday afternoons alone, and then down to Sean's pub for a cola and a talk with his dearest friend.

Anna felt nervous about starting her new job the next morning. Her thoughts drifted to Daire and how she never considered working as they lived in a little hovel in the middle of nowhere. She tried to remember details about where he lived, but could not recall anything. Anna reasoned there was no way to get back.

Maybe the police knew where she was found. Then, she could scout out some areas. She wanted answers from Daire. She did not understand why she had not experienced temporary paralysis since she ran away.

Could he have caused them?

Anna was shaken by the thought. Before she knew it, Father Donnelly had said his closing prayer and everyone said, "Amen." She took a deep breath and looked at Henry as he passed her down the aisle as they sang the last, depressing hymn.

Is this what his life is like?

She lost a little respect for Henry that morning. She could not believe he was part of such a dreary little church. Henry was embarrassed by the service and went to disrobe. He had apologized to Father Donnelly with pure humility the night before. Father

Donnelly was angrier with himself than with Henry, but he accepted the respectful apology and moved beyond it immediately.

"Thank you for conducting the service," Henry said to Father Donnelly as they disrobed.

"It was nice for me," he said politely.

They both knew it was more than *nice* for him.

"Are you going to see Anna today?"

"I'm going to leave that up to her."

Father Donnelly hoped Henry would make himself a little scarce that day. He liked the peace and quiet of his little cottage. It had been in an uproar for an entire week.

Their relationship was still on shaky terms, but would heal in a few days. Henry shook Father Donnelly's hand, and then walked out the back of the church.

Anna contended with a multiple of people who had introduced themselves to her. They shook her hand. A few little girls had also attached themselves to her; she laughed nervously.

"Princess!" they called.

"Why are they calling me that?" Anna asked an embarrassed mother.

"Oh, it must be because you're so pretty," she lied.

In truth, Henry had told all the girls his wife was a princess from another land when they were first married. The legend stuck with every girl in his congregation. She was Princess of the Fairies and the mother fairy had let her become a real girl because she loved Henry so much. The story was almost as good as reality, which none of the children could possibly understand.

"Princess of the Fairies!" One of them yelled out at the top of her lungs as she ran away.

"I'm sorry," her mother pleaded.

"No, it's fine," Anna replied.

A few women hugged her, but most of the people simply welcomed her as they shook her hand. Sarah stayed close to ensure everyone's behavior was to the specifics of her husband's directive.

Where in the world is Henry?

Henry snuck out the backdoor of the church and was on his way to his wife's tombstone. He had left his favorite tool there and he wanted to retrieve it before the snow ruined it. The walk was not far from the church and it gave Henry space away from Anna. He was embarrassed by the service and in no hurry to hear what she thought of it.

Father Donnelly and Sarah invited Anna over, but she felt they did not want her to accept. She politely declined and went around back to Henry's little apartment. Anna caught sight of Henry from the window as he walked away from the church as the last car left.

"Henry!" She called and ran after him. "Where are you going?"

"I was just going for a walk," he said when she caught up with him.

"Can I come?"

"Aren't you hungry?"

"No."

"Come on," he said as the last car rode slowly by.

He finally held out his hand since no one was around. She took it and Henry decided it was better to lose his spike driver than her, so he detoured toward the fields.

"Henry?"

He looked around, and then kissed her hand. She blushed a little.

"I almost kissed you last night."

He stopped dead in his tracks, looked pass her, and thought, *Why is she telling me this?*

"Why didn't you?"

She licked her lips because the cold air chapped them. It only made it worse.

"I feel so confused and I think you do, too."

"I'm not confused," he said without looking at her.

"You haven't fully mourned your wife, Henry."

"That doesn't make me confused."

Anna took a deep breath, and then her exhale made a cloud before her.

"Well, maybe I can't speak for you, but I know I'm confused."

"What about?"

"What about? Henry, what do I have to actually feel secure about?"

"Your heart."

"I don't even have that on straight."

"Yes, you do. You don't realize it because of that stupid man."

"He's not stupid."

Henry burned with anger and asked, "Anna, really?"

Anna was shocked at his reaction.

"I mean, come on . . . The man was drugging you! He was *drugging* you! What does it take for you to see people for who they really are? You're always thinking the best of everyone, but sometimes you have to stop and say, 'Huh, someone is drugging me, he might really be a bad guy!' or possibly, 'This man I don't know told me he was my husband and he isn't. Maybe, just maybe, he wants to get me in bed with him!'"

"Henry!" she cried

"I'm a good man, Anna. Why don't you want me?"

"I've only been here a week, Henry!"

"How long before you slept with Daire, Anna . . . A day or two? You seem to throw yourself on any man who shows the vaguest interest in you."

With that, Anna fell silent and stared at him with her mouth open. Her unbuttoned blue coat and red dress stood out in the white blanket of snow like a lantern in the darkness.

I'm an idiot, he thought.

This was the second time in two days Henry had lost it with someone he loved. He knew he had a breaking point, but he did not know his fuse was so short.

Anna finally trudged quietly away in the snow. His heart broke for the thousandth time. Anna brushed away free-flowing tears before they froze on her pale face. Nothing could have hurt her quite like what Henry had said.

She stormed into his little apartment, threw herself on the bed. *So, this is what he thinks of me. How does he know about me and Daire? The doctor must've told him!*

Anna felt betrayed and horrified. Her dear friend who she respected so much knew.

Henry sat down at a small table in Sean's pub where he had lamented all afternoon about his terrible comments to Anna. He was more than sorry—he was horrified by his actions and had tromped through the snowy fields around his childhood home for hours. His face was burned by the cold and his fingers trembled.

Sean put a cup of coffee before Henry and sat with his own brimming glass of stein. There was never any judgment from Sean—he accepted Henry's few faults with hearty love and friendship. He had, however, not seen the look on Henry's face in years.

"Tell me," Sean said and waited.

"I'm a moron."

"This is true," Sean agreed as all of Henry's boyhood friends might have. "This calls for some Rosemary Clooney if we're to have the moron talk."

Sean put a coin in his new juke box, and then sat down as Rosemary crooned in the background.

"I love her," Henry said and took a sip of coffee.

"So, do everyone. Rose is a good girl."

Henry smirked and confided, "Anna's in-love with her captor."

Sean shook his head and replied, "I've read that sometimes happens."

"It's crap."

"That it is. That it is. Me thinks you need a drink."

"Just shut up, will ya? Listen for once in your life."

"'Tis my job. Lay it out, brother."

"Should I just tell her?" Henry asked as he stared into his cup.

"Would it make a difference?"

"I don't know."

"What is the best case scenario for doing so?"

"She lets herself fall head over heels for me."

Henry winced. He needed a drink, but he would never admit it to Sean.

"Okay," Sean said.

He stretched his arms, and then leaned closer to Henry. "Worst case scenario?"

"She murders me violently."

"Sounds like a risk worth taking to me," Sean said.

He sucked something out of his teeth. Henry took another sip of coffee and imagined it was a dark beer.

"Now, you're going to catch me quoting the Bible once— right now and never again. That's it, all right, Henry. You remember that."

Henry snickered. Sean tried to remember it, and then said, "Do unto others as they'd have them do to you or something like that. Moses or somebody said it."

"Jesus said it."

"Well, whatever, it's all the same thing. The point is this, if it was you, would you want to know?"

"I *would* know. I'd be crazy for her instantly."

"Well, she's gorgeous and you're not exactly Clark Gable, if you haven't noticed. So, don't go thinking Anna should leap for joy when she sees the likes of you coming."

"I don't know what I'd want. I guess I'd want to know."

Henry had not thought about it in that way before.

"Then, tell her, man. Buck up and go get her!"

"I don't know. The doctor thinks differently."

"Who knows her better, you or the doctor? Go with your gut. You know her. She certainly deserves you and I've yet to meet another girl who did."

Sean lost his train of thought and winked at Clara, or possibly Cara, when she walked pass him.

"I thank God I'm Irish when I see the red-headed ones," he commented.

However, Henry was not listening.

"Besides, if you don't make a move, there'll be a line of men following Anna around and I'll be one of them."

"Shut up."

"I'm just warning you."

Henry reached out, shook his crazy friend's hand, and said, "I love you, Sean."

"Get out of my bar, you stupid protestant," Sean joked and slapped Henry on his back.

Henry did not confer with Father Donnelly and he did not pray. He did not do anything, but drive to his apartment. He had to tell her—it would change everything, but he still had to do it. He knocked hard.

"Go away, Henry!" she shouted.

"Anna, open the door! I want to talk to you!"

She locked it.

"Anna, I'm so sorry. I just need to tell you something!"

She did not answer.

"Anna, please,"

Still nothing. He begged for another ten minutes until his fingers became numb. He finally drove away. Anna was relieved and upset when he retreated.

She could not bear to see him because he had known what she had done the whole time. She was so embarrassed and was sure his beloved wife had been as white as snow. Anna was humiliated beyond what she could endure.

The next day was Anna's first day of work at the florist shop. Henry came in as soon as it opened. He was greeted cheerily by the twins.

"I need to talk to her, where is she?" he asked.

"She's in the greenhouse, but Henry she asked to not be in contact with anyone today. She doesn't look well. Clara almost sent her home when she saw her this morning."

"Give her this," he said as he handed Cara a sealed envelope he had prepared in case.

The note inside read:

Dear Anna,

I am an idiot. I am your friend. I am sorry.

Love,

Henry

As soon as Cara handed the envelope to Anna after Henry left, she shoved it, unopened, in the compost pile.

"Oh," Cara said with her lip turned up, "that mad, huh?"

"Yep," Anna replied.

"You know he's going to come back tomorrow, right?"

"Yep."

"What are you gonna do?"

"I'm going to go on with my life and forget he exists."

"That's kind of hard to do, Anna … being he's the preacher and all."

"Some preacher," she muttered.

Cara whispered into her sister's ear, "Lovers quarrel."

"I don't know how anyone can be mad at that man," Clara said, condescendingly. "He's the most precious thing to walk this earth."

"Yes," Cara agreed.

"Oh, he's precious all right," Anna said and threw her dirty towel on the counter.

The rest of the week went just as smoothly for Henry; he began to think he had ruined everything. On Tuesday, he was a fraction of a second away from accepting a beer from Sean. On Wednesday, he invaded the knitters club made up of five busybody seventy-year old women because he was lonely. There, he talked incessantly, which was more than unusual. On Thursday, he ate two entire pies in one sitting. Finally, on Friday, he pushed a letter under Anna's door.

It read:

Dear Anna,

Are you finished torturing me?

Love Always,

   Henry

She slid it back under her door without opening it. It fell into a puddle in front of him.

Saturday came and Henry had yet to see her face the entire week. He laid his head on Sarah's kitchen table as she made him an omelet. He had made one last ditch effort and left Anna the journal she had once kept of his encounters of God speaking to him. Anna had seen it on her way to work and tossed it on her bed, unopened.

Sarah thought Henry had lost his mind, particularly in light of his uncharacteristic behavior with her husband the day before his fight with Anna. Father Donnelly and Henry did not give her any details, as much as she pried and seduced them with her baking. Sarah assumed the worst.

She had not set her eyes on Anna all week either. She had sent Father Donnelly to see about her on Wednesday. He returned with a lovely report of a friendly, healthy Anna. She was annoyed Anna had not been to see her.

I certainly don't deserve being snubbed.

Yet, her husband had reported Anna sent her a warm hug and had asked for Sarah's forgiveness for not coming around all week. The gesture had not been enough for Sarah's hurt feelings.

"Do you want me to talk to her?" Sarah asked Henry.

"No," Henry said meekly.

Clara and Cara had asked Anna the night before to help them on Saturday. The Augustinian Priory was celebrating an anniversary and they had been asked to make a special arrangement of flowers. The girls were in high spirits as they decided to make things fun if they had to work on a Saturday. They broke out a bottle of wine and brought down their record player from their upstairs living quarters.

"We have to listen to the record Daniel sent us," Cara said excitedly.

Anna had an inkling who they were talking about because she had heard about almost nothing else the entire week. The twins were infatuated with a violinist who had played at the Clancy Music Festival a few months back.

They squealed as they read the album's cover which read: *To my fair-haired girls, from Daniel.* Clara squealed and kissed the inscription.

Neither of them had any idea who exactly he was interested in and often bickered about it. Anna had remained silent when they asked her to dissect Daniel's many strange advances. It was as if he toyed with the two of them.

Initially, the record started with a loud thud, and then the beautiful strokes of his violin lifted the three of them. As Anna worked on the beautiful, yellow arrangement, she stopped. Something was familiar.

"I remember this."

The twins stopped dancing with each other.

"I've heard this song!"

"It's a new song. I think it was written this year, Anna."

Anna searched her thoughts. She knew the song! She thought hard with her eyes closed. Then, as if a spike was driven into her heart, her eyes opened and she knew.

"What is this called?" she asked.

Clara checked the packaging and slowly read, "It's called . . . The Lake Isle of Innisfree."

"Is that a real place?" Anna desperately asked.

"It's a little island no one can live on up by . . . What is it by, Cara?"

"I know, it's a William Butler Yeats poem. What was the town? Oh, it's Sligo Town."

"That's right, it's Sligo Town. Do you remember something, Anna?" Cara asked.

However, Anna had left the store before Cara had asked the question. The two girls looked at each other and huddled at the window. They saw Anna run toward Dr. Lannon's house several doors down. Clara picked up her telephone and dialed Father Donnelly's number.

Dr. Lannon was the only person Anna trusted. She did not understand Henry any longer and did not know what the Donnellys knew. She knocked on Dr. Lannon's door as a couple stared at her after they passed by. He opened the door and asked Anna to come in.

He offered to make Anna some tea. She fidgeted, unsure about where to begin.

"I think I remember something," she blurted out as he led her to a small chair in his little cottage.

"Just a moment, my dear," Dr. Lannon said.

He rinsed his hands and put on a pot of tea. He needed a few minutes to wrap his brain around Anna's case. He had recently returned home from Mrs. O'Leary's bedside as she nursed a cold and ranted about how inconvenient it was for her to be sick.

"Now, tell me what you think you remember," he said gently as he sat by her and awaited the teapot's whistle.

"Well, I heard a song today and I think I remember it."

She was interrupted by a knock at the door. Dr. Lannon excused himself to answer it.

"Father Donnelly! Well, yes, she's here. How did you know? She's fine, fine. I'll let you know if we need you," he said, and then shut the door.

He returned, sat down, and begged her forgiveness. Then, he asked her to continue when the teapot suddenly whistled.

Anna grew frustrated and stood up as Dr. Lannon busied himself in his little kitchen. He tried to find the tea bags he claimed little people had stolen again. Anna walked around the little room and her eyes finally fell on a photo of the *very person* she was desperate to talk to him about. She grabbed the picture and started to hyperventilate.

Dr. Lannon walked in with a small tea tray and commented, "Oh, that's my son, Tomas."

Anna stared at the picture in horror as Daire stared back at her in a tuxedo as he held a violin in his hands.

"He's quite the musician. He got a music scholarship and became a doctor. He's in London working with a pharmaceutical company."

Then, Dr. Lannon turned and shuffled through a drawer.

"I have a letter from him. He hasn't written in a few months. . . ."

Anna fled as quickly as she had left the florist shop.

Daire, or Tomas, left me clues about how to find him! I'm in Daire's hometown! My doctor is Daire's father!

She stood in the middle of the street, dumbfounded. She spun around and looked for where to run. Then, it had hit her. The song she remembered was the song Daire had played for her—a clue in case she ever left him.

He's on the Isle of Innisfree like the song he played on his violin!

She remembered the poem was Yeats and quoted some of it. The song must have been written from the poem. She had to think. She knew the isle was inspired by an actual place.

She ran to Henry's little apartment and remembered there was a book of Yeats' poems. She did not realize how desperate she was to see Daire again—how much she worried about him, how much she needed answers from him—until that moment.

She uttered, "I have to find him . . . I have to go back!"

CHAPTER 24

"GOD, HELP ME FIND IT!" Anna whispered as she rummaged through Henry's hodgepodge of books.

Finally, a small book on Yeats and his poetry caught her eye. She found "The Lake Isle of Innisfree" with ease, read it, and found no help within it. Then, she read the side notes which stated: "The Lake Isle of Innisfree was inspired by an uninhabited island in Sligo Town's Lough Gill which Yeats called Utopia."

She rustled through Henry's things and found a map. The island was right by Sligo Town—*I found it!*

She packed one of the shopping bags which she had saved with a few things, and then counted how much money she had. *It might be enough to get there.*

The problem was Anna had no transportation to the bus station in Shannon. She rustled through Henry's drawers and found a key to his car. She walked quickly to the Donnelly's house, got into Henry's car, and drove off.

Sarah noticed from the kitchen window and called frantically for Henry to no avail.

Anna sped away and watched the rearview mirror for Henry to emerge and run after her.

I've stolen a priest's car . . . I'm going to hell.

Yet, she had to at least get to a bus station. She pulled up to the Shannon Church of Ireland and parked. She gave the keys to the rector and asked if he knew Henry. He did not, but he knew the Donnellys. He promised to deliver the car safely back to Henry.

She asked for forgiveness from the shocked rector, and then ran to the bus station. Anna waited impatiently for a bus which was scheduled to be there in ten minutes. It felt like ten hours. She was worried Henry was hot on her tail.

Sarah found Henry asleep in the spare room. She shook him awake.

"I'm sorry, I was up all night," he muttered.

"Anna took your car! Something is going on!" Sarah said frantically.

Henry stared at Sarah wide-eyed for all of two seconds before he sprang out of bed and grabbed his shoes. He bolted out the front door and found the Donnelly's car was gone as well!

Henry ran back into the house and yelled, "Where's your car?"

"Thad has it . . . I don't know where he is right now!" Sarah yelled back.

Henry ran out of the house, down the lane, and asked everyone he saw if they had seen Father Donnelly. He knew Anna was long gone and he could not follow her. Then, he ran to the floral shop. The twins tried to remember every detail of their last conversation with Anna. He grabbed the record album and read the back cover.

"Is this the one that was playing when she said she remembered something?" He asked frantically.

"Yes," Clara said as she tried to fight back tears.

He read it aloud, "The Lake Isle of Innisfree."

Henry searched his mind. There was nothing remotely like it in his memories of Anna.

She's remembered something with Daire!

"Where did she go next?"

Cara replied, "To Dr. Lannon's, I think!"

Henry ran down the road and stopped along the way to ask people where Father Donnelly had gone. He knew he would have to ask another parishioner for use of his or her car if he did not find him soon. He pounded on Dr. Lannon's door. When he opened it, Henry rushed in uninvited.

"Anna was here! What happened while she was here?"

"I don't know. She said she remembered something, and then left in a panic."

"When . . . When did she leave?"

"She looked at a picture of Tomas and . . ."

The room spun around and Henry felt he might faint. He grabbed Tomas' picture. The handsome man looked back at him. His former best friend's eyes penetrated his soul.

Is it possibly Daire and Tomas are . . . One in the same?

He ran out of Dr. Lannon's house and was stopped by Father Donnelly who was in his car.

"I need the car!" Henry demanded as he pulled Father Donnelly out. "Anna took my car somewhere!"

"What? Anna doesn't even have a license!"

"That's the least of our worries right now! I think she's going back to Daire!"

He pleaded, "My boy . . . let me go with you!"

Henry had already pulled away. He drove back to his apartment and burst into the room. On the bed, an open-page book revealed what he had suspected: the Isle of Innisfree. The island was very near where Anna had been found.

He ran out and headed straight for Sligo Town.

Anna looked out the window, her heart pounded against her chest. She saw the little bakery she and Henry had eaten in and held back a few tears.

I'll forgive him, she thought.

She had, after all, stolen his car. She felt it was retribution enough for his horrible words.

Why am I rushing off like this? He must be worried.

Anna shook the thought away. She had waited for answers and did not want to waste another second wondering. The confusion and not knowing frustrated her. She had almost allowed herself to get involved with Daire's pastor!

What are the odds? She sat stunned as her mind raced. *Does Henry know me? Did Dr. Carey somehow know to call Henry because Henry knows Daire?*

The thought was extensively unforgiving.

Is it possible Henry has known all along about Daire and kept me from him? Am I really married to Daire after all?

Anna had dismissed the notion after she saw him drug her food. *Is it at all possible?*

She could not quite figure it out:

Dr. Lannon would've certainly known if I'm his son's wife, wouldn't he? In fact, wouldn't the entire town know?

What if Daire . . . Tomas has gone out of his mind? Dr. Lannon seemed oblivious to the fact his son had taken residence underground; quite literally. Did he know about his son's delusions?

I need to get him help. What if I left him stranded? What if Daire had run out of food and had no way off of the island? I took his boat!

Visions of Daire dying from a fatal wound or malnutrition raced through Anna's mind. She thought of his tender hands on her back. She thought of the music which entranced him; the same music she had heard that morning.

It's divine intervention calling me back to him!

Sligo Town was hours away and there were several more stops to be made. Anna could hardly sit still as her seat companion changed three times during the bus ride.

She pushed away the thought Daire had drugged her and convinced herself he must have had a reason. *No gentle soul like his could've hurt me. Why had I abandoned him? What was I running away from? I love Daire!* Anna knew she tended to react with passion instead of common sense. She counted the money in her purse again. She had enough for the bus ride, but not much else. She did not know if she had enough money to get back if she needed to get help or rent a boat to even get to him. Anna prayed for help.

Sligo Town was bigger than Anna remembered. She was exhausted as she walked to the docks of Sligo Town's Lough Gill. She found a man with a fishing boat and gave him almost all she had left to take the boat out for an hour.

She saw the island from the shore and was amazed; her eyesight had improved so much since she had left weeks earlier. Also, there had only been a thick fog during her time on the island.

Anna yanked the cord to the little motorboat and guided it from its bow. She had butterflies in her stomach. She tried not to think about how mad Daire was. She wished she had brought a medical bag with her.

It was hard navigating through the water because the tide was rolling in. Anna almost got stuck twice, but maneuvered her way out desperate to get to the area where she had stolen his rowboat weeks prior. She searched the map and tried to remember the island.

She calculated she had spent three weeks away from Daire: one week in the hospital, and two weeks in Adare.

A-dare! Had Daire taken the name as another clue to me?

Anna gulped. He knew she might betray him and had bread crumbs placed for her to find him again. She looked up. There, sitting so innocently was a little island. She knew it right away, but she had previously thought it was far from a shore.

She dragged the boat up, stronger than before, and then looked around frantically. The island seemed smaller. Anna ran up the embankment, and then turned toward the place she and Daire had called home.

There, Daire stood in the snow—awestruck—and stared at her. He carried a load of firewood in his arms.

"Daire!" she yelled.

They each stood there—twenty feet apart—breathless. Daire did not answer. At first, he was not sure if Anna was real.

"Why did you drug me?" she yelled.

Daire was overwhelmed and dropped the firewood. She had left him and he did not understand why. He even thought maybe she had died during her attempt to leave. Yet, there she stood, healthy and more beautiful than he remembered.

"You have multiple sclerosis, Anna!" He yelled back. "I was trying to help you!"

She paused and tried to remember what he had told her before about the disease.

"You said MS was nothing to worry about!"

"I lied!"

She thought for a long time and replied, "I haven't had symptoms since I left! What does MS do?"

"It's unpredictable," he yelled. "I'm trying to find a cure!"

"Then take me to a hospital!"

"It's too dangerous to leave in winter, besides they can't help you like I can. I was worried you'd die! Your eyesight was failing, your limbs—"

"I'm fine!"

"You're fine now, but you won't be in a few weeks, or maybe an hour. You never know when it'll hit you!"

"I saw your father!" she yelled. "I was in Adare!"

Daire was unprepared and instantly panicked.

"He thinks you're in London! He didn't mention you're married to me!"

"I hardly talk to my father, Anna."

"You'd tell him if you're married!"

"No one wanted me to marry you because you were so sick. Come inside, Anna! It's freezing out here!"

"No! I want you to answer my questions right now!"

"I'm not going to scream back and forth like this; come inside!"

Anna took in a deep breath. She saw he was all right and his explanation seemed plausible. She looked at him as he pleaded with his eyes. She walked toward him and he held out his hand to her, but she did not take it. He still had a lot of explaining to do.

"Did you ever take me to Adare?" She asked as she walked alongside him.

"No," he answered immediately and felt more at ease, "I never took you home."

"Do you know the Donnellys and Father Henry?" she asked.

His blood chilled instantly and replied, "Yes, a little. I'm not very big on religion."

"I was hosted by them," she said with anger in her voice. "Tell me, Daire, why did you leave me clues about where your whereabouts?"

"I didn't do it knowingly," he said honestly, "but I hoped you'd come back to me. That's why I didn't leave. I have another boat on the other side of the island."

When they reached the hovel, Anna looked inside. She smoothed out her beautiful clothes, straightened her gloves, and wondered how to get down there without getting filthy. It was much smaller and dirtier than she had remembered.

Finally, she crawled in and looked at the fire with soup boiling on it—it smelled bad. She looked at the bed where they had slept together and suddenly she felt a terrible pang in her stomach. It was not at all as she had remembered.

She remembered a romantic little place where the two of them were alone and safe. What she saw with clear eyes was a hole in the ground.

Daire stirred the pot. She looked hard at him; he seemed small. She was used to Henry's size and the memory of him dwarfed Daire's stature. He sat down and looked at her with a sigh. She looked like a lady. He shook his head and snickered. She began to think coming back was a terrible idea.

"Have some water," he offered as he poured it for her.

She shook her head even though she was incredibly thirsty.

"No, thank you," she declined his offer properly.

He wondered if he could ever get her back to the way things were.

"He got to you, didn't he?" Daire asked.

He was referring to Henry. He knew Henry would give her the sun, moon, and stars if given a chance. He believed her clothing was a small sample of all he had lavished upon her.

"Who?"

"Henry," Daire said as he finally showed one of his aces.

Anna was stunned and stood still.

"I knew it," he said more to himself than her.

"I thought you said you didn't know him."

"I said I only knew him a little."

"Is that true?"

"No."

"How well do you know him?"

"He was my best friend."

Anna searched his face. He was totally complacent, his movements seemed relaxed. She became more concerned.

"You lied to me."

"Yes. I had to."

"What does that mean?"

"It means you're lost in more ways than your health, Anna," he answered with a sneer.

His demeanor became more rigid as Daire realized it was too late—he had lost Anna. He searched his thoughts for a way to salvage what they had—he knew her well. She was normally unrelenting with her questions. So, he came to the conclusion he had to start over with her. He thought about where he kept the serum. Daire knew he had to be discreet about filling the needle. He turned his back to Anna and fumbled through his shelves. He moved down the cups on the shelf, as if he was preparing for his meal, and found a small vile. He worked quickly.

"What does that mean?" Anna asked.

He filled the vile. "Your beliefs are so insane they're clouding your judgment to know what's real."

"And that's what you're trying to do for me . . . Help me?" Anna asked angrily.

He pumped out the first bit of serum, anxious the syringe did not have any air in it.

"Anna, I'm always on your side. Of course, I'm trying to help you."

Anna finally realized how long Daire's back had been turned to her. At once, the instincts God had placed within Anna were fully alarmed. Daire held the syringe slightly behind his back where she could not see. He came closer and she grabbed her arms to protect herself. He put his hand on the door and drew close to her face. She thought of hitting him, but did not want to aggravate him and make things worse. It was the wrong decision.

He kissed her neck, and then suddenly stabbed her with a needle. He whispered how sorry he was and held her close as she sank. Almost instantly, Anna could not move any part of her body!

She was only able to hear and see as Daire laid her down. She lay motionless on the little dirt bed with quilts. She watched as Daire refilled the syringe.

"Just in case," he said to her.

Then, he got into bed with her. She was totally immobilized. He removed her beautiful coat, and then started to unbutton the top buttons of her blouse.

"I've missed you so much," he said.

He took his shirt off and put his arm behind her head. All she could move were her eyes. He put his face down into the crook of her neck and breathed deeply.

"I'm so sorry, Anna. I was trying so hard to help you."

He lifted his head and looked at her. He moved the hair away from her damp face.

"I don't want to start all over with you. I want you to know that," he said and kissed her forehead. "You're so beautiful."

He took her hand and kissed it, and then held it to his bare chest.

"I want to tell you some things before I give the drug to you again. You won't remember what I'm about to tell you, but I just need you to hear it once."

He wiped his tears away and unbuttoned one more button from her blouse, and then brushed her jawbone with his hand.

"What they did to you girls was more than I can take, you know that? Henry could never know or understand it—we knew that. I was at the prison camp they put you in, Anna. You were in a terrible place where people were tortured to death for being Jewish or considered an undesirable. Then, there were people like you and me: spies. You and I helped so many people before we were captured, did you know that?"

Anna wanted to scream, to run. She wondered if everything Daire said was a lie.

He touched her lips with his fingers.

"I was a doctor and so they—the Germans—put me to work. My first job was at the prison camp where you were. The prettiest girls were put in brothels—horrible places where girls were raped. The most beautiful girls, like you, were for the SS.

"They had me sterilize you girls, but sometimes it didn't work. The conditions were beyond what I want you to know, but that was not the worst of it. The worst was when one of you became pregnant. I pray you never had to endure such a thing. Most died from what we were forced to do to them."

He covered her up with the blanket more and put his hand on her chest.

"Henry...Well, I don't think he even knew all you went through. I don't think you told anyone the whole story, not even Sarah. I knew, Anna, because I was there. I think I even remember you.

"I remember this one time they handed me a ticket. They said it was a reward for doing an excellent job. It was for twenty minutes in the brothel. I didn't want to go, but they told me I had to or I'd be put back in the camp as a regular prisoner. Henry never understood this."

He kissed Anna's ear, breathed into it, and whispered, "They put this stuff that burned like crazy on us as we stood there naked, and then told us to run to the door we were assigned. There was a soldier who opened it—he explained the rules, and then shut the door, but watched from a peep hole to make sure I abided. The girl just stood there, totally naked and looked at me. I saw every rib, every bone—she was being starved to death. It turned my stomach, Anna, but I knew they were watching.

"I got into bed with her; I just laid there and cried. It was like she was dead. I didn't do anything to her, I swear it. We were so weak, anyway. She had deep blue eyes which were glazed over."

Tears escaped Anna's eyes. She was so scared.

"I didn't want you to remember anything like that, Anna. When I knew you went through all of that, I tried to find a way to help you. I worked for a year to find this cure. All I wanted was for you to forget and lead a happy life with me. We'd eventually have left the island and had a wonderful life together, I know. I want to try again, Anna. I want to start all over . . . Have you love me again."

Anna screamed inside. She did not want to forget Henry.

"I can see in your eyes—or am I just hoping—you still love me. Why would you come back if you didn't?"

He touched her clavicle bone.

"I wish you could tell me what you want right now. Maybe, you'd even want me as much as I want you."

The car wheels squealed into the parking lot of the police station of Sligo Town. Panicked and flustered, Henry ran inside. He was told the lead detective on Anna's case was out on an assignment, so Henry tried to explain the case to another detective. Henry lost patience quickly and announced to every officer in the station he was prepared to give him one hundred pounds if he came with him—an army of twenty officers followed Henry in haste.

They gathered a few motorboats and Henry lodged himself on the stern as his small band sped quickly toward the Isle of Innisfree where he was sure his wife had gone.

They sped around the little island twice before one of them caught sight of a small tree in the middle of the water.

"You better thank God its high tide!" The officer who steered Henry's boat called out.

He did and they found the little boat Henry assumed Anna had taken. He jumped into the water before his boat successfully docked. Henry motioned for the band of officers to remain quiet, and then they split up. They were on the hunt.

Turn right! Something inside of him said. So, Henry quickly followed its leading without taking time to truly think through whose voice he heard. He saw a shed on a high hill, and then looked at a roof which sat atop the ground.

His eyes narrowed, as he remembered Anna saying she was underground. He knew it was the spot. He ran to the nearest officer and motioned toward the underground hovel, not wanting to alarm Tomas.

Henry raced down to the underground dwelling and kicked open the door. He scrambled in, his heart burst with anger. He pulled Tomas off of his wife and threw him to the other side of the hovel. Tomas' body smashed through the glass of his cupboard and blood began to pour from his head. Initially, he was in shock, but then grabbed the knife on the table.

Henry looked at his childhood friend as if he was a stranger. Tomas seemed possessed. Henry looked back at Anna who was undressed from the waist up and quickly covered her.

Henry! Anna thought, still unable to speak.

"What have you done to my wife!" Henry demanded.

Anna's mind raced, and thought, *Is he talking about me?*

"I've loved her like you never could!" Tomas yelled.

Henry turned around in rage, but Tomas was ready and stabbed Henry through his ribs with the knife. Henry gasped. Anna fought to get up as she watched the horrific scene, but she could do nothing, but watch. Henry doubled over. Tomas stabbed him again, this time in his arm. Henry rolled over. Finally, Henry threw a punch—a stunning haymaker—which took Tomas down.

The police ran in, held Tomas back, and secured his weapon. An officer went to Henry who was in bad shape. Anna lay lifeless.

The officers wrestled Tomas outside and threw him into the snow as three of them held him down and handcuffed him. It took a team to secure him as he flew into a supernatural rage.

Finally, a police officer reached over to carry Anna out.

"Stop!" Henry cried out. "I want to carry her!"

He got up gingerly and the officers looked at each other. There was no way he could do it. So, one of them stood in front of Henry and helped him carry Anna as he cradled his wounded arm.

"I've got you," he whispered to Anna.

The officer pulled her through the entrance hole, and then Henry covered her again after he barely made his way out—it was a strain. He helped the officer cradle Anna again and carried her quickly to the motorboat. Tomas watched from the snowy ground with hate-filled eyes.

Henry reassured her, "You're going to be okay. I'm here,"

Henry got into the boat. The police officer, who helped carry Anna, placed her in Henry's lap. Then, they sped through the marsh toward Sligo Town as fast as possible. They were fortunate for the light and raced through quickly. Then, the boat slowed and the officer called to Henry they had run out of gas.

Henry bent over Anna and secured her with the blankets. He pet her head as his blood dripped all over her. She was soaked in his blood.

"I have you," he soothed.

She did not respond; she could not.

Henry began to feel pain as the adrenaline wore off. He held his hand over his wound in his side to stop the blood, but his eyesight became very dark.

"I can't see!" He called out to the officer.

"You're in shock; you're injured," the man said when he realized the extent of Henry's wounds.

He took off his uniform coat and stuffed it around the deep gash in Henry's rib. He examined the cut on his arm and realized an artery had split. Blood came out like a tiny fountain and the officer took off his shirt and formed a tourniquet around his arm. Henry had him loosen it. He was determined not to lose his arm.

"Can't you paddle us?" Henry asked.

"Here comes one!" He shouted and waved his arms.

Other officers used their boats to push the disabled motorboat to shore.

"We've got him in the other boat!" An officer yelled out to Henry.

Henry started to lose consciousness as he slumped over Anna and finally collapsed.

CHAPTER 25

"THE GIRL IS NOT THE priority . . . Take him!" Dr. Carey shouted. "He's lost too much blood!"

Anna wanted them to flip her around on the bed so she could see Henry, but they did not think to do so. They all worked frantically around her to attend to Henry. Dr. Carey used foul language to direct the nurses.

"He's got to go into surgery now!" He barked as they rolled Henry out.

Anna lay on the cot alone and prayed, *God, please help Dr. Carey. Help him save Henry.*

She was covered in Henry's blood and a blanket. A million questions had been answered in a few seconds when Henry broke through the hovel door. One was who she loved.

Finally, three nurses and the doctor ran by her with Henry. She finally saw him and breathed in, hardly able to take the shock. His muscular chest was covered in blood. He was cut deeply in his side. His arm hung lifeless and was wrapped in bloody, soaked bandages.

He was unconscious, as a small, wooden cross hung from his neck onto the gurney. Anna wanted to scream and run to him, but she still could not move. All she could do was blink away the tears and wait.

A candy striper volunteer came by and grabbed Anna's chart. She went over to Anna and touched her arm.

"I'm going to call your family," she said.

Then, she left Anna with a young nurse who hooked up a glass bottle of IV fluids and shakily injected a needle into her vein.

"Dr. Carey has ordered lots of fluids so you can flush out whatever was given to you," she said. "I have to do a catheter as well. Blink if you feel any pain, okay?"

Anna blinked. She could feel, but she could not move. The nurse tried a few times and finally got a vein. All Anna thought about was Henry. He had said she was his wife!

Can it be?

Her breathing became labored and she closed her eyes as the nurse fiddled around. More important than any incredible piece of information, though, was if Henry was going to live. That, more than anything, was unbearable to Anna because she was the cause of it all; she had gone back to Daire!

What have I done?

Hours ticked by and Anna was still immobile. All she did was pray simple prayers and beg God to perform a miracle.

The nurse came back in and said, "If you can hear me, Anna, my name is Molly. They told me you might be able to hear me. Henry's still in surgery. Dr. Carey is doing all he can."

Then, Molly touched her leg through the blanket.

"I'll return in a little while."

Time slowly ticked by —Anna knew because she literally heard the clock. She was alone. Then, as if the earth had erupted, the door flung open at once and the Donnellys, Clara, Cara, Mrs. O'Leary, and a few other people Anna did not know rushed into her room. Sarah started to cry when she saw Anna. Father Donnelly took his sweet wife's hand.

"My dear, you must be strong," he said and looked at the others. "The nurse says Anna can hear and see us."

Then, Father Donnelly looked hard at Anna and said, "Blink once if you can hear us."

She did. Everyone watched awestruck.

"Anna, blink again if you can see us."

She did.

"So, let's do this, blink once for yes and twice for no."

She blinked once.

"Are you hurt?"

She blinked twice. It was a lie.

"That's good, that's good. Now, tell me, do you . . . know?"

Anna paused for a moment. She believed she knew what Father Donnelly had asked. She blinked once and the ladies started to cry.

"You know about Henry?"

She blinked once as a tear escaped.

"He's your husband."

She blinked once.

Sarah could not take it any longer and threw herself on Anna. She kissed her cheeks through puddles of her tears.

"We love you so much," she cried.

Sarah waved everyone out of the room. Father Donnelly went to find someone to tell him more. He knew nothing about what had actually transpired other than a police officer's account who was in the hall. Sarah shut the door, leaving the two of them alone.

"We're alone right now," she said as she tucked Anna's blankets around her shoulders. "I want you to tell me something. Do you know who I really am?"

Two blinks.

"All right, that's all right now. My dear . . . You were married to my son. He died and you've been my dearest, closest girl," she began to cry. "You're like a daughter to me. I thought I'd lost you . . . And here you are."

Two blinks. Sarah smiled.

Anna wanted to ask a million questions, but she could not. Then, she felt as though she needed to clear her throat. Sarah jumped and ran to get a nurse. Molly came in.

"Can you do that again, Anna?"

She did. Molly smiled.

"This is good," she said as the others came in and heard the good news. "The drug is leaving her; she may regain all her faculties. The doctor told me to watch for it. The police also got some valuable information from the man who did this to her. He said it was *temporary* paralysis."

Everyone sighed and thanked God in relief. Anna knew as much from her past experience.

"What did you find out about Henry?" Sarah asked as she touched her husband's chest.

Father Donnelly shook his head and began to cry. Everyone feared the worst.

"They don't know," he finally muttered out. "There's a chance of survival, but it's slim."

"We have to pray," Sarah said.

Word spread throughout Adare very quickly. Their friends piled into cars to travel to the hospital in Sligo Town to pray with Father Donnelly for Henry. Some townspeople accompanied others to await Henry's certain death. However, the majority believed he would be all right.

The hospital staff was divided. Some welcomed the convergence of visitors and brought cots and chairs for the people to sleep on. While others thought the amount of people was a nuisance.

By nightfall, when some of the villagers had gone to look for an inn, Anna was able to talk. Her voice was raspy, but understandable.

"What do you want?" Sarah asked.

"Clothes . . . Present from Henry on my bed."

"Someone will bring you some things; just rest."

The nurse gave Anna something to help her sleep. She fought sleep as long as possible. The Donnellys waited until everyone was settled or had left the hospital. Anna was asleep when they finally left to check into their room at the inn.

Anna dreamed for the first time since she left Daire. It was a simple little dream—a memory, in fact.

Henry was seated in a tall upholstered chair, reading a book. The fire was going and her eyes met his. She carried a serving tray which contained tea saucers and cups. Henry watched her as she looked around. They were alone.

"I have a present for you, Henry," she said and reached into her apron.

Henry looked more than surprised. He reached out his hands and took the small gift. He opened the little box and inside was a gold chain with a wooden cross.

"It was Jamie's," Anna said as he looked at her, moved. "I wanted you to have it."

Then, she walked away.

Sarah woke Anna as a few more nurses looked on.

"It's all right, dear," she whispered as Anna gasped in a panic.

Yesterday really happened—it's all so terribly real. I'm in a hospital.

"Can you move anything?"

Anna tapped her fingers. The nurses smiled at each other.

"Someone brought up your present from Henry. Do you want me to open it?"

Anna nodded. She already knew it was a book. Sarah slipped off the thin ropes.

"Henry's terrible with tying knots," Sarah noted as she tried to open it.

Sarah ripped off the paper and looked at the book. Then, she showed it to Anna. It was a small, red book which read: Henry's Dreams.

"He was trying to tell you who he was," she told Anna.

"Do you want me to read to you?"

"Not right now," Anna said weakly.

She did not want others to know her husband's secret thoughts.

"All right."

Sarah picked up the book and a small picture fell out. It was a picture of Anna in a bridal gown. She showed it to Anna who gasped. Then, she flipped it over and read: Anna Oliver, 1946.

Anna then knew for sure. It was, in fact, her.

Clara and Cara came into Anna's room and hugged her. Anna still was not able to put her arms around them.

"We were so worried," Clara cried.

"Girls," Father Donnelly said as he stepped into the room.

They all looked up, anxious for news about Henry.

"He's lost a lot of blood. The doctor says he needs a transfusion, but his blood type is very rare. Sean came and gave his, they're a match."

"How did he know that?" Clara asked.

"Henry's done it for him before," he said quietly.

Everyone soaked in the nature of who Henry was.

"She can shake her head now and move her fingers a little," Cara said happily to Father Donnelly.

"Getting better by the minute," Sarah whispered and kissed Anna's forehead. "I love you."

"The good doctor said it might be helpful to Henry and Anna if they were together in the same room. They'll be wheeling him in very soon," Father Donnelly said with uncertainty about how to prepare the girls for the gruesome wounds Henry had.

Anna heard the squeal of hospital bed wheels and knew they were bringing in Henry. When he was brought in, she saw he was covered from the neck down. The nurses steadied the tall, metal poles which contained his fluids.

Anna silently rejoiced. *It's so good to see him.*

She wanted everyone to leave them alone, but they all stood there and gaped.

"We're keeping him sedated," the nurse said. "He's had the transfusion and was sewed up really well. He keeps trying to wake up, so we've increased his sedatives."

"Why do you think that is?" Father Donnelly asked.

"When there's a traumatic event, patients often do that," she said calmly. "I think you all need to give the two of them some privacy."

They all agreed, although no one wanted to leave. Sarah laid the book on Anna's lap and kissed her forehead. Then, she went over to Henry and kissed him. Father Donnelly put his hand on Henry's shoulder, and then ushered his wife and friends out of the room.

Anna could finally move her arms.

"Henry, if you can hear me, I'm beside you."

Nothing.

"Nurse, can you move our beds closer?"

The nurse looked like was going to say no, but then changed her mind. She moved Anna's bed closer. She wiggled her toes a little and tried to shift to her side to no avail.

"The chart says you need to eat," the nurse stated.

She spooned Anna some soup. She ate to appease her.

"Try to get some rest," the nurse said and turned the light low. "We're going to keep him warm. The blood transfusion can result in patients being very cold."

Then, she noticed Henry shivered slightly. The nurse put another blanket on him.

Anna felt for Henry's hand and held it. It was bloody and dirty, but she did not care. She wanted to feel his skin. She wanted to know he was alive. Then, she fell asleep.

The next day a nurse came in and opened the drapes. Anna looked over at Henry, and then realized she was soaking wet.

"Hi, Anna."

"I think the catheter . . . ," Anna began as she pulled back her blanket.

She looked frantically at Henry. He had not awakened.

"Uh, oh," the nurse remarked casually. "That happens. We'll change you."

"I'm so sorry," Anna said as she put her feet on the ground and started to stand.

"Well, look at you!" the nurse chimed. "Looks like that terrible thing is wearing off! Do you think you can walk?"

"I don't know," Anna said, hesitantly.

The nurse put her arm around Anna to steady her and commented, "You're doing great! Let's see if you can make it to the bathroom so we don't have to put the cath' back in, okay?"

Anna settled down on her clean sheets and felt much better. She looked over at Henry who was totally still. She missed him, although he was right there.

"How long before you let him wake up?"

"Dr. Carey said he's concerned Henry will do too much too soon, so he's going to wait until tonight to stop the sedatives."

Anna thought about what it might look like. *Will he be angry with me?*

She squeezed her eyes shut and thought about the horrific scene she had witnessed. *What have I put Henry through? Why hadn't he told me from the first moment he was my husband?*

She had so much to say to him.

Beth and a few other nurses came in and greeted Anna as they pushed her bed aside to get to Henry's. They brought in buckets of warm, soapy water to bathe him. Anna watched as they took off his gown and revealed his chest. Beth smiled at Anna, and then drew the curtain a little between them.

342   *A Little Irish Love Story*

"We're going to get him cleaned up," she said and winked.

Anna heard the nurses giggle after one commented it was the best day on the job she ever had. They brought in bucket after bucket and changed the bloody water repeatedly.

They dressed Henry in a new gown and were careful to put another sheet on without moving him from the bed. It was not easy, but none of them seemed to mind. His lifeless body flopped around a little as they shifted him. Anna was scared they might injure him further, but they seemed confident about what they were doing.

Finally, they finished, pulled back the curtain, pushed Anna's bed close again, and smiled sweetly at her.

"We've wanted to clean him up for a while," one commented. "He's been such a mess."

Beth put some lotion on his elbows and hands, and commented about how dry they were. Another nurse cleaned his mouth and swabbed his eyes. Anna watched as they tried to rinse his hair in a bowl which proved to be too difficult.

"He'll be awake in a few hours," Beth said.

Then, she left.

Anna closed her heavy eyes. Hours later, she opened them. Henry's eyes gazed back at hers. She almost jumped out of her skin. She moved her mouth to speak, but was not sure if he was truly awake, so she kept silent. He looked back at her more deeply. She inched closer to him and held his face in her hands.

Henry did not answer, yet he kept staring into Anna's grey eyes. He knew there was something different in their interaction.

My love, he said inside.

Relief was not even close to what he felt at that moment. Anna stroked the sides of his face as she cuddled close to his side. They looked into each other's eyes and did not want to call the nurse or alarm anyone of his consciousness. They wanted the moment to themselves.

It was the same peace they had felt one night years ago when they felt the stillness the first winter snow brought. They looked out the window to see the white flakes against the black background and cuddled close in the same quilt. The silence could shake the world; it was a peace not of this earth. No words were more beautiful than their gaze at each other. Nothing more needed to be said.

As their spirits hung between heaven and Earth, they found so much in each other's eyes which had not been evident before. She was his hero, now he was hers.

Henry saw in Anna's eyes what he had longed for: she knew him. She might not remember him, but she knew him. It was all he had ever wanted.

CHAPTER 26

HENRY RESTED HIS HEAD AGAINST the white leather seats of his car. He faded in and out of blissful and painful sleep. He held Anna's hand. Sean drove quietly.

"Why are you sitting on your coat balled up like that?" he whispered to Anna.

"Because I can hardly see out the window," she said. "I hate sitting in the back. I always get car sick."

Henry smiled and remembered how she had always kept a pillow in his car to sit on in case she drove.

"I think you should've stayed in the hospital longer," she said, worried the drive back to Adare was too much for him.

"Ten days is enough. *You* should've gone home a week ago."

"I wasn't about to leave you."

Henry smiled and whispered, "I just want to be in a peaceful place where people can't descend upon us constantly. And the police ... They were relentless. I don't know how many times you and I gave our statements. I'm so tired of it all."

The number of visitors who came to see Henry was beyond what the hospital normally handled—every hour, at least another family came. He was not resting, but he had forbid Dr. Carey from ordering no visitors. He could not impose such a restriction on his dear friends.

The Donnellys had found a nurse and doctor to be on call during his recovery, but they were about thirty minutes away in

Shannon. Dr. Lannon had gone to be with his son as he prepared for his court hearing.

Anna worried about it, so she changed her thoughts almost entirely to the surprise the town had for Henry. She had wanted to be part of the planning, but had not left his side while he was in the hospital.

Sean drove through the prettiest town in Ireland—as the people of Adare insisted it was—and waved at many friendly faces. Henry was almost asleep and she hated to wake him. Henry felt the bumpy road and thought they were going back to the little apartment behind the church, but Sean had gone in the opposite direction. He stuck his nose up and opened his eyes.

Is Sean driving to the Manor?

He rubbed his eyes and looked around at the white fairy land before him. He had never noticed how beautiful it was until that moment. He watched his lovely wife swell up with tears as the car stopped.

"Do you remember it?" He asked with hope.

Anna still had not remembered anything about her past life. She shook her head and wiped away tears from her cheeks. It was so beautiful, more so than she had imagined.

"I feel like I do, but . . . no . . . It's just . . . knowing this was our beginning—"

"It's still the beginning," he said.

"No, Henry. This is our rebirth."

He smiled because she had said "our." It was *his* second chance as well. He was determined to be a better husband this time around, of this he was sure. He knew how to love her as he never had before.

"Why are we here?" he asked.

"You'll see," she said.

She smiled as Sean pulled the car past the castle-like home and headed toward a grey, stone house with a dozen windows which faced a pretty courtyard.

"Why are we at the carriage house?" he asked.

Sean stopped the car, jumped out, went to the other side of the car, and opened Henry's door. Anna tried to help Henry get out, but she was not much help.

"Do you think a wee thing like you can carry this massive creature?" he teased.

Henry chuckled underneath his breath and steadied his arm on Sean's large shoulders.

"You would've broken in half, that you would! Step aside, step aside," he said in good spirits.

"Why are we here, Sean?" Henry asked again.

"Faith, Henry, faith," he said tongue in cheek.

Sean perched Henry up and Anna stood beside him.

"What are you up to?" Henry asked Anna with a wicked smile on his face.

Then, Sean opened the door and Henry took in the enormous surprise. A dozen of Henry's dearest friends were in the carriage house with smiles etched on their faces. Henry took in the sight of them together. Then, he stepped inside and looked around the carriage house, but it looked a far cry from it. The beautiful space had been converted into a home.

The carved mahogany walls were a beautiful backdrop to the yellow and white pallet. The windows on one wall looked out over a courtyard frozen in time. The open beamed ceiling had a beautiful wooden chandelier. He knew a man in town who did woodworking had made it.

He looked at Sarah and smiled—he knew her décor. Then, he looked at each man full of warm pride for they had done the renovation themselves. Then, his eyes fell on the lighted painting over the fireplace. It had hung in the past over the Donnelly's mantle. It was the painting of Ruth which Anna had painted as a present to him on their wedding day. He realized the yellows in the wheat and pale colors of Ruth's robes were all over the house. Finally, he looked at Anna. She had been at the hospital with him almost every moment, so she had not seen the house either. Tears streamed down her face. It was *their* house.

Father Donnelly shook Henry's hand and chuckled underneath his breath, "Well, there were no more cottages to be had in town and Mrs. Donnelly would've killed me if I had offered your old cottage back."

"I heard that, Donnelly!" Sarah heckled.

"This is too much," Henry said with a catch in his throat.

He went to each person, shook his hands, looked him straight in the eye, and said, "Thank you."

Every person felt the weight of his thanks and love for them as if he was the only person in the room with Henry. Then, he turned to Anna. She looked at his arm in a sling, and then at his face—it radiated love and peace. It was as if Henry dwelled in heavenly places.

Sean offered his arm to Anna. She took it, and then he led her to a pretty, yellow print armchair and she sat by the fire, visibly tired. As wonderful as the moment was, she wanted everyone to leave so she could be alone with Henry.

"'Tis the life of a clergy's wife," Sean commented as he looked at people everywhere.

He sat in the twin chair opposite her.

"You know," he said and scratched his stubbly chin, "there's still time to run away with me."

"Running away didn't turn out too well for me, now did it?"

Sean was at first embarrassed by what he said, but then saw the gleam in Anna's eye. He remembered her sense of humor which he had always appreciated.

"Good you can joke about it, I suppose," he said, relieved.

"Sean, I'll never forget what you did for Henry. He would've died without you," she said about how he had given blood.

"He's done the same for me."

"What happened?"

"It's really an embarrassing story," he said and looked over at Henry as he talked to the horde of people.

"Then, I *really* want to hear it now," Anna said and put her head back against the chair.

"Mind you, it was on Christmas holiday—my first time back from the university. I got a very expensive law degree which I used to start my pub," he said tongue in cheek.

"Naturally."

"Naturally," Sean agreed. "I had this idea we'd go sledding—"

"Oh, I think I know where this is going."

"Why are you having me tell you this then?"

"Go on," she laughed.

"Well, it's like this. I was first because the rest of them were chickens. I'm not the smallest person in the world and I got some serious momentum going," Sean said.

He inched closer to Anna so no one would hear.

"Then, out of nowhere—God is my witness and Henry, too—a swan comes out of nowhere."

"I'm sorry, a swan?"

"Yes, a swan! They can be very aggressive, you know!"

"I had no idea," Anna laughed at his expense.

"Well, this swan—it must've had a ten-foot wingspan—starts pecking at my face while I'm sliding down! I was batting at him and swerving. So much so, I didn't see this telephone pole dead ahead of me."

"They had telephones in Adare way back then?" Anna interrupted and continued to laugh.

"Well, it was the first year for them," he said, and then saw her point. "Oh, hardy har-har, you're not too far behind me in age, missy!"

"I'm sorry, I'm sorry. What did the swan do to you?"

"Well, I went straight into the pole—the swan was unhurt. Me, however, I had twenty-five stitches in my skull, a concussion, a trip to Shannon, and a blood infusion from Henry."

"Have mercy!"

"Yes. It was terrible. I don't like swans, Anna. I'm telling you they're like these modern-day pterodactyl."

"They're not!" She said and giggled as Sean maintained a serious face. "You almost got taken out by a swan!"

"It's true. I did. Thanks to Henry, I'm here."

"You're a good friend, Sean."

"Yes, I am. Speaking of which, I'm going to get old lazy bones. He looks like he's wilting over there."

Sean rose and went to get Henry. He walked him over to the chair he was just in and steadied him down into it.

"I'm tired," Henry said with a sigh.

"I'm going to kick everyone out," Sean announced. "Attention, everyone out!"

Everyone looked as Henry hid a smile under his fist.

"Go down to the bar and I'll give you all a free beer! Did you hear that, Donnelly? I said, one, you greedy priest, one!"

Everyone laughed, gathered their coats, and were ushered out. Sean did not let them kiss or hug Henry again.

"By the way, you owe me five pounds for everyone's drinks, money bags," he whispered to Henry.

Then, Sean scooted the last person, Mrs. O'Leary, out with a small shove as she timidly called back, "Come to breakfast soon, Henry."

Sean smiled like a Cheshire cat at the two of them and poured himself a drink from their new icebox. Henry and Anna smiled at each other as he talked.

"Anna will take the day shift; I'll take the night. She'll be in the apartment behind the church like she has . . ."

Sean had discussed it at length with Henry a few days before. Henry believed as long as Anna did not remember her wedding vows, she had made none. So, the decent thing was to separate until she wanted to recite them again.

Anna shot up a look at Sean that terrified him and emphatically said, "I'm not leaving Henry!"

"Well, now," Henry said and held her hands. "Would you rather stay at the Donnelly's?"

"No. I want to be here with you."

"Well," Sean said and wiped his mouth with his sleeve, "that just wouldn't look right according to his Excellency."

"Look right? Henry, I've been with you every second these past two weeks in the hospital. I'm not leaving you now," Anna begged.

"Why don't you want to stay in the apartment, Anna?" Henry asked gently.

She began to fill up and he thought he knew the reason why.

"How about staying with the Donnellys if you're afraid?"

"I'm not afraid!" She shot back more forcefully than she intended.

"That's my cue," Sean said. "Give us a kiss."

He and Anna kissed each other simultaneously on the cheek. Henry smiled with his mouth agape at his friend's brazenness.

"What is it? Are you jealous?" Sean teased, and then kissed Henry all over his face. "See now? I love you, too, you rascal!"

Anna laughed which broke through the tension in the air. Sean loved doing that during difficult situations. Sean winked at her, and then took off. He shut the door, took Henry's car keys, and roared off to his pub to oversee the bar celebration for his best friend's return.

Henry twitched his head a little and motioned for Anna to come closer. She dragged over an ottoman and sat knee-to-knee with him. Henry took her hands and glided his fingers through hers. His heart beat fast; he tried to slow it down. The doctor had said rest, but with his beautiful wife around, he got a thrill from simply breathing the same air as her. He looked into her soft, grey eyes which were about to give birth to tears.

"Tell me then," he said so gently, it was almost a whisper.

He wanted her so desperately to put what she felt into words. He wanted to hear the words over and over again. She had yet to really say anything since he had rescued her. She had been so quiet and only spoke when absolutely necessary—she held her emotions tightly at all times. She finally looked down, not able to take his tender gaze one more minute. He was overwhelming her with his love.

"I just don't want to leave you," she said, uncharacteristically timid.

He smiled slightly and took what he could from it. Then, he brushed away the few straggly tears which had escaped her eyes.

"I don't ever want to leave you," he answered.

"Henry," she said, hesitantly. "Are we still . . . married?"

Henry paused. It had been the first mention about the topic. He knew she was aware in the hospital, but she had never spoken of it.

"That's a difficult question. In the eyes of the law: yes. If you want to ask if I think we're married, I think the best way to put it is I'm married to you. It's like that moment during a wedding when the husband has said, 'I do' and the bride has yet to make her vows. That's where I think we are."

"In limbo."

"No. I wouldn't put it like that. I wait in this beautiful moment. You wrote this poem when I asked you to marry me. It read:

Today, your heart held me in suspension
between heaven and Earth
by unseen wings of your words.
What are words?
Movements of sound embodying spirit,
taking shape as life and death,
love and hate.
Your words are so few.
But they are life.
Your words blow on my naked bones,
sewing on flesh,
forcing through my life blood.
You breathe into my mouth with your kiss.
No. I am not in the between.
I am in heaven.

He pushed back a black tendril behind her ear and looked at her again.

"That's where we are, Anna; this fantastically exquisite moment. I'm in heavy anticipation for your love."

She sighed, and then shut her eyes tight. He brushed her jaw bone with his fingers. All alone, they could finally let go. She held his face with her hands and kissed him. He stopped for a moment, looked at her, and then kissed her again.

Then, as fantastically as the moment had begun, it quickly ended. She turned away and looked at the fire. With Henry still in a frozen state of rapture, she spoke casually.

"I better go get some more firewood."

He looked at her, confused. However, then he remembered a very distant memory of her doing something similar. She was shy.

It was a rare sight, but he truly saw it.

"Please don't worry about it," he barely replied and cleared his throat.

"I'll just be a moment," she said, pleased she was back to normal for a few moments.

Henry glanced at the huge pile of firewood behind her.

"Anna."

"Yes?" She answered as she put on her coat.

"Please come here."

She looked at him strangely. It was not like him to ask anything of her.

"What is it?"

He decided to confront her.

"I know this is all strange and new, but I don't want to be parted from you, not for a moment. Please stay with me."

She immediately felt at ease, unbuttoned her coat, and put it beside her. He pulled her closer and had her sit on his lap. He kissed her again.

"So, this is the plan?" She asked slyly.

"Yes, this is *always* the plan," he said with a gleam of mischief in his eye.

"Well now, Father Henry, I don't know how becoming this is of a priest."

"Not at all."

"That's what I thought," she flirted. "Tell me something—"

"No, I don't think so. I'd much rather kiss you. You see, I've been waiting quite some time to do this."

Henry kissed her again.

"Suckin' face, finally I see!"

Sean's voice jarred them. Henry almost threw Anna off his lap.

"Well, it's about time!"

. "What in the world are you doing back here so soon?" Henry asked slightly annoyed.

"I brought dinner, you good for nothing," Sean said and held up bags of food. "One of the ladies of your fine parish made something for us. And I don't see Anna going anywhere tonight. Couch for me."

He put things into the refrigerator and mumbled, "And here I had that nice guest room all made up with warm, cozy sheets."

"What's that I hear . . . You mumbling about getting cozy?" Henry teased his friend.

"No, I was talking to myself about manly things!" Sean retorted. "Manly things you would know nothing about!"

"Sean?" Anna asked sweetly.

"Yes, beautiful," Sean said as a jab to Henry.

"I'd be more than happy to take the couch so you can have your comfy bed," Anna said with a gleam in her eye.

"Why don't you stay in your stupid husband's bed with him, huh?" He asked and knew he had crossed a line.

"Sean!" Anna cried out.

"Well, it makes no sense to me," Sean said into the refrigerator again.

Henry changed the subject and asked, "What did you bring?"

"Shepherd's pie."

"Henry doesn't eat meat."

"Well, Henry has my blood in him and he better feed it good, missy," Sean said, a little agitated.

"Sean!" Anna scolded.

"I'm sorry," Sean said insincerely. "I have a head of lettuce. Would you like to eat lettuce tonight, Henry?"

"That'd be fine," Henry said.

"Henry, can't you make an exception this once?" Anna begged quietly. She knew he needed the nourishment.

"You've been living on pudding lately."

"All right," Henry conceded.

"See, I told you he had manly blood in him now!" Sean said triumphantly.

"Why do you not eat meat anyway?" Anna whispered.

Henry looked away and twitched a little.

"I've never liked it in the first place, but after I burned down the barn and animals . . . I couldn't look at it anymore."

"I'm so sorry, Henry. You'll have to tell me that story some time. Do you want me to go out and get you something else?" She asked sweetly.

"No. Just watch. There'll be a vegetarian one for me. Sean likes to get my goat."

Anna smiled knowingly. She loved Henry's friend almost as much as Henry did.

"Dinner is served!" Sean said.

He slapped down their plates onto the new dining room table. Anna went and got the drinks as Sean eased Henry into the hard backed chair.

"Um, Henry," Sean whispered, "I'd highly recommend you send me home so you can be alone with your wife."

"You really are uncouth, aren't you?"

"Thank you," he said.

Sean sat and put a napkin in his lap. Anna smiled, innocent of the male rhetoric, and quietly folded her hands as if to pray. Henry stared at her for a moment. Sean looked at her confused.

"What are we doing? Are we praying or something?"

"Bless this food and the manly hands which brought it to us," Henry began.

Sean said, "Amen."

"And bless this house and our first night in it. May it be filled with You."

"And thirty-two babies," Sean added.

"And friends who know when to stop. Amen," Henry concluded. Henry looked down at his vegetable pie and smiled. He was home.

"Henry, I wanted to ask you earlier before I was so rudely interrupted," Anna began with a teasing smile, "Why don't you go back to the Manor? Why here?"

"Well, Anna, it's like this," Sean said knowingly, "Henry gave away his castle to his ungrateful extended family."

"Why did you do that, Henry?"

"It wasn't me anymore."

"Well, it sure could've been me," Sean said and shoveled a heap of shepherd's pie into his mouth.

"Why not?" Anna asked and ignored Sean's banter.

"Because I knew I needed to be close to my parishioners, not on some high and mighty mountain looking down at them. I also wanted my money liquidated so I could give more freely."

"Hey, Henry, give me a car," Sean requested as he chewed.

"No."

"Some friend," he mumbled and took another bite.

Anna hid a snicker.

After dinner, Sean cleaned up while Anna drove across the way to the apartment to get her things. She went back to the carriage house and unpacked quickly in the guest room with its pretty yellow wallpaper and floral quilt.

She wondered who in the town had made it for her. She ran her hand on the new, handmade dresser and bed made of a light wood. It was beautiful.

She scooted into the bathroom in her robe and started a bath. Anna touched the numbers on her arm after she undressed. She still wondered why some people were marked and others were not. She wondered if what Daire had told her was true.

Was I forced into prostitution in a terrible prison? No, it must be a lie. None of it makes sense.

"Can you please explain to me what I'm supposed to do?" Sean asked Henry in their quiet moment without Anna.

"Just stay," Henry said. "She can't lift me if I need help. I'm twice her size."

"You two are very odd, you know that?" He said in reference to the slow pace of their romance. "You're suited for one another."

Henry put his head back on the sofa.

"How am I going to sleep with her in the room next to me?" he lamented.

Sean smiled. The question had taken him aback. He loved it when he saw glimmers of humanness in Henry.

"How did you sleep in the hospital? She was right there, man."

"Sedatives," Henry responded.

Sean almost spit out his beer, he laughed so hard. He loved it when Henry joked, but he knew he really was not in this instance. His friend was head over heels for his wife. It was a miracle to behold in a husband who felt that way.

They sat quietly for a moment while Sean sipped his Guinness. They each thought about Tomas, but neither wanted to talk about it.

"So, she kissed you," Sean finally commented.

Henry smiled.

"What do you think it means?"

"It means my wife likes me," Henry grinned.

"You're a small minority—most wives don't like their husbands."

"What about you, old timer? Are you going to settle down or what?"

"It's a matter of deciding between the two prettiest twins in the world that's got me, Henry."

"I can understand that," Henry added as he thought about Clara and Cara.

"I can't tell them apart either."

"Yes, that'd be a problem. Well, I believe you're worrying for nothing because neither is interested in you."

"That's because they haven't seen my romance in action."

"Or lack thereof."

"You laugh, Henry, but you're the only one settled down out of us and look what it's brought you: misery."

"Not entirely," Henry said softly.

He hoped Anna was not listening to Sean's terrible speech.

"Love equals suffering," Sean lamented.

"That's true, but it's worth it."

"Haven't met one who'd make what you've been through worth it."

"She's out there, Sean. Just you wait. She'll kick your . . . bottom."

"Bottom? That's what you've become, a person who says bottom. Just like an old lady."

"Well, I couldn't think of a nice way to put it."

The two sat another minute and contemplated their fates.

"Do you hear her?" Henry asked and inhaled quickly.

"What?"

"She's singing."

The two sat completely still and listened to the little melody Anna was singing.

"Is she remembering that?" Sean asked.

"Yes."

"What's she singing?"

Henry listened another few seconds. Henry inhaled his tears.

"She's singing 'In the Garden.'"

The two froze as Henry mouthed the words to the second verse:

He speaks, and the sound of His voice,

Is so sweet the birds hush their singing.

And the melody that He gave to me

Within my heart is ringing.
And He walks with me, and He talks with me,
And He tells me I am His own;
And the joy we share as we tarry there,
None other has ever known.[3]

Henry bent over, put his face in his hands, and released months of pain. He cried in front of his dear friend. Sean sat motionless and beheld the miracle. He wiped away a tear of his own and looked toward the closed bathroom door where she sang each verse perfectly.

"Where have I heard this before?" Sean asked and tried to place the song.

"At Anna's funeral," Henry replied with muffled speech.

Sean had only seen his friend cry once in their lives. He remembered the night so well.

It was the night after Henry burned down the barn. He had asked to see Sean. Henry had put his massive hand on Sean's shoulder.

"We've been on the wrong side," Henry insisted and told him of his conversion. Then, he cried.

Sean choked down another sip of beer and waited for his friend to get hold of himself again. Henry stood and carefully walked a few steps to the fireplace. He put his arm on the mantle and looked into the fire.

"I remember Anna use to sing that song when she was at the Manor. She'd scrub the floors and sing. Her voice carried all through the house and I'd close my eyes, no matter what I was doing, and take it in. I think we all did.

"She told me one day the story behind the hymn and it stuck in my brain, you know, like the music became synonymous with her. She said this man was reading the Bible one day and was lead to his

---

3   Words: Miles, Charles Austin. 1912. "In The Garden." *hymnlyrics.org*. http://www. hymnlyrics.org/mostpopularhymns/inthegarden.php (Accessed August 29, 2013)

favorite verses about Mary finding Jesus in the garden after his resurrection. She told me it was her favorite New Testament story, too.

"She said the hymn writer was in his dark room—you know,
where he'd develop photographs—and he had a vision of those
very verses. When he came to, he penned the verses of the hymn,
and then later that day wrote the music."

"I didn't know that," a sweet voice chimed from behind them.

"I didn't know you were standing there, sweetheart," Henry said
as he quickly got a hold of himself.

Anna and Henry looked at each other, and then at Sean.

"Do you remember any other pieces of music?" Sean asked her gently.

"I don't know. That one just sort of came to me."

She combed through her wet hair with a fluffy robe on.

"Well, now, you have a beautiful voice," Sean said.

Anna remembered what Henry had told her, his wife had been
a soloist. She wondered what else was dormant inside her.

Henry looked at his wife with her long, dark hair wet. She re-
knotted her robe and walked back into her room. Henry sniffed
as he watched her go.

"She's remembering herself, isn't she," Sean asked, more a statement than a question.

Henry did not answer. He did not know.

CHAPTER 27

HENRY HANDED ANNA HER TEA as she sat down at the kitchen table in her nightgown and robe.

"Have you seen the rest of the house?" he asked.

"No," she replied.

Henry shifted in his seat and Sean got up to help Henry stand.

"I think you'd be more comfortable sleeping in the other room," Henry said to her as he weakly hobbled to the bedroom hall. He motioned for Sean to go back into the other room so he could talk to her.

"No, it's fine. I like the little room I'm in," she said.

She looked into the master bedroom where a huge, hand-carved poster bed almost touched the ceiling. It was raised as the beds of old used to be. Long silk drapes puddled at the floor and opened to the large windows all around.

"This is beautiful!"

"Change your mind? I'll gladly trade with you," offered Henry.

"No, I'll be fine, but can you even get in that bed? It's so high."

"There's a little step over there."

Anna entered the room and looked out the beautiful windows to the great Manor behind. She wished she could see it inside. Lanterns lit the drive and it looked like a dream in the snow. Henry reached around her from behind and held her while she looked out.

"What do you want to do tomorrow?" He asked and kissed her ear.

"Can we see it?"

"The Manor? Of course. My family is coming in tomorrow. They've been in Italy for months. Father Donnelly got a hold of them finally and they want to see me. You have perfect timing, you know that?"

"Did they know me . . . before?"

"Yes."

"What are they like?"

"Well, I have a cousin. She's very sweet, but not very reserved. Her name is Ashling. Her husband is a banker: Pearce is his name. They have two terribly behaved boys I truly adore. They call me Uncle Priestie because I'm a priest."

They chuckled.

"Peter is eight and Michael is two. Ashling is like a sister to me. She spent every summer with us and we're about the same age. So, she loves the house."

"What do they call me?"

Henry smiled. He hoped she would ask.

"They call you Aunt Cindie."

"Whatever for?"

"They think you're Cinderella—you know the fairy tale."

She did not.

"Peter started it and Michael knows no better."

"Were they named after the Biblical people?"

"No, actually, they were named after Peter Pan characters."

"Oh, that's funny."

"Ashling and I use to play Peter Pan a lot!"

"That I can tell . . . And who were you, Nana?"

"Oh, ha-ha," Henry said sarcastically.

He kissed her ear again from behind.

"Ashling was, of course, Wendy and I was Peter Pan."

"You seem too serious for Peter Pan," Anna commented.

"Yes, I didn't say I was a very good Peter Pan, but there was simply no one else. I also played every lost boy as well as Captain Hook."

"Sounds like a very busy childhood."

"Oh, yes, of course."

Henry's thoughts went to Anna's terrible childhood which she no longer remembered. He wondered if it was a good thing she did not. He held her tighter. She turned around in his arms. He almost lost his balance.

"Whoa, are you okay?"

"Yes," he chuckled. "You're making me dizzy."

"Goodnight, Henry."

"Please don't say that."

"Why?"

"Because you promised me long ago you'd never say it to me again."

"Why would I do that?"

"You made me have a very long engagement with you. I got tired of leaving you every evening."

"I'm sorry I don't remember my promises to you."

"We'll have to make new ones to each other."

She frowned. It was too much for her to think of making vows to Henry at that moment. She kissed him on the cheek and went to her room.

Henry looked toward his old house and tried to make sense of the day.

"Don't think you should be on your feet like that, old man," Sean said as he leaned against Henry's doorframe.

Henry began unbuttoning his shirt to change into his pajamas.

"You think I'm going to help you undress, you got another thing coming."

Henry ignored him and pulled off his shirt. He ripped off the bandage and looked at his side.

Sean swore, and then said, "That's huge!"

"Yeah," Henry answered as he carefully removed and threaded his bad arm through his shirt.

Henry showed Sean the other gash on his arm where he had tried to protect himself from Tomas. Sean shook his head and finally went over to help his friend—he had not realized the extent of his injuries. He knew, of course, Henry had needed his blood, but Sean did not realize until then how vicious the gashes were.

"Why did he do it?" Sean asked with deep pain the question which burned in their minds.

"I've been asking myself the same question. I just talked to the guy when he came into town this summer."

"I did, too."

"He seemed fine," Henry said, as he remembered an uncomfortable encounter in the drug store a week before Tomas took Anna.

"He didn't seem fine to me," Sean said while he bandaged Henry again.

"What do you mean?"

"He was anxious, like he was looking for a fight or something."

"Did he say anything suspicious to you?"

Sean thought for a moment. He had kept the encounter from Henry for a very long time.

"He was in love with Anna."

"When did he tell you this?"

"Almost the first day we met her at the Manor."

Henry pulled his t-shirt over his head, looked at Sean, and said, "You can't fall in love with someone after meeting her once."

"I don't know, Henry. He was pretty obsessed from day one."

"Why didn't you tell me?"

"Why would I do that?"

"I don't know . . ."

"It'd just come between you and . . ."

"He acted like he hated her. He said all kinds of terrible things about her when we got engaged. It just doesn't make sense, Sean."

"You know Tomas, he's a passionate human being. I never thought him capable of this," Sean added.

Henry sighed deeply. He suddenly felt as if he could run.

"Was I wrong to tell you now?"

"No."

"I want to kill him," Sean admitted.

"Imagine how I feel. Do you know how I found him, Sean? He was on top of my wife!"

Henry could not say anything more. Sean shook his head.

"I'm sorry, my friend," he said and grabbed Henry's shoulder.

Henry turned and looked back out the window.

Sean commented, "He's always been jealous of everything you had."

"Me? What about him? He had the looks out of us—"

"Hey, now, I'm pretty stunning."

"He had . . . I lost count of the number of women. He was a doctor. He got a full scholarship. He was a musician. What did he have to be jealous of me about? I'm an orphan who inherited a fortune I never wanted."

"Yes, we all feel very sorry for you, Henry. Push your arm through."

"Sean, I'm serious."

"You had Anna, you idiot! When are you going to get it through your thick skull?"

Henry pushed his arm through his pajama sleeve, ruffled his hair, and joked, "I have thinning hair, too!"

"You're getting fat, too," Sean teased, although it was not true.

Henry finally smiled.

"Hey, I love you, Sean," Henry said with a chuckle.

"What's there *not* to love?"

"Do you really want to stay while I change my pants?"

"I'm on the couch if you need me," Sean said over his shoulder as he left.

Henry tried to sleep, but he was not even close to it. Anger kept him charged—each time Henry closed his eyes, he saw Anna with her blouse open in Tomas' hovel.

He thought of all the times he had defended Anna to Tomas. He had wondered why Tomas had criticized her so much. Tomas must have been angry with her for not loving him in return. Henry was pretty sure it was the one and only rejection Tomas had ever felt from a woman.

A knock at the door made him jump.

"Henry?" Anna's small voice called.

"Come in."

She slowly pushed open the door.

"What's wrong, Anna?"

"I can't sleep."

"Neither can I, but you can't be in here, sweetheart."

"Why not?"

"Because it's just not proper until you get your memory back."

She walked toward him, climbed onto the bed, and sat beside him.

"I was thinking, Henry. It doesn't matter if I don't remember you. What matters is I know you."

Anna leaned forward to kiss him.

Henry woke up with a start. He had been dreaming.

"Henry, you split your stitches!"

Sean yelled him awake with a string of profanities. It was a dizzying difference between his dream of Anna and Sean's bad breath in his face. Henry looked down. Blood was everywhere.

"Anna! Anna, get in here!" Sean yelled as he put peroxide on a cloth and held it to Henry.

Anna ran in the room as she pulled on her robe and asked, "What's wrong?"

"Henry must've turned wrong or something."

"Oh no!"

"Can you dial the doctor in Shannon?"

Anna immediately left the room quickly to make the call.

"You're supposed to be all healed up, Henry! What happened to you?"

"Anna was a seamstress. Have her stitch me up."

"You've got to be kidding me."

"Just go get her."

"Anna, come here! Are you still on the telephone?"

"I'm just now dialing, Sean, what do you want?"

"Just hang up and come here for a minute," Sean called and shot Henry a harsh look. "Did you do this on purpose so she'd be close to you?"

"No!" Henry said, offended.

Anna entered and asked, "What is it? I was just about to get the doctor—"

"Just come here and look at this," Sean demanded and opened up the bloody sheet for her to see.

"Henry!" Anna uttered at the sight.

"You were a seamstress. You think you can stitch him up before he gets worse?"

"No! I'm not a doctor! Sean, he needs a doctor to do it."

"It's just skin, no muscle or anything," Henry reassured her.

"He's bleeding like crazy, I'm calling." Anna was adamant.

"See? She says she's calling the doctor," Sean said to Henry.

"Anna, come here for a minute," Henry pleaded. "By the time the doctor gets here it'll be at least an hour."

She uttered, "He's thirty minutes away."

Henry reasoned: "It's two o'clock in the morning. He's at least an hour away. He'll have to get dressed and get some coffee.

I've stitched up Sean enough times to know how to walk you through this.

"We'll call the doctor in the morning. I just want you to help me so I can go back to sleep, all right? Do you remember how to sew?"

Henry's gaze was convincing.

"Yes."

"Just take the needle and clean it good in the stuff Sean's got. Now, I'm going to push the skin together and—"

Anna panicked and protested, "I can't do this!"

"Yes, you can."

"Sean, do this!" She demanded and shoved a needle toward him.

"I'm not doing anything of the sort!" Sean cried out and held up his hands.

"Come on, baby, you've got this," Henry coached.

Anna threaded the needle and pushed it into Henry's skin. Henry winced.

"Why isn't it healing?" she asked.

"We'll ask the doctor tomorrow," Henry said.

"I thought it was all right when they released you?"

"I've been up a lot today. I should've rested more," Henry admitted.

Sean had to leave the room as Anna stitched Henry's wound.

"It hurts really bad, doesn't it?" Anna asked.

"Just talk to me a little. I'll be all right."

"Henry, did I write anything else poetry-wise?"

"Yes."

"Like what?"

"You wrote me quite a bit. When I read it, I feel like I'm looking into a mirror of my soul. It's like you're the spokesperson for my heart."

"Do you have any of the other poems I wrote?"

"I have them all."

"Can I see them?"

"Of course. I actually have one . . . Well, it's more of a letter . . . In my coat pocket. I keep it there all the time."

"Why?"

"It's my favorite."

"Why is it your favorite?"

Henry smiled and admitted, "Because you're my favorite."

"What?"

"You're my favorite. You used to say that to me all the time."

"What does it say?" She asked, unsure how to respond to his last remark.

"When you're done you can read it."

Anna worked for a few more minutes and asked, "Why did you have to stitch Sean up so much?"

"Because he got into a lot of fights and got tired of paying Dr. Lannon to stitch him up."

"Who did he get in fights with?"

"Me."

"Wait a minute! You guys fought, and then—"

"I'd stitch him up."

"Men are so strange. Why didn't he stitch you up?"

"He didn't have to. I was too fast for him."

Anna snickered, and then her eyes wandered. She watched Henry's chest move up and down with his breaths.

"Keep your eyes on what you're doing," he teased.

He was expecting a wild recant, or at least a zinger, but she looked a little embarrassed.

"What are you thinking about?"

"Nothing," she answered quickly.

"Are you all right about doing this?"

"Not really."

"Sean, come in and help Anna!"

"I'm almost done, it's all right.

"What do you want?" Sean called from the other room.

"It's really okay, Henry, I've got two left."

She finished stitching, and then looked at him.

"Just finish it off like you would a garment."

She tied and cut it. Then, she cleaned it again.

"You did a really good job," he said proudly.

She bandaged him again. He felt her hands brush against his skin. Nothing hurt when she touched him. She finished it off with lots of tape, and then put a towel under him.

"I think I bled into the new mattress," he said, concerned.

She picked up the sheet and looked under it.

"It'll be fine. There's a mattress cover on it."

"Good old Sarah."

"Where's the poem?"

"Oh, yes, the payment for your work . . . It's in the jacket over there."

Anna washed her hands in the bathroom, and then returned. She was quiet and serious. She reached into the inside pocket and pulled out the poem without searching any other pockets.

Henry smiled. *She remembered where it was.*

"I always keep it there," he added.

She took it out of the worn, red envelope and unfolded it as she sat on the tall bed by Henry.

"Dear Henry," she read aloud. "Today, I watched you as you pulled out your pocket watch and looked at it, winded it, and put it back into your inside pocket. Every man does that, I'm sure, but each motion, each movement, is somehow different with you. You're different. Everything you do, down to the simplest thing is beautiful. You're beautiful, John Henry. Anna."

She looked at him and asked, "Is this what you carry around with you always? Why?"

"You told me I was beautiful."

She looked at her words again. It was her handwriting, but she did not recognize the letter. She turned it over. It was written on scrap paper.

"Henry, I know you want me to love you again like this, but I've been through so much and I—"

"You don't ever have to explain to me."

"I need time."

"I know," he said patiently.

"Did I love you first?"

"No."

"When did you fall in love with me?"

"I thought you were gorgeous the first time I saw you. But, you know when I fell in love with you? You know the song you sang earlier? It was the first time I heard you sing it."

"I was scrubbing floors?"

"You were. You would've thought you were scrubbing the floors to the throne of God with that voice."

She smiled, looked down, and asked, "Why did I make you wait to marry me?"

"You wanted to be certain I was close to the Lord before I became your husband."

"Why'd that matter?"

"Ah, well, that's a question only you can answer," Henry replied and smiled.

"Henry," she said as she settled next to him. "Tell me about my life with you."

"I had a hard time showing you how I felt. One thing good which has come from all of this is I'll never shield myself from you again. My arms will always be open to you."

"Tell me, though, Henry," she said and closed her eyes, "what was our wedding like."

"Well, every person in town came. You wore a white dress with this huge skirt. Father Donnelly performed the service."

"What kind of flowers did we have?"

"Lily of the Valley."

"Oh, I love those."

"And we had purple roses and white camellias. Sarah stood up for you. She had a deep blue dress on. You wanted her to wear purple, but she wouldn't."

Anna smiled with her eyes closed. She put her head on the pillow beside him.

"Anna, are you falling asleep?" He asked and brushed her hair out of her face. "You can't sleep in here, honey."

"Mm?" she groaned.

"Come on, Anna. You need to go to bed."

Sean stood in the doorway with his arms folded and commented, "Kicking a beautiful woman out of bed, I see?"

"Come on, Sean, this is hard enough. Can you carry her?"

"Sure," he finally said.

Sean lifted Anna's small body out of the bed. She put her arms around his neck.

She mumbled, "I love you, Henry."

Henry turned white and looked at Sean's shocked face.

"Did she just say what I think she said?" Sean whispered frantically.

They looked at each other as Sean held Henry's wife. Then, Henry grinned.

CHAPTER 28

SEAN CAME BACK INTO THE room after carefully covering
Anna in her bed.

"She's been so quiet lately."

"I've noticed that, too."

"She's not herself."

"She's thinking. When she thinks deeply about things, she gets
quiet. Before she painted, she'd get even quieter than this. She used
to say, 'The more you know me, the quieter I become.' It's true.
She's really outgoing with people she doesn't know, and then goes
deeper inside herself the closer she becomes to a person. Sarah
used to say she'd go days without talking."

"I never would've thought."

"I saw it quite often, but a lot of it was my fault. I, too, went into
my shell a lot."

"She's going to have a ton of questions, Henry. I wonder why
she hasn't started asking yet."

Henry did not respond.

"I need to go in tomorrow. The pub is probably falling apart
without me," Sean said as he graciously changed the subject.

"Oh, I seriously doubt that."

Sean stretched and joked, "You two wear me out, you know.
Why can't I have normal friends?"

Henry smiled and shot back, "*You're* not normal."

"No, but I'm not complicated either."

"True, true."

Henry smiled again and chimed, "She loves me!"

"Maybe ... She was unconscious. Her brain might be malfunctioning."

"*You're* a malfunction!"

"Good night, beautiful," Sean said in jest as he strolled out and left his friend for the comfort of the couch.

Sleep did not come as easy to Henry as it had for Anna. The loud snoring on the couch indicated how easy it came for Sean as well.

He looked at the ceiling and prayed for a long time until his eyes finally grew tired hours later. He drifted off. He remembered how it felt to hold Anna in his arms and pray every night. Henry was not much of a sleeper, but he often pretended to be tired to have a chance to hold her.

His two weeks in the hospital had been filled with people in and out, spending the night in his room. It was not odd for him to awaken in the morning with a room filled with people who stared at him. Yet, one constant, Anna, was always there with her bed or chair pushed as close as possible to him.

What Henry found interesting was how few people acknowledged Anna. She became invisible during the hospital stay. It was as if no one knew what to say to her, so they pretended not to see her. Some nodded cordially, bid her good night, or good morning, but no one asked how she was. That is, except, of course, the Donnellys.

Sarah was somewhat of a nuisance the way she doted on Anna. She sat and brushed her hair, or told Anna a story Henry was sure she had heard a thousand times. It was all new, of course to her, but Henry knew most of them.

Father Donnelly had sat by Henry's bed and read him scripture until Henry thought he might scream. However, Henry sweetly and politely nodded his head and said, "Amen."

For the first time since his incredible conversion, Henry did not want to even listen to the Bible being read. It was a strange phenomenon. The one time he had needed its comfort the most, he wanted it the least. He wanted to stew in his anger and anguish, but Father Donnelly did not let him which also annoyed Henry. *Why doesn't Father Donnelly allow me a human moment?*

He had decided to push away from Father Donnelly for a little while and cleave to Sean who was real and vibrant. Henry was himself around him. There was something to say about the honesty spoken between the two of them. Henry was only real and honest with one other person, and the person was not Anna. It was God.

Henry's prayer times were filled with angry rants. He knew this did not make him a holy person, but he had to vent to someone. He reasoned since God already knew, He could certainly handle what was verbalized. It helped Henry to remain the contained man he was.

Henry had decided long ago not to tell Anna or anyone else his favorite scripture. Anna's was, of course, the garden scene after the resurrection. Sarah's was the story of Ruth, which was very fitting to her life. Father Donnelly's was Proverbs, which Henry found the least amusing of the scriptures. Henry's was the angry rant of Jesus in the temple. He loved to see the rage.

He understood Jesus more in those passages than any other. He read the other scriptures about Jesus' life with it in mind—Jesus had held his anger for years before releasing it. Henry purposely never taught from the passage. It was a secret he kept with God. Henry was, in fact, a loose cannon tempered only by divine grace and love.

Henry showered and dressed, but not without problems the next morning. Sean had forgotten about him and had spent the first hour of the day yelling into the telephone to his unsupervised manager.

Henry felt nauseous and disheveled. The shower had stung, one of the stitches had busted, and he had wrestled with his shirt. His

376   *A Little Irish Love Story*

pants were difficult to maneuver, but he finally got them on. It took everything out of him to get dressed.

Anna knocked on the bathroom door and asked, "Do you need some help?"

He quickly looked in the mirror and smoothed his hair.

"Come in," he said, happily.

"Good morning. How did you do last night?"

She unbuttoned the one button he had managed and spread his dress shirt open.

"Looks like you lost one. The doctor will be here in the hour," she said and smiled up at him. "Don't you want these bandaged again?"

"If you don't mind. The kit is over there."

She wore her blue suit Henry had bought her. She caught him staring at her dress.

"What is it?"

"You're beautiful."

"No, I'm not."

Henry shook his head, sighed, and asked, "Can you close the door for a minute?"

She did.

"Can you feel if I have a fever or not?" Henry requested pitifully as he sat on the lid to the commode.

"Do you think you have one?" she asked.

Anna quickly came to Henry after she closed the bathroom door with her hand held out to touch his forehead. He quickly grabbed her and cackled.

"Now you're in my grasp!"

"Henry! You'll tear your stitches!"

"Kiss me."

"Henry!" She protested and kissed him anyway.

"Good morning to you, too," Henry said.

Anna smiled and shook her head. She bandaged and buttoned him, and pushed her flyaway tendril out of her face a hundred times.

Henry was mesmerized and mused, "You've seen a different side of me with Sean and all. What do you think?"

"About what?"

"Do you like me even when I'm with my childhood friend?"

"Yes."

"Do you like Sean?"

"Very much."

"More than me?"

"No," she said and smiled.

"Oh, *really*?" Henry said as he took the opportunity to wrap his arms around her and rock her gently. "So you're saying you like me?"

"Of course, I like you, Henry."

His face became serious and he held her still. He wanted her to say she loved him, but she did not.

"Mrs. Donnelly . . . Sarah . . . made turnovers," she informed him.

"Apple?"

"Yes. Can I tell you something? I really don't like them anymore."

Henry smiled, kissed Anna's forehead, and said, "Then tell her."

"I don't want to hurt her feelings."

"You won't. She wants to please you."

"Henry?"

She took a deep breath and looked into his bright, green eyes.

"I'm so sorry."

"For what?"

"For what happened, for your injuries."

Henry sat speechless and asked, "What do you mean you're sorry? It's my job to protect you, Anna."

"Well, I release you from that job."

"You didn't give me the job, the Lord did. I don't intend on quitting a job I love."

"Henry, I'm not worth all of this."

"Not worth it? Anna, honestly, I think you lost some of your good sense as well as your memory."

"I'm saying all of this is because of me."

"So? Do you have any idea what I've put people through, what I've put you through for that matter? You're worth any price I could ever pay."

Henry held out his arms, but she shook her head as tears dripped down her face. He grabbed her and held her close.

"You're worth everything to me."

"Um, the police is here," Sean said on the other side of the bathroom door.

Henry looked at Anna, kissed her head, and muttered, "What in the world?"

Officer Hamm stood with his hat in hand and stated, "The police from Sligo Town called me out of bed this morning."

Sean snickered and looked at Henry who did not respond. Officer Hamm was as well-respected as a ham itself.

He was, indeed, the laziest person any in Adare had ever seen. He woke up at ten, went into work, and slept at his desk until lunch. Then, he walked around town waving to people in the afternoon and retired at four o'clock in the afternoon to his cottage. It was not yet eight o'clock in the morning. Sean figured it was the first time since his birth Officer Hamm had been up so early.

"I told them to call here, but they insisted I come up here to tell you in person."

"Let's have it," Henry said.

"Tomas made a deal. He's exchanging his scientific research and pharmaceutical developments for only one year in prison."

"Son of a—" Sean said and appeared as if he might punch through a wall.

"Part of the deal is he must confess everything. If he leaves out anything, he'll be rearrested and serve a full ten-year sentence. He's confessing today. The police have invited you and Anna up to hear it on the other side of a two-way mirror. Tomas doesn't know you'll be there. The police fudged it over a little with his lawyer."

Officer Hamm tried to hold in a burp from the breakfast he had wolfed down.

"It's at noon."

Henry and Anna stared at one another, dumbfounded.

"Well," Sean said and put his arm around Officer Hamm, "You must be exhausted."

"Yes, I am."

"Why don't you go on home and lie down for a little while to regain your strength?"

"I may just do that."

Sean showed him the door and closed it quickly.

"Well? What are you going to do?" Sean asked.

"He tried to murder you!" Anna said. "Kidnapping, drugging, and God knows what he did to me! He's getting a year? What if he comes after me again? What if . . ." she broke down and sobbed.

"What do you want to do?" Henry asked Anna as he held her.

"I want to go! I have a lot of questions I want answers, too!" She said in a muffled, yet terrified voice.

Henry was doing all he could to keep himself calm, but he was not doing well. Sean saw it in his face.

"Do you want me to go with you?" Sean asked underneath his breath to Henry.

He nodded. It was necessary to keep him from killing Tomas, mirror between them or not. Anna looked up at Henry. He knew the look; she did not want Sean to go, but for the first time in his life, Henry ignored her. He needed his friend with him.

Furious, Anna flew up and grabbed her coat.

"Where are you going?" Sean asked.

Henry knew better. She ignored him, opened the door with force, and nearly ran into the doctor Sean had called that morning who stood with his fist raised to knock. The small, old man had the face of a bulldog. He carried the little black case all doctors carried.

She almost laughed when she saw his expression. Anna immediately drew in her anger.

"I'm so sorry. You must be the doctor. Please come in."

Then, she went outside. She marched through the heavy snow. It was a cloudy day which made it feel colder; however, there was no new snow. She thought frantically.

Henry felt immediately trapped with the doctor. He knew his wife and the longer he left her to fume, the harder it was to calm her down. Sean had often commented she should have been a lawyer since he knew exactly what it took. It was almost impossible to win an argument with her.

The only time Henry had ever remembered winning was one time when she had made an iron-clad case. He had been totally lost for a comeback, and then she had seemingly out of the blue apologized. She had won, yet she said the Lord had told her she was wrong. So, she admitted she was wrong, even though she had convinced Henry she was right.

The doctor carefully put out his instruments, and then asked Henry to take off his shirt. Henry was in such a panic for the doctor to hurry, he almost ripped it off.

"Careful now," the doctor warned, "that's maybe why you're in this mess in the first place. Slow is better."

However, slow was not better. Henry calculated they had to leave in a half hour to get to the prison in Sligo Town by noon. The situation would have been easier if he did not have to get over the obstacle which was Anna's terrible temper.

The doctor sterilized his needle twice and talked about his times in the first war. Henry, who was usually an incredibly patient person, wanted to seriously injure the man.

Doesn't he realize what's at stake as he prattles on? Of course, he doesn't.

"Please, doctor, we have a terribly important meeting three hours away, if you don't mind being rather quick—"

"Shut up and sew, doc!" Sean added.

The doctor stopped for a moment, glared at Sean, and then threaded his needle. As the doctor carefully and slowly pulled each stitch through, Henry felt he had lost Anna all over again. He thought of sending Sean after her, but it would only make her madder.

No, he had to be the one to calm her. Henry asked God to help him, but God was not slowing down time which is what Henry truly wanted.

Henry finally could stand it no longer and grabbed the needle from the doctor. He tied off his stitches, and then snapped it off. The doctor was appalled.

"Bill me!" Henry said and put on his shirt without the bandage.

Sean grabbed the medical kit with bandages. He thought they might bandage him on the way. He showed the doctor out.

Henry bolted out of the house, paused, and looked around. He realized he was not only standing without help, but had also actually moved quickly! He blew big stacks of steam from his mouth in the chilled air. Then, he saw her. She was not far.

He tried to run to her, but immediately his side ached and he caught his breath and held onto the stack of firewood. Anna walked to him.

"How dare you!" She started without getting close enough to use a normal speaking tone.

Here we go, Henry thought and braced himself.

"How dare I?"

"How can you invite Sean? This is private, Henry!"

"I invited him because he'll keep me from killing Tomas!"

"Oh, that's poppy cock, Henry. There will be a hundred officers there—"

"Sean keeps me honest."

"God doesn't do that?"

Henry did not have an answer and begged, "Just trust me on this one."

"Trust you? Trust you? You conspired a lie which involved the entire town to keep the truth from me—"

"I was following doctor's orders—"

"Oh, shut up, Henry, when in the history of your life have you ever followed doctor's orders? Look at you! You've busted our stitches twice in two days!"

"Why don't you want him there?"

"Because I know some of the things Daire, or whatever his name is, is going to say!"

"So do I!"

Anna wanted to strangle him.

"I'm your husband and I have a right to know!"

"Oh, so now you're going to play that card. You're my husband, huh? Well, I bet you were a miserable one."

Henry was dumbfounded. She continued with sweet vindication laced in her voice.

"*You* don't even have a right to be there!"

Henry was taken aback once again and asked, "What do you mean?"

"Where were you in all of this? Why weren't you trying to find me?"

"I thought you were dead!"

"Love never gives up."

"Well, sometimes it has to."

"You're a piece of—"

"Listen to me, Anna, I love you! You know that! You know that. It doesn't matter what you remember, it matters what you know now."

"That's the biggest pile of—"

"Just watch your mouth and listen to me for the first time in your life, Anna!"

She stood as if she waited to devour him.

Henry continued, "You might not think I have a right to be there . . . I have no idea why, but you do. Now, let me tell you something. Just as much was stolen from me as it was from you. Your love meant everything to me and now it's gone."

"Just as much as me! My life was stolen from me, Henry! You'll have your sorry little life! I want my memories! I want to know things about myself every single person in this town seems to know! I want to know my secrets, my heart! I want to know why I paint, why I sing. But, I don't. See this!"

Anna showed him her arm with the numbers on it.

"Explain this!"

Henry did not want to.

"That's what I thought," she said softer, but in a tone which still made Henry's hair stand on end. "I want to know what the man who did this to me knows. I don't particularly want everyone else knowing more than me for once!"

Henry responded, "I know you think you have control over this, but let me tell you something, you don't. I'm going. The police invited me. I'm going. You want to take the car and drive in your usual hazardous way up there by yourself, that's fine! But, I will follow right behind you."

She had lost the fight. It was a terrible feeling for Henry. She walked away from him.

"Anna!" he called out, but realized he might, in fact, lose her the way he had always feared.

She did not turn around.

CHAPTER 29

ANNA STORMED TOWARD THE COTTAGE to get her purse. They had lost time. Sean was on the telephone, but was not yelling this time.

"I called Donnelly to tell him where we'll be. He wanted to go with us. I told him no way."

"Thank you," Henry said and hoped Father Donnelly did not take it as a rejection.

He missed Father Donnelly very much, but it was a strange time in his life; he really did not want to be fathered. It was not that Henry was not humble—far from it. He wanted to simmer in the moments he had to contemplate and work through his feelings in his time. Sean also gave some comic relief to the darkest moments.

Sean threw the medical kit in the backseat and commented the doctor was still preparing to leave in his car. Henry held the back door open for Anna, and then got in beside her. He started to unbutton his shirt as Sean sped away.

"Pardon my driving, sweetheart," he said to Anna, "this is a make it or break it moment. Bandage the idiot back there, will 'ya?"

Henry took his shirt completely off as the heat kicked up in the car. Anna stopped for a moment and looked at him.

"What?" he asked.

She did not answer. She just started to bandage him and worked quickly despite Sean's erratic driving. Henry carefully put on his shirt again in no time. Then, she looked out her window. Sean turned on the radio; started to sing, "It don't mean a thing if you ain't got that swing . . . ;" and put on his sunglasses, even though he did not need them in the cloudy weather.

Henry looked out his window as well. *How can she say I have no right to be at Tomas' confession? I almost died saving her from him. She's my wife! Everything that happened to her happened to me as well, or did it?*

He wondered deep down if losing her memory was the best thing to happen to her. If anyone can benefit from something like that, it was her. He had certainly not endured all the pain in life she had.

He looked at her stone expression as she stared out the window and gulped. He had lamented so many nights after her perceived death about his not having reached out to her more, given her more affection. He finally could not stand her being angry any longer. He reached across the leather seat and touched her hand with his finger.

She did not look at him, but immediately turned her hand over and revealed her palm. The small gesture was almost more than he could endure. It was a little thing they had done with each other. He smirked. She somehow remembered. He wondered if she remembered the next part.

She still did not look at him, but her hand was there and waited for him. He took his finger and started drawing letters in her palm which spelled: I - A - M - S - T - U - P - I - D. At the end of the letter D, she turned toward him.

"I know," she mouthed with a small smile.

He put his hand on his heart.

"I'm sorry, too," she whispered.

"Well, ain't that peachy?" Sean said with a mimicked southern drawl.

They laughed quietly.

"You two fight more than anyone I've ever seen. I thought Henry was over his hot-headed ways years ago until I saw you two in action. Was it always like this, Henry?"

"Yes," Henry said with a wicked smile, "but not with anyone else."

"I'm so special," Anna said sarcastically.

Then, the car fell silent again as everyone thought about the terrible confession ahead.

They pulled up to the police station in Sligo Town ten minutes ahead of time. Henry thanked the Lord. Each of them had stomach butterflies, but none as much as Anna. She knew what Tomas might say and dreaded it. She had tried so hard to keep those three weeks with him in that hole in the ground deep in her mind. She tried not to think of it at all, especially since he attacked Henry. Yet, she had so many questions she needed answers to and answers she did not want revealed.

Henry waved Sean's help away. He wanted to walk in under his own strength and took the concrete steps slowly. Henry put his hand on Anna's back and guided her gently inside.

"Sean, tell them we're here, I want to talk to Anna for a minute."

"What's wrong?" Anna asked as they stood in the ugly tiled entrance.

"I want to tell you no matter what he says in there my feelings for you won't change."

"Henry, you can't make such a promise."

"Yes, I can."

He nodded reassuringly at her, and then they walked toward the desk where Sean waited. Anna took off her grey gloves and coat, and draped them over her arm. She looked regal in her beautiful suit. Henry stopped to look at her for a moment. She was not the person who had lived in a hole with Tomas for three weeks. She was becoming the person he knew more with each passing day.

An officer took them to a small observation room with a few hard chairs and a table. One wall had a large window which was actually a two-way mirror. There were speakers on the upper parts of the ceiling so they could hear Tomas' confession.

On the other side of the two-way mirror was a room much like the one they were in. Anna sat down on one of the chairs, but the two men congregated on the right side of the room. Sean stood behind Henry in an identical stance: arms folded. They could have been brothers, but Sean had a baby face and Henry did not. Sean was also a bit bigger.

A stenographer came in and set up her machine at the table. She looked like she was a librarian as her cat glasses dangled from a necklace. She did not acknowledge anyone.

Then, a man came in who was heavier than Officer Hamm. He had on a grey suit held together by exhausted buttons—they were about to give up at any moment. He shook Henry's and Sean's hands, and then took off his hat when he saw Anna and the stenographer. He put it down on the table. Anna nodded at him.

"I'm the prosecuting attorney," the man in the suit said to Henry. "Are you Father Henry?"

"Yes," Henry said quietly and shook the man's hand.

It was then Anna noticed he had not worn his collar in quite some time. She did not realize Henry had murder on his mind and he could not bring himself to look like a man of the cloth with that kind of sin in his heart.

Anna then remembered why she was there. The nervous fluttering started again. All three were startled when the door to the other room opened and an officer led in the prisoner. Anna stood.

It's Daire . . . Tomas!

She knew it would be him, but somehow he was hard to recognize in handcuffs and a jumpsuit being led in by the police. Henry's face was white and Sean repositioned his feet. No one spoke. Then, they heard Tomas' voice.

"Why are we in a two-way mirrored room? Who's behind there?"

"A lawyer and stenographer."

"Why aren't they in here?"

"You're a dangerous prisoner, Dr. Lannon."

Hearing Tomas called Dr. Lannon brought chills up Anna's spine. Tomas looked out the mirror and almost straight at Anna, although he did not see her. She sat back down quickly.

The officers cleared the room, except for one who sat across the table from Tomas. He lit a cigarette, put the carton on the table, and then tapped it into the ash tray.

"Want one?" He asked Tomas.

"No, they make me sick. I wish you wouldn't smoke in here." Tomas said.

Anna did not recognize his voice. She questioned for a small second if Tomas was, in fact, Daire. The way he sat, the expression on his face, all of his mannerisms changed. She saw the metamorphosis in only a few seconds.

"Well, we want what we want," the officer said nonchalantly. "I'm Detective Andy Allen."

Tomas was slightly agitated, but he simply twitched his head.

"How about you take these cuffs off me?" he suggested.

Detective Allen stood, unlocked them, and took them from Tomas.

"Do you understand the document you signed?"

"Yes," Tomas said without emotion and stared hard at the detective.

Anna looked at Henry. He looked back at her, and then at Tomas.

"I need to tell you for legality sake you're to tell the entire story," Detective Allen started. "If the court feels you've left anything out, you'll be detained for ten years. Do you understand?"

"I understand, but what if it's accidental? Will I still be detained?"

"I'll try to prompt you for the information. If we believe you've willingly held back on anything, the contract is void."

The officer leaned forward with his cigarette in his mouth.

"I'm a detective, you worthless—I don't think anyone who's as brilliant as you can possibly make a mistake in this confession."

"I want another person to confess to!" Tomas yelled out.

No one came. Detective Allen smirked through his cigarette.

Henry already liked the interrogator. He turned and smirked at Sean who thought the same. Anna, however, wanted him to be gentler on Tomas. She was afraid, if provoked, Tomas would tell more than she wanted known.

Detective Allen explained, "I was chosen by the prosecutor. It's me or ten years in prison. Want to talk now?"

Tomas smiled, realized he had lost, and sneered, "Where do you want me to start?"

"I think the question on everyone's minds is why."

"Why what?"

Detective Allen paused, and then spelled things out, "Let me tell you something. If you think I'm going to play this game you're grossly underestimating me. I'm tired, I want to go home, and if you aren't done in an hour and a half because of your shenanigans, I'm calling it. Whatever we have, we have. Whatever we don't, you can go back to jail for ten years and think about how you wished you had pooped while you were still on the pot."

"I'm in love with her," Tomas answered.

"And when did this delusion start?"

Tomas frowned, rolled his eyes, shook his head, and answered, "As soon as I saw her."

Detective Allen asked, "She's pretty, huh?"

Tomas did not answer, but said, "She's the other half of me."

Anna's spine tingled and the feeling ended in her fingertips. She hated her feelings for him.

"Spare me," the detective said through his teeth which held his cigarette.

He opened the file in front of him and noted, "She's married to your best friend. Is this her?"

He held up a black and white photograph of Anna and commented, "Gorgeous girl—so, you were jealous."

"No."

"What was it then?"

"We loved each other."

Henry turned around to Sean. Anna looked at them.

"You believed she loved you back?"

"She did. No one knew, but me. She was all high and mighty because of her religious beliefs, so she'd never admit it to another soul, but I knew. We silently came up with a pact that we'd act like we hated each other in front of everyone else."

Tomas chuckled to himself.

"Henry tried to convince me to like her—he couldn't stand when I'd say bad things about her. So, he began to tell me things about her, but it only fueled my fire for her."

Anna looked at Henry. He began to well up with tears, his arms were crossed and his index finger curled around his mouth. He did not know what to believe any more. Neither did Anna.

The thought she had harbored secret feelings for Tomas and they had kept it from Henry was more than he could endure. Especially since he had no idea if it was true or not. He knew Tomas had come on to her before she and Henry were married, but he did not know what happened afterwards.

Anna was also bewildered. It made her crazy to not know her heart. One thing was certain, though, it was obvious she had feelings for him while she was his captive. The question was if she had feelings beforehand?

Then, she began to feel betrayed by Henry. *How could he tell everything to Daire?* Things she was sure only Henry knew, Daire knew as well. They looked at each other again and pushed away feelings of betrayal.

"What kind of things did he tell you?" Detective Allen asked.

"He told me she smuggled Jews across the English Channel during the war. One night, she was taking a mother and a little girl across. Before they got to the boat, they were found out. The mother and the girl were shot immediately in front of Anna, and then she was taken to a concentration camp. She was there for almost two months before the Americans came in. I don't think I need to tell you what they'd do to a girl who looks like that."

So, what he told me the day I went back to him was all true, she thought.

Detective Allen sat still. Everyone in the other room froze as well. The stenographer stopped typing. The lawyer reached over and put his large hand on Anna's shoulder, and then took it away. Henry looked at the floor. Anna finally found the courage to look at Henry.

Is this all true? Did he know all of this?

She knew from the look on Henry's face he did.

How could he keep this from me?

He had kept so much truth from her she began to ponder if she should lump Henry and Daire together.

"I was also in one," Tomas said and showed the detective his numbers.

She rolled up her silk blouse and looked at her arm. *The numbers . . . That's what they are. I'd been a prisoner of war?*

Henry put his face in his hands. He could not take it. He never wanted her to remember what happened to her. He would have even given up the memories she had of him in exchange for her not remembering.

"I don't want her here for this. Can we look over the document?" Henry begged the lawyer.

"You don't get to make this decision, Henry," Anna snapped back in a whisper.

"They can't hear you," the lawyer said. "You can talk at a normal volume."

"I'm staying," Anna said frankly.

"She always wore long sleeve blouses, like she was ashamed." Tomas continued and winced. "We were at the same camp, but it wasn't similar. What she went through was worse than me."

Detective Allen asked, "How do you know that?"

"I was moved pretty quickly out of there into a camp with other Allies. In fact, when the Germans heard I was a doctor, they put me to work. I had pretty regular meals. I didn't get to sleep much and it's a little hard to perform surgery with a gun to your head, but you learn to do it."

"But Anna?"

"You can only imagine," he said and became human suddenly. "When I found out where she was and what happened to her, it was like she melted into my soul. She became part of me after that."

Anna twitched her lips in anger. *I'm not like you. I'll never be like you. I'll never understand you.*

The detective glanced toward the mirror, but Tomas did not notice.

"When I held her, we were perfect together, like she was my missing puzzle piece," Tomas said and looked more like Daire to Anna when he talked about her.

Tears started to fall down her frozen face.

Detective Allen rolled up his sleeves and took a deep breath. He was well aware Henry was listening.

He demanded, "Get back to it, Lannon."

"I felt she could love me if she *let* herself, but she was this religious fanatic and turned Henry into one as well. I've never believed in God. If I did, I'd hate Him, so for God and my sake, I tell Him I don't believe in Him.

"I didn't want to see Henry go down the road of being a fanatic like she was, but more than anything, I wanted her to truly see what she believed in was make believe. It really is ridiculous, you know."

"I'm catholic," Detective Allen said gruffly.

"Exactly. These people give their lives for a fantasy land. I knew if I could help her see it was all a lie, she'd see I was the one for her."

"So, let me get this straight," the detective interjected, "you were under the delusion this girl was not letting herself fall in love with you because you were not a Christian?"

"Precisely. I also believe the only reason Henry became one was to win her."

Surprisingly, Sean huffed at the claim and said, "We all know better, Henry. Never have I ever known a more honest person."

It was a rare thing for Sean to dole out compliments, so Henry took it. He needed the reassurance. Henry was more outraged with each passing moment. To hear Tomas say how much he loved Anna was unbearable.

"I believe the reason she held on to her religion is because of all she had been through. It became this crutch to her, except it was a crutch that demanded her life and our love. I knew if I could take her out of her head and show her, she'd see the truth."

"The truth being what?" Detective Allen asked.

"That I'm hers."

Anna's blood raced. She tried to control her breathing, but it seemed to take over the room.

"Well, I suppose it was better for her to cling to God than turn into a psychotic person like you."

Tomas sat limply and stared angrily at the detective. The detective smiled.

Then he said, "All right, so tell me about the drugs."

Tomas scratched the stubble on his face and said, "I'm a chemist. I work in a research lab in London, but I couldn't get over what I had seen in the war. Other men couldn't either. I saw men who I knew to be absolutely brilliant go totally insane from the memories. I remember one night I woke up from a night terror and thought maybe there was a drug I could produce to help cut off memory nerves to give these men some relief.

"I began experimenting with rats. It was very hard to tell if it worked, but I used a method where before the drug was given I'd teach them a trick. Then, I'd give them the drug. They forgot the trick. I knew I was on the right path.

"I just needed a subject so I chose some of the worst cases: men who came in to the hospital totally lost. When I gave them the drug, they didn't remember anything, yet led rather normal lives. I envied what they had. I wanted to forget, too."

"Why didn't you pick yourself?"

"If I had, I wouldn't have remembered the experiments, now would I?" Tomas replied incredibly annoyed there was someone less intelligent in the room.

"So you picked Anna Oliver."

"When I went home for a holiday, I stayed with my father. I watched Anna. Henry was ignoring her. It was absolutely painful to see. Here's this beautiful girl reaching to him repeatedly and he put her off. He'd be off to some person's house for some ministry he had to do. He had given up his beautiful house for a little cottage to be near his followers. He used her like she was his maid again. I hated it so much."

"Did Anna confide in you about all of this?"

"She didn't have to. I saw it myself. There was this moment when she looked at me—you know, straight in the eyes. Those grey eyes of hers were so sad and I had never seen her like that. Then, one night, I was walking by their cottage and saw her sobbing."

Tomas shook his head, outraged.

"The bastard was breaking her heart! Hadn't she been through enough to have to beg a God who doesn't exist to get her husband to give her any kind of attention?"

"So, you took her," Detective Allen concluded.

"There was a lot of prep to actually do it. I knew I needed a place where she wouldn't be found. So, I chose the island because I love Yeats and it was out of the way."

"What does that have to do with anything?"

"There's a poem he wrote about it. Read a book or something," Tomas snapped. "It took me a while to take everything we'd need out there."

"No one questioned this."

"I was discreet."

"Did you plan when you'd take her?"

"I had to be ready when the time came, and I didn't know when. I prepared my father by telling him I was waiting on word from a college to write about a fellowship. I'd then produce a letter I had contrived on demand and be able to go without a hint of suspicion."

Detective Allen fast-forwarded his interrogation, "Tell me about the night you took her."

"The night was really warm. Everything was quiet because an old man had died in the village. She and I seemed to be the only ones who weren't loitering around the widow's house. I was walking by her cottage—"

"Why is that?"

"I wanted to be close to her."

"Go on," the detective said.

"And I saw her get into her car and start fiddling around with the radio. I wondered where she'd go that late alone, so I got into my car and followed her out to Ballybunion Beach. I pulled in about a block away. It was dark by then, but it was a full moon so I still saw her."

"Did she see you?"

"Not at first. She started taking off her clothes until she was down to nothing, but her underwear. Then, I watched her play in the ocean for a while. It was beautiful. I knew it was the right time. I finally walked over to her clothes.

"She saw me, and then hid a little in the water. She told me she was cold and asked me to please go away while she dressed. I told her I couldn't. She'd have to come and get them. She hesitated for a while, but I knew the water was freezing and she'd give in."

Tomas smirked in retrospect.

"She was quite a sight coming out of those waves. You'd think she'd hurry out and cover up, but that's not like her. She walked out like she wore a royal robe. God, I love that about her."

"So, you grabbed her when she got close?" the detective probed.

"No. I waited and she came up to me and took her clothes. As she took them, I had a syringe of a drug I'd perfected years ago which causes temporary paralysis. I held her close while I stuck her. I cannot tell you how good it felt to hold her, and then have her totally go limp. I left her clothes there and picked her up in my arms."

Anna gasped. She tried very hard to hide it. She looked up at Henry who stared angrily at Tomas. The lawyer put his hand on her shoulder again and she looked back at him with a face, wet with tears. He nodded to comfort her, but she could not be comforted.

"I laid her in the back of my car. I had a blanket back there and covered her up. Her eyes were really eerie because I wasn't aware she'd be able to see and hear me as I later found out. I drove back to Adare. I saw Henry's car on the road and knew I didn't have much time.

"I left her covered in my car and went in my house to present my father with a forged letter from London. He congratulated me on my fellowship and I packed my bags quickly. He thought I had to catch a train right away, but I left for the Island of Innisfree.

"It actually couldn't have worked out better because as I was leaving, the entire town was getting into cars to go help Henry find her. By the time I got to Sligo Town, it was the middle of the night. I easily put her on my little boat and took her out to the island. I remember the feeling of carrying her into my little house and starting the fire. I knew she'd come around soon. I hadn't given her very much of the drug at that point because I didn't want her paralysis to become permanent.

"I looked over at her and realized we were alone for the first time. So, I uncovered her to look at her. I took off the rest of her things and watched her breathe. Her eyes were moving slightly, so I looked at them closely. She scared me to death when she looked straight into my eyes. I didn't realize she could see until that moment.

"I remember smiling at her and thinking she might not have ever let me do this to her because of her religion, but she sure wanted me to."

"Did you take advantage of her?"

"No."

"Why did you want Anna Oliver?" Detective Allen asked, annoyed and unconvinced by Tomas' last answer.

"I told you. I wanted to erase her memories because I love her."

"Did you do this?"

"Not at first. I was giving her too low of a dosage. The first time I gave her the drug, she remembered just about everything within a few minutes. In fact, when the paralysis wore off, she attacked me."

He showed the detective a scar.

"I had to inject the paralysis drug again. Then, I realized I didn't really know much at all about the chemical. I also needed to stage something in case she started asking questions. So, I came up with the tree backdrop."

"Which was?"

"Well," Tomas said, almost excited to tell the detective, "I had this idea to put her in this tree in the middle of the marsh. She'd recover from the paralysis there after I injected her with the memory loss drug. I could tell from a distance whether or not she remembered anything if she called out to—"

"Her husband."

"Yes."

Detective Allen asked, "Did she call for Henry?"

He paused and admitted, "Yes. She'd scream for him and I'd have to go and get her to start all over again. She'd tear me up."

Anna began to sob uncontrollably. She looked at Henry who stared at Tomas from a few inches in front of the mirror. Sean looked at her with gentle eyes and nodded. The story made more sense to everyone.

"Several times you tried this?"

"Five times."

Everyone gasped in the room save Henry, who remained motionless.

"So, she'd cry out for Henry, and then what would you do?"

"I'd eventually shoot her with a stun gun, and then go and get her. You know, this was for my protection. She'd fight me otherwise."

"Naturally," the detective said sarcastically.

Tomas asked, "May I continue?"

"Please."

"I remember her waking up the last time and she didn't know a thing. It was wonderful. I immediately saw in her eyes she trusted me. Then, as the weeks went on, she fell in love with me."

Anna's rage climaxed. *Tomas could've killed me with all he did to toy with my brain!*

"So, your plan was working."

"It was."

Tomas smiled to himself.

"Will her memory return to her?"

"Probably not. Of course, the drug is still in experimental form. With the mice, their memories finally came back after a few weeks, but they were on it a much shorter period of time, in a very small dosage.

"What I believe the drug does is kill the nerves that go to that part of her brain, leaving the rest intact. That's why she can remember things she's learned. As long as there are no personal factors involved in the memory, she can retain it. If you were a doctor, I'd be able to explain it further."

Detective Allen said, "Tell me about everything you gave her besides the paralysis drug and the memory drug."

"I gave her a drug to keep her eyesight dulled."

"Why?"

"I didn't want her to see how close land was if the fog ever lifted."

"You didn't want her to be able to escape."

"Yes, that's true. It caused a radiating light to come out of everything as well. It was a side effect."

"How often did you use the paralysis drug?"

"When she'd try to hike to see what was around, I'd put a powdered form of the paralysis in her food so she'd need me to carry her back home."

"How did you explain this to her?"

"I told her she had multiple sclerosis."

"What else?"

"I gave her a drug to loosen her up, especially when she started to lose her temper. It's about as effective as a few beers, but doesn't have the hang over."

"Why?"

"Why do you *think*? It tore down her walls, so she could do what she wanted to do," Tomas smiled, but tried to hide it.

Henry gasped, unable to take it all in. Suddenly, the entire room shook! Everyone turned and realized the sound was Anna breaking through the glass with the chair she had been seated in!

Tomas leaped out of his seat and the detective's eyes were wild with shock. Anna screamed and her eyes locked intensely on Tomas'. Then, she ran out of the observation room immediately.

"What's she doing here!" Tomas yelled in panic.

Officers burst in to restrain him. He fought them off as one hand clutched the glass around the broken mirror. Blood began to flow out of his hand down the glass.

Tomas cried out, "Anna! Anna, I didn't know you were here! Anna!"

Two officers finally subdued Tomas on the floor and handcuffed him. Henry and Sean stood frozen as they watched the officers restrain Tomas on the floor as he screamed Anna's name.

Henry slowly walked up to the open glass where Tomas could see him. Tomas looked up at his best friend's face and had only seen that expression once before during their fight in the barn. He knew Henry wanted to kill him and felt it deep within his tortured soul.

Henry looked into Tomas' fear-laden eyes. He thought of killing him, *I can jump through this window and break his neck.* Henry knew he would be jailed. *It's worth it—he'll be out in a year to terrorize Anna again.*

Then, Henry heard a small ringing in his ears and the entire room filled with murmuring voices. Things began to darken into shadows. He thought for a moment hate had taken him over and he was yielding to it. Yet, as the shadows came Henry felt his pounding heart soften. Everything stopped in time.

Then, he felt a hand grab onto his collar. His vision became radiant and he immediately realized he looked into the eyes of the most bloodied human being he had ever seen. There was a man beating the bloodied face with a cat of nine tails. Then, Henry knew who it was.

Lord! Henry yelled from within.

"*I have taken the punishment for Tomas upon myself,*" *the bloodied Face said.*

When his mouth parted to speak, blood poured out as if he had a mouthfull. Henry could hardly make out where his eyes were.

"*Even those who have hurt you, my beloved Henry, I have even taken on their punishment as well.*"

Henry's vision returned. No time had elapsed for anyone else. Yet, strangely Tomas saw the immediate change from one blink to the next in Henry's eyes. The officers pulled Tomas off the floor and he faced Henry.

"*Henry,*" *the Voice whispered inside of him,* "*reach out your hand and touch Tomas. I love him as I do you.*"

"*God, I can't. I'll kill him,*" *Henry thought with great fear.*

"*Reach out your hand, Henry.*"

The murmuring grew louder.

"*Prayers are being offered for you to forgive. Can you hear them, Henry? If you believe in grace, stretch out your hand to prove it to Sean and Tomas.*"

Henry fought back every instinct to disobey. This was the one time, without question, he knew it was God he heard. So, Henry reached his hand through the opening toward Tomas who stood with his hands cuffed behind his back. He was held by two officers who had reasoned Henry deserved an opportunity to hurt Tomas.

They gave Henry that chance and held Tomas tighter as Henry's large hand reached through the hole Anna had created. As Henry reached in, he felt an unexplainable, supernatural love radiate from heaven and pierce his outstretched arm.

Love beyond logic took over as Henry put his hand on Tomas' wet cheek. Henry felt God look through his eyes to see the man God had created Tomas to be. What Tomas felt was beyond fear into a realm only explained as hell-terrifying. In that moment, whether he ever admitted it or not, he knew God existed.

"What you have meant for evil, Tomas. God meant for our good."

Henry withdrew his hand quickly, and then walked out the door. The officers who held Tomas looked at each other. Sean froze for a moment and watched his best friend leave the observation room. He walked over, looked at Tomas, and then punched him square in the face. Tomas had a black eye later that day.

"That's for Anna, you son of—!"

Henry found Anna as she stood on the steps of the police station. She held herself tightly with the cold air visible as she breathed. Henry did not hesitate. He went straight for her, put his arms around her, and held her close. She held her arms crossed at her chest. She did not know if she wanted to hit Henry or hug him, so she let him embrace her. Then, her tears came hard and heavy.

"Why did you tell him all those things!" She demanded through muffled sobs. "If you'd kept your big mouth shut, none of this would've happened!"

"I'm so sorry," he said and kissed her head. "Please forgive me, I'm so sorry. You have no idea how sorry I am."

She instantly felt warmed by him and stretched out her arms under his coat to put them around his body. He winced as she grazed his wound with her hand, but the love he felt far surpassed any pain he physically felt.

She seemed so small, so fragile. He had never seen her in such as way in the past. He had always looked up to her, marveled at her strength. However, she needed him. It was a beautiful, terrible moment for him.

Anna's heart beat in her ears. Henry had not told her about any of her past.

Did he wish I didn't have to remember those things? Does he love me so much he wants me to live a life filled with beauty?

With Daire, she had felt something sweet in her heart toward him. She realized so much of it was pity. With Henry, however, every cell in her body came alive and sang his name. She wanted to crawl inside his heart and never leave.

Sean stood and watched them. Then, he put Anna's coat around her and went to the car to start the heater.

CHAPTER 30

THE PARTY OF THREE SAT quietly in a café and drank tea and coffee. They did not look at each other.

"I'm sorry, but this isn't cutting it. I need alcohol after all that happened today," Sean finally said.

"When we get home you can have all you want," Henry remarked.

Sean stared at his coffee and thought about the moment between Henry and Tomas.

"Henry . . . Back there . . . What the hell?"

"Remember once you asked me what grace is?" Henry asked Sean. "Well, that's what it looks like."

"Not a big fan so far," Sean said.

Anna looked down at Sean's hand and asked, "What happened to your knuckles?"

Sean grinned. She did, too. Anna leaned over the table and kissed him on the cheek. Sean leaned back, put his hands behind his head, and looked at Henry with a stupid grin.

"I'm Lancelot," he said.

"Thank you, Sean," she said.

"Your boyfriend here tenderly touched Tomas' cheek," Sean complained.

Inside, however, he admired Henry for doing it. He had never met a finer man than John Henry Oliver.

Henry shook his head at Sean. He did not want him to tell Anna how he had reacted to Tomas. He thought she might hit the roof. However, she looked at Henry with soft eyes.

"I couldn't help it," Henry said to her. "The Lord took over. He knew I would've killed him if He hadn't."

She nodded. The one thing she had felt so guilty about was being intimate with Daire, but he had admitted he drugged her to do it. Somehow, as angry as it had made her an hour ago, it made her feel better.

As Anna had listened to Tomas explain those three weeks, actually a few months total including the times his serum was unsuccessful, it was therapeutic in ways she had not imagined. Still, there were so many disturbing things she had yet to process and grief to work through.

For the moment, though, she allowed herself to think only about a few things. First, she was with Henry. Second, the coffee was very hot. Third, Sean had punched Daire. The latter had brought great joy to her. Henry winked at her to tell her everything was all right.

"Oh, no!" Henry exclaimed suddenly.

In unison, Anna and Sean said, "What?"

"I forgot about Ashling!"

He got up quickly and asked to use a telephone.

"Hello? It's me, Mrs. Fitzgerald. No, no, it's all right. I know why you didn't visit. Please don't get upset. Can I talk with Ashling?"

He looked at Anna as she sipped her coffee. She was so beautiful; he lost his train of thought.

"Ashling it's me. Ashling . . . Ashling, don't cry. Please don't cry. I'm fine . . . You did? Oh, I'm so glad you got in. I was worried you were waiting for me. No, I wasn't there because we had a visit from the police and had to come to Sligo Town to listen to Tomas' confession. Yes, she knows all of it.

"Do you still want us to come over tonight, or are you too tired? Of course I will. I'll ask Anna. I don't know if she'll be able to. I love you so much, Ashling. Don't cry again . . . I know you would've been here. I'll see you soon. It'll be about eight . . . Is that too late for the boys? No, don't wait for me for dinner . . . I love you, too."

Henry returned to the table and sat down with a sigh.

"Well, she didn't get into town until this afternoon, so we're fine. I thought she'd get in this morning or late last night and be waiting for me. She's been terribly worried. She got word a few days ago about what had happened."

"Why did it take so long?" Anna asked.

"She was in Italy and there was no telephone in the countryside where they were renting."

"Why were they in Italy?"

"Her husband was in Venice for business, and then they decided to take a holiday. Ashling is very big on being with her family. She didn't have that growing up with her parents, so she has the whole family every year go somewhere secluded where they can get closer."

"Well, I say if you have the money, hire a nanny," Sean said. "I'm hungry. I haven't eaten one thing today."

"I don't think I can eat," Henry said.

"I don't think I can either."

The thought of food was more than Anna was able to take. The coffee was almost too much to get down.

"Well, nobody asked either one of you. Waitress, bring me one of those fattening things in the glass over there . . . That one with the nuts on it."

Sean ate the sticky bun in less than four bites and handed Henry the bill.

Sean drove Henry and Anna home as they sat in the back seat again.

"How are your stitches doing? Do you think we should stop at the hospital before we leave?" Anna asked.

"Because we miss it there so much?" Sean asked.

Anna unbuttoned Henry's shirt. Sean looked in the rearview mirror and said, "You two behave yourselves back there."

She took off his bandage and ran her fingers over the wound. She looked at his chest, and then stopped. He took her hand and laid it on his heart. She cleared her throat.

Anna barely squeaked out, "It looks better than it did this morning, but I'd feel better if we had another doctor look at it."

"If I need someone, tomorrow I'll drive into Shannon. Tonight, I want to see my family."

The word family was felt a knife in Anna's heart. That was something she still felt a deep longing to have. She drew back her hand and Henry buttoned his shirt. Then, he took her hand again and kissed it. She put her head on his chest and closed her eyes.

Anna woke to the bumpy road on Adare grounds. She pushed slightly away from Henry's chest and looked out the window. It was dark already. Henry had prayed for her while she slept for the Lord to give her peace. She had slept well for the last three hours and he was thankful. It was a miraculous peace after what she had been through.

"Can I take the car tonight?" Sean asked when he dropped them off at the carriage house.

"Of course."

"I'm going to go see if the pub is still standing."

He drove off and left the two to enter their home without him. Henry lit a fire while Anna took off her coat.

"Do you want to go over to the Manor?" he asked.

"No, but I don't want to leave you either."

"I can wait until tomorrow."

"No, no, that's all right. I'll go."

"Let me tell you something which may help you. I hate to tell you about your past relationships because I want you to form them yourself, but this one is very special. Ashling's like a sister, as you know, although we're cousins. However, your relationship with her is even more special. You two bonded immediately.

"She came to stay after our wedding and you two were insepa- rable. She was very close to you. She's extremely upset she wasn't here during all of this. I think the reason she left Venice to take the month in the countryside is because she couldn't deal with your death.

"Everything reminded her of you, as it did me. She couldn't be here. I thought I'd have to sell the Manor. She didn't want anything to do with it. I haven't seen her in two months which, to me, is like years with all of this happening. Anna, she's your best friend. You can feel safe being yourself with her. You can fall asleep on the couch over there, no one will blink. There's no formality."

Anna felt better the more Henry talked and said, "I want to go. I want to change beforehand."

"Of course."

Henry looked longingly at his wife, but he dared not touch her while they were alone.

"Just wear something comfortable, all right?"

Anna took a deep breath and changed into silk pants and an angora sweater. She slid some Vaseline on her lips instead of the crimson lipstick she wore earlier and put on flat shoes. She tried to imagine what her best friend was like.

Henry had put on a sweater and jeans when she came out.

"Hi, beautiful," he said and grabbed his coat. "I called Ashling. She's so excited we might have to hog tie her! She's been cooking something for us."

Anna felt she could actually eat. She and Henry stood on their front stoop and put on their gloves. Then, they started down the cobble drive to the beautiful castle before them as they held each other's hands. Oil lamps lighted their path and it began to snow.

"Are you all right walking?" She asked Henry.

Henry smiled and assured her, "I'm fine. Actually, I was thinking about something. There was this one time when you and I . . . Well, we weren't you and I yet. I was walking on this road and looked up. I saw you in the window. You waved to me with this big smile and I remember thinking you were the happiest person I had ever met. When you told me all you had been through, I really had to ask why."

"Do you still think I'm the happiest person?" she asked.

"No, I don't . . . That worries me tremendously."

"It's been a lot to contend with, Henry."

"It has, indeed. Anna, you've been through worse."

"Henry, I don't want to ask this question, but it's really bothering me. You know other men have been with me."

He stopped and quietly said, "Please don't bring this up."

"I want to know . . . Before me . . . Were there any other women?"

"No."

"Did you take any girls out?"

"No."

"Why not?"

"I'm not exactly good with women."

"You've mentioned that before, but I think you're quite good with me."

"Well, I have some history with you. I'm not exactly shy around you."

He paused for a moment and looked around.

"Anna, all great love stories come from tragedy and pain. Finding love is like finding a little flower in the snow. It's truly appreciated when it's rare. Then, it captures our heart and never dies."

"Where did you get that from?"

"I don't know," Henry said, embarrassed.

Anna giggled and said, "You're a little corny, Henry."

"Yeah. . . ." Henry said as his face turned red.

"Henry," she said and looked at him, "I love you."

Henry looked at Anna. He knew, but somehow this time it felt different. He actually saw his wife in Anna's eyes. He touched her shoulders, and then kissed her as snow fell on their lips.

"I can't feel my lips," he finally said.

She laughed a little and said, "Neither can I."

Henry opened the kitchen door and Anna went in. It was all she had imagined it to be.

A young woman with bright red hair turned around swiftly from stirring a pot. She reached out and held Anna in her arms before Anna even really saw her face. She held Anna so tightly she immediately felt loved. The young woman finally pulled back and wiped tears away.

"I can't lose you," she said and nodded her head. "I'm no good without you. The thought of the rest of my life without you . . . I can't do it, Anna, I can't."

She held Anna again and kissed the back of her head.

"I love you so much!"

Henry unpeeled Ashling from Anna, and then she gave him a gentle embrace. She immediately began to scold him.

"You scared me half to death, you know that! Do you know what Donnelly's letter said? 'Dear Ashling, Come soon. Henry has been stabbed. Did you get my letter about Anna? Regards, Donnelly.' Apparently he had written five letters, but that was the only one I got. I ask you, what was I to make of that?"

She looked at Henry with bright blue eyes and freckles on her nose. Her round face and gap between her teeth were a sure giveaway about how adorable she had been in her childhood years.

"I had to get Pearce to drive us up to the nearest town so I could use the telephone. I got Sarah to tell me the whole story. I was at this inn—I'm sorry let me take your coats and sit down you two—and I fell into Pearce sobbing. He had to have Sarah explain the whole thing to him again because I couldn't talk. Henry, can you imagine I couldn't talk!"

She hugged his neck again and kissed him on the cheek.

"Do you know me at all, Anna?" Ashling asked without emotion.

"No, I'm sorry."

"Well, that'll change after tonight. Consider yourself warned."

Anna smiled shyly.

"The Donnellys are here, too. They're at the end of their coffee, but they wanted to stay to see you two. Come on, they're in the library."

"What are you cooking?" Henry asked as he strained his neck.

"Oh, the sauce! Oh, just go . . . I don't have to show you around your house. Give me another kiss will you!"

Henry kissed her on her dimpled cheek and held Anna's hand as they went into the library.

Sarah got up and kissed them. Father Donnelly warmly hugged Henry.

"I've miss you, my boy!" He said with a break in his voice. "I've prayed for you every minute I've been awake."

"And then I've been up praying when he's snoring," Sarah added.

"Thank you. We can certainly feel your prayers," Anna said as she always had.

They each noticed it immediately and looked at her lovingly.

"I'm such a mess," Ashling blurted as she came into the library, wiped down her apron, and then took it off.

"Ashling, will you be a dear and warn the boys I'm in terribly bad shape and they can't jump on me," Henry whispered into Ashling's ear.

"Take off your shirt, I want to see."

"Ashling, I'm not taking off my shirt!"

"Take it off, Henry!"

Henry sighed and complained, "I've taken off my shirt for more people this week than I have my whole life!"

The Donnellys did not defend him. They were interested in seeing his wounds as well. He finally sighed, started to unbutton his shirt, and took off the bandages. Everyone gasped, except Anna. She looked down at her feet.

"Boys!" Ashling called.

Henry heard the thunder of their feet on the stairs. Henry braced himself. Father Donnelly stood by the doorway to intervene. Everyone waited in heavy anticipation. Finally, the older of the two was caught by Father Donnelly and Ashling caught the little one by his suspenders.

"Uncle Priestie!" they echoed.

"Now, look at your poor, old, Uncle Henry. He's messed up!" Ashling began.

"Uncle Priestie, you're truly splendid! Let me see how gross you are, Frankenstein!" Peter said.

The littlest one started to cry. Ashling consoled him.

"That's right, Michael, he has a boo-boo. Now, listen, if either of you jumps on or hurts Uncle Henry in any way, Father Donnelly's going to give you a swift kick in the rear!"

"I am?" Father Donnelly protested.

"They're not scared of us, Donnelly, go with it!" Ashling said as Michael tried to squirm away.

"You hear?" Father Donnelly said to Peter loudly.

"All right, all right . . . Let me at him."

Peter ran toward him. Everyone in the room gasped. Then, Peter put out his hands and pretended he was going to touch Henry, but he did not. Ashling laughed. Michael followed suit and pretended to touch Uncle Priestie without making contact.

"Give me a hug," Henry said and they put out their hands as if to hug him, but did not touch him.

"Aunt Cindie!" Michael squealed.

He immediately nestled on Anna's lap. She touched his red hair. "No heaven. No heaven," he said.

"I'm sorry, Anna," Ashling said. "When we told him you went to heaven he screamed, 'No heaven!' over and over again."

Peter stared at Anna.

"Hi, Peter," she said sweetly.

"How do we know it's her?" he asked.

"Peter!" Everyone said in unison.

"How do we know? Let me see your tattoo," he said.

Everyone was in shock, but no one said anything. Anna looked around the room, and then pulled back her sleeve. She showed him her arm.

"All right, anyone could've done that. Can you prove it another way?"

"What do you suggest?" Anna said.

Peter had a freckled face, like his mother's.

"Aunt Cindie use to tell me something all the time. Do you know it?"

"Peter, she doesn't remember anything, dear," Ashling said.

Henry was agitated with his nephew.

"You use to say, "Peter, you're a—"

"A prince . . . Peter you're a prince," she said with more of a melody in her voice.

He nodded. Then, he cried.

"Don't go back to heaven, okay?"

Anna filled up as well. *I remembered something!*

"I'll be such a good boy. Just don't leave again."

She held out her arms to the child and he almost fell into them. She petted his dark hair as Ashling cried into her apron.

"One day when she's very old she'll go, but she'll stay with us for a long time," Ashling said to her oldest son.

"Ashling, something is burning," Sarah commented.

Ashling flew back into the kitchen.

"I better go help her," Sarah added and patted Anna's cheek before she left the room.

"What did you find out today?" Father Donnelly asked Henry.

"Boys, will you go draw a picture upstairs of your favorite memory with Aunt Cindie?" Henry asked.

They hustled upstairs.

"Father," Henry said sweetly and intentionally, "I prefer not to discuss it yet. I'm raw and so is Anna."

"I understand. Are you all right?"

"Yes, I am surprisingly. I don't know if it'll hit us tomorrow or not, but for now, I'm fine. Are you all right, Anna?"

"I'm tired, but I feel the same way as Henry. I had my moment of crazy anger, and then it dissipated. I don't know when I'll truly be able to take it all in."

"There'll be a time for you both to work through all you've learned. I believe the Lord is giving you an oasis tonight. Do you think you can enjoy your family tonight?"

"Just seeing Ashling is medicine to me," Henry said.

"It always is," a tender male voice said from the doorway. "She's my medicine as well."

Henry stood.

"Please don't get up," Pearce said and shook Henry's hand. "Forgive me, I was on a call and didn't hear you come in."

He then turned to follow Henry's gaze to Anna.

"My dear," he said with sweetness similar to Henry.

"Anna, honey, this is Pearce," Henry introduced them.

"I figured as much. It's so nice to meet you."

Pearce was taken aback a little, and then offered his hand.

"It's miraculous to see you, sweet Anna," he said quietly. "Are you well?"

He did not know what to say.

"Yes, just a little tired."

"How are you, Henry?" Pearce said even more gently to him.

"You missed the show. I showed my battle scars."

Pearce looked at Henry with true esteem in his eyes and said, "You've become what every man dreams he'll be to his wife."

"Thank you, Pearce."

"Get in here!" Ashling yelled from the dining hall.

They all entered and their faces were lit by Ashling's beautiful table and candles all around.

Pearce sat down beside Father Donnelly who slapped him on the knee, and then squeezed his shoulder.

"Truly miraculous," he said again.

"I've burned them all!" Ashling's voice boomed before she appeared. "But we're still going to eat them and everyone's going to ooh and ah!"

"Use lots of sauce, people . . . Lots of sauce!" Sarah exclaimed as she bustled in holding a huge tray of black calzones.

"Boys!" Henry called.

Michael came down with his footie pajamas on. He held his picture in his hand and climbed on Anna's lap.

"Aunt Cindie," he said as his little nose ran.

She took her glove out of her pocket and wiped it.

"Yes, love?"

"Hold."

She picked him up. He rubbed his eyes.

"Kiss both my sweepy eyes," he said.

She did. Then, he slid down and ran to find his mother.

The entire family sat around the great dinner table to eat a slightly burned meal.

Pearce prayed, "How can we thank Thee, Lord, for these Thy bountiful miracles? We can only stand in awe of who You are in our lives, knowing we live on the holy ground of love. Bless this food and our precious time together as a family."

"Amen," everyone whispered.

Sarah wiped her tears with her napkin and commented, "Why you didn't go into the ministry, Pearce, I have no idea. That was beautiful."

"Well now," Pearce said quietly. "It has not occurred to me much. I feel as though the honest work of a banker can be as much of a trusted ministry as a priest's ministry."

"Too true," Father Donnelly said as he touched his glass with Pearce's.

"I took a cooking class in Tuscany," Ashling said without the slightest bit of snobbery. "The chef said if he was giving me a grade, it'd be a D minus. I hated him, but these are good, right?"

Everyone agreed, except Henry who snickered. Ashling showed him the food in her mouth as she had when she was six, and then kept eating.

"You're the worst, John Henry Oliver!"

"Anna," Pearce said sweetly as she started to slow down on her enormous calzone, "you said you were tired earlier. Would you like to stay here tonight? I know my wife is counting on it."

"I'll be fine at the carriage house," Anna said.

Ashling had been on a high from the moment she had seen Anna, but suddenly felt low she did not jump at the chance as she might have done before.

"Tomorrow," Ashling said. "I thought maybe you'd stay tomorrow then?"

"Anna, why don't you stay here," Henry said.

Anna looked at Henry in awe.

"I'll have Pearce bring your things."

"Of course," Pearce said.

"I'm so tired and want to sleep in my bed," Anna said.

She knew as soon as the words came out of her mouth they were not true.

"Then, you have to stay here, in your old room you had with Henry," Ashling said, still a little offended Anna did not want to stay.

"Uncle Priestie!" Michael said as he awakened suddenly from a twilight state on his father's lap.

Henry smiled at Michael. Henry did not want to leave Anna, but he knew they could not be alone either.

"All right," Anna said sweetly as she ran out of excuses.

"Yay!" Ashling cheered and clapped.

"I feel a bit like a vagabond," Anna said to Pearce. "Henry has moved me around quite a bit."

"My dear, he's protecting you," Pearce whispered.

"From who?"

"From him . . . He loves you very much, but you two really aren't married any longer. I'm sorry, I hope I haven't overstepped."

"No, not at all," she said.

"Isn't my Pearce wonderful?" Ashling said dreamily.

"He's wonderful because he's exactly like me," Henry said.

"Oh, hush, Henry!" Ashling protested.

"You said it yourself, you little bugger!" He continued as he mocked Ashling's voice, "Pearce is perfect because I looked and looked for a man like you, Henry. God found and delivered him to me. He stuck this gorgeous ring on my finger and we're going to live happily ever after!"

"Shut up, Henry!" Ashling said and threw her napkin at him.

Pearce smiled humbly and said, "I'm always honored to be compared to you, Henry."

Henry smiled and replied, "Same here."

"What about me, Ashling? You didn't want to marry someone exactly like your rector?" Father Donnelly protested.

"Eww!" Ashling squealed.

Everyone laughed.

"There are a lot of good men around this table," Sarah said and kissed her husband.

"Except for Peter, of course," Henry teased.

"Hey!" Peter retorted.

"Pearce is more serious than Henry. They are tenderhearted, but Henry's got an edge to him." Ashling said and winked at her husband who blushed. "And of course, Pearce is the most handsome man on the planet!"

He was, indeed, very handsome.

"I think this little one is done," Pearce said to his wife.

Michael sucked his thumb with his eyes closed and rested his head on his father's chest.

"Let me take him," Ashling said.

"I've got him."

"Aunt Cindie!" Michael insisted when he woke up heavy-eyed.

Anna held out her hands and Pearce handed his son to her.

"Do you want me to put you in bed, sweetheart?" She asked and kissed his curly, red locks.

"Sing," he said.

Everyone stopped and looked at Anna. She quickly got up and carried him out of the room. She went into the foyer and stood at the bottom of a grand staircase.

"Michael, darling, where's your room?"

"I don't know," he said.

She went back into the dining room and looked at Henry.

"I don't know the way," she whispered, but everyone heard her. The image of her being lost in her house haunted them for a moment. Ashling finally stood and offered to go with her.

"He's so sweet," Anna commented as they went up the stairs together.

"Yes, when he sleeps he's the sweetest thing in the world," Ashling stated.

Anna giggled, and then kissed the little boy again.

"Just through here," Ashling guided Anna into a room decorated to look like it was out of a story book. "I don't know if Henry told you, but I'm perfectly obsessed with Peter Pan. I had the nursery decorated right out of the book."

"All you need is a Wendy," Anna said softly.

"Oh, I'll always be Wendy!" Ashling retorted with a chuckle.

Anna laid Michael down in a crib, and then covered him with a blanket.

"You're still in love with Henry aren't you?" Ashling asked as she looked down at Michael.

"I've fallen in love with him," she admitted.

Ashling smiled and said, "Anna, Henry's in all aspects my brother. He's annoying and wonderful all at the same time. I adore him, but when I thought you were gone . . . I couldn't even look at him because when I looked in his eyes . . . All I saw was his love for you. It made me miss you so much I wasn't there for him like I should've been. I left when he needed me most. The Donnellys stepped in as his surrogate family, but I want to tell you . . . To tell you I'm sorry."

Anna instinctively opened her arms, embraced Ashling, and said, "No one in his or her right mind would ever hold it against you. I do have one question, Ashling."

"What's that?"

"Is Henry Peter Pan?"

"He was a terrible Peter! I think he's more of a Captain Hook!"

"All right, if Henry is Hook, and you have a Peter and a Michael, and you are Wendy . . . Who does that make me?"

"Tinker Bell, of course."

"I was afraid of that!"

"With your temper," Ashling joked, "your bravery, and your wonderful love, you're her through and through."

"You're crazy," Anna said as she laughed.

"Want to see your room?" She asked, excitedly.

"Yes!"

Ashling scurried down the hall with her, opened a door, and turned on the lights. The room was gorgeous in yellows and had a huge chandelier.

"Oh, it's beautiful, Ashling! It reminds me of what they did to the carriage house."

"I know! I popped my head in there earlier. I think they were trying to make you feel more at home."

"Well, it's beautiful, Ashling," Anna said again.

She looked at the beautiful bed and was ready to get in and sleep.

"Let's go downstairs and say goodnight to everyone. You don't have to wait for Pearce to get your things. You have some clothes here."

"I do?"

"Yes, of course. Even after you two moved out to the cottage, when we'd come into town for holidays, you two stayed in your old room. I gave Mrs. Fitzpatrick and Cook the night off. I'll light the fire for you later."

Anna and Ashling went downstairs together and went back into the dining room where Sarah had already cleaned up. Ashling thanked her, and then told her husband not to worry about Anna's things.

Anna stood and held the back of her chair; she was, hardly able to look at Henry. She was home, she knew, but it was only when she looked at him she felt it. Somehow, though, the feeling frightened her. She was afraid she would find out it was all a hoax, even more elaborate than Daire's. It was all still a lie, too good to be true.

"I don't want to leave you," Henry whispered to her.

The admission made her want to fly.

"I know," she said.

"Will you be at church tomorrow?"

"Is it Sunday already?"

"Yes," he chuckled. "I've convinced Father Donnelly I'm all right enough to do the service. Please don't tell him the truth."

She smiled and said, "I look forward to it."

"Walk me out?"

Henry had Anna take his arm and they told everyone goodnight like they had for so many years of their married lives. Everyone smiled at each other and silently reminisced of times which seemed so long ago—much like that night. Sarah kissed Anna twice on her cheek, and then held her for a long time.

"I miss you, baby," she said and squeezed her again.

Henry shut the kitchen door behind them, and then realized Anna did not have her coat on. He wrapped her in his, and then kissed her. He quickly took his coat back and waved at her as Pearce drove the car around. It was a short ride, but they all knew Henry should not walk. He needed to rest as much as possible.

Anna waved, shivered, and then went back into the warm kitchen. Ashling was pouring tea for herself.

"You'd think Henry and Pearce would be so close since they're so similar. They respect each other so deeply, but it's not really a friendship, you know? I wish it was, though."

"Why did you want to marry someone like Henry?" Anna said as she sat on the bench.

"I didn't. I wanted to marry someone as flighty as I am, but I fell madly for Pearce, and then realized when I brought him home to meet Henry and his parents they were extremely similar."

"Strange."

"Not really. Henry's my family. We tend to pick those who are like our family members, don't you think?"

"I don't know."

"Oh, I'm sorry, dear," Ashling apologized as she realized Anna had no point of reference since she had no family.

"No, don't be. I like it when you talk."

"Want some?" She asked about the tea.

"Please."

"Well, Pearce is this quiet, humble person, but he's very good with numbers and people trust him. I remember when Henry told us he was going into the ministry, I wasn't happy. Henry is the best man in the world besides Pearce. I couldn't imagine him getting any better through his conversion, but he did. Did you know Pearce and I became Christians through Henry and you?"

"You did?"

"Yes, of course."

"Why?"

"Why did we become Christians . . . Is that what you're asking?"

"Yes."

Ashling was taken aback by the question and replied, "We thought to ourselves if you and Henry are an example of what God is like we'd like to know Him."

"That's a very incredible thing to say."

"I know it is. It's also true."

"What did we do that was so wonderful?"

Ashling sat beside her and answered, "I've never seen someone forgive like you, Anna."

"What do you mean?"

"That's the motto you and Henry lived by. It's written on the mantle in the library."

Ashling walked Anna to the library. She touched Henry's big arm chair. Ashling pointed to Henry's handwriting. It was very small print, but it was there: Love gives up its own rights.

"Lofty words," Anna mumbled.

She thought about her lack of forgiveness toward Daire which she believed she would always have.

"You've lived them. Look at your tattoo, Anna. You forgave every one of those men who hurt you in the concentration camp. You forgave them. You wrote them letters of forgiveness. That's when we began to believe."

"Why would I forgive them?"

"That's what we said."

Anna breathed heavily.

"I'm so tired, Ashling," she said weakly.

Ashling put her arm around her and said, "Come on, let's go to bed."

Ashling walked Anna up the stairs and lit the fireplace in her beautiful room. Then, she pulled out a nightgown from her dresser.

"I'm going to go get your tea; I left it downstairs. There's a washroom over there."

When Ashling came back up the room with tea in hand, Anna was already in bed.

"Here's your tea, Anna."

"Ashling, will you stay with me tonight?"

"Of course, I can."

Ashling undressed down to her slip and settled down next to Anna in bed.

There was a long, soft pause.

"We were close weren't we?" Anna asked finally.

The pretty orange glow of the fire settled on Ashling's sweet face.

"Yes," Ashling confirmed and wiped away a tear.

"I was wondering if you'd answer some questions for me."

"Of course."

"Tomas . . . Did I have feelings for him?"

It felt strange for her to say his real name. Ashling turned over on her side so she could see Anna.

"Well, you dive right in like you use to, don't you?" She joked and smiled. "I think so. Honestly, Anna, you never said it outright. I think you had some feelings for him, but they were nothing compared to what you felt for Henry."

"Did I flirt with him or something?"

"Goodness, no. You each kept your distance, that's why I was suspicious of your feelings.

"He was in a prison . . . A concentration camp?"

Anna had recently learned the term and did not understand all it entailed.

"Yes, but not long. They found out he was a doctor and he began to work in the German hospitals.

"Do you know if he was in the same prison as me?"

"I don't know. You were in a . . . Much different sort of place. Fortunately, you arrived toward the end of the war; otherwise, you probably wouldn't have survived."

"How did I get back to London after I was released?"

"Sarah found you and she brought you home."

"Was that quite an ordeal to find me?"

"She says God told her where you were."

"That seems a little far-fetched."

"Not for Sarah Donnelly."

"So, I went back to London. My husband had died already."

"He died very early on in the war. You began working on the Channel the last year of the war. You didn't want to leave Sarah, but you knew you had to help. You told me you couldn't sleep at night until you did it."

"Why was it so important?"

"The Germans were killing Jews, Anna. They were trying to—"

"I don't think I want to hear this right now."

"All right, what do you want to know?"

Anna thought for a moment and asked, "I was close to God?"

"Yes. Very."

"What exactly does that mean?"

"Everything you did was like a love letter to Him. Your songs, your art—"

"Are any of my paintings here?"

"A dozen."

"Will you show them to me tomorrow?"

"Of course."

"Ashling . . . Why didn't I have any children?"

"I don't know."

"Did I talk about it?"

"No."

"That seems strange."

"I'm pretty open about things like that, but you're not."

"I wonder why."

"You're just different, Anna."

"Did Henry ever talk about it?" She asked carefully.

"Yes, once. He said he prayed for a daughter like you. For some reason, he got this notion in his head he wanted three daughters named Sarah, after your mother in law; Elizabeth; and Rita."

"Most men want boys."

"Henry wants to have mini-Anna's I think!"

They laughed a little.

"He loves me, doesn't he?"

"You think!" Ashling said with a smile.

"Ashling, thank you for being so open with me tonight. I can see why we were so close."

"Goodnight, Anna."

"Goodnight, Ashling," Anna said and took her friend's hand on her pillow.

CHAPTER 31

ANNA SLEPT WELL THAT NIGHT. It was a wonderful thing to have such a good evening after such a terrible day. Anna awoke to the chaos only a Sunday morning with small children getting ready for church brings.

"Peter! Peter, get that suit coat on or so help me!" Ashling yelled and then sang out more gently to her husband, "Pearce, go eat, you'll be starved if you don't by the end of the service!"

Then, "Michael, why are you naked again? I just dressed you for the third time!"

Anna found a pretty dress in her closet and changed quickly. She needed to help her friend as much as possible. She did her hair and put on makeup she found in the dressing table drawers.

"Ashling, what can I do?" Anna called as she rushed out of her room.

"Go eat!" Ashling yelled.

"How can I help you?"

"Here, take Michael. He needs to eat," she said.

She handed Michael, who was naked, to Anna with a ball of clothes. Anna immediately started to dress him.

"Peter, I see you and you're wearing sneakers! What are you wearing sneakers for?" Ashling snapped and hustled after him.

"Hi, Aunt Cindie!" Little Michael said with his thumb in his mouth.

"Hello, my love. Are you hungry?"

"No!" Michael screamed.

"Well, that's too bad now, isn't it? I guess I'll have to eat breakfast in front of you!"

Anna carried Michael into the kitchen. She walked in with a smile to the smell of cinnamon buns in the air. An older, pretty woman turned around.

"Hello," she said with a shocked look on her face.

Pearce was reading the newspaper said underneath his breath to Anna, "Mrs. Fitzpatrick."

"Good morning," Anna said, and then put Michael in his high chair.

"No eat!" Michael yelled.

Pearce looked at Michael over his newspaper and ordered, "You will be hungry, my boy."

"No eat!" Michael yelled again.

"It's no problem," Anna said as she sat down with some chocolate milk and a cinnamon bun. "I'll eat Michael's breakfast for him."

Anna bit into the bun, and feigned supreme pleasure, "Ooh, it's so good . . . Ah!"

Michael stared at her astonished, and then sobbed, "Aunt Cindie's eating my breakfast!"

Anna laughed underneath her breath. She gave it to him, and then poured herself some water.

"It's good to see you," Mrs. Fitzpatrick said. "Do you remember me at all?"

"No, ma'am, but maybe we can catch up later?" Anna suggested sweetly.

"Get in the car!" Ashling ordered as she came in like a hurricane. "We're going to be late!"

She wiped Michael's face and grabbed him out of his high chair.

"I'm hungry!" Michael wailed.

"Here's a bottle, Ashling."

Mrs. Fitzpatrick had filled it with chocolate milk.

"Life saver!"

"Are you coming with us?" Anna asked Mrs. Fitzpatrick.

"I go to mass on Saturday nights," she replied.

"Anna!" Ashling screeched. "Come on!"

Anna squeezed up against Michael in the backseat as Pearce drove calmly and Ashling fiddled in her purse for her reading glasses which she did not have.

"Henry's doing the service!" She said merrily to Anna over her shoulder. "It'll be packed! Don't think he'll save us a seat, either! We'll have to stand if we're late."

Anna had witnessed how crowded the church was when Father Donnelly had spoken the one other time she had attended. However, nothing prepared her for how crowded it was when Henry preached—straight out of the hospital!

They were twenty minutes early and barely found a seat together in the last pew. Anna was fortunate enough to get the seat which swung out slightly toward the wall so she had a perfect view of the podium.

People came in, and then Pearce and Peter gave up their seats to older women as Michael bounced on Ashling's lap. As cold as it was outside, it began to get warm inside. People stood in the corridor, ushers brought in all the chairs available. Somehow, they managed to seat everyone.

The bells rang, and then the beautiful sound of Henry praying in the doorway echoed through the church. The organ began and the processional started. Anna stretched her neck to see Henry. She smiled.

Ashling looked at Anna after a few lines of the hymn and smiled, too. Then, those in front of her turned around and looked at her. She did not realize she was singing "The Church's on Foundation" without a hymnal.

The Church's one foundation

Is Jesus Christ her Lord;

She is His new creation
By water and the Word:
From heav'n He came and sought her
To be His holy Bride;
With His own blood He bought her,
And for her life He died.[4]

Henry walked onto the platform and looked out over his congregation. Anna knew he was searching for her face. Finally, after he scanned the crowd, he saw her. She beamed at him. Then, he realized what he hoped for: she was singing.

When Anna sang the third verse: "Mid toil and tribulation, and tumult of her war," he winked at her. She had sang the entire song without a hymnal.

The congregational singing grew quieter until at the last verse it almost whispered the song as parishioners listened to Anna as she sang. Henry watched her, as many turned to get a peek of her. She, however, did not notice because she was totally lost in the words and melody and on Henry's sweet expression.

Finally, after prayers and readings from the Bible, Henry stood at the pulpit. He shuffled his notes.

"I don't feel as though I have to preach after that first hymn."

Everyone chuckled quietly.

"The presence of the Lord is truly here, isn't He? I'm very honored and glad to be back here in the place I love the most to serve and love you. It'll still be a bit of a struggle for me to concentrate on anything, but the miraculous events of this past month. I know God will anoint me as needed."

Father Henry smiled at his congregation with love in his eyes. He dared not look at his beautiful wife or would lose his train of thought. He also knew from careful prayer this was his most important sermon.

---

4   Words: Stone, Samuel John, and Music: Samuel S. Wesley. 1866. "The Church's One Foundation." *Hymnal.net.* http://www.hymnal.net/hymn.php/h/833 (Accessed August 29, 2013)

"Mrs. O'Leary read a little while ago an excerpt from the book of Ruth, which you all know is very dear to my heart."

He looked down at his paper, paused, and then began to read, "In the midst of battles, miracles, lists of names, and hundreds of rules, is nestled a slim group of stories about love within the Bible. They are few, small, and easily missed, yet we gravitate toward them, memorizing them when we're children. These stories were written and recorded by the Holy Spirit. Why in the world would the Holy Spirit care about love stories? Why not simply read the genealogy and be done with it? Why are these stories even in the Bible?"

Henry looked at his flock which smiled. He had not seen a more beautiful look on their faces.

He continued, "It's because our stories . . . Each of our stories is a love story, a divine romance. As long as each of us has waited to find love, some still wait. However, nothing compares to the amount of time God has waited. If we believe He's infinite and always existed, then think about infinity *before* the earth began. That's how long He longed for us. That's a lot of time to ache for someone. It's a lot of time to want.

"Then, after an eternity of longing, He picks out a very small portion of the enormous expanse of time and space, and He begins . . . He begins by singing. He sings, 'Let there be light!' and feels the melody over His romantic dawning as we feel the melody in our souls when we experience the dawn as well."

Henry paused.

"I feel music when I see the one I love."

Everyone smiled at each other. Anna choked with joy.

"Then, He began to make a beautiful home for His love. He made each thing by hand, marveling at how she'd love each little animal and flower. He knew, in particular, I'd love Lily of the Valley. I can see him smile and think of me as He's making the first one.

"Then, He stopped, took a deep breath and began to make a man who looked like Him. I can see Him sitting back, watching His precious child daily and realizing his little boy had the same feeling of loneliness He had for so long. Being the loving father He is, He decides to make a woman. Then, He watches their love story unfold. Still, somehow, even with His children around, He still longs. What's He longing for? He longs for His love, the Church which acts, talks, breathes, and moves in Him. That's what He longs for.

"You can feel Him dream about His love to come as we see the saturation of His prophetic future in each of those beautiful romances in the Old Testament. You can particularly feel His longing in the book of Ruth. This book is my favorite. What's so interesting about this story is it begins not as a romance, but as a deep, true friendship between an older woman and a younger. You can feel Ruth's tears when she says, 'Don't ask me to leave you, for where you go, I'll go. Your people will be my people and your God, my God.' That's where this story begins, with their devotion to one another."

Sarah began to fill up with tears as she sat on the first row.

"Then, Ruth takes the most humble position she can find. She must support Naomi at all costs. She's basically a beggar, the lowliest of workers: a gleaner. She picks up the refuse the workers in the field leave behind. Then, she takes home her sparse strands of wheat to ground, bake, and serve them to her dear friend, Naomi. What's beautiful about this is the most eligible bachelor in all the land, a prince of Israel, notices her. She must've been quite striking to be noticed by him. Remember, she was a beggar.

"Can you see Jesus wanting to jump out of His throne as He watches! He gets so excited at this point. 'Yes,' He says, 'that's how I found you, My beloved people. You were beggars, but you're beautiful to Me!'

"Then, Boaz blesses Ruth and tells his workers to leave handfuls of the wheat on purpose for her to gather. This is where the romance begins: with generosity. Isn't the Lord so generous with us?"

Henry paused and looked at his notes, as if he had lost his place. Yet, he had not—he held back tears.

"Boaz, though, is a shy man. Ruth, in her boldness, decides to hurry things along and she sleeps at Boaz's feet after the harvest celebrations. He's had too much to drink and she makes the excuse she's protecting him; however, it's actually a marriage proposal. In those days, when a younger woman uncovered the feet of an older man and slept crosswise from him, she was signaling she wanted him to marry her!

"I can see Jesus now getting *so* involved in this story. He wants us to want Him in such a way. He's longing for the day we want Him to come into our hearts and become His! Yet, like all love stories, there's a problem. The problem is there's another man in town who is closer in relation to Naomi and the law said he must have first grabs at Ruth. So, Boaz goes to the man and the man says he's all for it when he hears he can have this beautiful woman, Ruth, as his wife and all the property her father-in-law used to own in Israel. Until, of course, he realizes marrying Ruth is actually a bad thing.

"Ruth is a foreigner and if he marries a foreigner, he has to give up his inheritance. He quickly does the math and decides it's not in his best interest. However, Boaz doesn't think about his best interest. He only thinks about Ruth, whom he loves.

"Jesus has done the same for us. He has never thought of His best interests. The only thing He acts upon is *our* best interest. Isn't that amazing? Isn't that romantic? Do you hear His heart thumping as He watches their wedding day? You can see Jesus, sitting on His throne, and then standing, craning His neck to see and hear the entire story take place.

"It reminds Him of what He's promised: His love story with us. He longs for you and me! The story reminded Him of His incredible love for us! That's why it's in the scriptures . . . Because He *loves* that story."

Henry looked at his congregation again.

"May our lives be an example of His romance . . . May our love stories be like Ruth's . . . May they show the world who He is. When our hero slays the dragon and whisks us off to his castle, we feel it in our bones because it's *our* story. He's our Hero, our Love.

"We must remember who we are. We are His beloved. We have been adored, longed for, cared for more than any of us can ever imagine. We are His."

Henry finally looked at Anna. Tears streamed down her face—she understood Henry. She felt waves of love go through her like the waves of the sea. Anna felt the Holy Spirit move her heart. *This is what heaven is like.*

"Here's my heart, God, take and seal it," she whispered.

There was a closing hymn and a few other formalities, but Anna did not notice. She was lost in prayer. She rested her head against the wall and closed her eyes. Finally, she was home.

It took a full thirty minutes, but finally everyone had left after the service. They each greeted Father Henry and Father Donnelly as they stood at the back of the church. No one came near Anna, not even Ashling, because she was surrounded by a holy cloud which no one wanted to go near. It was an instinctual thing which had been felt by those who knew.

They knew God was working in Anna's heart which was strange for them to witness. The one who had been regarded as the most holy person in the parish needed Him as much as the rest of them.

Ashling was the last to leave and kissed Henry goodbye. Then, Henry sat by his wife and waited.

"That was beautiful, Henry," she said. "I know now why you became a priest. It deeply touched me."

Henry put his arm around her as they stared at the stained glass window at the front of the sanctuary.

"I'll let you in on a secret which every person in this room knew, but you. You wrote that."

Anna looked at him in shock. He nodded.

"You wrote it to me for our anniversary and the Shannon paper published it with our first love story. Everyone has read this before—some know it by heart."

Anna sat for a long time. Then, Henry got up.

"Here are the car keys. I'll be at the Manor."

"Henry," she said as she reached for his hand and slipped the car keys back into his hand. "I want to walk. Can you give me some time?"

Then, he left. Anna went to the apartment in back of the sanctuary and sat for a moment in the armchair.

"God, is this real?"

There was only a quiet hush around her.

"How have You made me into a happy person despite all I've been through?"

Quiet.

Anna stood, searched for answers, and looked through Henry's books. Nothing jumped out at her. She was restless.

Where's this God everyone tells me I'm so close to?

She thought she had felt Him in the church earlier, but she thought maybe the feeling was her remembering what she wrote. She had no previous memory to base anything on. She lay down on the small bed and looked at the ceiling.

"Show me what's real, God," she said.

Nothing at all happened, so she stood and left. Anna began to walk the few miles of fields between the church and the Manor. It was a beautiful walk. She stopped at one point to delay the journey and survey the white beauty around her.

"He makes all things new," she said aloud out of nowhere.

Anna did not know where she had heard the expression, but in one small sentence everything became clear. She closed her eyes. All revelations are within the cross and this was no different.

"I'm alive with Christ," she said.

She looked into her mind's eye where she saw His death and resurrection. She felt a rush of light come from within her as if she was resurrected with him. She opened her eyes with a start.

"Hello, Anna," a voice said from behind her.

She jumped and turned.

"I'm sorry. I didn't want to frighten you."

A tall, old man with spectacles over his beautiful green eyes greeted her with a warm smile.

"It's all right," she said.

"It's beautiful," he said as he admired the outskirts of Adare with her.

"Yes, it is."

"Do you have a camera?"

"No, I don't think so," she said.

"Can you check?" he asked.

She knew she did not, but she checked her bag any way. There, to her amazement was a camera.

Ashling must've planted it here for some reason, she marveled.

"May I take your picture with this scene in the background?" the stranger asked.

"Of course," she said.

It was a strange request, but Anna stood and the sweet man snapped her picture. He handed her back the camera. He stopped and looked at her as they held onto the camera. He looked like Henry, but maybe sixty years older.

"We see a snapshot of what's real here on Earth, but there are moments when we truly experience heaven on Earth. Those are moments documented in our hearts, even if our minds don't remember them. One day, you'll be standing in America and you'll think back at this moment as the most concrete miracle. Everyone needs something real to hold onto when faith has to be as strong as yours."

Anna looked away at the landscape, thinking.

"Sir, have we met?" she asked.

She turned toward him, but he was gone. She looked around and marveled at what had happened. *Am I going mad now?*

She looked at the camera in her hand which indicated one picture had been taken. She ran to the Manor and burst into the kitchen.

"Henry!" she cried.

Everyone she loved was gathered together. Henry stood.

"I need to get this film developed!"

"The shops in Shannon are closed on Sundays."

"I have a dark room," Peter commented.

Everyone looked at each other. It was true.

"Good boy!" Anna said as life beamed out of her face. "Come on, let's do this!"

The entire family waited outside the dark room. Anna prayed inside while Peter carefully developed the lone picture. He swished the photographic paper in different fluids, and the image began to appear. It looked rather normal. It was a picture of her with the backdrop of snow.

"Just give it a minute," Peter said as she reached for it.

Then, Peter hung the picture to dry and finally opened the door.

"It's an ordinary picture," Anna said, disappointed. "I thought it'd be a miracle or something in the picture."

"Who took this?"

"A man, just now . . . He acted like he knew me, but when I turned to talk to him, he was gone."

"Anna, I watched you every minute from the church to here from a window. No one was walking with you." Henry said.

Anna was confused and said, "I don't know him. He was walking in the snow with me."

Henry suspected he knew what had happened.

"It's the picture of a person who died and is now alive, Anna. This picture is the first since you disappeared. *You* are the miracle, sweetheart," Henry said.

Anna went back into the kitchen and sat with the damp picture. She thought for a long time. Henry finally came and sat next to her. The rest of the family, including the Donnellys and Sean, crammed in the doorway so they could hear.

"If you saw no one, maybe I'm crazy," she mumbled, "because I talked to him. Wait, how can this picture exist if he hadn't taken it?"

"It was an angel, Anna," Henry said frankly.

Anna looked at Henry with an expression of disbelief. He smiled.

"You'll see it one day," he said.

He knew she was starting to understand her faith.

"Henry, I feel like God is . . . Chasing after me. Is that a crazy notion?"

"No."

"I can feel Him."

"Yes," Henry said plainly.

"Do you feel Him?"

"Rarely, but you used to constantly."

"It feels like . . . It feels like when you hold me," she said.

Henry smiled toward the band of people behind Anna.

"Come here," he said and held out his arms.

She got up and put her arms around him. She felt something in his breast pocket.

"What's that?"

"It's nothing," he said nervously.

"Come on, Henry, be smooth!" Sean shouted.

Anna turned and finally realized they had an audience.

"Hey, come here," Henry said and pulled Anna close to him again.

She gasped and put her hands to her face. She suddenly realized what he was about to do.

She blurted, "That's a ring in your pocket!"

Henry shifted his weight on his feet. He was more nervous than the first time he had seen her.

"Well, yes, but come here," he said.

She looked at him with joyful, wide eyes.

"You're going to ask me to marry you!" she said again and looked at the family.

They all grinned.

"Henry!" She said and threw her arms around him.

"Just come here, will 'ya?" he urged.

They looked back at their family and friends gathered together with same stupid grin on their faces. Everyone chuckled as Henry pulled her out the door.

"Where are we going?"

"Just come with me!" Henry insisted.

She marveled at how well he was moving around. He hustled her to their new home—the carriage house—and opened the door for her. Inside was a sea of flowers. Every kind she knew was in the cottage.

"Henry!" she yelped.

"So," he said even more nervous, "you were supposed to come home with me tonight and I was going to open the door and ta-da! And you were supposed to come over here . . ."

Henry led her by the hand to the far side of the room.

" . . . And read this," he said as he handed her a card.

She opened it and read: "The winter is past, spring has come."

She turned. Henry was on one knee and held a little box.

"And then, you were supposed to turn around and see me here on one knee—" he started.

Anna started to cry. He got up and put his arms around her.

"Why are you crying? You knew I was going to ask you ten minutes ago!" He said and chuckled.

"I'm crying because I had doubts ten minutes ago you were going to ask me, but now I know it's real. I want to marry you, Henry!"

Henry slipped the ring on her finger and kissed his wife.

For more information about
Amy Fleming
&
A Little Irish Love Story
please visit:

www.amyfleming.org
www.facebook.com/authorfleming
@amyflemingbooks
authorfleming@gmail.com

....

For more information about
AMBASSADOR INTERNATIONAL
please visit:

www.ambassador-international.com
@AmbassadorIntl
www.facebook.com/AmbassadorIntl